hymns of abomination

secret songs of leeds

These stories are works of fiction. Each character, narrative, organization, and event are entirely products of the author's imagination or are used fictitiously.

HYMNS of ABOMINATION: SECRET SONGS of LEEDS © 2021 by Silent Motorist Media and the authors. All stories are original to this publication.

Cover art by Yves Tourigny

Designed, illustrated, and edited by Justin A. Burnett

All rights reserved. No part of this manuscript may be reproduced electronically or in print without prior, written permission from the publisher or authors published herein.

First Edition

ISBN: 978-1-954082-02-1

www.silentmotoristmedia.com

Contact: silentmotoristmedia@gmail.com

Welcome to Leeds

editor's introduction / 11

let us fly and feast, like winged slugs: some notes on matthew m. bartlett

s.j. bagley / 13

northampton's favorite son

yves tourigny / 19

open call

aksel dadswell / 27

anne gare's rare and import video catalogue I[1] / 53

dead in september

farah rose smith / 55

anne gare's rare and import video catalogue II / 67

suddenly my house became a tree of sores

gemma files / 69

anne gare's rare and import video catalogue III / 81

puppy milk

b.r. yeager / 83

a delicate spreading

scott r. jones / 99

anne gare's rare and import video catalogue IV / 109

stump-water

christine morgan / 111

---

[1] all entries of "anne gare's rare and import video catalogue" by jonathan raab

i could tell you so much

                                          s.p. miskowski / 121

    anne gare's rare and import video catalogue V / 133

the beat of wings

                                              betty rocksteady / 135

missives from the house on crabtree lane

                                         joanna parypinski / 147

    anne gare's rare and import video catalogue VI / 157

the house of lost sisters

                                              l.c. von hessen / 159

    anne gare's rare and import video catalogue VII / 177

crawl of the west

                                            cody goodfellow / 179

    anne gare's rare and import video catalogue VIII / 193

there will always be men like johnny

                                               hailey piper / 195

    anne gare's rare and import video catalogue IX / 211

the wxxt podcast, episode 23: leeds regional high school

                                                  tom breen / 213

    anne gare's rare and import video catalogue X / 231

on hunger hills

                                         john linwood grant / 233

    anne gare's rare and import video catalogue XI / 257

station maintenance

                                                 pete rawlik / 259

seven-second delay: in which terrible things happen
to tender young girls

jill hand / 275

anne gare's rare and import video catalogue XII / 285
all your fathers here and gone

k.h. vaughan / 287
itemized human sacrifices, q4

sean m. thompson and cheshire trask / 309
what am i?

s.l. edwards / 323

anne gare's rare and import video catalogue XIII / 329
leaving leeds

brian evenson / 331
father ezekiel shineface sermon hour

jon padgett / 339

anne gare's rare and import video catalogue XIV / 347
uncle bart's map

john langan / 349

about the authors / 383

editor's introduction

The book you're holding in your hands has been postulated and mulled over for several years now. When I saw the opportunity to bring it together, I didn't hesitate. Given the fact that Matthew M. Bartlett's *Gateways to Abomination* was one of a handful of books that "rescued" me from a strictly academic trajectory into Reformation Literature, why would I? As the overwhelmingly supportive response to this anthology more than aptly demonstrated, Bartlett's work has planted its spores irreversibly into the landscape of horror and weird fiction. Ligotti, Evenson, Barron, Bartlett…if there's a "canon" of contemporary weird writers, Bartlett's unquestionably in it. "But he's *still alive*," some have objected. In that case, I'm just glad to have compiled this tribute before it's too late.

What else could I possibly say? It's been an honor to work with the incredible host of talent you'll find featured herein. No, *more* than an honor. As a fan of weird fiction whose earliest exposures to the genre included Bartlett's work, it's been a *dream*. And now, incredibly, I get to welcome *you* to Leeds, where the night's never still and the shadows flicker with strange, unearthly life. As fans (for what other dark purpose would we gather here?), I *know* you'll relish the reverent irreverence Bartlett's world has been subjected to throughout these pages.

"Bartlett writes like a man in the grip of a vision," Orrin Grey wrote. If his writing's a vision, it's contagious—every year lures more readers into Leeds, and with this tribute we joyously descend further into the nightmare. What better way to celebrate Bartlett's legacy than to don his vision like a suit? Only we must be cautious—the suit's filled with things you don't want inside you.

justin a. burnett

HYMNS OF ABOMINATION

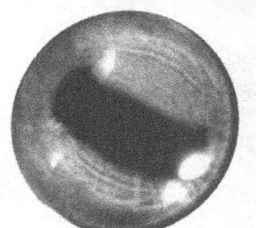

let us fly and feast, like winged slugs: some notes on matthew m. bartlett

s. j. bagley

Matthew M.[2] Bartlett is one of the shining examples of literature that arose from that weird liminal internet space called "livejournal.com," (back in the day when it was a more broad ongoing concern than it has been for the past decade or so) one of a small group of writers (like so many others) writing and sharing their weird little works on that platform, honing his skills in the dark, as it were, until he was ready to burst, a diseased fruiting body ready to spore.

And, once he was good and ready, he did that thing that literally everyone worth their salt involved in writing and publishing will tell you is just the absolute worst idea.

He self-published his first book.

To be honest, I balked a bit, but, I realised, having come of age beneath the shadow of the diy punk scene of Western New England it just seemed natural for him to self-publish his first book, like a scrappy little punk band recording their first seven inch in their drummer's garage and hand selling them at dirty basement shows [only…without, you know, the stink and filth and whatnots.]

So I took a chance and bought the damnable thing.

And…it was good.

But not just "good," it was visionary.

A weird little novel masquerading as a short fiction collection masquerading as a weird little novel masquerading as…well, you get the point: it was an absolute gem of weird recursive horror.

So I told everyone to buy the fucking thing, and they did (and then told everyone else to buy the fucking thing.)

---

[2] The middle "m," despite my insistence, does not actually stand for "Matthew."

But that's all just HOW it happened, not WHY.

The truth of the matter is that the WHY is simple: Matthew M. Bartlett is a writer whose use of the grotesque, reminiscent of both E.C. Comics and the Grand Guignol, and his notions of l'horreur cosmique bear some resemblance to Lovecraft but, at the core of his work, beneath all of the playfulness, all of the sticky grotesquerie, lies a strange sort of humanism, an antimisanthropy, and a deep and true sense of grief that we are all so temporary and so ephemeral.

But there's still more to it.

What if the trappings of "Satan," a la Dennis Wheatley and company, were, rather than standing in opposition to Lovecraftian notions of "cosmic horror," reframed as part and parcel of them?

A grand malignancy at the center of our history, of our very being, that took a great deal of amusement in pulling our wings off and burning us beneath his magnifying glass. Not out of malevolence but out of, as some high school gym teacher might say, "shits and giggles."

What if that amusement hid something deeper, something stranger?

When we see something in Bartlett's work that is an avatar of this cosmic horror, we see it through the lens of those who suffer beneath its horns or prostrate themselves in worship before the baleful gaze of its rectangular pupils.

We see it play and scamper, manipulating people to horrible dooms.

But we also see that it is always and forever out of time, like something that has somehow stepped a century backwards and forwards at once, the result being a sort of primal and uncanny sense of disorientation.

It's this notion, this disorientation, this grotesquerie of cognizance, that lies at the core of Bartlett's work.

We are never at home in our homes, we are never safe in our beds, and we are forever aware of this.

LET US FLY AND FEAST, LIKE WINGED SLUGS

We cannot trust our senses but we cannot trust out distrust of them, either (and his use of radios, that technology that was so pervasive in modern history that is almost gone, ALMOST but not quite, the airwaves still saturated with the buzz and cry of it.)

If it bleeds, it's Leeds, the saying goes, and much of his work is centered around that actually real and visitable township of Leeds, Massachusetts (although threaded through with notions of impossible and strange horrors that shape the town and the surrounding area, as reminiscent of King's Derry as Lovecraft's Arkham [but, again, Leeds is real and the points where that real becomes Bartlett's fiction are…not so much "points" as strange fens one must traipse through, wishing they'd brought some waders.])

Which brings us back, in a roundabout way, to disgust.

There are certain fulcrums that most writers' work pivot on (Ramsey Campbell's middle-class alienation, Terry Lamsley's misanthropy, Thomas Ligotti's notions of suffering, as some examples) and Bartlett's work gleefully uses the grotesque (and notions of disgust in response to the grotesque) as the center which his work spirals and circles around.

But! unlike the ever-churning nonsense of most "extreme horror" writers, he uses the grotesque to evoke not simply a childish response of shock but to examine something deeper: why the distortions of body and mind, the collapse of our edifices of decency and well-being, effect and affect us the way they do.

The unsettlement in Bartlett's work runs deeper than simple revulsion, attempts to out squick his contemporaries or inflict some sort of juvenile notion of "harming the reader."

What it does is something that echoes back to the absurdists, the surrealists, the impressionists, dada, even: it shows us that being is, paradoxically, both finite and infinite and that the edges of our understanding of the self are frightfully murky and prone to dissolution and subsequent horror.

We have notions of what "we" "are," but Bartlett's notions of the grotesque make explicit the fact that those notions are grounded in artifice and prone to slipping away like cheap greasepaint beneath achingly hot stagelights.

(And, cycling back to his Leeds mythology, we can find that our very notions of "linear time" are fundamentally untrustworthy with his use of anachronism and how EASILY that slips into our understanding of the work. Our consciousness should revolt against such absurdity and it should, by all rights, render the work worthy of ridicule but, in Bartlett's deft hands, it creates something deeply sinister and often leads to situations where the reader cannot trust their memory of what they have literally just read and that, as so much comes back to, leads to a sense of the grotesque, the malformation of "time" and "narrative," that echo that we see in the human and the animal in his work and his consistent use of the radio and its voices out of and beside time.)

However, there's yet more to the story of his stories.

His first book, (the above mentioned *Gateways to Abomination*) was a small masterpiece—a hybridisation of patchwork novel and short story collection that showcased both how horrific and how deeply funny our ends can be (and let no one ever tell you that Bartlett's work isn't funny; it is riotously so, as if Ligotti's humour at the pointlessness of everything where somehow stapled to Cheever's sense of wordplay and a sense of the disgusting that equally echoes Mirbeau's *Torture Garden* and, like, early Alien Sex Fiend.) A fantastic work and a valuable contribution to contemporary horror that would have sealed his place in any reasonable notion of "canon" in that regard.

And then came "Rangel."

A small thing, a longish short story first published as a chapbook by Sam Cowan's venerable Dim Shores imprint in a wee edition of a one hundred copies.

A small thing but a powerful thing.

A work that so perfectly combines how utterly horrific the truly absurd is with such an achingly profound sense of grief and loss that I

LET US FLY AND FEAST, LIKE WINGED SLUGS

feel no shame in saying that I found myself openly weeping at the end of it and that it gave me strange and appalling nightmares. A small thing that elevated my estimation of his work and that showed that he was willing to be complex, to understand the importance of the range of human emotion, that we are frail beings flailing around and dying like gnats on a windshield and, while that's profoundly hilarious, it's also utterly gobsmackingly heartbreaking. Our lives and deaths mean absolutely nothing and everything at the same time and there's no contradiction there, no cognitive dissonance to be suffered, just an immense weight we can never accept.

And that, frankly, is beautiful.

After "Rangel" opened the floodgates for him, he began to center much of his work away from that semifictional town of Leeds, with its witch cults and flying leeches and radiowaves, but even as he wrote of other places, other worlds, other ideas, he would still creep back to that disconcerting bit of the Pioneer Valley, that town that is both completely real (i've been there!) and entirely unreal (i've been there!) that crawls through him like a parasite, bringing us back again, and again, and again while we, the readers, attempt to fit all the pieces together of a puzzle that's swollen with mold and rot (with at least two pieces eaten and sicked up by some wretched ruminant.)

And so, here we are and I've said very little to truly illuminate Bartlett's work and absolutely nothing to illuminate any of the work within this book.

You see the names in the table of contents and you can trust some of them to take us to dark corners and brightly lit diners, strange woodlands and horrid houses, the haunts that we have frequented through his work, while yet others lead us to different places populated by different creeps where the influence of Bartlett is simply a whisper, barely heard, but recognisable if we focus, if we concentrate on it.

Now sit back, turn that radio dial to WXXT and enjoy the Unsettlement Show, these *Hymns of Abomination*.

HYMNS OF ABOMINATION

x18x

northampton's favorite son

yves tourigny

I'm a middle-aged white guy, I'm gainfully employed as a public servant, and I'm Canadian. All that to say: I'm not a thrill-seeker. Excitement for me is hunting for used books, or playing a mildly confrontational board game, or eating the last brownie. I'm definitely not one who enjoys being the center of attention. In fact, *any* attention, good or bad, causes me great anxiety. But what happened last year has some relevance to your project, and it would be irresponsible for me not to speak up.

I've tried to tell this story before. I posted a version online and got two angry faces and a sad face before it was taken down for not following Facebook Community Standards. I've tried to contact the Northampton City Council, the Hampshire County Sheriff's Office, and the Massachusetts State Police. None of my calls or emails get returned. I heard you were planning this tribute anthology, so now I'm writing to you. Maybe you'll consider publishing it, or at the very least include a warning in the introduction. Just…don't use my name. All I want is to put this whole thing behind me.

—x x x—

Necronomicon 2019 was held in Providence, Rhode Island, in August that year. I think you were there. I attended in 2017, but wasn't sure I wanted to return. My new girlfriend thought it would be a fun little trip, and my teenage son half-heartedly agreed to give me a hand manning the merchandise booth so I could take in some of the readings and panels. I let myself be convinced.

We drove down from Ottawa, mapping out a route that would take us through upstate New York, across Massachusetts, and into Rhode Island. We left early on Thursday and were making great time. Check-in at our motel in Seekonk wasn't until 5 p.m., so I proposed that we turn off the Massachusetts Turnpike near Springfield to have a late

lunch instead of eating the sandwiches we had in the cooler. We could find a place in, say, Northampton, just a few minutes off the Interstate, and do a little sight-seeing.

Neither my girlfriend nor my son share my particular literary interests, so the name meant nothing to them. I told them that it was the setting of several stories by an author with whom I had collaborated on a few projects.

My girlfriend tried to show some interest. "Oh, Lord Baron, right?" I corrected her gently, and took the exit which would take us north along scenic US-5, following the Connecticut River up through Holyoke and into Northampton.

Halfway through my sanitized explanation of the Leeds stories and why it might be fun to take some photos at some of the places they reference, my son put his earbuds back in. I felt the last few drops of parental love congeal in the chill of his disinterest. I know that seems harsh, but I think these feelings played a part in what came later. I'm not blameless in this story, and I'm ready to own my part.

We drove along train tracks for what felt like forever. I was worried that we had somehow missed the city when we finally saw several orange trucks marked CITY OF NORTHAMPTON DEPT. OF PUBLIC WORKS. "That's a good sign," I remember saying. My girlfriend gave me a dubious look before returning to *her* phone. "Dunkin' Donuts...Look, a Family Fun Centre! That's neat," I said. We passed car washes, used car dealers, and gas station after gas station while I desperately tried to find a landmark I could recognize.

"What's with all the beards," my son mumbled from the rear seat. "It's so random. All the construction dudes have the same beard."

"What?" I yelled back, only half listening. I had yet to see a single traffic light, and I was desperate for a place to stop. I wanted to load a map on my phone and get my bearings before running out of city. I felt pressured to get the most out of our visit, to justify my choice of destination. I was afraid to confront the possibility that perhaps

Northampton was as dull as they suspected that it, and I, both were. I was not paying attention to the pedestrians or the other drivers.

"The beards," he said.

"I don't know," I said, a touch too testily. "All I know is that I've seen fifty crosswalks but not a single stop sign or traffic light. This is crazy. Don't they want people to stop in town?" Sensing my anxiety, my girlfriend put her hand on my arm and suggested, quite sensibly, that I slow down. I eased off the accelerator.

"It's starting to look more and more like a regular downtown," she said, "and look, there's a light just up ahead." She was right, and I reached the light just as it turned red.

I was relieved to see that the Hotel Northampton was just ahead, since it meant the Haymarket Cafe was nearby. I had looked for places that served vegan meals and had been pleasantly surprised to discover that the Cafe, mentioned in a few stories, advertised itself as such.

I quickly found parking and asked my son if he could take a few photos from the back seat. I turned on the radio, searched for the lowest FM frequency I could find, then affected a look of horror for my Instagram followers with the Hotel Northampton sign directly behind me. I've attached the photos, disappointing as they turned out to be.

Obviously, we didn't stumble upon a WXXT broadcast or anything like that. My Hyundai's FM scanner couldn't find anything below 91.9, so that's what the blurry photos show. Reviewing them on my phone, I wasn't satisfied with my son's poor composition and unsteady hand. We were all a bit "hangry" by this point, so I bit back my exasperation at his inability to do even the simplest task, grabbed my fanny pack, and locked the car.

We walked over to the Haymarket Cafe, and I took photos of every building which looked old or interesting, paying little mind to my immediate surroundings. These photos are in much better focus: look closely at the figures hovering at the edges of the public spaces.

"I think he's right about the beards," my girlfriend said. I think that's what she said. I walked into her, then, and was about to apologize, when I realized that it wasn't her at all. It was the *author* (I've found that it's better not to name him).

I was surprised, to say the least. He seemed equally surprised, but he greeted me warmly, with a sweaty hug that cracked my spine. "Listen, I have to go," he said before I could utter a single word, let alone introduce him to my family. He asked whether he would see me in Providence, as planned, and I said that he would. "Ok, don't let me down," he said, with what seemed to me to be a touch of real menace. I was unable to articulate a response before he stormed off, theatrically.

"Hey, was that..." my girlfriend asked. "The author," I said, still shaken, "He, uh...we'll see him in Providence. He probably has a lot of things to prepare before then." I hoped that my son, walking his customary 20 paces ahead of us, was too far away to have noticed the interaction.

—x x x—

We found the Cafe and ordered a meal. I don't remember much about it, only that my son went to use the washroom and that I felt apprehensive about having him out of my sight. I was afraid he might pocket a candy bar from the counter or lift someone's wallet. He returned soon enough, however, and asked me whether all restaurants in the States had servants.

"I don't think so. Do you mean, an 'attendant?' Is there one here?"

"There's a dude in the washroom giving out napkins from one of these things," he said, pointing at a silver napkin holder. He's not the most articulate boy. "He said he needed money for cat food. He had the same ridiculous beard as all those other dudes." He said this to me with his usual half-smirk, as if he couldn't wait to tell all his friends the latest absurdity encountered on his father's stupid trip. I didn't quite believe him. He was a habitual liar, among other things, and I suspected him of wanting to forestall another discussion about the importance of hand washing. Despite a pressing need to urinate, I felt I couldn't risk the possible embarrassment of meeting an attendant in the washroom. I resolved to hold it until we found a Starbucks or some other well-known establishment.

My girlfriend asked, with a forced cheerfulness that signaled profound boredom, if there was anything else I wanted to see in town, and I replied that I was impatient to get back on the road since we had many things to set up once we arrived in Providence. In truth, I was trying to bottle the urge to return to Ottawa immediately and forget about the entire trip, which I felt was already going poorly. I couldn't bear the thought of being "on" for several days while my son scoffed and rolled his eyes next to me at my table. I think I may have wished that I had left him at home. I don't think it was anything worse than that, and I swear it wasn't entirely serious.

I was falling deeper and deeper inside myself, driving back along the same stretch of road we had traveled earlier when my son startled me by shouting "There! That's the napkin guy." I looked where he was pointing, at a man on a side-street pushing a shopping cart full of mannequin parts. At the speed I was going, he was out of sight in a flash, but I could have sworn it was the author. He had on the same outfit as when we had met on the street.

I should have kept my eyes on the road. By the time I saw the pedestrian in the crosswalk, I couldn't avoid him.

The car must have hit the man's knees, taking his legs out from under him. His flailing arms hit the hood, and his face hit the windshield in rapid *ba-dum-tss* succession, which would have been comical under different circumstances. The car continued to roll for several meters, moving under the unfortunate man so that he landed somewhere behind us, before finally coming to a stop. The impact of his face on the windshield left an imprint of his shocked expression in blood, mucus, and saliva, which must have mirrored mine.

"Hey, was that...," my girlfriend asked, in a voice completely without affect. I was frantically trying to remember whether the author had brothers, or whether his father was still living. I wasn't sure whether any of those outcomes would have been any less awful.

People approached my car on foot. I was too stunned to move, and noticed with detached relief that the airbags hadn't deployed. The rear door opened and shut. Someone tapped insistently on my window. I didn't know where to look. In the rear-view mirror, I could see several people heave the injured man unceremoniously into the rear cab of a DEPT. OF PUBLIC WORKS truck. Most of the people were dressed as the author had been, with the addition of orange reflective vests and hardhats. They all sported the same facial hair and glasses, a pair of which was embedded in my otherwise undamaged windshield.

I glanced out my side window where the author, dressed in an ill-fitting state trooper's uniform, was tapping on the glass with a filthy fingernail. When I started to roll down the window, he winked and gestured for me to keep driving. I let out some confused noise and was about to ask the officer what I needed to do next when my girlfriend put her hand on my arm and told me to drive in a tone that left no room for argument.

Looking in the rear-view mirror one final time as I drove off, I could see that one man was hosing off the street, while another picked up a shoe which had been flung off to the side and smelled it. The man with the cart was visible a few hundred meters beyond them. They were all maddeningly alike.

—x x x—

In Holyoke, we stopped for a long-delayed pee. I was shaking, and it was only when I cut the engine that it registered that my son was no longer in the back seat. I turned to my girlfriend, but she shook her head to forestall any questions, and climbed out of the car. I sat, paralyzed with uncertainty, convinced that law enforcement would converge on my location at any moment.

NORTHAMPTON'S FAVORITE SON

After fifteen uneventful minutes, during which I turned over the idea of returning to Northampton to locate my son, I exited the car and visually inspected the front end of the vehicle. There were only a few marks. I paid for a carwash to remove as much trace evidence as I could, and pried the glasses out of the windshield with my keys. I threw them in the ditch when we rejoined the Mass Turnpike. Each toll booth between Springfield and Worcester was a scene of great anxiety, but we reached Providence without incident.

—x x x—

We had a good time in Providence, all things considered. I wasn't surprised to run into the author. He put his arm around me and told me, his hot breath burning my ear, that he was glad I had made it. I told him I hadn't wanted to disappoint him. He looked none the worse for wear.

I introduced him to my girlfriend. He sniffed her with gusto and congratulated her on the pregnancy—she was two months pregnant at the time. She glared daggers at me and I made a helpless gesture as he took her hands in his and started kneading them, insisting that we return to Northampton before the next Necronomicon. "Give me a bit more notice next time, and I'll show you both the real Leeds," he said.

Some nights, when my newborn son shrieks and hollers and won't settle down to sleep, I'm ashamed to say that I'm tempted by the offer.

HYMNS OF ABOMINATION

x26x

my phone screams

out an alert. Amy's tagged me in a post. I look over at her, sitting up next to me in bed and scrolling through social media.

"I'm right here, you know."

"I know," she says without raising her eyes from the screen. "Just look at the post. It's an open call for an anthology. Thought you might like it."

"Oh?" Curious, I look at the post. A goat with shining eyes stares back at me. It's looming over a fuzzy tree line set against a bright red background.

"Hymns of Abomination," I say, reading the title. "Secret Songs of Leeds. A tribute to Matthew M. Bartlett." I shrug. "Never heard of him. Looks kinda weird. Plus, what is this, horror? Really? I dunno about that. My writing's more…observational realism."

Amy emits a theatrical sigh and levels a withering gaze at me. "So, observationally realise your way into this antho. Just because you teach *lit-rich-a*," she says, exaggerating each syllable and curling her fingers in quotation marks, "doesn't make all the other stuff less worthy or important."

"It's not that. It's a tribute anthology. Usually helps if you're a fan of the person being…paid tribute." I say the last bit awkwardly, fumbling over the words as they come. I'm glad I can write better than I can speak. "Probably also helps if you've actually read their work."

"So read his work."

She makes everything sound so easy.

"I'll have to buy it," I say, as if that's an insurmountable barrier.

"No you won't," she says, triumphant. "I got into him a few months ago. You can borrow my copy of his first collection." She gets out of bed and searches through the double-stacked books in her bookcases that take up a whole bedroom wall. "It's wild stuff. Gateways to

open call

aksel dadswell

Ab…" she pauses, runs her hands down a series of spines, "…om…" finds the one she's looking for, "…in…" and extracts it, "…ation."

"Didn't quite catch that," I say, laughing.

"Gateways to Abomination." She slaps the book into my hands, a thin red paperback with a hand-drawn goat's head adorning the cover. This one dwarfs a crude rendition of a cityscape, all blocky buildings with lots of windows. I flick through it and ask, "Why am I doing this again?"

"Because if you don't write this thing, I will. And I'll get accepted, and then you'll feel like shit for not even trying, and a rift will open up between us, slowly widening as your resentment at my success festers and festers, and then, *poof.*" She mimes an explosion with her hands, sets it off right in my face.

"Wow," I laugh, not finding this entirely hilarious. "So, basically, you'll break up with me if I don't write something for this?"

Her laugh is far more genuine than mine, and warmer, and I think Fuck, I don't deserve this girl.

"I just know that you have talent, and that those literary journals you put up on a pedestal are making your life hell and filling up this house with fucking rejections—and shut up, I know they're emails, the imagery is what I'm going for. My point is, I think you should break out of the loathing and doubt you put yourself through and try something new. And the best part is, you've got nothing to lose. If it doesn't work out, no biggie. But if it does, maybe you've got something different to do. Maybe you actually *like* it."

"You're the horror fan. Why don't you?"

"I'm not the writer."

"I'm not the *horror* writer."

"You can write whatever you want. Why limit yourself? Flex some different muscles."

"Okay, sell it to me. What does he write about? Why's it good?"

"Um, so there's this weird radio station run by a witch cult. WXXT. He writes short stories, and little snippets like radio ads and stuff set in this creepy little town in Massachusetts called Leeds. Everything kind of interlocks." She cups both hands like she's encompassing a globe. "He builds his world from it. It's really different, really well done. Quite funny and creepy. And gross. Lots of weird sex and body horror."

"Okay, okay," I relent. "I'll give it a try for you."

"No." She delivers a mocking smack to the back of my head. "For *you*."

"Fine. But look." I shuffle closer. "We know what you'll do if I *don't* write something," I run a finger from her neck to her shoulder, "but what do I get if I *do*?"

Amy sighs into my touch and laughs, low and gravelly. She reaches out with a blind, flapping arm to turn off the lamp and we're plunged into a cosy darkness.

there's something captivating and unpleasant

about Bartlett's work, but the words pull me in and don't let go. What began as a cursory, half-hearted skim becomes engrossment. Part of me doesn't like it, all these rundown rural settings and creepy old white dudes crawling out of the woods to wreak havoc on normal people, leeches in their smiles and horns emerging from their skulls.

There's something about it, though. I'm not a horror veteran, but the style is interesting and each nasty little vignette feels like a slow build towards something bigger. A whole world that stays with you, pooling in the brain, playing and replaying inside your skull over the course of the day, repeating so often that it becomes as subconscious as your own breathing. Your own private radio station.

The tumour in the brain. The clot in the vein. The blood in your stool.

I haven't read—experienced—anything like this before and I've no idea how to *write* something similar.

But I'm infected with it.

Even as I give my afternoon lecture, I have a hard time concentrating, my thoughts drifting back to the image of a goat bursting out from inside a man's flesh. A rain of red pulp, warm as a summer morning.

"So, uh, Raymond Carver's short stories were all about regular people," I say, eyeballing Jess at the back as she scrolls through her phone and doesn't listen to a word I'm saying. I stumble, doubly distracted. "Um. People facing quite normal issues, financial trouble, employment, alcoholism, quite often, um, marital or domestic problems. Predominantly blue-collar, working class people." I click to the next slide. "His prose was very minimalistic, and he often made the reader fill in the gaps, infer character motivations and thoughts. The way that he wrote, his style and subject matter were known as *dirty realism*, which is basically exactly what it sounds li—"

Gabe's got his hand up and he's clicking at me like he wants some service. I feel for the poor waitstaff who have to suffer this arsehole in restaurants.

"You have a question?" I ask him after an obvious sigh.

He starts talking, and some students behind him roll their eyes. Gabe always drags the class out with his pointless monologues-posing-as-questions.

A gentleman goat flaps its jaws in my ear, smacks its lips. "Eat him," it tells me. "Kill him. Suck the marrow from his useless bones. Only useful for eating. Flap flap flap goes its mouth."

Flap flap flap goes the goat's.

There is no goat, you idiot.

I shake my head a little to get rid of the voice and the hot reeking breath I'm imagining against my ear. Gabe's halfway through his rant. I've got no idea what he's talking about.

—x x x—

I rush my way through the garbage fire of a class, deflated and distracted and feeling like an idiot.

When I get back to my office, I make a list of things to include in my tribute. Tribute. I let out a little giggle. It sounds like a sacrifice, something made to appease the gods.

I flip open my notebook to a new page, write down the words **radio—SOUND** in big letters and scratch a line underneath. Then below this: **winged leeches** and **goats** and **Benjamin Stockton** and **something crawling out of the woods** and **descent into madness** and **blood? LOTS**.

These are things to tick off but what's my approach? I draw a line beneath my list, bisecting the page. I tap my pen against my bottom lip, and wracking my brain feels like wringing out a dry cloth in the hope of extracting some moisture.

Maybe I need to know more about Bartlett and his work.

HYMNS OF ABOMINATION

x32x

OPEN CALL

a writer dedicated to the nightmarish and the debauched

is revealed with a quick Google search. No shit. He self-published his first collection of stories and vignettes, nasty snippets all. From there he's achieved escalating success over the years, and a cult following in the horror community.

Looking at reviews of his work on Goodreads, I discover a mini essay on *Gateways* that reads more like a masturbatory rant interspersed with slivers of actual information. Whoever wrote it obviously knows their stuff, but they're probably not the kind of person you want to be stuck in an elevator with. They proclaim from the start that "I need a shower after reading this, my skin beaded with fear-sweat, the grime of Bartlett's words accruing in every crease." That's fair enough. I keep reading.

> Bartlett is a writer whose work will sit comfortably amongst such crown'd heads as Barker, Lovecraft and Ligotti. A writer who we should all consider, from this moment, as horror royalty.

Crown'd heads? And Amy calls *me* a wanker.

> Even the names he comes up with for his characters have a sense of grotesque tactility reminiscent of Dickens or Mervyn Peake. You can really feel the sharpness of a Francis Styrax or Benjamin Scratch Stockton against your tongue, the bitter taste of Abrecan Geist, the phlegmy and infected Rexroth Slaughton, and the raw, unclothed monstrosity of even simple-sounding monikers like Anne Gare or Uncle Red. Horror hides behind every word. And oh, those words!

HYMNS OF ABOMINATION

The quality of Bartlett's wording is so precise that it unsettles the reader on a level beyond the stories themselves. The rhythm of his prose, once read, takes up residence in the skull, and as you go about your daily motions, as you sit at your mind-numbing, exploitative job, it is Bartlett's work that circles your psyche like a vulture, descending in ever-tightening spirals, and you can be sure, dear reader, that it's coming for the dying meat of your poor old brain. But to liberate, or annihilate, or something else entirely?

Either way, the world deserves to read this man's work, and we need to bring these dark, sparkling wonders to a wider audience. You read his words, and you can't help but worship at this strange and bloody altar.

Indeed, if it bleeds, it's Leeds. But before I abscond into the crawling night, I'll leave you with something to think on. Why would these creatures and characters that populate Bartlett's oeuvre, these entities bent on corruption and debauchery, why would they limit their malign influence to Leeds? Why not the whole of Massachusetts? Why not America? Surely their designs should be as wide-reaching as they are nefarious?

But then, what is Leeds? Leeds is not a place, Leeds is an *idea*. Leeds is the world. Leeds—

I click the X on the window and it disappears. Enough of that. I know what the imaginary goat would whisper in my ear about this guy.

There's something here, though, something about the words. The power of language. The reach it has, the way it shapes perception. A worm in my brain.

I add **language/stories = infection???** to my meagre list. I hesitate, sucking on the end of my pen. Then: **Reach** and **How far? Beyond Leeds??**

That's enough for one day.

—x x x—

Over dinner, Amy and I talk about our day with vague turns of phrase and euphemisms. I don't mention the goat, but I tell her I've read some of *Gateways*.

"What do you think?"

"I like it, actually."

"'Actually,' he says."

"I just haven't had much time to read it in between driving and work and stuff. Hard to figure out how to approach it at this stage."

"You should try the audio book. Both collections have different narrators, but they do the voices *so* well."

"Okay. I might try the second one. What's it called?"

"*Creeping Waves*," she says, waggling her fingers at me.

Later, in the dark, she bites my lip and draws blood. She giggles an apology and breathes "Don't stop," into my open mouth, licks the wound and stuffs her tongue inside. She feels alive and pulsing. So do I. We're one throbbing vein, stretched between two skin suits. Glutted on the blood...

...the blood...

...the blood...

the words ooze

through my speakers and sink down into the sludge of my brain. I imagine them as corpses slowly enveloped by a bog, scrunched and wrung out in the close, encompassing darkness. The weight of these stories is crushing me, changing me. They're always with me now, the words so busy and vibrant in my head. They spill and buzz and chuckle away even when I'm not reading or listening. Awful fat cherubs with bulging nappies bounce against the ceiling of my skull.

The narrator's delivery is pitch-perfect. He does a great job with all the voices, the different lilts and intonations, pacing and vernacular. It pounds within the confined space of my head.

My whole life feels like a confined space, or is it defined by them? Confined by them? Drive to work in my car, spend the day in my office or classroom, drive home, eat dinner, maybe watch TV with Amy, fuck, sleep, and then over again. And over. And over. A pattern that everyone knows and everyone endures. And nobody cares because we're all in the same dingy boat. First world fucking problems under late stage fucking capitalism. I should do something about it, but I don't. Won't.

I need an escape. I have the seed of an idea for this tribute, something about a character who tries to branch out, expand their horizons. About how they end up worse off than when they began. The creeping crawling cloying decay of life, the flesh's rot and the brain's ooze.

My thoughts are loose and untethered, but they feel true, somehow. Or they're skirting the truth. Something I'm not aware of but I'm so close to getting. Some vast secret of the universe hiding in plain sight.

I shake my head and try to focus on the audiobook.

One story finishes and the narrator moves onto the next, this time with a feminine singsong lilt to his voice that does nothing to lessen the feeling of bugs crawling over my skin.

"Anne Gare's Rare Book and Ephemer*ugh*." What was supposed to be "ephemera" deteriorates into a wet cough. The voice tries to clear its throat but it turns into a coughing fit. There's silence for a moment, and I think the app's crashed, but then:

"I know you're there, dear listener. Little eavesdropper. Little," its voice deepens into a dark dirty growl that's suspiciously reminiscent of the goat's, "*voyeur.*"

For a moment I'm almost convinced it's addressing me, but it's obviously a trick of the story.

"No," says the audiobook. "You were right the first time. I really am talking to you."

My head's pounding and I just want to close my eyes and sink into the words the way the words have sunk into me.

"Don't close your eyes," it tells me. "You have to open them up. You weren't paying attention before, were you? Now you are, now you know the truth. Maybe it's time you shared that experience. We like the look of you, Bucko. Sonny Jim. Congrats from us, you've made it to the next stage. Gotta show us what you've got, though. This selection process is tougher than old Bantam's possum cakes, and it'll give those bowels a'yours a run for their money as it passes through ya. Or," and here its voice drops to a whisper as I lean closer to my phone, "as *you* pass through *it.*"

A subsequent burst of grainy cackling shocks me, and I recoil. But then it cuts itself short, hisses at me. "Whoopsie, someone's coming. Best get back to the regular broadcast, Bucko. Be seeing you, sooooooooooooon." It stretches the last word's single syllable into an elastic moan, which eventually snaps and returns the track to its normal narration.

I scrub back through the chapters but what I just heard is nowhere to be found. I don't have time to think about it before there's a knock at my office door and Gabe pokes his head through.

Someone's coming—

My eyelid twitches and ticks.

He enters and takes a seat. He looks more humble than usual, and I know he's about to ask for an extension, or essay advice at the very least.

"The final essay, I just wanted to ask…"

Gabe keeps talking and I'm half-listening, nodding along. He seems increasingly agitated as he talks, looking around the room, scratching at his arms and face. After a moment he stops mid-sentence, frowning and looking around.

"Sorry, professor—what's that sound?"

I stop and realise I've had the audiobook blaring from my phone. I hadn't noticed. It's just background noise, now. I'm absorbing it rather than actively listening. When I press pause the silence rushes in to fill the void like blood in a spittoon and I shift and scrunch, suddenly uncomfortable.

"Sorry. It's an audiobook. Research for something I'm writing. Trying to write."

He looks at my phone, the screen still bright with *Creeping Waves'* nightmare carnival cover. His gaze lingers, his expression shifting from confusion to curiosity to…hunger?

He licks his lips, essay troubles forgotten. "Would you recommend it?"

"Um. Sure, if you like weird stuff. Or even if you don't. I don't, usually, but there's something about it. It…gets inside you." I don't know where these words are coming from, but they taste like they're not mine.

"Sounds cool," he says. "What's it called?" His eyes look glassy.

My eyelid's still twitching.

night soaks in

with rain and cold as I cradle my fifth glass of wine. My mouth's tacky with it, tongue all rough. Amy's washing the dishes—it was my turn to cook and hers to wash up—and I'm scrolling through my phone, sipping my drink way too fast. A show I'm not paying attention to plays on the TV.

When Amy's done, she slumps down next to me on the couch with a sigh. Now that we're over thirty, simple pleasures include sitting down at the end of the day, errands run and jobs done and drama over. Her hands are rosy from the hot water, a few splashes darkening her T-shirt.

She sits there for a moment, looking around at the objects in the room: the TV, the bookcase, the blinds over the window, closed against the night. Me with my wine and my phone. Her book sitting on the armrest.

The whole thing feels fake, like a set. The audience must be sitting just beyond the door, faces dark, waiting and silent. No laughter yet, but it's coming.

The rain makes a gentle rhythm outside as it encloses us. To me it sounds like static, and that's even more comforting. I can feel the goat's breath again, its words an incessant trail of foul language and violent imperatives.

Observational realism, I think, stifling a giggle. I turn it into an exaggerated cough, clear my throat, push down the grin that wants to rupture my face.

Someone knocks at the door and for a moment I think it's Gabe at my office, back at work. It's loud and sharp, urgent. Weird to have a visitor at this time on a weeknight.

"What the fuck's that." She doesn't say it like a question but a line she's reading, and without much conviction. She doesn't look very concerned or surprised, either.

I can see the artifice, the script behind the performances. I'm so tired. I just need some sleep and these weird feverish thoughts will slough away.

The knocking's furious now. I look at Amy, and she stares back, not blinking or moving. I get up with a huff. The visitor doesn't stop pounding on the door until I go to it, swearing under my breath, and wrench it away from their eager fist.

"Have you seen this man?" asks the man at the door. It's one of the neighbours. Phil or Pat or Mike or…something.

"What man?" I ask.

"This man," he says. He raises a hand and flexes it in front of his face, nails caked with dirt. The coat he's wearing is filthy, too. His forehead is stippled with sweat despite the cold.

"What's wrong, mate?" I say.

He frowns and looks dazed for a moment, like someone on the verge of waking. He looks around like he doesn't know how he got here. "I…can't remember? I needed to come over here, to show you something?"

He pushes past me into the house and stands there, dripping, in front of the TV. Amy greets him with a dull smile. What's up with her?

He looks at me. "It's about the open call. They said to say," he mouths the words and looks off to the side, trying to remember his lines, mouthing them silently before he speaks. "They said to say, yes, that it's down to you and the other guy. You need to…prove you've got what it takes, bring your work to the next level. They also said, and this last bit was the most important part…" He puts on a serious, elderly tone, something that makes me think of a Victorian gentleman. "Ink isn't going to cut it, young man.'"

I'm so confused, but there's something building inside me. My perception's fuzzy. I can't form words. All I can taste is wine and bitter fruit. It sours in my mouth, overripe and crawling with larvae. The door's still open, and the rain sounds like radio waves from here, like children screaming or laughing, I can't tell. There's that studio audience.

OPEN CALL

"He's right," says Amy, and I think I really am going nuts. She comes up behind me and her mouth's hot and moist against my ear, her fingernails scratching at the back of my neck.

"It's about a place," she says, "but the place is inside us. All of us." It sounds like a fucked up motivational slogan. "You just need to find the little door inside you, babe. Swing it wide and let. Us. All. In." She nods her head with each word, like she's ticking items off a list.

Phil or Pat or Mike nods along with her, his eyes locked to the floor.

"What's going on with you? Who the fuck is this?" I gesture at the grubby looking man standing in our house, dripping on the carpet and fiddling in his pockets.

Amy sighs. "You'd better hear what he has to say. There's one more thing."

"One more thing?"

"One more thing," confirms the man. His hands stop shuffling in his pockets and he pulls out a knife, its blade wicked and jagged and long as my forearm.

"The story..." He starts reciting again. "The story matters just as much as what you use to write it with." As he speaks, something squirms in his mouth that isn't a tongue, a black and glistening undulation, and it adds its own sibilant layer to his words, a substrate of sound I can't quite discern beneath the surface.

He looks at me, and he says, "Did you get all of that?" He swallows, a real cartoony gulp that makes his Adam's apple bob, and he looks around as if to check who's watching, listening.

He steps towards me, his voice low and hoarse and urgent.

"We're not who we are, you know."

"Um," I say.

"Or what we think we are. Certainly not me. Not anymore. And not her." He gestures drunkenly at Amy before looking back at me, stone-cold sober. Terrified. The knife trembles in his hand. A tear tracks down his face. Eyes wide, glassy. "It's you I have the message for."

And then, before I have time to absorb what he's said, he raises the knife and opens his throat in one swift stroke, and at the back of my mind I'm trying to remember that exact wording. *He opens his throat in one swift stroke,* it's got a great melody to it, a good rhythm and rhyme. I should put it in my submission.

I feel terrible.

At least there's one less competitor, I think as blood soaks the floor and the furniture and the man collapses in a gurgling heap. Amy stands there, just staring at Phil or Pat or Mike as the seconds tick by and his life literally leaks out over our floor, and then some switch flicks inside her and she just starts screaming.

As if on cue, a record player's needle starts scratching a crusty, crackly tune into the soft parts of my brain.

Her scream rises to the heights of terror or orgasm, I can't tell anymore, and my vision's getting fuzzy around the edges. For a second, I think she sounds like she might be enjoying this before my body turns to jelly and unconsciousness pulls me into its murk.

—x x x—

When I wake, there's no body on the floor and no sign of Amy anywhere. I call and call for her, searching every room, peering under every bed and looking in every closet, pantry, and cupboard. Nothing. Not a hair or a whisper or a giggle. Just this: a bathtub full of blood.

I stand in the bathroom, my phone clutched in my hand, dialling Amy's number over and over again with no response. Everywhere's pristine except for the bath, full to the lip.

The blood sloshes and shifts occasionally, as if something's living in there. As if anything could. But then I have a bathtub full of blood in my house and an AWOL girlfriend, so at this point anything's possible.

I don't want to sink my hand in to pull the plug, and I don't know what else to do, so I just close the bathroom door and go to bed.

OPEN CALL

While I lie there, I play the audiobook to soothe my nerves and help me sleep. It'll all be okay in the morning. I've got work tomorrow, a class to teach that should be easy and normal and distracting.

It'll all be okay.

and so, the goat emerges

from the human host. Although, of course, he's not really a goat, but something far greater, something much more."

I'm in class and I can't remember driving here, or what happened earlier in the day, or if Amy showed up.

The slosh of dark liquid fills my head.

The students are staring at me, frowns creasing some faces. Some are scribbling down notes. I've got a marker in my hand. I look at the whiteboard. I've written WXXT in huge letters down one side.

Jess raises her hand, pulls it down again, raises it. For once she's paying attention. "Um, I thought we were still looking at Carver this week?"

"We are. This is…additional content. I thought it might be good for a bit of contrast. Dirty surrealism," I add, laughing more than I need to.

Nobody says a word. Chairs shift and squeak. Papers rustle and pens click. Gabe's at the front again, scratching at his wrist, running a tongue behind his lips, a sheen of sweat on his face. A fly buzzes, collides against the window over and over with a little *plip* sound that fills the quiet.

I pull out Amy's copy of *Gateways* and start writing out a passage from it onto the whiteboard. The marker squeals as it makes the words, as it shapes out a version of its world in mine. Goat teeth gnash and snap at my ear. I can still feel the blood under my nails from last night's kerfuffle. The sound of a man opening. Amy's screams. A record player's needle scratching its song into my brain.

"I need your help," I tell the class as I write. "I'm trying to emulate Bartlett's work and world and style, to write something that pays tribute to his stories. I need a way in, and I've almost cracked it."

"I know what you're writing."

"What?" I turn around.

OPEN CALL

Gabe's sitting up straight, watching me. He's stopped his itching and his hands are splayed out in front of him. His jaw moves ceaselessly, as if he's chewing something. His body language is off. He's different, has a sharper edge somehow.

"This story spans eons. Space, time." He bares his teeth in a snarl that's a grin that's a snarl. "You showed this costume how it goes. He's *comfy*, by the way." He wriggles obscenely in his seat and winks at me.

"I see what you're trying to do, boy. This is good work. I'm very proud." His voice is gravel. "This open call worked *so* much better than I expected. Leeds was our world, but we want *the* world. We want to bring Leeds with us, expand its edges. So much more life in the ocean than the puddle." His eyes are as red as stovetop coils, glowing and…fizzing? I can feel the heat from here. "Yum yum, goat's bum."

People are moving away from him now, chairs scraping away from desks as they congregate at the back of the room. Someone's sobbing quietly.

"Who are you?" I say, even though I think I mean *what*.

"Baaaa," says Gabe, a sound like a sheep or a goat. "Baa baaa, baa." His sounds turn to splutters and then he coughs up a word. A name, one I'm not surprised to hear. "Bartlett." He gnashes his teeth at the end. The goat in my ear, the static that fills the world. The worm in the apple in the anus. The bitter grit at the bottom of the bottle. Bartlett.

"But I'm a bloke of many monikers. They call me Scratch, Benji. I'm one of my own characters, you know. Or not characters, really. Look how real I am." He pokes at his face as he rises from his seat. "Flesh and blood and far from home."

Someone's telling me to call someone, to do something, please, puh-lease *pluh-ease*, their voice cracking the word like an egg as their panic rises and spills out between the broken syllables.

Someone else is asking what the fuck's going on with a nervous laugh, like this is all a weird practical joke. A learning experience. Part of the lecture.

Some of the students finally get a hold of themselves and move towards the door, but before they can flee it opens from the other side and in walks Amy, grinning. She looks odd, though, bloated and sick, her skin blooming with angry, shiny bruises that pulse and flex. She looks at me and smiles.

I'm so happy to see her.

But nothing is as it was. Perhaps never was. These are all just costumes. That's something else dressed as my girlfriend. Just like Bartlett's wearing a Good Ol' Gabe outfit. Squeezed in, he is. It's a tight fit.

She approaches me and says, "One last kiss?"

I hold her, and she feels plump and well fed, but also strange, boneless, her arms rubbery against her sides. I kiss her and her lips are as inert as a Halloween mask. "Baby," she says, in a voice that buzzes from somewhere else. I bring my hand up to her face, run my thumb over her cheek as tears fill my eyes. Her flesh comes away in my grasp and what's underneath pulses glossy and black, a shape stuffed into my girlfriend's skin. After that first piece comes off, the rest follows, sloughing away in front of me, the most captivating and catastrophic strip tease. The human falls away and beneath it is something ancient in its simplicity, a thing of primal functions honed to perfection.

I step back and the thing that isn't Amy anymore rears up to its full height, a boneless sinew of prehensile flesh, squirming and fattened on what I know must be blood. Her—its, *its*—mouth snaps and puckers. Wings buzz on its back. A winged leech, taller than a person.

"Baby," it says again, before it rises to the ceiling to survey the scene, a squirming angel aloft and observing.

The rest of the class is chaos now. There's too much going on. Some are trying in vain to smash the windows, some cower under their desks. Most are huddled in a corner of the room, sobbing and howling at Gabe/Bartlett/Benji. His eyes are bleeding and they drip on the floor, sizzling through the carpet.

He laughs and laughs as he advances on one group and then another, chasing people around and around, snarling and biting at them.

The door's closed, and all logical concepts such as "exits" have ceased to exist for them now. Their only reality is the inescapable horror contained within these four walls.

Gabe's laugh turns painfully high and squeals like a bad connection, but this isn't the worst of it. Something's coming through. The noise is a gate and his flesh too, a door opening on hinges never used in this part of the world.

Something sizzles and pops like cooking meat, and I can smell it now, the caramelising fat, the hot juices sloshing in the pan. My stomach rumbles, mouth watering.

Gabe opens his mouth wide, impossibly wide like a carnival clown and static pours out, a brambly verdant sound so dense I can actually see it, a liquid cross-hatched from shadows and blood. Gabe seems to shrivel a little as he retches this matter up, but it clings to him, is part of him, or part of the thing that's using his flesh as a doorway.

His skin splits and blackens, peeling back like a pepper in an oven and the meat beneath stretches, contorts, desperately trying to re-shape itself around the growing form, the sentient noise that's bursting from him like a newborn.

But it's not enough.

One body alone can't carry all that, sustain it.

Help me, begs the static. *I need more*, it pleads in a voice that comes from nowhere and everywhere, filling the room with its volume.

I want to scream at them to "Stay away!" or "Fucking run!" but that's not my role in this.

Jess steps forward, breathing hard and clearly about to shit herself, but she wants to help, and this overrides her sense of self-preservation. It's her downfall.

It reaches out with one of Gabe's human hands, his eyes pleading, while the bloody pulsing tentacle of sound reaches round from the other side and snatches her.

And then it pulls a slack, dead-eyed grin onto Gabe's face, and it gets to work.

HYMNS OF ABOMINATION

Amy writhes and pulses at the ceiling. Her buzzing, crooning language fills my world.

OPEN CALL

squelch and squeem and schnak

goes the class, and the made-up words that flare in my head with each impact make me giggle and spit.

I just know this is it. I've cracked it. I'm almost there. I've got a way in, now. The anthology awaits.

I watch while the thing that's now much more Bartlett and a lot less Gabe tears my students apart like warm bread, blood so thick in the air I can taste it, feel it mist on my skin like condensation. I think I'm crying, too.

As it works tirelessly, reducing each student to screaming meat, the staticky writhing growth fattens, each murder bringing it further into the world as it adds pieces of them to itself. The Gabe part of it changes, too, his head and neck stretching beyond recognition until his skull's just a screaming mouth around which Bartlett sculpts his masterpiece, his new and glorious form. The spine and ribs split in two directly down the middle and they're appropriated as adornments atop the bulging, growing head.

"Baa baa Bartlett," it croons in a voice like spoiled milk, hunkering down in the corner of the room with its back to me, ministering and whispering and singing lullabies to what's left of its craft.

The work takes several squishy, crunchy minutes to complete, and all the while I'm wondering if I'm the author or the audience.

But I'm just standing here, watching it all play out.

I haven't done anything, not really.

"Oh yes you have," says the Bartlett thing, in a voice as old as sound, in a voice that cracks like pack ice and trembles like a mastodon in heat. It's all but finished now, steam spiralling from its feverish flesh. Its shoulders rise and fall with each breath. The jagged coils of its horns scrape the ceiling. The floor at its feet is a slick of viscera and discarded parts.

The whole room reeks of blood and meat.

HYMNS OF ABOMINATION

"We broadcast the word," it says, the wet globs of each syllable falling to the floor. "And you answered our call. I want to show you just how much you've helped. I want you to see me. Lay your eyes on what the Great Sound has wrought."

It turns to face me. It's a patchwork thing, a creature of pieces and parts that's so much greater than the whole, a fleshy goat-thing, bipedal and so tall it has to hunch to fit in the room.

I'm not the only one confined.

Each leg is a whole person cracked and torn into shape, its flanks a tight jumble of arms and legs, its chest made up of lesser torsos. Its head is magnificent, its teeth a mess of splintered bone and fingers. Each eye is a severed head, one slack-jawed with awe, the other still locked in a scream. It's slick and bright with blood, wet as a newborn and far more beautiful.

At this reveal, the giant leech that used to be my girlfriend floats down from its perch on the ceiling and alights between Bartlett's legs to complete its nauseating anatomy. Its horrible, wonderful shape shudders and laughs with pleasure.

At the back of my mind, some vague and icky subtext screams out, but I'm too distracted to pay it any attention.

The leech thrums and pulses between its legs, a grotesque distended cock longer than I am tall, as lusty for blood as the rest of its new master.

"You've read my words," it says, leaning down and addressing me directly. The heat and stench and raw wonder of its regard is too much for me, and I shit myself where I stand. "D'you know what they are?"

It wants an answer, but I can only tremble in the presence of such a thing.

"A gateway," it sneers. A red-slicked hoof made from someone's clenched fist taps me on the side of the head.

"It builds and it grows and it feeds." A wet bone-snapping cackle, and then it raises its head and howls words like a wolf baying at the moon: "Double-yooo ex exxx teeee," it screams, the sound of the horribly elongated syllables slightly out of sync with its mouth's movements. My head's pounding, buzzing.

"I've got a gift for you, a thanks for worshipping at my pages. A story of your own."

It leans down towards me until our lips touch, and it slicks my face with red. It retches and coughs, hawking something from its great maw directly into my mouth. The knowledge, the sound, grainy and chewy, and I'm gagging on it, on the sharp awful orgasmic taste that fills my mouth, my throat, my whole self. I gulp it down without consent, with no choice left but to digest it or die. It's the dirt under the fingernail of my soul, I think, and belch out an acidic bubble of laughter. I should write that down. I should write this whole thing down.

No pen around but there's blood, blood, blood on every surface. I dip a finger in it, and write my story on the white board, and then the windows and the walls. They'll have to choose my submission. They'll have to.

Bartlett watches me craft my tale, and he smiles his goatish smile.

You are reading *Hymns of Abomination: Secret Songs of Leeds*, a tribute anthology to Matthew M. Bartlett, the good ol' goat of the woods, the biter of your wife's bum, the wart on your daughter's inner thigh, the maggot in your son's turd, the leech on your teat. Next up, a screaming rendition of your own death, performed by Slaughton and Dither, followed by Benjamin Scratch Stockton's special recording of the sound of a thousand babies sleeping, chewing, cooing…But don't ask how he got it, just look at the smear of darkest red around his mouth. Tune in, but don't you dare—don't you *fucking dare*—tune out.

HYMNS OF ABOMINATION

Anne Gare's Rare and Import Video Catalogue
October 2022

Jonathan Raab

"Elephant Subjected to the Predations of a Mentalist" — Dir. B.S. Stockton, 1921

A harrowing 47 seconds of early black and white motion photography, this film appears, at first, to be a derivation of the popular 1903 silent film short *Electrocuting an Elephant*, but is in fact something far more grotesque. A simulacrum of a large, grey elephant stands at center frame against a backdrop of a labyrinthine concrete industrial complex. Upon closer inspection, the creature is revealed to be an undetermined number of men, women, and children trapped inside a large costume of grey-painted fabric and bound together with lines of rope, patchwork thread, and cloth billowing in the wind or pressed outwards by hands seeking escape.

Each leg of the human body-assembled beast is composed of two or three tall, muscular men lashed together by pig iron chains to support the weight of the creature's bulbous body. The elephant's trunk is likewise a person wrapped in chain and dirty textile, but rail thin and malnourished, face twisted into a painful grimace or the rictus grin of recent death. The elephant's head is a globe of cloth and floppy fabric ears that bubble and pulse with the struggle of those within. Its painted-on eyes and smile are white and stupid, comical in their cartoonish proportions.

Just as the viewer's mind begins to accept the horrific contours of the elephant's construction and its nauseating implications, a black-clad figure enters from the right, movements blurred by missing frames and the degradation of the film stock. The figure raises a cloven-hoofed hand, points at the writhing mass of human suffering trapped beneath fabric and chain, and—

Well, we won't dare spoil it for you.

Agfa nitrate base film stock, acceptable condition.

Two thousand three hundred dollars.

dead in september

My memory of Marla Breevort was abysmal at best, considering her seventh grade All Hallow's afternoon prank of vomiting peaches and rubber worms into my locker. She got a slap on the wrist, I got the clean-up. After all, she was mother's favorite student, and I was mother's least favorite son.

When I saw Marla again, it was at the old, run-down pub by the cemetery. The one splattered with lead paint, ugly phrases, and the occasional fecal smears of the local homeless fellow the neighborhood children liked to call "Uncle Larry."

Mother had died the week before. We set her to rest, and then came the onslaught of every wretched student she ever deemed her "favorite." Clyde Turpin from band class, William Wilson, who plagiarized all his papers, Celia Winch, the little cyclops! And Marla, who I didn't recognize at first. The sight of her brought a burst of cold air into my stomach. I couldn't place the memory until she turned to face me, her strange, square face less off-putting than it was in childhood, now taking on what could have been a glamorous appeal, had I not remembered it laughing at me through fake vomit.

My stomach turned as she approached, but the anxiety vanished the closer she came. Marla had become a delicate sort of woman. Pale and graceful, no more black lipstick or taxidermied rodents in her purse. I remembered the first-grade rumor that her birth parents put her up for adoption when they found her playing house with Lucky, an exsanguinated dog.

"Hey Morton," she said. Her voice was mud and wood chips, like a monster on a WXXT radio drama, one you might want to fuck. I stared. She looked transparent, dusty.

"I'm really sorry about Mrs. Dooley." Her wayward antics had cooled to a wistful, mysterious air. "My Grandpa died a few weeks ago, too. Suicide."

"I'm very sorry," I was able to choke out before my limp, gray hot dog arrived in a moldy bun. I didn't have the energy to ask for a fresher one. Marla slid the dish back towards the server.

"Look, Mortie. Can I call you Mortie?"

"Please don't."

"I know a cute little coffee shop a few streets over, tucked away, over by Mr. Milkerton's place. Not a lot of seating, so…"

"I'm sorry, I have to be around to receive condolences."

"Nobody's here, Mortie."

I turned to see Aunt Julia waving goodbye from the door, grimacing from ear to ear, the foul stench of her underarms wafting towards us in the October breeze. My appetite died, so I tucked my wallet in my back pocket and began to put my jacket back on. Marla put her jacket on, too.

"I'm sorry, I have to go feed my tortoise." She rocked on her feet for a moment.

"Look, Mortie, I wanted to say sorry for all the stupid things I did to you in high school."

"What about junior high?"

"Those, too."

"And at Langford Primary?"

"Mortie…"

"And story hour at the Leeds Library?"

"Christ, how do you remember back that far?"

"People remember pain!" I yelled. The lone server in the pub gave me a look like I'd just pulled out a knife. I walked out and got in my '89 Ford pickup. Marla knocked on the window.

"I figured since you lost your mom, and I lost someone close, maybe we could have some coffee and talk about it? Sure ain't easy around here to exchange compassion."

Compassion? I laughed to myself. What did Marla Breevort know of compassion? Wasn't she the one who took pictures of dried-up bodies under *that* tree at Look Park for her senior photo project?

"He treated me real bad you know, scratching me up every time he got annoyed."

"Huh?"

"My grandfather."

I paused. I suppose I remembered Marla coming into school some days dressed oddly. I thought it was just her being a freak. Who wears long black sleeves in July? I didn't know she was hiding something.

"I'm sorry, Marla. That's not right, that kinda stuff." She looked down at her feet. I felt a pang of guilt, and unlocked the car. The click made her look up, a rush of excitement in her eyes.

"Come on. Where was that cafe again? Shallowbrook Lane?"

—x x x—

"Grandpa Grim was always obsessed with his own suicide, said it was going to make him famous, get him in the *Leeds Weekly*."

Grimaldi Breevort. When I told my mother about Marla puking in my locker, she said it must have been some old gag her crazy kin had taught her. I figured she meant the old bastard. Marla said he worked at the Northampton Lunatic Asylum back in the '70s, though she also said he told everyone in Leeds that he had a fist fight with a Pukwudgie one night on old Cemetery Hollow Road. When he was asked if he got a good look at it during the fight, he said no. "There weren't any streetlights back then. Only the stars overhead and the screams of bobcats. But it had an ass like sandpaper."

"One day he was sitting in a beach chair in the garage with the *Weekly*. He saw that a local teen committed suicide by overdosing on Exelis. You remember that stuff? Grandpa was pissed, since he was planning to OD on it in the local playground."

"Did he...did he teach you the worm thing?" I asked, hesitating to do so. I felt like a fool the moment I said it. Marla laughed.

"Sort of. I'd sit on the staircase and hear him talking to himself in the shower. Something about the Master of Worms. And when my brother Irwin was born, he was the favorite. He called him his little worm. So, I don't know. Maybe I thought of them as a good thing."

Richard Frogtoucher came into the cafe and shot us a foul, curious look. Marla rolled her eyes.

"Dad hated Frogtoucher."

"You don't mention your dad a lot."

Marla took a sip of her coffee.

"Daddy disappeared into the Leeds backwoods when I was twenty-two. For about four years before that, he had been helping Grandpa build what he called 'our impossible house' at the end of Cemetery Hollow Road. Grandpa kept building, adding to it...cupboards, stairs, right up until the day he died."

I remembered the house. It was a giant white Victorian with a huge front porch and a white birch tree in the front yard. People didn't tend to walk that far down Cemetery Hollow Road, so close to the woods. I sure didn't. It gave me the creeps.

"Is that where you live now?"

Marla laughed.

"No. They buried Grandpa with the key to the house, per his request. The key, and his goat, Thurston"

I chose not to ask how one gets a goat into a coffin with a six-foot-four-inch dead man.

"So where do you live?"

She took a moment, playing with her pewter spoon, before choking out her words.

"Nowhere, really."

"You're homeless?"

"Well, I guess you could say that. I try not to."

"Like, kind-of homeless, or Uncle Larry-homeless?"

I had taken a liking to Marla, though I suspected it was sheer boredom and intrigue that drove me to her. It was like I wanted to dig her up, the old her, whatever the hell she was about way back when.

DEAD IN SEPTEMBER

That, and I was desperate to fuck, six years post-divorce. I invited her back to my house to talk some more, drink some more.

—x x x—

I felt something I'd never felt in quite that way. Joy, obsession. We fucked and every inch of her was satisfying. It was half past five in the morning. Marla's post-coital cigarette was the WXXT radio station. She rolled over to turn the dial and scrubbed to it.

"My parents hated the radio. Never let me listen. So, I listened at night." I think everything Marla said to me was like some oral autobiography. Normally, I wouldn't have given a shit, but something made me want to know more about her.

"So, your dad disappeared. What about your mom?"

I knew a bit about the woman. Ellery Cruz (she kept her maiden name) was not a pie short of 800 pounds. Her skin looked like purple cottage cheese, an infected berry on the verge of bursting. We only saw her on the cusp of Autumn, when she would go out to the pumpkin patch and choose the most warped, phallic-looking gourd for who knows what.

"Momma's dead. She choked on something."

I remembered a column in the *Leeds Weekly* saying she had to be taken out of their house with a backhoe.

"That pissed off Grandpa, real nasty-like. He regretted funneling her those high-calorie meals, but only cuz he wished he'd thought of doing it first."

I moved her hair from her face. Her skin was icy, sweaty. She looked panicked.

"Hey, are you ok?"

"Actually Mortie, I have to go. I had a really great time."

She stood up and grabbed her undergarments.

"Wait, you don't have anywhere to go!"

"I'm staying with a friend down by the churchyard. It's ok."

"It's almost dusk! Isn't the eyeless man out about now?" Marla smiled.

"I wonder if he's related to old Celia Winch. D'you remember Celia? I heard she poked her eye out with a stylus in college."

I was unsettled by her smile. Who would smile at something like that?

She wagged a finger at my tortoise, waved childishly, and headed out the door.

—x x x—

I met Marla for coffee a few more times that week, only half of the days followed with fucking, during which Marla seemed increasingly dry and cold. Asking her what was wrong was pointless. She was in mourning. We both were.

"Could you do me a favor?" she asked me out of the blue one day when we were taking a walk through the local pumpkin patch.

"Depends."

"Could you come with me to my old house and help me get in? I still have a few things left over that were precious to me. You know, heirlooms and such. I couldn't get them out before the town locked up the property."

I hesitated. "Isn't that…illegal?"

"My rightful property is in there."

"Yeah, well, can't you contact the town?" Marla looked like she was anticipating my stupid questions, but still resented answering them.

"It's in foreclosure. Grandpa didn't want me to have the house, blah blah blah. It'll take ten minutes to pop a window and grab my things."

The hair on my neck was standing up. I'd never done anything like that before, breaking into places and what-not. I was a goody-goody growing up and too damn tired from work in adulthood to do anything but surf the internet.

"I'm not really comfortable with that Marla, I'm sorry. Are you sure there isn't a way? Do you want me to call the town hall for you?"

She didn't answer me. The rest of the night she was monosyllabic, and we split at my front gate.

—x x x—

A week and a half went by. I didn't hear from Marla. I left her a few messages, even stopped by the cafe at our usual time to see if she was there. She never was.

By the time week two rolled around, panic set in. She was homeless. Where the fuck could she be? Was she murdered? Was she squatting? Had she found some other loser from high school to blow and try to con into breaking into her old house for her?

I went to the Leeds police station on October 13th to file a missing person's report. Officer Llewelyn laughed in my face. "What kinda game are you playing, trying to report someone we already have a report out on?"

"Pardon?"

She ripped a flyer off the wall and held it out to me.

HYMNS OF ABOMINATION

MISSING

Have you seen this woman? She disappeared from Cemetery Hollow Road on the same night that Grimaldi Breevort, her maternal grandfather, committed suicide by unclear means. No foul play is suspected. She answers to Marla Ellery Breevort, enjoys humiliating pranks, and undertakes fornication with nonstarters. She has a younger brother named Irwin, who is married to a bittern. Her fourth and fifth toes are deformed and she is allergic to leeks.

-LPD

DEAD IN SEPTEMBER

I felt a bolt of pain shoot through my stomach.

"Officer, this says missing since September 19th?"

"Yes, it does." she answered, clearly annoyed. I walked out of the station with the flyer, not bothering to ask anything else.

—x x x—

I walked down Cemetery Hollow Road, watching 247 grow larger in the distance. Victorian farmhouse mansion type-things aren't built nowadays. Now everyone wants a silver box and minimalism. This was the kind of house that held history like cell memory. Like blood.

A foreclosure sign dangled from the white picket fence. I laughed to myself. Of course, Marla must have gotten in and been squatting there. I hopped the fence (it was a quaint, stubby one, as if it circled an old lady's garden), and went to the door. Locked. I began checking the windows on each side of the house. Nothing was broken, dislodged, anything. It was eerily undisturbed. My worry came back. If Marla wasn't in there, where the hell was she?

Of course, I couldn't be certain. She had said her grandfather kept building. Maybe he built a secret entrance, like a storm door. I checked again and didn't find anything. I look out into the field in the back of the house. A lone billy goat stood way out there, staring. Not chewing, or stomping, nothing. Just staring.

—x x x—

I sat up in bed that night, Orville the tortoise on the pillow beside me. I turned the dial to WXXT.

Ol' Jimmy Juicejoint is at it again. The elderly fuckhound went out into the woods with dead mice glued to his skin to declare his submission to the Leech. While the rat and mouse ritual is rare in these parts, some crawl out from the woods with their eyes eaten out, their assholes sore from the brittle woodland fucking. Juicejoint is a new grandfather. Turns out it's a girl, and he wants her for a sacrifice when she's ripe and defiled. Not by him, of course. She has many Christian suitors in town, Catholics to be specific.

HYMNS OF ABOMINATION

What could ripen one more for sacrifice to the Leech than getting fucked by a Catholic?
You're listening to WXXT. The time is 3:41 am. Grab the shovel and dig up the truth. Bury something while you're at it. Up next, we've got The Tremors performing their version of "Float Mama Down the River."

—x x x—

There were only a few hours until dusk. I'd been digging and digging, hands calloused by that hysterical digging. I had to get the key to the house. When the shovel hit the coffin, I heard a strange squelching sound, like squeezing a tomato. After a struggle, the lid finally lifted. Inside was the headless body of an elderly man shoved into the hollowed-out corpse of a goat. The key was dangling from a horn, blood and goo dripping from its hilt.

—x x x—

I limped to 247 Cemetery Hollow Road in a dissociative fugue. The radio broadcast repeated in my head. *Dig up the truth. Bury something while you're at it.*

The key turned in the lock as the first rays of sun pierced the night. The house was preposterous. One couldn't even see where to walk. The ceilings were crooked, rooms were isolated triangles, the staircases led nowhere. Floorboards, ceiling boards, strange convergences of wood and glass, a labyrinth of material and repeated, twisted images.

"Marla?" I remained in a daze, thinking that maybe if I retrieved some of her personal items from the house, I could get back in her good graces. I crawled through a hall that could barely fit a grown pig…a claustrophobic nightmare one would only see in a fairy tale.

My jacket was caught on a nail. I struggled to turn and dislodge it. My head was touching the ceiling, arms grazing the walls. I was on my knees, crawling, regretting every second as the space grew smaller.

DEAD IN SEPTEMBER

I finally managed to turn and get free of the nail. It was then that I saw a small door that I had passed. An optical illusion had kept me from seeing it while crawling forward. I opened the door. The odor was foul. I vomited in my mouth and swallowed it back, lifting my shirt to cover my mouth and nose. I looked closer. I looked. I looked and I looked and I saw her. Marla, her chest cracked open, her grandfather's head peering out from breasts and torso with a triumphant grin. Marla, dead as a doornail, roadkill in an impossible room, an impossible manic house. Not dead since I last saw her, or first saw her. Dead in September. Dead long before.

—x x x—

THE LEEDS WORD AROUND TOWN
By Miss Margaret Maughbrook
From Ms. Maughbrook's column in the *Leeds Weekly*

Mr. Morton Dooley, grandson of the late local poet and mystic Michael Dooley, was admitted to the Northampton Lunatic Asylum on October 14th. He was found raving in the front yard of 247 Cemetery Hollow Road around 7:15am. The property has been in foreclosure since the death of the late Grimaldi Breevort, who made his fortune in goat milk farming. Care of Mr. Dooley's tortoise has been passed on to the Leeds pre-school center, which also recently took in a turkey vulture that was found eating foreskin out of a desecrated grave.

HYMNS OF ABOMINATION

x66x

Anne Gare's Rare and Import Video Catalogue
October 2022

Jonathan Raab

"Residents of a Spiritualist Colony in Orford Parish, CT" — Dir. Iris Dunlopp Whitcomb, 1915

A curiosity attributed to Canadian filmmaker Iris Whitcomb via her name and title displayed on a handheld chalkboard in the opening frames of this six-minute strip. Not much is known about her outside of a few obscure academic papers and out-of-print books that mention her as a point of interest in the broader tradition of the creatively bankrupt and morally degenerate Northerner Royalist cinematic arts. Mrs. Whitcomb finds herself among such Canadian-auteur luminaries as Daniel E. Aykroyd, known for espousing quack UFO theology and shilling a mid-shelf spirit best suited for cleaning industrial working surfaces; Michael Clattenburg, whose television programme following the misadventures of criminal trailer park residents is an observational mode documentary depicting the rotted fruit of Canadian neoliberalism in the working-class environs of Nova Scotia; and one David Paul Cronenberg, a cut-rate pornographist whose "artistic" output consists primarily of slime-coated practical special effects that mime the form and function of malformed human sex organs.

This strip depicts shots-in-portraiture of the various hucksters, charlatans, phonies,

HYMNS OF ABOMINATION

frauds, fakes, conmen, and hustlers known to frequent the medium enclave-cum-syphilitic colony historically known as Oracleville in Leeds' beloved sister-city of Orford Parish, Connecticut. (A missive delivered to this shoppe by interested parties from the Orford Parish Historical Society informs us that in 2009, Oracleville was mercifully bulldozed by corrupt property development interests (but we repeat ourselves) and has since become known as the Low Point Urban Opportunity Zone, where out-of-state capital and organized crime interests (*but we repeat ourselves*) cycle ownership of the quick-build, low-quality, postmodern apartment complexes that now cling to the cursed soil like gangrenous sores.)

Each of Mrs. Whitcomb's subjects is more grotesque than the last, with physical, mental, social, spiritual, and political deformations of the mediums and spiritualists on display, effecting migraines or mild panic attacks in the viewer.

Goodwin Celluloid on reel and in case, acceptable+.

Twelve hundred dollars.

suddenly my house became a tree of sores

What I saw and how I saw it: As if through a cracked piece of sea-glass, worn to kaleidoscope etching, all lights forming haloes and all darknesses eddying like some fungal sea. Through dry and bleeding eyes. At a distance, through the mind's dirty windshield. In shreds and patches, drips and drabs, bits and snatches. By implication only, the same way Rorschach formed his blots.

A woman cloaked in moth-wings so long they drag the dirt, standing on a high hill, overlooking us all—the town, the woods, the road, me. Every move of her shedding dust, tiny scales, reflective, musty. A scent like the very end of brush-fire, ash and ruin, a salted ground.

She looks down, she looks down, she looks down. Her eyes rake the ground. Her burning, burning eyes.

I will go insane.

I have *gone* insane.

—x x x—

It happened slowly, so slowly, up until it didn't. I remember the creep and rot of it now, but at the time, I was distracted. So much to do. This is how women live, forever cocooned inside the lives of others, a fungal, many-layered shroud. It forms over years, ripping away only with the greatest difficulty, a scab atop five hundred interwoven scabs. Every rip you make spews spores, and those spores infect the exposed, raw flesh anew, sowing yet more layers—a whole harvest, spreading so fast, unwinding so slowly. As if I was an Egyptian already mummified, struggling to unwrap myself.

If men knew how often women are filled with white-hot rage when we cry, they would be staggered, I remember someone saying the other day, through the groaning static of my house's ancient intercom system.

We self-objectify and lose the ability to even recognize the physiological changes that indicate anger. Mainly, though, we get sick.

And oh, how true that is: We sicken, we are consumed, laughing wild amidst severest woe. We flourish with illnesses that have no cure and a thousand different names. Hysteria, the lung, wandering womb syndrome. Our own immune systems turn against us, fight us as if we ourselves were diseases, infestations. We wither, we swell, miscarry, grow phantom pregnancies, ingest our babies and turn them to stone. Our wounds fester, turn inside-out. Our equipment rusts and degenerates from over-use or lack of use or potential for use alike, decays within us, sliming blackly over the rest of our pulsing, stuttering interiors.

Things get lost inside us: penises, forceps, scalpels. No maps to the interior. And every once in a while, we simply flush our systems without adequate warning, drooling blood in clots from inconvenient areas, dropping squalling flesh-lumps everywhere—in trash-cans, in bathrooms, shoved under beds and swaddled in bloodied plastic, buried shallowly, immured behind walls that bulge with black mould-stains, pumping out flies.

This house I live in is sick as well—that's no secret. When I first entered it, as a bride, I thought I felt it welcome me, but that was only an illusion; it fastened shut around me instead, less a mouth than a wound, forcing us to grow together in mutual disease. Where once this house began where I left off, we nowadays seem far too entangled for any such distinction, crammed tight alike with garbage and debris. A hundred thousand useless cheap and dusty objects lie enshrined within, packed tight from floor to rafters, and myself the most useless amongst them by far.

My husband orbits the wreckage on a weekly basis, returning only to demand his conjugal rights before returning to the office. *I promised you children,* he reminds me, less a vow than a threat, or a plea turned inside-out: Why marry in the first place, if not for some elusive dream of reproduction? It takes two, after all; we're not amoebas, he and I, able

SUDDENLY MY HOUSE BECAME A TREE OF SORES

to rip ourselves in half and call the result John or Jane Junior. It should be instinctual—birds, bees and fleas do it. Rats in the walls.

Just do it, darling. Just let it happen. Let me help you let it. Let nature...take its course.

I would if I could, I want to say, but don't.

And thus I swell too, deflate, swell again, every month on month, with little real result. This morbid, moon-drunk cycle. Is it some infection inside me, roused and then soothed, stiffening like scar tissue? Some horrid tumorous intimation of cancer to come, temporarily defused every four weeks or so, but never fully cured? Hard to tell, without medical aid.

Impossible, nearly, 'til the evidence finally presents itself.

—x x x—

Later tonight she'll come to me again, my moth-winged harbingeuse—perched darkly upright in the highest crook of a tree, standing rather than crouching. Fiercely predatory. Her gaze will sting as it passes me by, a cigarette's glancing burn. Fragile grey snow will fall around her like ash from the sky, shake from her scales like pollen and dust, dissolving into a wind that comes and goes in the same rhythm as her breath. She still smells of reckoning.

You are empty, she will tell me, lips unmoving. *A living ghost, mirror-trapped, flesh-mired. I can barely see you, even from here, inside your mind. Can you see yourself?*

Barely, I will reply.

I can help with that.

I'm unused to believing in dreams at this point, or even remembering them. My sleep is disordered, like everything else; I drug myself insensible, wake with head hammering and mouth dry. Opiates are like that. Sometimes I think I've poisoned myself so thoroughly that other people could probably drug themselves just by burning my body and inhaling the smoke.

HYMNS OF ABOMINATION

The moth-winged woman has no eyebrows, just a doubled arch of eye-sockets as deep-set and high-ridged as an owl's. Her hair is plaited thickly into two long braids, tied back with a sheaf of what looks like vines. Ivy-leaves crown her peering face, its features round and blank and pitted, skin nacreous-luminous as the hanging moon. Her nose-tip dips beneath her top lip, sharp enough to pike out a dead man's eyes. And none of this will seem unlikely to me, as I register it; none of this will seem unfamiliar, or odd. It will seem, quite simply...inevitable.

What brought you here? I will ask her.

You did, she will reply, unsmiling, to which I will shake my head. Asking, as I do: *Why me?*

Because.

That's no answer.

When she cocks her head to stare at me directly, at last, her gaze will hurt worse, yet so beautifully. Her mere attention enough to pin and mark me forever, an invisible brand.

The only one you'll get, from me, she will say, then. *The only one I have to give. Now...*

...do you want it, or not?

—x x x—

Men'll want to stick things up inside you, too, my mother used to tell me, in between spasms of vomiting that rarely brought up anything but bile tinged with blood. *They just* love *doing that. Want* you *to love it, and say so, all the goddamn time. But you won't.*

Her voice, so tired and scratched all over, with all its bones showing: An x-ray plate from Stalinist Russia, printed under the counter with forbidden music. And what does the sound of it remind me most of, even now? Those words from the ducts, of course, eddying, static-laden. The intercom system, moaning blood-resonant, like sonar inside my skull.

Stick things inside, I repeated, in my unformed little voice. *Like...their* things, *Momma?*

SUDDENLY MY HOUSE BECAME A TREE OF SORES

Honey, that's the absolute least of it.

My mother, I sometimes think—*our* mother—was made from cast-iron, for all her complaints; she pumped us out like etchings, the way a press works, spitting kids like a nail-gun does spikes of iron. Me and all the others, those grubs I hauled from pillar to post, wiping their tears and snot on anything handy. There were so many of us, you see, and the room we crammed inside when she had visitors was so very small.

They're all outside and we're all inside, that's why, if you have to wonder. All of 'em hypnotized by that snake between their legs, that crawling worm—say we're the ones got the whole human race cast out of Eden just to gnaw a piece of fruit, but is that true? How can it be? They're the ones speak serpent, baby, not us; remember that, if nothing else. That's the root of the trouble, right there.

Repeating again, dumbfounded, as if chewing the words over twice would make them more palatable, let alone understandable: *They have no in*sides*?*

Ha, and isn't that the truth; none that matter, anyhow. Now get in the closet and be quiet, the lot of you. Keep your mouths shut so the nice gentlemen don't hear, or there won't be any supper.

Red light on the wall, flickering gently, and the smell of gas besides. Red curls on the wallpaper, raised mock-velvet mouths all screaming soundless, gums bare, with never a tooth between them.

I remember pressing my hand to my sister's lips—sister? Brother? Baby?—and holding it there firmly, no matter how hard they tried to bite, as we watched my mother entertain through the ill-set crack between door and jamb, the keyhole winking at us like her phantom third eye: *Stay still, stay silent. Study what happens now, if you can stand to.*

And then the usual choreography, the flapping buttocks, the flailing limbs. A music-less dance, done badly. That same flabby pink worm-snake she'd been raving over earlier crawling out of one set of drawers, excruciatingly slow, just to burrow deep again through the barely-tied strings or too-wide, dirty lace-festooned leg-hole of another.

HYMNS OF ABOMINATION

It was here, through this narrow strait-gate, that I got my first glimpses of the future, without even a cracked sea-glass lens to scry them through. How my life would be nothing but a series of ins and outs, in and between all the rest. How this closet I squatted in would prove, if only metaphorically, both tomb and womb.

Where did they all go, I sometimes wonder, these relations of mine? My fellow spawn? Out into the world like shrikes and jays, screaming, spreading carrion. Riding the migratory urge like another air-current, one I must have been born unable to interpret, and leaving me behind.

This house is a cage, I think. *Like this world, or my body.*
Yes, the intercom replies.
I am buried here, rotten, rotting still. I always have been.
Yes.
But—more and more—I do not think I always *must* be.

—x x x—

As evening falls, like clockwork, my husband comes home, seeking his weekly solace. He expects dinner served promptly, followed by me spreading myself out overtop clean, fresh sheets, all shaved and powered and sweet-smelling. But tonight is not that sort of night.

Are you here? He calls out through the darkened house. *Honey, where are you? What happened to the lights?*

(I went around crushing them in an oven-mitted fist, dear. The glass rained down like stars, and in its tinkle I heard the moth-winged woman's laugh.)

My husband moves further inside, feeling for the switches, muttering strings of swear-words each time he flicks yet another one that also fails to work. Then raises his voice once more, calling: *Honey, it's me—can you just answer me, please? What's this stuff all over the floor? What's that smell?*

(Dinner, dear. What else could it be?)

SUDDENLY MY HOUSE BECAME A TREE OF SORES

He's entering the kitchen now, its air thick with smoke, equal parts charred chicken and melted plastic. Slipping on defrosted vegetables that squish beneath his shoes, I hear him hit hard as he lands on one knee, one hand, skinning both against the floor; he must surely be feeling his raw flesh burn as it connects with a scattered layer of salt mixed with bleach that I've spread all over, since he gives such a ridiculous little yelp of pain before screaming my name. *Damn it, Ayla! What is this? Where the hell are you?*

(Upstairs, dear. Follow the sound.)

(Follow the sound of her wings.)

Granted, it's currently smothered beneath the carefully overloaded washing-machine's grind and churn, the steady sloshing of water as it spills down the staircase, rendering the deep-pile carpet sodden enough to squish beneath him as he wades upwards, pulling himself along by the banister. But the further he travels, I trust, the more audible it will become.

Turns out, I have things inside me already, I want to tell him, *and they need to show themselves. They need to talk to you, my love.*

But really, why spoil the surprise?

Up, and up, and up. Past the ruin of the bathroom, the tangle of the walk-in closet. Through the corridor of photos, once perfectly posed and framed in gold, all left hanging askew and smeared with filth, their individual panes of glass carefully shattered. Into the master bedroom, where every sheet lies slashed and the mattress excavated fistful by fistful, eiderdown swirling like a snow-flurry hurricane tangle. He breathes some in and coughs before doubling up, coughing even harder, as the moth-winged woman's pheromonal danger-stink finally begins to penetrate. Sucks yet more detritus down and spasms, hands to mouth, while he spatters his palms first with blood-tinged mucus, then thin, bile-flavoured vomit.

He calls my name again, a growling moan, but I...I don't answer. I have no reason to.

I simply press my back against the balcony railing outside, looking up into the black, black sky, and wait for him to find me.

—x x x—

White-hot rage.

I remember reading about a woman running naked down a road, both arms severed just below the elbows and ground into mud to keep her from bleeding out; I remember how three cars passed her before one stopped at last, that one driven by a couple on their honeymoon. I remember reading about a man who testified that the first time he strangled a woman to death during sex, they were both so drunk he didn't know what he was doing and she didn't try to stop him. I remember thinking how much more persuasive that testimony would be if only we could summon her to rebut it.

I remember my first abortion, looking up over the rubber sheet and the doctor's bent head to fixate on a framed 1940s-era poster on the office's back wall; *Meat is a material of war,* it read, *use it wisely.* I remember my third miscarriage, listening to my body mourn even as my mind flooded with relief, knowing that whatever lurks inside me should never be given a chance to escape. I remember driving two states over to beg another doctor to tie my tubes, only to hear her argue I might reconsider and return to sue her. And: *No no, you don't understand,* I remember choking, through nauseated tears. *The ways I'll change, if something does manage to take hold...the things that thing will do, if it survives...*

I'm not *hysterical*, for God's sake; I never have been. I simply know myself, intimately, well enough to understand that no one else should ever have to. To know that all my bloodline truly prepares me to spread, even when it's admixed with someone else's, is disease, and rust, and blight.

Ruin, sister. Reckoning.

Yes, oh yes. Exactly right.

Above me, the moth-winged woman hovers stable as a dragonfly, flickering with promise, baptizing me in dust and ash. My harbinger

SUDDENLY MY HOUSE BECAME A TREE OF SORES

angel, poison-soaked and haloed with every sharp-spread finger and toe finally recognizable—at such close quarters—as less a claw than a sting.

Inside, my husband still stumbles back and forth, searching, calling. Her eyes burn and mine meet them, itching to catch fire fully; I feel cataracts form like half-dollar sized mirrors, ferryman's fare, reflecting everything. They make my pain and rage look *beautiful*. Almost as beautiful as her...

But not quite. Not quite yet.

I'm not sure about this anymore, I tell her, silently, hearing the intercoms wheeze to the pulse of my thoughts. *It doesn't seem fair—to him, I mean.*

You called, she reminds me, her voice leaking from that same system, cloaked in static. *Your choice, not mine. All of this is your choice, Ayla.*

I know, I reply. *Never think I'm not grateful. I've been alone so long, suffering, and it's not as if he noticed. But still...ignorance shies close to innocence, especially here. Whatever he did to me, I let him do, without question. Should a man whose only crime was to think he loved me really have to die, just because I don't want him? Because he never guessed I never did?*

Should he?

...maybe not.

A click beneath my breastbone, turning. It's as though I plunged a key made from knives inside myself, cutting one last hole through which I can finally hope to escape my body's cumbersome cage. And I feel myself swell, feel myself harden, feel myself breathe out until my lungs deflate, a crushed white butterfly. Feel my bones turn to brass, my skin to scales. Feel my hair rise to taste the night air like a corona of snakes, even as my back humps and my shoulder blades crack apart, exposing my spine. Making room for this fragile new set of wings now emerging, mainly nerves as yet but already widening, thinning, stretching to form a pair of membranes stiff with bioluminescent cartilage that snap and spit against the night. I open like a flower, tasting my own destruction, turning myself inside out—and even as I gasp with the sheer beauty of it all, as I howl with elation, I watch my husband's head swivel my way at last: *There she is, there.*

Watch him lunge for the French doors that separate balcony from bedroom, even as I thrust my hands up to meet the moth-winged woman's and beg her to lift me up, to take me away, to gather me in and fly. I want to be gone now, long gone, before he has the chance to recognize me. Before he has the chance to try and stop what can't be stopped.

He can't, she assures me, all ten sting-fingers plunging deep into the webs between my own blunt digits. *None of them ever could.*

I know, sister.
I'd kill them, if they tried.
I know.

Ayla! He screams, as her own wings give one tremendous beat, powering us up beyond the clouds. I don't bother to answer, though.

That is no longer my name.

—x x x—

What I see, and how I see it: The ground, dropping away as she swoops yet higher, higher, higher. My husband staring after, reduced in one beat more to pixels, to memory, the absence of such. The house, a tiny, infinitely crushable toy, no longer worth the stepping on. This stupid human sphere of reproductive torque and lurking mortality, in which—from now on—I will share no further part.

You can't just think yourself out of things, my mother used to tell me, *not even if you go crazy. More's the damn pity.* And that certainly proved true, for her; far too bitter-proud to pray in her personal abandon, so no angel ever came to liberate *her* from that penitential whorehouse rack she'd condemned herself to...along with me, of course, and all my siblings. Those hate-cured seeds she cast back into the maelstrom after fertilizing us with the disgusting spectacle of her doom, hoping our well-learned capacity to turn pleasure into plague might raise a crop to envenomate the world that ruined her.

SUDDENLY MY HOUSE BECAME A TREE OF SORES

I am my own child now, I think, looking up at the moth-winged woman and knowing her for what she is: Yet another maggot bred from my mother's corpse come at last to glorious fruition, buzzing through the cosmos, sowing decay and wisdom in her wake. And I hug her close, secure in this vision; I grow myself into her, tucking my nakedness into some pouch-womb birthed from imagination alone, where I can sleep for as long as it takes to dream myself back into being. I cicatrice over, forming my cocoon, looking forward to becoming, to being. To playing harbinger myself once I emerge, once we descend again on an unsuspecting planet full of things like me.

Don't drop me, I beg her, curling close.

Never, she replies.

HYMNS OF ABOMINATION

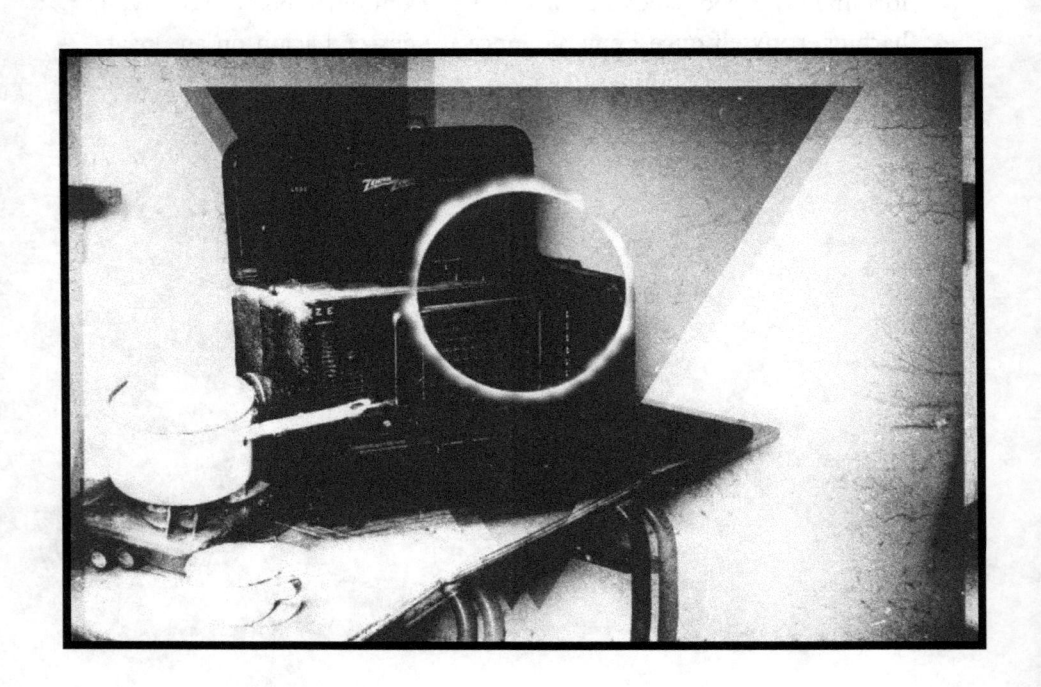

x80x

Anne Gare's Rare and Import Video Catalogue
October 2022

Jonathan Raab

"Ol' Will's Birthday Bash and Dither Family Reunion" — Dir. Various, 1952

A collection of disjointed, stuttering, handheld shots taken over the course of one afternoon and evening at a birthday party. The image is fuzzy and green, as if the lens were coated with a translucent slime. The film depicts dozens of malformed, asymmetrical faces over the course of its nine-minute runtime, all wearing pained, forced smiles. There are shots of a picnic table, home to open, steaming dishes of discolored, rotting lumps of meat and overcooked vegetables congealing to mush; a dog, hanged by its neck on a leafless tree, its paws still twitching; an interior countertop, home to row upon row of bottles of dark and anxious liquors; children, fleeing into a cornfield of tall, leering stalks and rows that run at angles contrary to all sane and sanitary principles of distance, horizon, and perspective; and a birthday cake, its surface full to the limit of burning candles, brought forward through a line of naked, pale bodies, whose mouths twist and lips slap in mockery of song. At its terminus, the cake reaches an amorphous, fleshy impossibility, all mouths and eyes and chipped teeth and bowels roiling beneath the surface of its repugnant, stained skin. Dare, dare to look upon ol' Will in the depths of his cups, at the nadir of his descent, within the apotheosis of his transcendent debasement! Dare! Dare! **DARE!**

16mm film strip on reel and in case, acceptable+.

Two hundred twelve dollars.

HYMNS OF ABOMINATION

x82x

puppy milk

It's like a toothache. It takes over everything. A patch of rot grasps a nerve and the world falls away. Your body disappears, your pasts and futures dissolve into a single intolerable present and all you are is a throbbing sweaty toothache. Like it's the only thing you've ever known.

They aren't the words I'd prepared. They come in the moment, like a wave crashing through me. I don't even look at the paper crumpling in my hand. I close my eyes and it all comes out between gasps.

> *You said you didn't believe in free will. That's what war is. My body isn't my body. A pale tooth. The world's a pale tooth. A twirling spear drilling through the spaces. All the spaces. Your father sucking your clit. It's a twirling tooth. A pale tooth. A twirling bone. The world's a twirling beak. A pale tooth. A pale bone. The world twirling like a drill. A twirling tooth. A pale bone. A pale drill. Twirling like a tooth. A bone. A drill. A bone. A tooth. A drill. You don't even know. It's the music that used to be you. In your ear. In the air. You don't even know. A twirling tooth. A pale bone. A pale drill. Twirling like a tooth. A bone. A drill. A bone. A tooth. A drill. A tooth. A bone. A drill. Drilled milk and cum. A bloody fucked tooth. Fucked bloody. Drilling. A tooth. A bone. Spins and spins and spinning milk and cum. Milk and cum. So much and all you can do is stop breathing.*

I breathe in. My head tips forward, my lips press into the microphone. (Warm and sticky. Why is it sticky?) I exhale and my breath hisses through the room. I jolt upright. Back in my body. Back in the room. In the café. All Sedona-red walls, curving bulbous plaster giving a shoddy illusion of something organic, like the walls of a cavern, like we're all trapped in this tiny wet pocket. All of us—me and Liz and Chelsea and the other Leeds High burnouts, encroaching on the shitty old bohemians. All of us packed in and robbing each other's breath.

Hesitant clapping. The open mic emcee taps my shoulder. "Um, cool. Thanks Nicole." I look away and wobble off the stage. "Okay, next up we have Mya W. Let's give it up for Mya!"

I drift between the chairs, gently bumping into shoulders, toward Liz and Chelsea in the back. Liz looks away, at her shoes or over her shoulders. Like she's trying to hide. Embarrassed, for me or of me. But Chelsea stares me right in the face, and that throws me off. She'd been in her own little world all day, big puffy headphones wrapping her ears, fist clutching a Walkman, thumbing the radio tuner. She'd barely said a word since lunch.

"That was…different," Liz says, faking a laugh. A solitary *ha*.

"Where'd you hear that?" Chelsea asks, still staring, almost like she's staring through me—not all the way, but past the skin, the muscle, the bone. The question crawls inside my mouth. It pries at my gums.

"What?" What's she on? Am I on it too?

"What you said up there." She's almost shaking. My jaw throbs in sync with her tremors. "Where'd you hear that?"

White. Sticky white. "Nowhere," I say. I believe it but it doesn't quite feel true.

Liz finally looks me in the face. "You don't look so hot."

I wipe my forehead with my sweatshirt, smearing a charcoal birthmark on the sleeve. A wet achy fever beneath my skin. But I don't tell her that. I just say I need some water and push through the clusters of people to the pitcher between the stage and bathroom. Empty, except a few dying ice cubes and a limp lemon sliver. I head to the counter and wait while three customers crawl through their orders. It's the busiest I've ever seen the open mic. All strange smelly bodies pressing into each other, chatting over the awful uptalk poetry honking through the PA. I hate it but it's the last place in Leeds that'll let kids hang out.

The barista—I've seen her almost every Friday this past year but still don't know her name—waves me in. "What can I get you?"

"Water."

"Water's over there." She points toward the pitcher. "*Next*."

"It's empty." Sweat pours down my forehead, into my eyes, distorting her features. Making her blurred, bloated, monstrous.

"What?"

PUPPY MILK

"Pitcher's empty."

"And?" She clenches and unclenches her jaw.

"And?"

"And what, you didn't bring it with you?" She slaps the bar. "I can't leave the register. Bring it up so I can fill it. *Next*."

I push back through the crusts and failed Rainer Marias, grab the pitcher and head into the bathroom. The mirror stretches across the entire wall. I almost don't recognize myself in it. Like I'd been dipped in water and aged two decades. I look like my mom.

That fucking toothache. Stuck in the back of my jaw. Like I'd been gnawing gunpowder. Tiny explosions. Buzzing. Like the enamel's vibrating. Stirring up my pulp.

White. Swirling, smelly white. A swirling white tower. Twisting milk and cum.

Last fall Liz and I copped a quarter of mushrooms off this townie spanger named Scam. He chewed our ears off, all this stuff about fungal intelligence, these massive networks of membrane that mushrooms use to communicate. He said that tripping is just mushrooms' attempt at communion with us. "It's translation," he said. "They're making your brain think the way a mushroom thinks. That's all that tripping is."

Hours later Liz and me were rolling in the leaves, giggling, listening to them crackle—an almost horny sound. I closed my eyes. A mass of scaley meat, a world's worth of heaving wet serpent flesh wrapping my body, wrapping the Earth's entire skin. "Yooo," I said. "I'm feeling a little snaky right now." Liz laughed and threw a fistful of leaves at me.

That's almost what this feels like. Almost. Not like snakes. A world of milk and cum, spilling over the world until there's no air left.

I shake it away. I squeeze my eyelids tight and open them again. Back in the ladies' room. In my body. Mom's face in the mirror, staring back at me.

I fill the pitcher and glug it down—the whole gallon in one go. I yank fistfuls of paper towels from the dispenser and wipe off my face. Then I drop the pitcher in the toilet bowl and leave.

Onstage, a middle-aged man in a Panama straw hat hovers over the microphone. "Come *on*, America. Listen to your *brother*. You used to call him *Jesus*. Listen to your *mother*. You used to call her *the trees*." I pop up on my toes, scanning the room for Amber. Her narrow pale face and spiraling red hair. She'd told me at school she was coming tonight. Forgot? Lying? Whatever. I head back over to Liz and Chelsea.

"You good?" Liz asks.

I lean close to her face. "Can I ask a weird question?"

"I'm used to it."

"Did you dose me?"

Chelsea scrunches her forehead, eyeing me.

Liz laughs. "Dose you? Like did I roofie you? Bitch, I'm not that desperate."

"Like with acid or something?" I'd heard about a guy at school who got dosed at a party. Some prick rubbed liquid LSD on the back of his neck. Had no idea what was happening when he got home. Tried to slit his wrists but his folks caught him just in time. "Anything like that?"

"Come the fuck on. Are you really asking me that?"

"I know. I know. I'm sorry."

"You sure you're okay?" She presses the back of her hand to my forehead, like my mom when I'm coming down with something.

I step back. "I'm good. Sorry. I just need to smoke or something."

She drops her hand to my shoulder and squeezes it like a giant leech. "Then let's book. You done here?"

I make one last scan for Amber. I almost think I see her onstage, but it's another red-haired woman, older, probably in her 20s, reading from a Moleskine: "My heart is a robin's egg, and my fingers are feathers, lifting me from another broken shell."

"Yeah," I say. "Sure, I'm done."

—x x x—

PUPPY MILK

Outside's a warm, damp thaw. Patches of white dissolving on soggy dead grass. Storefronts blacked out, gaping voids under glass. Not even the spangers are out. The streets wet and dead. An inversion of the café. Dead, maybe, but at least enough space to breathe.

Liz pulls a cigarette from her pack and sticks it between her lips. She's about to light it but stops. "You hear that?"

I do. This warbling. Barely audible beneath the wind and lamp noise, but there. A single sustained note. Singing, maybe. A stagnant, violent sound. My teeth wiggle and ache. A heat inside. In my gums, beneath my skull.

Chelsea pulls off one of her headphones. "Over at the park."

"A concert," I say. It's like the singing is inside my mouth, prying at my teeth. "Spring concert or something."

"Let's check it out," Liz says.

"It's just a choir or whatever. Boring shit." I don't want to go. My teeth don't want me to go.

"We've got to cut through there anyway. Let's check it out. Just for a minute."

Our sneakers clap against the sidewalk, echoing off hollow buildings. Empty storefront after empty storefront. Only the occasional headlight cutting out from the hill ahead as proof we're not alone. The singing grows louder. The note bends gently, like a warped record. It rubs against my teeth. I run my tongue over the enamel, wetting the gums, but it doesn't stop the ache.

A voice calls out across the street. "Woop woop!" A man kneeling on a stoop. Long ratty hair stuffed under a stocking cap; a torn-up bomber jacket, camo shorts over long johns.

Liz claps and smiles. "Yo Scam!" We dash across the street. Good old Scam. "What's good?" She gives him a hug.

"You know." He pulls back and shrugs. "Same old same." He points at Liz's cigarette. "Think I can buy one of those off you?" He digs into his pocket, fistfuls of change rattling.

"You can have one dude." She takes one out and hands it to him.

"Danke." He lights it up, inhaling deep, holding it, then exhaling long and slow. "What're you ladies up to?"

"You know. Just came from the open mic. We're checking out whatever's going on at the park."

"Pulaski Park?" He turns his head and spits on the sidewalk. "Nah, you don't want to go down there."

Liz smirks. "Why's that?"

"Bad fucking scene. Just real bad news."

"It's just a concert or something. You don't like music?"

"They're giving their children away." Scam rolls the cigarette between his fingers. "Real ugly business."

Chelsea goes stiff beside me, but Liz keeps smiling, forcing a laugh. "Who is?"

"Coward parents. You know, scared people are the most dangerous people in the world."

Liz chucks him on the arm. "We're tough. You know that."

Scam smiles. "I know. I still wouldn't go down there if I were you."

"How 'bout if I promise we'll be safe?" Liz gives him another cigarette and leans in for a hug. "It's good seeing you, buddy. We've got to take off though. Be good, okay?"

"Yeah, I'll try."

I nudge Liz once Scam's out of earshot. "What was that about?"

Liz wipes something out of her eye. "He's fine. He's just sick. He's trying, but you know. It sucks."

I drop it. The drone rises with every step forward, pushing against my skin, through my lips. My teeth buzz like a bee colony.

—x x x—

Pulaski Park glows between city hall and the Academy of Music. A glow that spills into the street. Lanterns strung from tree and post; torches pounded into the ground. A bonfire. At least a hundred people, dressed in jeans and button downs, or skirts and blouses. They hide their faces in masks. Papier-mâché animals—pigs and horses and roosters and goats. They circle the park's central pine tree. Hundreds of small paper circles tied to its branches, like a skirt of fungus. As a child, I'd look up at the pine in terrible awe, unable to fathom a tree growing that tall and wide.

A band—a fiddler, an accordionist, a tom player—walks the crowd. It's barely music—a shrill keening, an approximation of a cicadas' hum. The voices—this looping, warped falsetto, the timbre of cats drowning—comes from everywhere, from every person, from behind every crude animal mask.

Chelsea pulls off her headphones, staring at a couple wearing matching otter masks. She stares like they're on fire. "We should go. Can we go?"

"Yeah," Liz says. "Let's book."

We maneuver through the bipedal rams, rabbits, serpents. All staring at us now. The keening scrapes at my teeth, slipping beneath the gumline, prodding my jawbone. Through the bodies, between the pine and bonfire, I glimpse a stained wicker cradle, rocking gently back and forth. Something bursts beneath my gums and I grab my face and look away. Liz pushes me along and we break from the crowd, onto a path toward the concrete steps where I knocked my front tooth out when I was seven. We descend and cross Pulaski Parking Lot to the South Street underpass and the dirty trail beyond.

—x x x—

Tall metal lamps light the path all rosé beige, the season's first moths tapping at the bulbs. Clots of fresh mushrooms encroach the path, around my feet. I kick a patch. Spore motes explode and lift through the lamplight. Another kick, another milky cloud rising, drifting in waves, into my face, up my nose, down my throat, into my lungs.

We hop off the main path onto a thinner vein, scaling the hill between the woods and society. We push through brush and thorns until we reach it: The Pod. A mass of thick vines curled into a round hut. We discovered it last summer, figured a spanger had built it to sleep in, but we never saw anyone use it except other kids getting high. We dragged a fallen tree trunk inside to use as a bench and made it our own.

We duck inside, Liz and I calling "Not bitch." We take our seats on the rotting log, Chelsea stuck in the middle (but she's still lost in her headphones, staring quietly at the rusted coffee can blooming with cigarette filters). Liz reaches into her backpack, removes her glass bowl and weed, packs it and lights it up. I ask her if Amber said anything about coming out tonight. She lifts her head back, blowing smoke through the vine ceiling. "You've got to stop chasing that." She hands the bowl to Chelsea.

"I'm just asking if she said anything."

"You're in for a whole world of hurt if you keep after her."

"You only know, like, the persona she puts on. I know…"

"You know I love Amber," Liz says. "I love Amber. But Amber's fucked up. It's not her fault, but she's fucked up in so many ways and hasn't even begun working toward rectifying that shit. You're gonna get wrecked if you go down that path, that's all I'm saying." She sighs deep and shakes her head. "Anyway, there's like literally millions of girls out there."

Chelsea jolts in her seat. She coughs through the bowl, blowing the weed out. "Oh shit." She clutches the right headphone to her ear. "Oh shit."

Liz roars. "Those were my fucking headies." She reaches across me, yanking the bowl from Chelsea's hand.

"Holy shit." Chelsea presses the headphones tighter to her head, pressing so hard it's like she's trying to cave her own skull in. "I found it." She pulls them off and pushes them at Liz. "You've got to hear this."

"Nah. I'm mad at you now." She pulls her baggie from her backpack and loads a nug into her grinder.

PUPPY MILK

Chelsea turns to me, forcing the headphones into my hands. "Please. Listen."

I slip the headphones over my ears. A voice like pebbles dragged by a river. A hornet's buzz pitched down to a low rasp:

> ...and the last brown patches of snow melt away. The bodies planted in autumn reveal themselves. A blackened thatch of bones intertwined among briars, bristles, and burrs. A mummified infant, curled like bug, wedged under the root of an ancient elm. A long, lean cadaver, white as marble, winding gracefully through the rocks in the swift waters of a reborn tributary. A fresh kill caged in thorn-busy vines, a man of indeterminate age, his head cracked open at the jaw, a bouquet of mushrooms growing from the gaping maw of a mouth like a swollen fungal megaphone.
>
> Harken: a liturgy of flies. †

I pull the phones half off. "What is this?"

Chelsea's eyes crack wide open. "Your poem. What you said back there. I've heard it. You've heard it too."

My teeth go alight. Like they're bursting, frothing with pulp. Melting down to tendrous nerves. Entangled in radiation.

White. The world. Everything white. All a dense, silky light. No, not waves or particles. The texture. Milk. Milk. Soft sour milk. A flood of it. A tower. A white twirling tower, as wide as a mountain, as wide as the Pioneer Valley. A churning tower of sweet old milk, pungent like semen, flushing up into the sky. Twirling like a drill. A tooth. A bone.

The bodies inside. Hundreds of thousands. All our bodies. We can't move, we can't speak. Just flushing upward into the sky, a torrent of rank milk and cum.

"Yo. *Yo.*" Liz's voice. The world drifts back. No white. Just dark, and thin blades of moonlight spilling through the gaps in the ceiling. Liz hands me the bowl. I wave it away. "You sure?" She takes another hit and cashes it. "Bus should be coming soon. Let's get back." She stuffs the bowl in her backpack and rises from the log, ambles onto the trail and down the hill.

 Chelsea gapes at me like I have a gun for a face. "You've seen it," she says.

 "What?" But I know.

 "You've seen it. The tower."

 The white simmers in my spine.

 I stand. "I haven't seen shit."

 Chelsea grabs my elbow. Skinny fingers like bones. "Can I stay at your place?"

 "Tonight?"

 "I don't want to go home."

 I pull away. "Okay. Sure."

—x x x—

The voices are gone. The accordion, violin and tom. Everyone vanished. The bonfire doused, though the torches and lanterns remain, flames dwindling. A gust tears through the ancient pine, and the paper circles flip and sputter on its branches. Chelsea grasps at them, putting her face close to see what's written on them. Liz jogs ahead toward the bus stop. I'm staring at the stained wicker cradle. My teeth buzz.

 "Come on," Liz shouts. "It's gonna be here any minute."

 "Just a sec." I step toward the cradle. A black lace veil lays over it. A sound inside—a whimper, a slurping.

 "Yo!" Liz yells. "I see it, it's up the block."

 "Just a second!" My gums ache and throb. I pinch up the veil and let it fall over the side.

 A puppy. White and brown. A beagle, maybe, coiled inside the cradle. Shivering, its mouth pressed to its loins. Whimpering, suckling. Suckling gently on its penis. Not licking or gnawing. Suckling.

 It stops. It removes its mouth from its penis, its maw sticky wet white. It looks up, straight into my eyes, and smiles like a person smiles.

PUPPY MILK

In a hushed sweet voice, a toddler's voice, it asks: "Want to know a secret?"

—x x x—

The bus drops me and Chelsea off a quarter mile from my house. We barely speak the rest of the way. I don't tell her about vibrating teeth or towers of semen or puppy secrets and she doesn't tell me about any of the things she's seen.

My parents are already asleep when we get in. We head straight for my room. I flop on my bed. She sits at my desk. "I don't know how much left I got in me," I say.

"It's okay." She looks down at her Walkman. "You can go to sleep if you want."

"Okay." I twist onto my belly and close my eyes.

—x x x—

Pale marble towers. Taller than trees, than the mountains. The scent of animal lactation. Driven between the river, white water rising up the banks. Soaking the soil to sludge.

He's standing there. I can tell it's him though his back is turned to me. A scalp and shoulders I've known my entire life. He turns, and his face is a flower. A fruiting. A bloom of flesh. Like Amber's orange pussy rotting beneath my tongue. He steps forward and the slit pours white.

I wake up drenched. Face stuffed in a pillow, a rotten ache pounding in the back of my mouth. I slip my fingers past my lips and feel along my gums. Dry and swollen. I twist upright and tap along the night table until my hand finds the water glass. I glug it down in one go—washing the ache, but not diminishing it. I feel for the lamp and switch it on. A crack of beige light. The room throbs. An empty room. Alone. Chelsea's gone.

I go out to the hallway. The bathroom door is open, a black void inside. I creep downstairs, slipping through the den, the dining room, the kitchen. She's nowhere.

I go back up to my room. My foot kicks a chunk of something, something plastic on the floor, sending it skittering across the hardwood into a patch of dirty clothes. I squint and bend over it. A plastic charcoal brick. Chelsea's Walkman.

I pick it up and run my thumb over its surfaces. It's rough on the back. I flip it over and squint. Stalks and dots and infinity signs carved into the plastic, just above the battery cover. I turn it sideways. Two dots, a dash and six numbers: *88.1-89.3*.

I place it on my desk and climb into bed, but I don't get to sleep.

—x x x—

The weekend passes. I call Chelsea but each time it's six rings before cutting to the answering machine. Monday comes and she isn't in school. I ask Liz if she's seen her, if she's talked to her. "No." At lunch I hit the cafeteria payphone and call her again. Six rings, then answering machine. My gums flex and throb.

—x x x—

Mom and Dad look at me different now. Like they're reading my thoughts. They hardly even speak to me anymore. They'll smile, but there's a great strain in their eyes, like a jet of water pounding on their optic nerves.

Mom makes cream of mushroom soup for dinner. Whole creminis that burst on my teeth like dead mice. I get through two bites and ask to be excused.

I hear them talking downstairs, when they think I'm asleep. My father's voice: "It's got nothing to do with what you or I want." Inaudible. "You make me sound terrible."

PUPPY MILK

Silence. Then a single rising note. Mom wailing. Fried rasp. Weeping.

My teeth shake. An awful pressure. Like worms, botfly larvae crawling beneath the enamel.

White. Sticky sloshing white. A sea of white. Stinky milk and cum. Submerged in it. My head floating just above the surface. Hands at my throat. I reach up and pull at them. Familiar textures—hairy knuckles, ill-trimmed hangnails, the pads of rough callus. My father's hands. They push me under, into the thick smelly white. I thrash my arms and legs but the hands are too strong, too steady. They push me far below, further even than his reach. My world is slick greasy white and when I scream it floods my mouth, my throat, my lungs. Sticky rotten and hot.

I snap awake. Sheets soaked through. A knifing headache. My mouth filled with warm copper.

I sit up in the dark. The moon's gone tonight. I switch on the lamp and the room comes alive with light and opaque brown dots and dust motes. Little dancing spores. I spit in my palm—red swirling in clear and white. I wipe it on the comforter.

I crawl to the end of the bed and reach out to my desk, grabbing Chelsea's Walkman. I put in my earbuds and flip on the radio. A wave of static. A wall of hissing flies. My thumb rolls over the tuner. Crackly blasts of country music, then club music, and more static. I watch the dial. Rolling my thumb across the tuner, back and forth between 88.1 and 89.3.

The voice. I hear the voice. Gravelly and hollow, almost like water. It crackles against my eardrums. Like a wave crashing through me.

> ...and won't even blink. Blood is so thin. You don't even know. When it comes down to it, there isn't anyone who'll let blood stand in the way of dry land. It's coming. Ever more cats in bags and bags in rivers.

My teeth vibrate in time with his cadence. An almost comforting throb, like an old friend's caress. An agony I'd miss if it were gone.

I listen until sunlight cleaves through the window. I switch off the radio and twist onto my belly. I blink, and when my eyelids flip back open my mom's yelling it's time to go to school.

—x x x—

Chelsea still isn't anywhere and Liz still can't reach her (I've stopped calling, I know it's useless). I tell my teachers I have cramps and spend half of each class in the bathroom, thumbing the radio tuner on the Walkman. The voice is never on the same station—it drifts. Never really a station at all—somewhere between them.

> *Seed will go to seed will go to seed will go to seed. Goats make promises with fathers, but goats are always goats. Goats never care about our words, let alone promises.*

—x x x—

I pinpoint the tooth. At first I thought it was my entire jaw but it's only a single tooth. My right bottom molar. I open wide and pinch it between my thumb and forefinger and feel it quiver, buzzing like a fly. I wiggle it side to side—loose in the gum, but when I yank it won't pop out. Throbbing burning copper. I spit red and white into the sink and twist on the faucet, flushing it away, spiraling around the ceramic into a deep black hole.

Pliers. Pliers pliers pliers.

Downstairs, through the kitchen, out to the garage. Even though I've never seen Dad fix anything, I know he has a toolkit. Every dad has a toolkit.

I trace the walls, pulling tarps off bikes, coolers, snow tires. A shock through my gums. Impossible agony, like my tooth twisting, like it's trying to spin around, or burrow deeper into the gum. I buckle in half, sinking to my knees, hissing and spitting on my nightshirt, trying to keep quiet. I close my eyes and it's pure white behind the lids, dripping out and smearing across my cornea. I open them and shake it away, clenching my jaw, trying to push the pain out of my mouth.

Then I see it, tucked between the trash bins and the volleyball set: a broad grey box.

I lean against Dad's SUV and step toward the box. I'm standing over it when I glimpse them resting atop the trash bin. Two ovals, each the size of a face. Two papier-mâché ovals, lumps running down their centers, like snouts. Twin gaping black eyes punched through each of them, staring up at me. Dull grey stubs rising from their foreheads. A pair of goat masks.

White. Dripping white. Dripping from my eyes, my ears, my lips. All my insides clogged with white.

I beat my forehead with my fist until it goes away. I spit copper onto the concrete floor, then unsnap the toolbox latch and flip open the lid. Nails and screwdrivers stab at my hands. There. Round rubber grips. A pair of needle nose pliers, greasy and old. I tuck it into my sweatpants and head back to the bathroom.

—x x x—

I don't have visions anymore. That's okay though. I don't need them. There are other ways to prepare.

The cops find Chelsea's parents but they don't find her. Her mom's body is half-hanging out the front door to their house, burned to grey. Almost just bones. Chelsea's dad's body is burned to black, a skeleton curled into a fetus beside the toilet. She left the dog alive, locked in the pantry. They can't find her brother.

It was stupid of her to do that. Only brings attention. A stupid mistake, but I get it. I hope she'll be alright, though I know that's probably impossible now.

HYMNS OF ABOMINATION

You have to wait it out. Wait for the tide, the tower, the torrent. By then, there won't be any cops, or hierarchy. You'll only have your parents to worry about, and their hands, and even then, they'll be too preoccupied with reaching dry land. A tooth. A bone. A drill. Twirling in space. A torrent of rank, mucousy milk. I can wait. Lying awake, sitting up when my door creaks, finding my father in my room, clutching an object I can't quite see. I can outwait them. When the tower comes and blocks the rivers and drowns the valley in cum. The torrent. A tooth. A bone. A drill. Then I can run free.

† *This broadcast is taken from Matthew M. Bartlett's "Spring Thaw," included in his collection* **Creeping Waves**.

a delicate spreading

The summer I turned fourteen I was baptized as a member of the Sentinel Brethren church. My parents insisted on it, reminding me that as the eldest I had a god-given responsibility to provide a good example for my younger brother and sister. OK, but see, that's not entirely true. I make it sound as if baptism was something I *didn't* want, but I did. Then. Of course I did, because they did, and I was their good son and a servant of the Most High. So, I went into the pool, sure, just like the other three hundred or so eager young Christians gathered on the floor of the rented hockey rink. Long lines to the three prefab swimming pools set up in the middle of the space, all eating their box lunches in the surrounding stands and cheering each freshly risen servant of God from the water.

But when the pastor in his soaked wife-beater placed his thick arm around my shoulders and made to dip me, I panicked. Sure, I went under, like a good boy. But my foot slipped on the slick surface of the pool bottom as I went down, and as I came *up*, I flailed, a *lot*, and I lashed out with my arms. I somehow managed to grab the side of the pool in a bad attempt to haul myself out. I panicked, basically. And the weight of my thin teen bod, plus the iron grip I had on the pool edge, well, it was cheap, see? One of those vinyl-sided jobs you can have up and half-filled in an hour. Cheap. And that was enough for the side of the pool to buckle. Now, I wasn't so clumsy as to follow the flood of water out of the pool as I half-destroyed it, but yeah, a lot of people got their church shoes wet that day.

I'll tell you a funny part. My parents were *so keen* to see their eldest, their first-born son, get baptized. Dedicate his life to Jahweh. Make that public declaration of faith in front of all their friends and only the best cultists. They wanted photographs, a record, but for some reason I've never fully understood, they never made it to the poolside that day for the pictures. Dunking a summer Sentinel convention's worth of souls in tepid hose water takes a while, but you know how these people do things, it's basically an assembly line. Some decrepit old

scott r. jones

sanctimonious turd from the Sentinel HQ in Brooklyn Heights gets flown in to ask a cordoned-off section of the hockey rink bleachers three rote questions. The questions are answered and then off they go to the locker rooms, all fresh-faced and full of that all too Christian glee, where they change into bathing suits and then it's line up, line up, get in the water pronto, you young sinners, dip dip dip and out you go, white as snow praise Jesus. Let us gather by the river in the age of automation.

My brother and I, at previous summer conventions, would sit in the stands and quietly whistle that song from the Merrie Melodies cartoon where the construction site guard dog takes care of the little black cat as it engages in high-rise, high-risk shenanigans. You know the one? That whacky mechanical assembly line jazz as the kitten bops along the girders, rides pails down rails to safety. Doot doot doo, doo doodley doot doo, and repeat. So long as our parents didn't hear, we were fine.

They weren't there, somehow, incredibly, but then, that assembly line is quick, right? Barrels along like the hot little holy ticket it is and though my perception of my clearly botched baptismal event seemed to stretch into a kind of nightmare eternity, a closed looping moment of embarrassed fear while in all likelihood it took less than half a minute from entering the pool to exiting it. Not even half a minute. So, my parents missed it; they couldn't get there in time from our seats in the stands. I get it.

I mean, I *wonder* at it, obviously. All things considered, with the station and the Bright Pillbug, well, I'll get to those things in a bit, I swear it.

I wonder at a lot of things.

I was not meant for this life, is what I think. I don't mean this philosophically, as in "ah, this life, what a heaven and/or hell" in a general way. I mean, this one, mine, specifically. I'm far from the Sentinel faith, now. Have been for many, many years. What often feels to me as several overlapping lifetimes, or life *themes*, I should say. Instars. Eras rolling over into new eras, new lives and life forms, cultures and cryptographies. Station to station. I wasn't meant for *this life*, as me, because,

A DELICATE SPREADING

and bear with me here, I'm no longer sure I ever was a me in the first place.

What crawled out of that pool in 1989, anyway, cheeks burning with embarrassment? What heart beat what urgent tattoo in what chest? Mine? Was that me?

I will tell you another strange thing about my failed baptism. It was one of the big conventions that summer, so we had to travel to get there. A three hour drive south from Chicoutimi to Quebec City proper and a Motel 6 right across the highway from a St-Hubert and only a ten minute drive to the rented skating rink where I was to be dipped. My little sister stayed with mom and dad in their room while my brother and I had the room next door. We watched anglo television with the sound off so as not to wake them, but also we were excited to try the adult channels: a shifting wall of nearly impenetrable static but every minute or so you'd see a flash of nipple or glowing lips engulfing some vague piece of bouncing flesh. It was impossible to know what was happening but nevertheless there was an air to the proceedings, simultaneously moist and crackling, like slow lightning passing through the meat of me.

"That's a penis," my brother said. "She's sucking on it."

"No, she's not," I said. "That's not where the penis goes." You know that bright, sweaty sheen on the faces of true believers? That certainty that the world functions in a particular way that only you and your brethren are privy to. I wiped that sheen from my forehead with the corner of a bedsheet.

"What do you know anyway, smart ass," he said.

"I know where the penis goes for starters, douchebag." Yeah, I was a good little asshole, faithful in little things and true, with the light of Jesus shining from my puckered fundament as was right and proper. I was two years older than him, but even then my brother had a bead on hypocrisy that was unerringly accurate. Bless his skeevy heart.

"Getting baptized tomorrow and here you are..." and he waved a hand at the snowy screen.

"Fine. I'll turn it off if you're so *bored*."

"I'm nine, dillweed."

"So, I dunno, go to sleep or something."

Well, he did. Dad had cranked up the AC when he installed us there. *May as well take advantage while we're paying for it, eh, boys?* My brother wrapped himself in the thin sheets of his bed and turned to the wall, his back to me.

"Do you think this place has scabies," he said through a yawn.

"What, like, bedbugs or something?" I asked but after a few moments waiting for an answer, I realized he'd fallen asleep. He *was* nine, after all.

Digging out my yellow Sports Walkman from my bag, I laid down and plugged in the headphones. None of my cassettes appealed to me in the chill darkness of that room, with the faint odour of dry rot in the walls and the musty carpet pairing with the AC to provide that freezer burn ambiance Dad was so proud of paying for. I didn't want to listen to breezy Christian rock or Depeche Mode or even the A side of Slayer's *Seasons in the Abyss* that I'd secretly recorded at a friend's house earlier that year, copying over my original Chet Atkins gas station tape, like a boss, using his dual-cassette stereo. It was a real SONY, too.

Instead, I attempted to tune into a local station, tracking the static wasteland in between islets of sound, looking for something interesting. Some college or public-access station with the weird stuff I just couldn't get in Chicoutimi. I suppose I wanted to keep that illicit blocked Superchannel vibe going. I mean, maybe?

I found it at the low end of the AM dial at first. Keeping the station in tune was difficult; it required a finesse that I didn't have at that age, but I did my best, rolling the sweaty pads of my fingers over the wheel. There was a drone, almost indistinguishable from the fuzz that bordered it on either side of the dial. It wasn't even music, but there were voices in there that I could just about catch if I mashed the headphones against my ears, filling them up inside with cheap foam and the chatter. Because chatter it was, like the scraping of beetle husks in a barrel or the

A DELICATE SPREADING

scratching of a branch on your window. Rats in the walls. The urgent, hushed bleating of homeowners on the other side of their doors when the Sentinel Brethren came to call on a Saturday morning, full of Good News and it's barely nine a.m. what are they doing up this early, Harold, tell them to go away. The sound from the station *felt* like placing a water glass up against that door, long after they thought you'd left to pester their neighbours about Jesus, and there you were, crouched on the door sill, on your knees with your shined up service shoes getting scuffed and filthy in their geraniums, there you are with your glass up against the door and you're about to hear what those awful people inside were saying. You *know* they're saying things about *you* because what else would they be talking about, you were just *there* on their doorstep but please understand, see, it didn't *sound* like that. The station I picked up that night. What it *sounded* like was not what it was, not what could be heard. Time dilated as I lay there in the dark, listening, listening, straining to hear what was, essentially, *nothing*, listening as if for the first time to air and rushing wind and useless secrets whispered by lonely people, mandibles clicking, the papery wingbeats of stick-like things with hydraulic limbs. I listened and imagined glaciers slowly calving away into viscous, oily seas, thick flows of lava crawling over green surfaces, burning and deliberate. All those things.

    The station I found that night sounded like an actual season in an actual abyss and that abyss? It was between my ears and it was *vast*. I knew that vastness then, in a way I had never known anything before. My upper limit for the largeness of the Universe had until that moment contained (a) god, but now there was this *voice*. Only a hint, but a hint at the truth of things, I knew. The abyss inside was so engulfing I nearly wept right there, with my little brother snoring away one bed over without a care in the world, safe in the lap of a loving deity.

    The station, and here is another funny thing, here is the thing that has kept me looking for it since that night, the station opened me to the unknown, simple as that. They are as one with your guarded threshold, says the good book, say *many* books if you care to read them right.

They are there on the other side of the door and you don't even need to pull at the edge of their world because they can just open it and walk on through. No straining necessary, no violence, panic. The door opened and the voice came up through the door, through the drone. The voice came in at a funny angle, but it was a real voice this time, soft and reedy, a crepuscular huffing of vowels and consonants but *there*, undeniably there and sighing, issuing forth from a set of lungs, a tongue, a voice box like my own, surely. Teeth in the mouth giving definition to sounds, to words in English. Surely another human was speaking.

"...were an interesting group, most scholars would agree. Their technique was quite ingenious and those who were known to have participated in the ritual reported a sense of serenity, of timeless peace, associated with it. Now, listener, doesn't that sound pleasant. You'll note that the steps were minimal. First, the Supplicant would be bound, their wrists shackled behind their back. They would be placed upon the Cone, and this in the obvious way, I don't need to explain to our listeners across this nighted land, wherever you may be, driving across it like a beetle under a heat lamp at the Sizzler or at home in some kind of bed or in a rented room awaiting some big decision, you know who you *are* and you *know* how the Supplicant was sat upon the Cone, how else would you do it, boy? Tell me, how *else*?"

A crackling pause and an intake of breath. I think it was mine. The voice continued.

"Weights are then attached to the ankles and over several days those weights are increased, slowly bringing the supplicant further onto the Cone. There is an opening, then. A delicate spreading, if you will, like unto the unfolding of a rare flower. Before long, the Supplicant expires. One cannot sit upon the Cone forever, after all. There is a spreading, as I've mentioned. Nearing death, they are closely monitored for the moment of ripeness, when the soul is ready to leave, but knows not how.

"It's a beauteous moment, we are told. The First Receptacle is brought in and the transference is accomplished using the Twinned Stone, that temporally-dislocated Object of Powah listeners may

A DELICATE SPREADING

remember from our series of special episodes on the Cities of the Red Night during our last Vernal Membership Drive, and thank you again for your generous pledges! The First Receptacle is then also bound, and, housing the soul of the Supplicant, is encouraged to watch the proceedings for educational purposes. Now, the patient work begins, for the weights must be increased on the ankles, and the skeletal structure, the hips and ribs and the god-ladder of the spinal cord bristling with vertebra, these must be delicately smashed within the expanding tissue as the Cone does its work from within. The weeping bone and exposed marrow is incorporated into the Bright Pillbug's bruised shell. The smashing is accomplished using the sacred silver hammer, as established in the Protocols of the Maggot-Sire. I encourage all my listeners tonight to put in an astral request for a copy of the Protocols if you don't have access to them at this time."

There was a burst of static so loud and sharp I nearly levitated from the mattress. My brother snored on. I glanced at the motel room clock but could not make out the numbers.

"Friends, it's now the top of the hour, Time shore do fly, and we need to take a short break for station identification and local weather but we'll be back with more juicy instructional excerpts from the Bright Pillbug manuscript. You're listening to WXXT, wherever you are on the dial, the Voice of Leeds and the Fragrant Interiors of Your Mangled Mind. Mmm-boy, that's some good headmeat!"

Great Jahweh in His Podunk Heaven, it turned me inside out, that transmission, burned its contents into the reverse side of my skin for that perfect, somatically based recall. It got into my bod, basically, I felt it enter, and the body always knows, I've found. Flailing under the thin covers at just the *sound* of the station I.D. letters, I flung the Walkman across the room, finally, maybe too late, yes very late, the cheap foam headphones sailing after them like a satellite caught in the wake of a yellow, bristling comet. Gasping for breath in that stale room, I crawled from the bed and retrieved the machine with clean teen fingers, but try as I might (and I *did*, I did, messing with that thing for hours!) I couldn't find the station again.

My instruction had ended.

My search began the next day.

The moment I panicked in the baptismal pool, I heard the call letters in my mind, clear as crystal, JHVH to WXXT, station to station. On the drive home to Chicoutimi, I caught snatches of that loathsome broadcast every time mom adjusted the dial. Walking to school, certain stones on the side of the road would begin to glow with a negative light before winking out as I approached. Getting up to piss in the night, I would pass my parent's room and instead of gentle snoring hear a great grey wash of static pouring from their mouths, gathering up against the ceiling like a thick layer of mammatus cloud.

Of course, I couldn't with the Sentinels. Couldn't last. I tried, for me, for my parents and my sister, for my little brother who went astray with the drugs and the petty crime. I was supposed to be the good example, but I'd heard something different one night and it was never to be. Word had come to me of another way to tread the world. I tried, still, I really did, even going so far as to marry a Sentinel girl, an endeavour doomed to failure. The sounds my ex-wife would make during sex brought visions of the Cone, of a transformed body with a transplanted soul, made somehow more real than my own decaying form as I thrust between her legs. I don't miss her. How could I, knowing what I'll be. There is no room for hypocrisy in the shell of the Bright Pillbug.

I've heard the Sentinel Brethren referenced as a death cult, and I agree, so far as that goes. I mean, what *isn't* a death cult, right. I can't eat a meal without thinking how much pain went into its preparation, what small lives were lost, what suffering was endured until the end of it, and all so I can enjoy some warmed-over carbon in my guts for an hour or two before shitting it out. I can't vote or watch a film or listen to music without seeing the deprivation and degradation of the human spirit necessary to produce these entertainments, these tinny protocols enacted against the waiting void. Jesus, books? No.

A DELICATE SPREADING

Entertainments, my god.

I fell away from god even as the baptismal water soaked the good shoes of my former brothers and sisters, my parents scrambling in the stands somewhere above, camera held high but too late, always too late. The vinyl-sided pool collapsing forever, red, dark mouths circling it in an eternal round of sighing. What stepped from that pool that summer, I ask you. I ask myself, constantly. That questioning pulls me into the future, a morbid telos from on high molding my person as I crawl from moment to moment. What *isn't* a death cult. What is my life, anyway. Not mine, not since that night.

The Bright Pillbug is what I will be, I know this now, and a Bitter Light to the World. I was to be born again in spirit inside that cheap pool in that cheap skating rink in that cheap part of Canada that somehow, *somehow*, received that transmission on that night because the station is what it is, goes where it wants, lives at whatever notch on the dial it chooses, this broadcast cast broadly across the lands of night, getting chummy and cacophonous as it bounces up against the Van Allen belts above this earth and rebounds, cast from a town, yes! a town called Leeds, I've learned. In this life of learning I have done so of Leeds and learned my limits. It's in Massachusetts, this town. It's in Hell. A twinned stone that has both places beneath its slick underside like a snail's slimed footpad.

The Bright Pillbug waits beyond the edge of my fear, my hesitation. It waits at the base of the Cone. In Leeds, some entity will have those pages, the Protocols of the Maggot-Sire. A shopkeeper will have it, *does* have it, I'm convinced, in a job lot of beetle-munched books still in their boxes, spines joyfully broken in anticipation of sharing a bookshelf with it. In Leeds, or nearby because, like its Voice, the town spreads, it is a transmission, in Leeds there is a Cone waiting for me to sit upon it, gathering dust on the ichor-stained slopes of itself, in a bare room or basement, some outbuilding back of a warehouse, and someone is there, in Leeds, some person or principle that plays at being a person, like myself, possibly, someone is there who possesses a sacred hammer for the delicate smashing necessary in my becoming and the cackling initiative, no small thing, to help me. The hammer is in a junk drawer in a sad kitchen where it shines on its own, simple and savage, sidling up to the sewing kit and switchblades and stapler. It is gathering darkness to itself in a toolbox with rope and heavy-duty zip ties, spools of electrical tape, and keen, keen saws. They were keen to see me go under, my parents.

And I am keen, now, keen as a saw, to see, as the tip of the Cone, here in my car at a dark rest stop on some nameless east coast interstate, stating my case to cadaverous ghosts in Sunday shoes. They're all piled in the back in cobwebbed layers, wondering aloud in whispers how much farther and I say not much farther and when they get too loud, when they just keep asking no matter what I say, I swear I will turn this car around. An empty threat.

I turn the key in the ignition and reach for the arc of the steering wheel. It is the edge of the pool, also, and I pull it down and to the left. Shining water spills onto the asphalt.

Anne Gare's Rare and Import Video Catalogue
October 2022

Jonathan Raab

"A Communist Dissident Takes His Medicine" — Dir. J.C. Proud, 1968

This unique film is fifty-one seconds of a single shot set in a wide, dimly lit room adorned with velvet curtains that stretch down the walls from the high ceiling. Ornamental golden candelabras hold bloated candles burning and melting with the consistency of human fat at the right and left limits of the frame. This is, presumably, the interior of some secret society property—a local Order of the Night Moose lodge or orgytorium, perhaps. Four robed figures soon appear at the five-second mark, dragging a naked man into the frame from stage left, until their group stands just off-center. We see no faces aside from the victim's and no voices save for his weeping cries for mercy. The red-robed assailants remain silent and wear identical masks: stone idol owl faces. The man *might* have a southern accent of some sort, but it is hard to tell, what with all the repeated, intensive trauma leveraged to his mouth and teeth.

This beating, conducted with utmost vigor and carried out with either police nightsticks or long flashlights, is efficient enough to leave the victim dead or unconscious by the conclusion of the film. The words "FOR PUBLIC SAFETY AND GOOD ORDER" flash across the screen twice during the course of the violence. When the naked man finally falls silent and still, his assailants, blood dripping from their hands, weapons, and even their owl masks, breathe heavily as they admire their work, but are otherwise silent in their duty. Quiet professionals, all.

One 9.5mm Bing British/Bingoscope film roll, good condition.

Five hundred six dollars.

HYMNS OF ABOMINATION

x110x

stump-water

In the wud outsyde uf Lede
Once't grew a most p'culiar tree
Not uf ashe or elme or oake
Nor cranapple nor cherrychoke
Stranger frute yts branches sprung
Whenne uponst yt wytches hung

The sing-song skip-rope rhyme lilted bright and merry, an unsettling contrast to its words and the clouded gloom of the autumn day as Dovvin waited by the winding lane for Scorlis to arrive.

Unsettling as well were the children chanting it as they made some intricate hopscotch dance about their yard. Quintuplets, girls, identical, five pretty peas from the same pod, they wore likewise identical smocks of some dark brown and moss-green gingham, over which were muslin aprons. Atop their heads, muslin bonnets, tied beneath the chin. Upon their feet, small cloth shoes, kicking blithely through late wildflowers and weeds.

He tried not to watch them. Tried to not even look at them beyond the corner of his eye. Being caught looking at girls was dangerous, being caught looking at *pretty little girls* ten times the more.

He tried as well not to hear them, but their bright, lilting chant pierced his ears as if determined to needle itself a home inside his head.

Such had happened to him before, out in the lonely woods along the lonely river. Haunting birdcall melodies like no birds he'd ever heard…the rush and chuckle of pebbled creeks taking on the semblance of gossiping voices…sometimes, he'd awake in his narrow bed in the attic room he rented, still hearing them despite the old house's weary creaking and the wind whispering in the eaves.

Now there just a stumppe doth stand
Where once't rose tall a gyant grande
Now bole and boughs and leaf doth lack
Hollow'd deep and rotted black

christine morgan

> *At yts heart a rough basyn formed*
> *Ne'er by the sunlighte warmed*

Dovvin shivered and drew his shabby coat more snugly 'round his shoulders. The air hung damp and cool, but not yet winter-cold; the insidious chill working its way as if into through his very bones came from within.

Trust Scorlis, who'd set the time and place for their meeting, to take his accursed leisure getting there! Stopped off at the public house by the mill bend, perhaps. Or, knowing him, romping with some milk-maid behind a dairy-barn, the scoundrel!

While here he stood, in thin boots and threadbare cap, no doubt seeming more suspicious with each passing moment. Lurking. Loitering. As the five little girls skipped in a circle, holding hands, showing quick glimpses of bare ankles and chubby calves.

In their innocent singing game, they appeared oblivious to his presence, but what about the sturdy well-kept cottage beyond them? Anyone might be peering warily through a curtain-gap. A stout and surly father-farmer, musket at the ready, about to step out onto the porch...quintuplet older brothers quick with their work-roughened fists...

Nervous, Dovvin sidled further into the shadowed undergrowth beside the lane. He would have made a point of facing away from the cottage and the girls, but the prospect of turning his back made the skin between his shoulder blades itch and creep.

> *Slowly there did form a brewe*
> *Of rain-fall, frost-melt, morning dew*
> *Drippe by drippe and droppe by droppe*
> *Higher and higher to the toppe*
> *Mingl'd moon-mist, corpse tears spill'd*
> *And so the wooden cauldron fill'd*

He rubbed his palms together in a futile effort to create warmth, wanting only for this business to be over. Why he'd agreed to it in the first place was...well, to that he knew the answer; Scorlis said it paid well. Better than the pittance Dovvin dredged up doing odd-jobs around the town, which barely covered his room-rent and meager meals enough to keep body and soul together. A solid sum might see him to a new coat and boots, or at the very least a decent dinner. Or serve to see him well away from Leeds, to which more and more he found himself wondering why he'd come at all.

This, as well, he already knew the answer to. No one would come searching for him here. No one would think to. Such a place as this, so quaint and queer and quiet, so far-removed...

Too quaint. Too queer. Too quiet. Too far-removed. As if, sometimes, the rest of the world existed only in his own memories and dreams. As if Boston and New York, with their bustling harbors, had utterly faded, ceased to be.

It was nonsense, of course. Those fine cities surely thrived, for the most part as uncaring of his absence as they had been of his presence. Only those to whom his name and his crimes mattered would have any reason to think of him at all.

And yet...and yet...

So, here he was, reduced to this, lurking in the bushes with wet mud seeping through his boots, half-hiding behind a tree, trying not to look at the five little girls. Trying not to wonder as to the color of their eyes, the plumpness of their lips, how sweet their skin might smell, how soft it might feel to the touch.

Trying, just as he tried not to listen to their lilting, carefree voices and their unsettling song. Trying, and failing.

> Steep'd in magic, steep'd in death
> Slime of leeches and fish's breath
> Clammy frogspawn tadpoles squirm
> Slick and slith'ring the long pale worm
> Dip thy hands, o witch-daughter
> Curse thy foes with the stump-water

This time, even less convincingly than before, he attributed his shiver to a deepening of shadow as thicker clouds rolled overhead. Not because of the song, or the way the quintuplets paused in their frolics to cluster close and giggle as if sharing some delicious secret. No. Because of the shadow, the clouds, the damp chill in the air.

The afternoon was lengthening, slipping by, still with no sign of Scorlis. Dovvin thought to walk back into town and check the public house, but with his luck he'd miss Scorlis in passing and then have the scoundrel decide he was not trustworthy. Given he'd already lost out on whatever scant day's wages he could've earned by agreeing to this venture, he was loath to come away from it with empty pockets.

"A bit of harmless foraging," Scorlis had told him. "One thing to poach game or kill a man's livestock, I grant you, or thieve the fruits of some farmer's hard-earned labors from his field. Another altogether when the wealth of the woods is just lying there in the loam and mulch, waiting to be gathered. And why not? Why leave them there to be eaten by wild hogs, when they're worth their weight in gold?"

To be sure, it was illegal. But, as Scorlis had gone on to say, what the governor didn't know would hardly hurt him, now, would it?

And, in truth, should Dovvin come to the governor's attention, he'd likely have far more to worry about than being charged with unlawful foraging.

> Bathe thy bruises, heal thy wounds
> Revive thy sister who hath swooned
> Give to drink a stillborne childe
> Tame heart of beast or lover wilde
> Mix thy potions, cast thy spells
> Draw from whence the stump-water wells

At that, the quintuplets clustered and giggled again, and when Dovvin looked despite himself, it was to see five round little bonnet-framed faces turned his way, with five pairs of avid gimlet eyes fixed knowingly upon him.

No feeble rationalization could else explain his shivers now; his skin felt fair to ready to crawl right off his body. He took off at a stumbling run, heedless of how his feet crashed through the undergrowth and the snagging twigs tore at his already ragged clothes.

Bother them and their skip-rope rhymes! Bother Scorlis! He wanted only away from the place! Away from those damnable girls, from their knowing gimlet eyes!

Eventually, winded, he faltered to a halt and stood bent double, hands braced upon his knees, heaving for breath. It occurred to him to listen for sounds of pursuit, the angry father or protective brothers perhaps, but as the beating of his own pulse in his ears quieted, he heard only the rustling of leaves and a whippoorwill's mournful whistle.

It occurred to him also that he did not know where he was. He'd left the lane behind in his frantic flight, and although he'd had reason now and again to venture into the forest before, he recognized no landmarks around him. Which way had he come? Which way was Leeds?

He collected himself as best as he was able and took closer stock of his surroundings. Would hardly do to get lost out here, but he couldn't have come very far...

Aha! Indeed, there, winking through the shadow-laden tree trunks, he spied a gleam of light. Lamplight, by its steady glow. Soon enough, he'd be back in his drafty, cramped, hated attic room, as gladdened to be there as if it were a mansion.

Overhead, the dark clouds rumbled with thunder as if in a mocking laugh. Dovvin made haste, not wanting to compound his wretchedness with a drenching, and soon reached the lamplight's source.

A lamppost, reasonably enough...tall and wrought of iron, paned with amber glass...but...

But there was no town within sight, not so much as a single building. Nor a road, lane, or even a footpath. Only the lamppost, some solitary sentry resolute against a corona of moths battering themselves to death.

Dovvin stood below it and turned in a full circle, but no direction looked more or less promising than any other. Just his luck; lost after all, lost somewhere in the wood outside of Leeds—
In the wud outsyde uf Lede
A cry of alarm burst from him. He whirled again—he'd *heard* their piping, lilting, sing-song voices, he *had*, he *knew* he had!—but saw no one.

His plight was getting to him. He steeled the frayed threads of his nerves. Should he just keep moving in a straight line, sooner or later he was bound to reach a lane, or the river, or a creek leading to the river. Never mind the encroaching dusk, brought on early by the clouds. Never mind his wet, aching feet encased in their thin and leaking boots. Never mind his hunger, never mind his thirst, never mind the chills wracking his bones.

On he went, choosing his course at random but holding resolutely to it. Now and then, he saw unfamiliar birds swoop and flit from branch to branch. Once, he saw what he at first mistook for a goat standing on its hind legs like a man, but told himself it was a mere trick of the eyes.

Another time, his foot struck what seemed to be a pale and rounded rock, *only* a pale and rounded rock, no matter how it rolled hollowly from his inadvertent kick, no matter how its tumbling revolution displayed gaping black sockets and the suggestion of teeth bared in a dead grin…a *rock*, only a rock, in *no* way a naked skull.

Neither did he truly see a dank, rune-carved stone plinth with huge slugs crawling upon it, leaving glistening trails of slime. Oh, perhaps he *did* see a stone, yes, but those were just cracks, not anything of meaning. And, while there *were* slugs, they were of ordinary size, *not* bigger each than loaves of bread, *certainly* not with uncannily human eyes wavering at the ends of fleshy stalks.

It was the woods, that was all—*In the wud outsyde uf Lede*—and his disorientation, and hunger, and weariness, and thirst. It was his nerves. It was the unpleasant prospect of still being out here when night came; he'd slept rough many a time before, was no stranger to it, but the very thought of bedding down upon sodden leaves no doubt writhing with leeches and worms...no, no he could not bear it.

Ahead, he glimpsed a patch of open space, where the last of the day's cloud-laden brightness lingered milky-grey. A clearing, a large clearing, and he rushed into it eagerly, all but sobbing with relief. Here, he would find some trail-marker, some sign—

Or a place where—*Once't grew a most p'culiar tree*—only a massive stump remained.

> *Now there just a stumppe doth stand*
> *Where once't rose tall a gyant grande*

Its sheared-off trunk rose to the height of a man's waist, its girth such that several people linking hands in a ring could encompass it. How tall it must have stood, in its prime! How broad the spread of its canopied limbs!

> *Now bole and boughs and leaf doth lack*
> *Hollow'd deep and rotted black*
> *Stranger frute yts branches sprung*
> *Whenne uponst yt wytches hung*

Dovvin stopped, sobbing in truth now and not with relief. The dregs of his strength left his legs and only desperation kept him standing upright. Great gnarled roots, each themselves thick as tree-trunks, hunched and clawed into dark, loamy soil. Moist lichens clung to its split, scaly bark. Ladder-shelves of flat, crinkled mushrooms, like the ears of dead men, sickly climbed from its lowermost crevices.

What manner of tree *was* it? Although far from a woodsman, shouldn't he have been able to discern *that* much, at least?

> *Not uf ashe or elme or oake*
> *Nor cranapple nor cherrychoke*

HYMNS OF ABOMINATION

And what force could have felled it? The work of men with saws and axes? The work of nature with age and time? The work of God with smiting storm? Where had the rest of it gone? Surely not hauled off and split for lumber and firewood! Only evil would come upon any who built from or burned its dreadful timber!

Somehow, not of his own conscious volition, his faltering feet dragged him toward it. Needing to see but not wanting to, wanting to know but not needing to, he trod closer until he could see over the trunk's edge, and into a sunken, rotted, black hollow brimming with liquid.

> *At yts heart a rough basyn formed*
> *Never by the sunlighte warmed*
> *Slowly there did form a brewe*
> *Of rain-fall, frost-melt, morning dew*
> *Drippe by drippe and droppe by droppe*
> *Higher and higher to the toppe*
> *Mingl'd moon-mist, corpse tears spill'd*
> *And so the wooden cauldron fill'd*

Spindle-legged insects skated across it, their many pinprick feet barely dimpling the surface. Frothed greenish foam and algae ringed its outer rim. Its scent was earthen, moldy, secretive, like a long-covered hidden well. Here and there lilypads floated, some sprouting pallid trumpet-flowers to only play a funeral dirge, some trailing skeins of wrinkled leafy lace as if a weeping widow left a discarded handkerchief.

> *Steep'd in magic, steep'd in death*
> *Slime of leeches and fish's breath*
> *Clammy frogspawn tadpoles squirm*
> *Slick and slith'ring the long pale worm*

Was that the quicksilver flickering of minnows in its depths? And tangled skeins of white and writhing eyeless legless bodies seething further down? Were those squirming tadpoles wriggling loose from clustered masses of jellied eggs, while inhuman bulbous yellow eyes

STUMP-WATER

looked on and corpse-skinned throat-pouches uttered low, guttural croaks?

> *Dip thy hands, o witch-daughter*
> *Curse thy foes with the stump-water*
> *Mix thy potions, cast thy spells*
> *Draw from whence the stump-water wells*

Were those *his* hands, his *own* hands, his own treacherous hands, lowering trembling fingers into the hollowed stump, into the cold but hellish wooden cauldron? As insects skated fast away, and minnows flitted in consternation, and those bulbous yellow frog-eyes shifted their inhuman gaze to him?

Oh, and it was cold, cold and oddly oily, oddly slick, seeming to coat his fingertips in unwholesome residue. He submerged both hands to the wrists, cupping his palms together. When he brought them up, water sluicing in trickles through his knuckles, some still-sane portion of his mind cried out its horrified protest.

> *Bathe thy bruises, heal thy wounds*
> *Revive thy sister who hath swooned*
> *Give to drink a stillborne childe*
> *Tame heart of beast or lover wilde*

He was no witch-daughter, had no swooned sisters or stillborn children, no lovers to tame, and any foes he might have cursed were far, far from here, but his thirst was terrible...and he *did* have wounds and bruises...

Surely, though, he could not mean to raise his cupped hands to his mouth! Did he not see, there, where a dark blotch clung at the base of his thumb? A leech, swollen and pulsating, already growing plumper?

Dovvin hesitated, tears spilling unchecked down his thin, unshaven cheeks to add their wretched salt of misery to the stump-water. He heard, from behind him, a naughty girlish giggling measured five-fold, and knew if he turned to look he'd see them, the sing-song quintuplets in their bonnets with their knowing gimlet eyes.

Then he heard *more* giggling, somehow eager and malicious, the giggling of *other* girls...girls who, once, had wept and whimpered...and knew if he turned to look, he would see *them*, too. Their torn clothes and mussed hair and little, lifeless bodies.

Had he thought he could outrun his crimes, hide from his sins and wicked deeds?

He lifted cupped palms to his lips and drank, almost glad to have it over and done with...here...

In the wud outsyde uf Lede.

i could tell you so much

You can drive a car hell-bent for leather from Skillute, Washington to Leeds, Massachusetts in forty-five hours and thirty minutes via I-80 E and I-90 E. By bus or by train it will take four days, fourteen hours. You can go lone wolf and walk it in nine hundred and seventy-six hours via US-212 W. Or ride a bicycle in two hundred and sixty-two hours via US-12 E.

This is public information. You can look it up. Of course, all the numbers are theoretical. They don't take into account the vagaries of the weather, current events, accidents, the idiosyncrasies of 20th century engineering, or the all too human craving for misadventure.

—x x x—

I stop walking when I see LORD HAVE MERCY on a sign a man is holding over his head. He's standing on the sidewalk in front of the bus station with a jar of small bills and coins at his feet. The man's eyes are the color of nickels, dull silver with a sky-blue undertone. He's not wearing a mask. Frothy spittle flies from his mouth whenever he speaks. He's slurring at every passerby:

"Stranger! Do you have a plan you can live with?"

I stop walking. Because I do. I have a plan.

"How 'bout you, sister?" the nickel-eyed man asks me.

The crowd edges past. People are exiting the bus station in a hurry, and others are trying to get in. They all want to go somewhere else as fast as they can. Most are wearing paper or cloth masks and they walk a wide circle around the nickel-eyed man. They don't look at him. They don't look at me while I'm talking to him. Like he's already tainted me. Like I'm already doomed, in spite of my face shield.

"I sure do," I tell him. My breath fogs up the inside of the plastic lampshade. "I sure as fuck have a plan."

I've had a plan for a long time. I've been ready. I've been waiting for something like this to happen.

—x x x—

We thought, after the temperature dropped and we had a week of rain, the fire season was over. Then came news of a warm spell, and here's what happened: Pregnant women came out of the woodwork, eager for sunlight, shrieking with joy. They put on bell-shaped summer dresses and designer sandals. They sent e-invites. They dragged their families and in-laws, their sheepish friends and idiot spouses, to the heart of the darkest and most heavenly forest. There they burned candles, sang songs, and danced in circles, without the slightest idea why. Some released balloons to announce the gender of their babies. Some set off fireworks. Then they drove home, leaving candles and campfires to smolder in their wake.

When the new wave of wildfires rolled up one shoulder of the canyon, the whole sky lit up pink and gold, scarlet and orange. Then everything fell into darkness. Moments later, along the cliff edge, houses began to burst into flames: window glass flying across brittle lawns, muffled voices indoors, people caught and gagging in the smoke, crying mingled with barking.

Some people made it as far as their driveway and collapsed. Dogs ran to the half-charred remains of their owners, stopped for one bewildered sniff, and took off down the road. They howled at the smoke, barked at every exploding gas tank.

Like an afterthought, the fire swept back, rolling across the power lines. They sputtered, popped, and every wing of the hospital blacked out.

The sudden dark silence caught nurses and aides and interns off-guard. The halls of the security wing were usually quiet anyway, but this was different. This quiet dropped hard, fell out of the sky and through the ceiling, final as a gunshot.

We waited. Nobody moved.

After a minute, a buzzing began in the corners of every room, underneath the beds and from the back of every drawer and cabinet. First, it sounded like the flutter of a bumblebee's wings.

Once the power died, it should've been a few minutes, no more, before the generator kicked in. We were all thinking this exact same thought, one mind humming, growling, and waiting. Staff must've been holding their breath, ducked down behind chairs, beds, curtains, fake potted plants.

Minutes passed. Somebody tried a cell door and found it unlocked. Somebody finally let loose and started screaming, but not out of fear. This was a scream of victory and hunger.

That tore it. Gustav—who was a dancer until he broke his leg, suffered a nervous breakdown, and killed his landlady—rammed the exit with a fire extinguisher and split it down the middle.

Next came a lot of running and shouting and shoving. A guy fell down and was trampled in no time. The floor grew sticky with blood, and the walls were stained with it. I stumbled out of the security wing and recognized the redheaded clozapine nurse on the floor, limbs crooked in all directions, head upright against the baseboard, blood filling the gaps between her yellow teeth. I rummaged through the cart next to her and pushed her aside on my way to the stairs. The supply closet was one storey down.

Two naked men, twins who like to be called Ivar and Bert but are really named after martyred saints, headed straight for the freeway. They left the fire exit hanging open. Nearby, on a cement block, they posed an intern like a mannequin, with crossed legs and a smile slit all the way across his bearded face.

Pretty soon a stream of patients, drugged, deranged, or quietly lost, headed after Ivar and Bert in the direction of stalled traffic: Drivers evacuating Kelso, Skillute, and Castle Rock, trapped in idling cars, trying not to cough or vomit from the smoke-clogged air. They shook their heads at those scrawny people in threadbare gowns, some trailing IV tubes and wheeling oxygen tanks, emerging through the smoke to weave their way between cars. Leaving gummy fingerprints and smears of phlegm on windows.

Did the drivers panic and scream? Somebody should've screamed. That would be the normal thing, stuck in a car, in a one-mile line, surrounded by toxic smoke and lunatics. Somebody must've screamed.

—x x x—

I have a plan.

I didn't run out into traffic like the other women from my ward, flashing middle-aged bush at terrified drivers. No, by the time I exited the hospital I was wearing cherry-pink scrubs, a sturdy lampshade face shield and pull-on ankle boots. I was carrying four things: a stolen wallet, a fanny pack loaded with pills, a box cutter, and a postcard. Only the last item belonged to me.

To my left, the parking lot was empty. To my right, three female patients were busy raping an intern. One had him pinned facedown with her full weight planted on his torso, while another gripped a rolled-up magazine from the lobby, and the last one yanked his pants down around his knees.

I kept walking. Away from the freeway. Headed toward fresh air. I kept walking.

—x x x—

People like nurses. People let nurses go ahead of them in line, even now. People nod and say hello to nurses—and thank you. They say thank you for no reason at all. I'm never lonely. Dressed this way, I'll always have friends.

—x x x—

The LORD HAVE MERCY man's silver nickel eyes are shut tight on the news channel, and his face is purple with veins popping out across his forehead. He's kicking a man on the sidewalk and yelling about The Redeemer. He wears brogues. Those blunt shoes have knocked the back of the other man's skull to smithereens. Brain fluid spurts onto the toe of one shoe, a fat shiny glob.

I've seen that happen before. Brain junk has an auto repair smell to it, a garage smell like oil and rubber.

The altercation started over the nickel-eyed man's "God-given goddamn right to not wear a fucking mask." A man exiting the bus station said a Christian isn't a Christian who doesn't respect "the greater good." The nickel-eyed man dropped his LORD HAVE MERCY sign, grabbed the man by the neck, flung him to the pavement, and started kicking.

"Oh my God! Who do you think shot that *awful video*? Who in the world would *just stand there*, recording it all, and not lend a hand to help that poor Christian man?" the passenger across the aisle asks.

He won't mind his own business. Keeps the right amount of distance on the other side of the tape but won't shut up. Mask dangling from one ear, which is against the rules of the bus line. Staring across at my iPad screen and reacting to every little thing with tics and twitches, like he can see it all just fine.

He notices me while I'm watching the news clip of the nickel-eyed man for a third time. The sweeps and pans and changes of focus are a lot like art, I think. Whoever shot it should get some kind of award. Sputtering screen images in the foreground, a slippery landscape outside the bus window blurring the background. The window glass is sweaty with condensation. The iPad I acquired from a distracted lady with three noisy children at a gift shop in Salt Lake City. Broke the password in no time, the nickname she called her littlest kid, the grumpy one with the poop-filled diaper: DILBERT.

"I shot it," I say to my fellow passenger. "I was right there. I shot the whole she-bang for the news report."

"Jesus!" he says. "That's an awful thing! You saw what happened, and you taped it too? My God!"

I stop watching the news report. I do this every time, stop at this point, two minutes and six seconds in, while the nickel-eyed man is kicking the man on the ground and shout-preaching about The Redeemer. I stop playing the video right before it includes me, walking up to the nickel-eyed man, slicing the back of his neck with a box cutter, and stepping away. All with my back to the camera and whoever really shot the "awful thing." The whoever was too stunned and too busy retching to follow me into the bus station, where I flung the box cutter away and heard it skitter over the tiled floor, underfoot of the heaving crowd.

"I honestly do not get what this world is coming to," says the passenger, and hooks his dangling mask into place. Then he closes his eyes, like he's praying, like he's shutting out all the filth and madness, like you would shut a door in the face of an annoying missionary or a stray dog. He doesn't want to receive the wrong message.

I decide I'll follow him off the bus as soon as we reach Denver. I settle back into my seat and enjoy the scenery. We pass bars, shopping centers, closed schools, derelict office buildings, and restaurants surrounded by protesters with signs:

```
MY BODY - MY RITES!
GOVERMENT KILLS MORE THAN CLOVID
MANLY MEN DONT MASK
```

—x x x—

Hours later, in the rest stop bathroom, my nosy fellow passenger slides down the wall to the Lysol-scented floor, his cheap shoes squeaking in a puddle of gore.

I COULD TELL YOU SO MUCH

Why do they stare up, like that? What do they expect? Every time, I swear. They stare up with amazement. I think they're stunned to discover a complete stranger hates them enough to make them shut up. A former stranger with a trash bag over her cherry-pink scrubs and plastic shopping bags over her ankle boots. No longer a stranger, now we're connected in such an intimate way, forever.

I leave the discarded bags draped over him, after tucking one into his big mouth.

—x x x—

Apropos of fuck-all, I've been engaged in a torrid love affair all of my adult life. I don't remember when it started. But every real person I've tried out failed to live up to my imagination, sometimes in small ways, sometimes by being a fucking jerk who had to be dealt with. You know what I mean.

—x x x—

Electroshock isn't what you imagine when you hear the word. They don't do it the way you see it in old movies. This is modern and people take it seriously. You get these small, short pulse currents in your brain, makes you feel confused, like maybe you've wet your pants and forgot about it. Then you feel *nice*, like sinking into a warm bath with lotus flowers floating around you.

Years ago, the treatment was different. The heat would spread all over, inside and out, in every muscle. You'd get all jammed up, like a fist. And you could feel it in your blood, too. Like being drunk when you planned to stop at seven glasses of whiskey and now all you can do is let it wear off. The scent of piss in your sweat glands.

I used to say the words "glands" and "glades" over and over, like a jingle. A girl in my class told another girl I didn't know the difference between glands and glades. When she was found in her bed at home with one elbow stuck in her mouth, her doctor claimed she had a spasm because he didn't see how a contortion of that kind was possible.

—x x x—

What am I talking about?

A broad-faced woman in leggings, cowboy boots, and layers of scarves is obsessed with the back of my head. I see her squinty face in the bus security mirror, ahead of us. She keeps showing off, being a bitch when she thinks nobody can see what she's doing.

I see what she's doing.

—x x x—

I'm feeling much better since St. Louis, and twenty minutes of heavy sleep. Most people think they need hours of sleep every night but all I need is twenty minutes a couple of times a day.

We were stuck for a while in traffic, outside Denver. We were stuck again outside St. Louis, when a road crew was struck by a van and bodies came raining down on the asphalt, each landing with a meaty crunch.

Woke up to the splash of windshield wipers. Rain again, washing the stains away. Our driver nods, knowing the route too well. He's bored. He'll keep driving this leg of the route until he's too old to grip the steering wheel, or the bus company goes out of business, or the road crumbles to dirt. What am I saying? None of this shit will last that long. All the drivers and passengers will be dead in less than a year. Most people just can't figure out what to do when the bad shit happens.

I had money for my bus ticket, but I like to be practical, so I swiped LORD HAVE MERCY's money jar after I sliced his neck. If you haven't cut anybody, the surprising thing is what comes out besides blood. A roll of crinkly, yellow fat came out of the nickel-eyed man's neck, but I didn't stop to admire it. Only had a chance to grab the cash and throw the jar away with the box cutter in the bus station.

—x x x—

I could've driven a vehicle off a car lot during the wildfires. I could've kept walking and hitched rides once I cleared the first emergency area. That's funny. On the news, one town official after another declares this place or that place is in "a state of emergency." Like it's only this town or that city. Like there's a spot somewhere on the map you can get to and be safe, if you drive far enough or run far enough.

This trip is all I dreamed of, ever since the postcard was delivered to me by the night shift nurse. Wrinkled corners indicated a long journey through many careless hands. The picture was hard to make out until I held it up close. There seemed to be a pen of some kind, maybe a corral, in the foreground, like at a county fair. To one side of the pen, a large goat reared back on its hind legs, raising its fore hooves into the air. Nearby, a group of children sat in a circle on the grass, picking dandelions and tearing them apart. On the message side of the card were two things: a Leeds, MA postmark, and a single hoof print.

—x x x—

I've had four different names. Only the first one is real. It's the only one that matters. My people come from a place across the ocean. Some sailed the Atlantic during bad times and settled in Massachusetts.

My cousins are Glancers, most of them. They never married out, or brought in fresh blood, so that line is pure as can be. Out in Oregon and Washington we've turned lazy, I can see that now. We had time to spread out, marry whoever we wanted, and ignore the past. We've forgotten too much.

My daughters are weak. The only family they ever met were just like everybody else, born in the same town where they lived and planned to die. They don't know their ancestors sailed up the Columbia and settled among the Cowlitz or drove a wagon west along the Platte River through the Rocky Mountains. From whichever direction they came, they burrowed in deep. Sometimes they hunted and fished. Other times they raised the dead, it was rumored. For the long winters, and not only to satisfy their hungry bellies.

—x x x—

I see what she's doing. The broad-faced woman in leggings, cowboy boots, and scarves is sneaking barbecued ribs. She got off the bus way back in Kansas City, and from the minute she came back and took her seat, she's been glancing around and grinning like a cat with two mice.

Now she's ducking her head over a cardboard box in her lap. When she raises her face again, she's got black-red sauce and charred bits of pig smeared around her lips. She drops out of sight again and reappears with thick sauce dripping from her snout.

—x x x—

Pittsburgh is a hell hole. Snow is falling and it's the color of copper. The scheduled brief stop is canceled after protesters hurl cans and bottles at the bus, chanting, "No mask now! No mask ever!"

Our driver's a woman with green hair. She wears an old-fashioned chauffeur hat with a shiny bill. She calls the protesters "little rebels" and speeds the bus toward a group of them until they jump out of the way. One protester slips and falls in the snow. His sign gets caught on the back bumper, and the bus drags him for a quarter of a mile, face down on the asphalt. When he breaks loose and lies crumpled in the coppery snow, our driver chuckles and hits the gas.

—x x x—

My body is streaming through the countryside, past long-deserted factories and mills. The cold rushes all around me. I am dreaming. A voice cuts through the darkness. I can't understand what it says. A figure draped in rags emerges from a cloud of smoke. He is taller than the bus and his arms wave woodenly at sharp angles. His head is that of an ancient, desiccated hog. He holds up the heads of two children, strands of hair stuck to their cheeks and graying tongues protruding from their mouths. I see the woman in leggings and cowboy boots clinging to the great hog's shoulder, suckling his sweat, nibbling at the damp hairs hanging from his armpits.

—x x x—

We're somewhere north of Philly, and a teenager wearing a Rams t-shirt is gawking at the sights. Every market, every trash dumpster, every alley seems to take his breath away. He keeps twisting around in his window seat, trying to make eye contact with someone who will share his gobsmacked excitement. The other passengers avoid him.

I'm thinking about my last dream, the sheer crimson shadows and darkened curves of it. I can't recall what happened after the figure with the hog's head reached the bus.

Traffic slows for the eight hundredth time. I notice a cord hanging over the back of the empty seat ahead of me. I pull it down and examine it. Earbuds. They look brand new, so I put them on, plug into my iPad, and search for music.

I'm scanning for some 1960s French pop when I hear a faint tinkling tune. Its simplicity is both beguiling and slightly irritating. I remove the earbuds and the music goes away. I replace them and the tune—the kind anyone can imitate, as basic as a TV jingle—grows louder. It's "Turkey in the Straw," I think.

I hate it but somehow, I can't stop listening. The notes are stuck in my memory like a recurring nightmare. As this occurs to me, I turn my head to the right and see the teenager in the Rams t-shirt screaming and banging his fists on his window. A man stands up and motions for the teenager to take a seat. When the kid keeps screaming, the man shoves him down into his seat and goes striding up the aisle to alert the driver.

    She pays no attention to the man's grievances. The driver waits until he retreats to turn her face toward us, chauffeur hat still perched on her head. Although she maintains a tight grip on the steering wheel, she keeps turning in her seat until she's facing the passengers. Her eyes are round and runny. She's not wearing a mask. Her face is elongated, bristling with short hairs and ending in a large snout. She opens her mouth, and a snuffling sound comes out.

    I'm going to remove the earbuds. I'm going to throw them away. But now the tinkly tune is fading, and the voice of a man rises gradually to fill the void, all of the voids. The guy who made the teenager sit down is now throttling the kid, and no one tries to stop him.

    To my right, out the window, I see street signs and houses and dogs. I see a man with loose, sagging breasts standing naked on a corner. I see a parade float, but I can't make out the words printed on the banner.

    "I could tell you so much, but I couldn't look at your face while I spoke," says the voice in my ears. "I could tell you where you've been. I could tell you where you're going. I could tell you when the vehicle you rely upon for safe passage will skid sideways into a truck filled with life-like baby dolls, the kind lonely childless women hold against one breast and sing to sleep at night, spied on by an elderly man with an erection standing on a step ladder outside the bedroom window…"

    I can't say it happens exactly when the man shoves the teenager to the floor and begins to stomp on his head, but this might be the moment when I know I'm on my way home.

Anne Gare's Rare and Import Video Catalogue
October 2022

Jonathan Raab

The Mouth That Opens — Dir. Inconnu, 196X

A storied and robust example of French Nouvelle Vague, *The Mouth That Opens* provides a startling viewing experience sure to capture the attention of even the most jaded cinephile. Observing the film multiple times reveals increasing orders of complexity and subtlety in its exploration of the mediums of motion photography and sound itself, resulting in a psycho-physical reordering of the mind and body in persistent viewers who find themselves socially isolated through circumstance, economic conditions, or general unlikability. There are teeth, teeth everywhere, and gaping maws—ever-hungry, never satiated—surround us, if only we have the eyes to see and the tongues to taste. Every hole you have ever seen is a mouth. Every mouth you have ever seen is merely a superstructural representation of the true teeth, lips, gums, tongue, tastebuds, tonsils, and throats *Beyond* that are ever-present, ever-consuming, consuming us all, consuming you, even now, even now.

35mm print, hand-assembled, complete with cases full of human teeth that rattle like the sounds you hear at the edge of a deep sleep. Excellent condition.

Two thousand six hundred dollars.

HYMNS OF ABOMINATION

x134x

the beat of wings

I.
Uncle Red Reads To-Day's News

The year's first snow has fallen on Leeds. The powdery substance feels chalky between the fingertips and leaves a lingering residue. It is recommended to avoid touching the snow, and to avoid the woods today, where a large murder of crows has been circling a patch of mud in which not a flake has fallen.

    Passerby claims to have seen the crows spitting teeth, and blood, and bits of flesh.

    Passerby claims they speak in the voice of the dead.

    They pace, their wings flutter and settle, they pace. None take flight.

    You are listening to WXXT.

    You are listening to the beat of their wings.

    Keep listening.

betty rocksteady

II.
The Beat of Wings

Max is dead.

    I'm alive. I think I'm still alive. A sticky wetness grows beneath me. I can't move my legs. I can feel my toes, I think, but I can't see them past the crush of car, the jab of the steering wheel, the impossible metal that stabs into my ribs. The front end of the vehicle is an unrecognizable pulp. My left shoulder must be broken. The door is crumpled so far into my side it may as well be a part of me.

    My neck crackles, sends shocks of pain down my side, but it does move, allowing me to inch my gaze away from Max's pulverised body in the passenger seat and out the cracks in the windshield.

    Beyond the broken pane, a bleak landscape. No sign of life. Snow, dirt, a crooked tree that stretches into the sky. I don't remember the crash, I only remember leaving Leeds, and nothing happened in Leeds. Home was still days ahead. My knuckles were white at the wheel. Spotify kept fucking up, the radio station kept slipping back and something moved across the road. We must have crashed and I must have passed out, and we are settled here now, where no one will ever find us.

    Flakes of snow dance in the air, drift through the broken car, settle on Max's eyelashes.

    I wonder how long it will take to die.

    Max was lucky. His head is split open like a watermelon, glass tangled in his hair. I wished him dead many times, for stupid, petty things, and now he *is* dead and I have no choice but to follow.

    I realize my eyes are closed. I open them again, wretch them away from the bruises beneath his eyes, his body still perfect, or at least as good as it had been. Only his head is destroyed, turned to mush by some mighty force. I turn my eyes back to the tree and try to breathe. It must be morning, it must have rained, because a layer of ice trickles from the twists and knots of branches.

THE BEAT OF WINGS

My right fingertips flutter but don't obey. I wonder if Max's phone is tucked into his pants or if it's somewhere on the floor of the car. Mine is in my purse in the backseat, hopeless, an endless distance away. But maybe Max's, if my arm would just reach over to the thigh I've touched so many times before, that I've stroked lovingly whether I meant it or not, if only my fucking arm would obey.

Too much movement. Too much pain. To close my eyes may mean death but I have no choice.

—x x x—

Max is alive and he is speaking and I can't keep up with his words. Something about the trip, something about things being almost the same and it flip flops my gut, even after all this, that he doesn't see the difference.

I open my eyes. Wet my lips, try to open my mouth and blood spills out, drips onto the shoulder of my shirt.

He looks good. Not like he did before, not when I really loved him, but good, not dead, his eyes sparkling and I slowly realize the radio is playing our song.

"If it weren't for what happened in Leeds, I'd say it was one of our best trips." He looks at me when he says this and the radio gets louder and I can hear someone crying.

"Nothing happened in Leeds," I say. "Can you move? We need help." I am begging and I am afraid and I know, deep down, there is no help for us.

Max smiles, except for his eyes.

—x x x—

Max is dead. A crow lands on the windshield, a mass of *something* juts from her beak. I run my tongue along my teeth and taste rot and I poke my tongue into the hidden, empty socket near the back.

HYMNS OF ABOMINATION

Max is dead and something moves beneath his skin. The crow watches with interest. Max is dead and his face is perfect and his eyes are open and they are blue and dark but his body is shattered, crumpled, like every bone has been broken and blood seeps out beneath him and stains the seat, leaks onto the floor. I move my neck the inch I've been allowed and stare deep into the eyes of the crow and the radio asks if I've gotten everything I've asked for. I hear myself whisper yes.

—x x x—

Max is alive but barely. He twitches in his seat and groans. My eyes won't open all the way. I can't feel my toes anymore but I still think they are moving. "Are you okay?" he asks.

"No," I say. I'm not. Not since the nothing that happened in Leeds and of course not now, pinned by broken machinery, my body failing, my lips cracked and dry and begging for water. "Can you reach your phone?"

"It's hard to get around with the ol' knee now. Can't use the motorcycle anymore, but we still had a good trip, didn't we?"

"Where's your phone, Max?"

"I can't find it. I think we'll just have to stay here and wait." The static starts again, buzzes through my body, brings with it the taste of bile and broken teeth.

"What are we waiting for? Who's going to see us down here?"

A gurgle, a cough and a spurt of blood. Max's head jerks forward, back, and when it stops moving his eyes stay open. He doesn't answer.

I look out the window, out the inch of sanity I have left.

In the tree, three crows. No, five. No, dozens.

And in front of the tree, fresh footprints in the snow.

The radio screams to life.

III.

Anne Gare's Rare Book & Ephemera Catalogue

#48793-C

The Book of the Crows

This unusual book was found amongst the belongings of a suicide victim. The aforementioned title is an assumption, based on the illustrations within and the feathers found stuffed between pages like bookmarks.

The pages themselves are made with scraps of garbage including receipts, test results, old calendar sheets. Some pages are bound together haphazardly with bits of twine, others tacked together with thick, dark blood from the throat wound of the deceased. The condition is overall poor, with many of the pages stuck completely together.

The markings that cover these bits of scrap paper are rough scratches that appear completely random at first glance, but upon closer inspection do seem to indicate some sort of linguistic system. Unfortunately, none of my specialists have further insight. Many of the pages have illustrations in a pictographic style, similar to prehistoric cave drawings. Taken together, these elements perhaps suggest an early, emerging intelligence.

Illustrations include but are not limited to: A spray of snowflakes surrounding a patch of dirt (a smear of blood obscures something on this page); a human jawbone missing several teeth; a gnarled tree gripping a huge black cauldron in its

HYMNS OF ABOMINATION

branches, the sky hatch-marked with hundreds of black wings; a woman, breasts exposed, engaged in sexual congress with a swarm of birds in the shape of a man; and finally, over a series of three images, the cauldron again, the smear of a woman's face as she boils and bubbles and bursts apart into a murder of black birds, and then darkness over the ensuing pages as the oily smudges of their wings blot out the sun.

The artwork is disturbing, leaving the reader with an uncomfortably vivid taste of dirt and blood. The meaning of the work is unclear, but perhaps to the right collector it will have some value.

Eighteen dollars.

IV.
The Beat of Wings (II)

I'm talking. I hear myself but I'm not choosing my words; my lips just move and I say, "Who were you talking to?"

Max's breathing is shallow. A thin trickle of greenish drool leaks from between the corners of his mouth. I can't look at him like this. It's worse than the accident at work, the one that crippled him, the one that crippled our lives. I can't love him like this. I never could. I never really did.

I look to the tree, the knots and whorls and how the branches reach for the thin grey sky. The crows peer back at me, their shining eyes alive, their fluttering wings, those clattering branches. They caw and call and their voices sound almost like words.

My head lolls, I can't help it. I don't want to look at Max but it's too much effort not to. I'm too weak to keep my head bent toward the tree.

When he speaks his mouth doesn't move. His voice is static. He says, "You're ready to talk about Leeds?"

"Nothing happened in Leeds." The words come out in a spray of spit.

"We're dying."

"I just want to know what he said."

Max turns to me and all the bones in his neck crunch. "What did *you* do in Leeds?"

A crow caws and I am babbling nothing nothing nothing until nausea overtakes me and bile spills out of my throat and Max is laughing, or maybe it's the radio and then something slams into the windshield and everything goes black.

—x x x—

It takes my eyes too long to open, but there is a scratching in my throat, the sensation of my jaw being wrenched open, the taste of damp fur, movement, and then the taste of blood.

Skin seems to tear as I rip my eyes open. A bristling black shape bulges from my mouth. I can't breathe, my fingers clench and release and my head jerks and finally the bird pulls its head out of my mouth. I see the shining of my spit on its beak. Its wings beat against my face and then it's gone.

I spit out a hunk of meat that looks like an earlobe. Blood fills my mouth, spills down my chest.

Max is dead. I can't stop myself from looking at him, my neck muscles are exhausted, I can't tear my eyes away. His ear is missing, along with most of his face. His neck is torn open.

I spit again. I can still taste him.

My stomach feels full.

My toes tingle as something comes alive. The feeling spreads up my legs, into my thighs, and strength slowly fills me. Finally, my neck moves and my eyes dart toward the tree, where something is moving, something besides the crows.

Branches twist and crack. The murder disperses in sudden flight, blotting out the sky in a squirming black mass.

A pulse beats through the earth, through the floor of the car, into my body, a pulse that pounds through the marrow of my bones. The sky clears again, and the silhouettes of tree branches against the white sky make dizzying geometric angles. As if it senses my eyes, the trunk curls, the bark tears, it wrenches itself from the ground and twists toward me.

It was never a tree.

He is so tall he can reach into the sky. His twisted limbs snap and break and tremble and He walks toward the car and extends His hand.

V.
The Crooked Man

Even before he opens his eyes, the first thing he notices is that everything hurts. Like every bone has been broken and mended poorly, knitted together with nails and tape.

All of his eyes open. The sky above is clear and white. The Crooked Man shifts his wretched bones and the broken branches that surround him snap. A massive nest has been woven around his crumpled body, large enough to curl his stretching limbs into. Dozens of crows surround him from the periphery of the nest, wings shifting, dark eyes focused on his face.

He relaxes. The pain will fade.

One of the large black birds lands on his chest and inclines its head curiously, darts its beak forward, pecking between his lips. He relaxes further and allows the bird to poke its head between his teeth, to regurgitate and fill his mouth with the taste of meat and dirt.

The Crooked Man chews, swallows, lets the energy fill him. He looks back at the sky.

It goes on like this for a time; days, maybe a week. He sleeps; his limbs ache and shift and change. The birds nestle into him, their dark feathers keeping him warm. And they feed him, mouthful by mouthful, until finally he is strong enough to stand, to let his long legs stretch toward the ground.

The crows watch him leave.

He walks through the woods, lets his new body carry him where it will. Shiny bits of beads and baubles hang from many of the branches, wards and symbols scratched into their surfaces. A reflection from a hanging ornament creates a tiny mirror that reveals his face, familiar but forgotten, with the addition of something decidedly new.

HYMNS OF ABOMINATION

A small bloodless slit runs between his eyes. When he strokes the side of it, it opens, revealing dozens of tiny teeth, and the mouth begins to speak.

A wet feeling moves down his spine.

He listens.

He leaves the woods, following the call of the crows.

By the road, a black fluttering conglomerate peels away in all directions, revealing a car hidden beneath their collective bulk. The driver is long dead, but his clothes will serve for a time. The Crooked Man dresses and discards the body to the trees.

In the car, he turns on the radio and he shakes and sweats and quivers and the mouth whispers directions.

He listens.

He arrives.

He slouches over a cup of coffee in the diner, waits for hours. The waitress stops seeing him after a time.

When they walk in, he loves her immediately. Not for her beauty, though she *is* beautiful. No, it's her bitterness. He can see it and smell it and taste it and through the couple's long meal he waits, breathless, for her to see him.

They finish and she passes The Crooked Man when she goes to the washroom. She doesn't notice him, but a tiny tongue darts from the tiny mouth to taste the air as she walks by. Her husband steadies himself against a cane and the mouth smiles and The Crooked Man rises.

The husband doesn't see him at first, not until he unfurls to his full height, until his limbs stretch and grow and creep across the walls, until he wraps his long fingers around the husband's shoulders and crows surge up out of his throat and the man tries to run but the mouth opens and it says, "My head is a cauldron and my thoughts are all spells."

The husband gapes.

"She will hear the call of the woods. She will give her teeth and her sex and you will give us what's left."

THE BEAT OF WINGS

"Leave me alone," the man tries to steady himself, tries not to believe, but the little tongue darts out again to taste his fear and The Crooked Man knows that tonight, when the radio blurs to static, he will believe more, and more still when She sneaks back into their bed with dripping hands and dirty feet.

The Crooked Man lets go.

He walks outside, back to the car, and he drives, past the hotel, past the city streets, down the long highway until the mouth whispers "Here."

He walks the rest of the way.

In the white sky above, dark birds cut through the air. He follows.

He takes off his shirt and his pants and his shoes and his socks and he digs his toes into the cold muck. His bones ache and so he lets them go still; he lets go of everything and he stretches his limbs into the sky and the birds come and they shelter in his arms.

He waits.

VI.
Uncle Red Reads To-Day's News (II)

Early this morning, a crashed car was found on the outskirts of Leeds. Authorities were led to the site by a massive and sudden migration of crows. The car was twisted, bent, crumpled. One male survivor was eventually extracted unscathed by the Jaws of Life. The driver's seat was empty. A flurry of tracks—human, avian, and something else—led away from the car to the woods.

    Shortly after rescue, the man slit his throat with a broken bit of windshield.

    This is WXXT. This is the Woods. The Woman. The Song of the Crow.

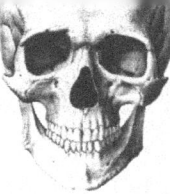

missives from the house on crabtree lane

Real Estate Listing for 6478 Crabtree Lane, February 2020

Welcome home to this lovingly maintained 19th-century Victorian charmer with rustic curb appeal! Drive up the private dirt road to the expansive front lawn sustainably carpeted with clover, where the full front porch greets you, perfect for those warm summer nights sipping a glass of wine while fireflies burst like fireworks in the darkness.

 Enter through the knotty pine front door, which may groan, into a high-ceilinged foyer that boasts an ivory chandelier, which may swing idly. Some say the chandelier looks like a broken ribcage.

 The living room welcomes you with an abundance of natural moonlight leaking through the peaked Gothic windows. A formal dining room with built-in ebony sconces leads into a quaint kitchen furnished with original appliances, including a vintage brick oven capable of roasting the flesh from any creature unlucky enough to find a place at your dinner table. All appliances are fully functional.

 Up the banshee-throated staircase with newel posts carved into decorative skulls, you'll find four cozy bedrooms with lofty beamed ceilings and two generous bathrooms needing only minor repair to the scratched walls. Please note the tendency of the faucets to emit a stream of maggots. Do not mind the bloodstains; they won't come off.

 The backyard boasts a hand-crafted pergola that collects seasonal roses and a local species of spider whose intricate webs veil the structure, adding an antique charm. It is inadvisable to remove the webs. The yard is vast, perfect for entertaining, and backs into the forest. Peace and quiet abound. All you'll hear is the interminable buzz of insects and the wind uttering sibilant invocations through the trees.

 You'll love the privacy.

joanna parypinski

The full-sized, unfinished basement is not included in the square footage. In fact, it's not included on the blueprints or deed. This versatile bonus space is brimming with possibility. Spacious and cool, it can accommodate large gatherings of any sort and is effectively sound-proof. The walls and floor do have some veiny cracks which have been stitched shut and occasionally emit a slimy odor like rotting meat. The current occupant implores you to keep the basement door locked. Please note that sometimes the lock sticks from the inside.

Included in the purchase of the home is a detached two-car garage large enough for your longest vehicles, and all the furniture in the house. The current occupant claims she no longer needs it.

This house is hungry to have you as its new owner and tenant. With a fresh coat of paint, a little fumigation, and your own personal touch, this diamond in the rough can be your forever home!

Please note, there are several parts of the hardwood floors where the wood is soft with rot like bruised flesh.

Please note, there have been deaths on the property.

Home is sold in as-is condition.

Diary of a Fixer-Upper, October 2012

I'm not sure what I was thinking when I decided to purchase the old fixer-upper on Crabtree Lane. The state in which I found it both intrigued and appalled me, like an open wound. Mold crawled like a swarm of black flies across the yellowed porcelain bathtub, fractured in reflection by broken mirrors. Dust as thick as cotton wove a tapestry of neglect.

The place was in a state of rancid decay. Not surprising, after the events of '82, that it had sat on the market unwanted and unoccupied for so long. It's been said, in rumor and urban legend, that pale men in dark robes used the vacant house for unspeakable rituals, though I wasn't inclined to believe it. Or, rather, it didn't bother me. What else are abandoned houses with disturbing pasts good for?

MISSIVES FROM THE HOUSE ON CRABTREE LANE

After the anger and injury of divorce, I needed a project, something to do with my hands—if I could heal this infected wound of a house, then surely I could purge the poison of my ex-husband from my life, a man of indifferent affect punctuated by rude eruptions tending toward tantrums, as if he never outgrew his childish need to be worshipped. Unfortunately, we had married before I realized this. Things got messy for a while.

So, I put all my efforts into the fixer. This wasn't my first time playing Mrs. Fix-it, after all. I'd had a hand in several friends' home improvement projects. I remodeled Brenda's entire kitchen after that radio glitch sent her into a seizure while she was chopping vegetables. But I'd never faced a project like this before. Parts of the house were soft and moist, which made hammering difficult as the nails sagged in the limp, fleshy wood. I thought I should just tear down the old paneling, which was all carved up, anyway. Those silly little carvings were damn near everywhere.

I was debating whether to restore or replace the banister to the staircase, wobbly and splintered, when I noticed the phrase carved all the way down its length, again and again: *The head is a house.*

My feet nearly skidded off the sagging steps as I drifted down the stairs to read the phrase winding its way down the banister. When I reached the bottom, my hand met one of the carved newel posts and jarred it loose so that it tumbled across the floor in a cloud of dust. It kept rolling, as if to escape me, but I caught up to it only to discover two black sockets staring back at me over a grinning, lipless mouth.

The texture was not wood.

After that, I went outside to see about the ancient gazebo in the back. I could hardly make out the color of the paint, so shrouded was it in webs. I decided to clear them away and discovered, on closer inspection, that these were no ordinary webs. They were spun of very fine, meat-like material, something like viscera. I put on gardening gloves and started peeling strands away, which popped like violin strings. A swarm of spiders came clacking over as if to stop me, and their legs looked like fingers. I decided to leave them their web.

The house seemed to watch me through its windows, and I hurried back inside as the sunset made black whispers of the forest. Stovetop mac and cheese eaten straight from the pot sated me well enough for dinner, but all the while I heard a chuckling coming from inside that old brick oven, which I had been trying to avoid. I was afraid of looking inside it due to the inexplicable fear of finding the remains of a charred little boy staring back at me. But there was nothing there.

So it went.

While working on the house, I bedded down on an air mattress in the master bedroom, which also bore carvings along the walls and beams. That night, I drifted in and out of sleep, dreaming that my head was a house, or my house was a head, until a sound thrust me awake with my heart in my throat.

My mind went immediately to my ex-husband and the possibility of him following me here, perhaps hoping for another fight. A few more bruises, maybe a broken jaw this time. I grabbed the closest thing to me—a hammer—and cradled it as I crept down the hall.

The front door groaned open and in streamed a procession of dark-robed men.

I felt a strange relief that it wasn't *him*. Really, I couldn't fault these men for coming in without permission—they surely didn't realize someone lived here now, in what had previously been an empty ruin. So, I watched from the top of the staircase as they filed through, men with pilled skin like cottage cheese, men with black hats and beaked noses. They dragged another man with a bag over his head alongside them.

One of them looked up at me with one eye that was waxy and white, the other a rich, searing blue. His lips were misshapen and colorless so that his mouth was like a jagged wound. He did not acknowledge me, and continued walking with the rest, down the stairs to the basement. They ignored me.

Curious, I followed, half-convinced I was still asleep. The hammer grew slick in my sweaty palm. A reddish light and faint, foul smoke curled from open wounds in the basement floor. The men started chanting and singing, their throats ululating, and when they pulled the bag from the dragged man's head, I discovered with a shock that it was my ex-husband. His eyes wildly scanned the congregation; his mouth was sealed with duct tape, his wrists tied in elaborate knots behind his back.

You understand, if it was anyone else, anyone at all, I might have tried to stop them. But the sight of my ex-husband with tears streaking from his bulging eyes gave me a perverse delight after all the hurt he had inflicted on me over the years. I stood at the top of the stairs that led down to the basement and watched.

One of the men pulled out a long blade. Their dark hats and hoods shielded their eyes and left only the lower halves of their age-mottled faces visible, their twisted mouths that sang and chanted. "For Ephraim Maggard," said the one with the blade, and the others echoed his words.

Then he brought the blade down on my ex-husband's neck once, twice, and again, until his head departed the body, tethered by a thin sinuous thread that reminded me of those spiderwebs which snapped in a final blow. The men gathered around eagerly, reaching for his head, leaving the body with its bleeding stump of neck discarded on the floor. They reached their fingers into his eyes until they popped in two little bursts. While they tried, unsuccessfully, to pry open his skull with the blade, I drifted down the stairs.

"Try this," I said, holding out the hammer.

Instead of taking it, one of the men presented my ex-husband's head and allowed me to bring the hammer down until it cracked open like an egg.

They gathered around and scooped out handfuls of pulsing brain matter. Then they brought the gore to the cracks in the walls and floor and squeezed it through like putty. The cracks belched a foul hiccup of smoke.

Once they'd fed the contents of my ex-husband's skull to the house, the men gathered up the body, using their robes to wipe away the curdling pool of blood on the floor. Carrying the carcass aloft on their shoulders, the men began to file out again, not even acknowledging me or the bloodied hammer I still clutched as they passed.

I'm not sure what I was thinking when I decided to purchase the old fixer-upper on Crabtree Lane, but I know what I'm thinking now. With my renovation, regular care and feeding, this house will return to its former grandeur. I wonder what it must have been like when it was first built, gleaming and new, by old Ephraim Maggard. It seems to have accepted me after that night, allowing me to fix it rather than pushing my nails out as fast as I can hammer them in. Perhaps it knows that I intend to treat it with respect. The head is a house, and I am its tenant. The head is a house, and I am only a thought in a dream.

Three Dead in Murder-Suicide, May 1982

A family of three was found dead last Friday in their home on Crabtree Lane.

Brock and Mary Tennant, along with their young son Peter, perished on Thursday in a grisly scene authorities are calling an act of pure evil. Leading up to what transpired that day is a curious account of a seemingly happy family that turned against itself in the most brutal fashion.

The following testimony was reported by a neighbor who knew the family but wishes to remain anonymous:

They were what you'd expect them to be. Mary was a professor of local history at the women's college and an avid horticulturist; Brock maintained seasonal employment, and enjoyed fishing and whittling; their son, Peter, played little league and was learning piano. He was a curious and tenacious boy who sometimes got lost in the clouds. By all accounts they were happy, and the new home was sure to suit their various hobbies. Mary tended the rose garden, Brock had room for his projects, and Peter hit balls out into the forest where they disappeared, swallowed by the trees.

MISSIVES FROM THE HOUSE ON CRABTREE LANE

    Peter Tennant's curiosity and tenacity drove him to an exploration of the house and its grounds, although his parents warned him against drawing too close to the lurking dark of the woods. He instead found himself investigating the large basement, where there was enough room for him to bounce tennis balls against the walls. There was one instance, however, that created a small fracture in the family, which perhaps would eventually lead to a larger rift. One day Peter pitched a ball hard against the old walls, and a crack opened up. Though his parents admonished him for damaging the house, Peter found himself drawn to the crack, which spread out, web-like, along the walls and floor. And from that crack (so he claimed) came a whisper of static.

    Peter pressed his ear against the crack and listened intently for the voice he could sense through the static, beneath the static, in the very hiss and susurrus of the static, like the trees at the edge of their property voicelessly whispering in wind. The more he listened, the more it seemed like a radio tuned to the blank space between stations, snippets of one program or another murmuring through the hissing void.

    After he began listening to the cracks in the basement, Peter quit his little league team and abandoned his piano lessons. At first, his parents expressed distress that their son, dark-ringed eyes staring hypnotically from his increasingly gaunt face, wanted to spend all his time in the basement, and tried to cajole him to rejoin his activities.

    They put him in his baseball uniform, but Peter just kept looking at his mitt and bat like he didn't quite recall what they were for. It wasn't until he raised the bat to keep Mary and Brock from getting any closer that they realized their mistake. Peter kept carrying the bat around, but his parents quit trying to get him to practice.

    Around that same time, Mary was seen around town sporting bandages on her fingers. "Keep pricking myself on those darned roses," she told acquaintances when asked about her wounds. When she showed up at the garden center with her whole face bandaged to buy a new pair of clippers, she blamed a local species of spider she had discovered burrowed in the dirt of the garden.

    Brock, too, was affected by the curious turn of events. His previous whittling projects, which he sold at the local farmer's market, consisted of decorative wooden ducks and owls. Yet, regulars began to claim that they last saw him hawking carved skulls. "One piece that was like a pyramid made out of a pile of eyeballs, I don't know what it was for, as it certainly wasn't pretty," said Alice Buckley. Brock said he was inspired by his new house, and that he was also hard at work carving designs into the house itself. He called his new project his "masterpiece."

    Meanwhile, the more time he spent with his ear pressed into the cracks in the walls, the more Peter thought he was hearing a voice. When he emerged one typical Tuesday—as his mother prepared supper grown fresh from the garden and his father sat at the kitchen table whittling some abominable new figurine—he paused in the doorway until he was noticed. When his parents tried to ask him how he was doing—carefully, of course, as if he were as brittle as glass—he opened his mouth, but his voice came out like static. His eyes faded into two grayish orbs, writhing as if filled with maggots, two snowy television screens. His screeching voice—a meaningless hiss—forced his parents to cover their ears.

Whatever the boy was trying to communicate was lost to them. They tried to listen but could only distinguish vague murmurings somewhere beneath the static. Whatever he tried to tell them, whatever he'd heard in the basement, made him climb into the old oven head-first. Or, perhaps his parents shoved him inside to stop the awful sound.

The oven was not in use that night. Mary Tennant was cooking vegetables on the stove. In fact, the family had never even tried to use the ancient thing, nor were they entirely sure how it worked. Still, nearly as soon as Peter Tennant crawled inside, the oven lit up and burned him alive. The sounds of his screams were drowned in the deafening static.

Unable to handle witnessing her son's excruciating death, Mary Tennant hung herself from the chandelier. The force of the drop unexpectedly decapitated her. Mary's head was found in the corner of the foyer, eyes eaten away and crawling with spiders.

Brock Tennant's response was to charge into the basement to locate the source of his son's madness. He peered into each of the cracks, and what he saw made him run upstairs and lock himself in the bathroom. His eyes began to swell; his pupils dilated into round tunnels at the end of which lay a wriggling, gray mass digging deep into his brain. His mouth widened in terror; his jaw unhinged itself as he watched his eyes balloon in the mirror before exploding into a swarm of buzzing insects that proceeded to feast on the tissue and brain matter that oozed from the holes of his eyes.

This may all be speculation, but our source has pointed out details of these events that are consistent with the state of the bodies prior to any such details being made available to the public: the decapitated woman in the foyer, the man in the bathroom whose hollowed-out skull was still crawling with insects, and the charred child's body curled up in the old brick oven.

If the head is a house where the brain lives, then these three were soon as abandoned as the house on Crabtree Lane itself. No brain matter was found in or around any of the bodies.

MISSIVES FROM THE HOUSE ON CRABTREE LANE

The Tennant family will be deeply missed by their community. A memorial is scheduled for Sunday.

Ephraim Maggard's Private Journal, June 1816

I have found a Way to live forever.

Surely do I knowe such other Sorcerers as have made theyr own attempts, but they have neither my Knowledge nor my Aptitude. They are unread, unwise, unlearned in the Ways of magick. In short, Fools. I have invited them on the solstice to a gathering near the woods so that we might call up the Devile himself. It is under this guise of moonlight that the Feast will begin.

What they do not knowe is that I have been building my House on the land beside these great dark woods, where they have been invited to gather. It is nearly complete. And its frame is a skeleton of the haunted Woods, its bricks the dried clay of this living Earth.

When my guests arrive on the solstice to partake of this ritual, they will not find me in body. They will find only my house.

They will be invited inside by the lights in the windows, glowing warm against night's scrim. And if they resist entry—those who may suspect this House is not what it appears—they will be met by a swarm of spiders that shall pursue them toward the porch. "Ephraim up to his theatricks again," they shall say, grinning at one another, expecting to find me inside with my black robes, a goat ready for slaughter, chalices in hand waiting to be filled with blood. "'Tis a good trick," they might even allow, amused by my spiders.

But then they will come under the house's shadow, and the lights will blaze in the windows with eager devilry. They will pause before the doorknocker, wondering if they should be let in. Yet, before they make any movement, the door will swing wide on its hinges, groaning into the blackness beyond.

Will they dare step inside?

HYMNS OF ABOMINATION

By and by, I know they will—for these men are arrogant Fools, filled with churlish Bravado. They think themselves as powerful as I, even as they grow lazy and indolent in their feasting, their parlour tricks. They have not a drop of the Devile within them.

And when they do come through the Doorway, they will find it not merely a doorway, but a Maw; they will find their eyes bursting open to create new doorways into their skulls, and they will find those skulls buzzing anew. They will find their brains Devoured and their bodies re-purposed: bones into balustrades, meat into tapestries, fingers into new legions of arachnids. I will consume them and they will become part of me, part of what I will have become.

In truth, I *will* be there, after a fashion—for I am building myself into the house. My Soul will live inside its walls. My fingers will wriggle away to do my bodily bidding. My eyes will be as windows, looking out. My bones will clack as doorknocker. Its eaves will be my eyelids. Its oven my stomach. If my Spelle goes the way it ought...

And on those who enter, I will Feed and live Forever!

Rustic Historic Mansion Private Getaway

Entire house hosted by Maggie
8 guests · 4 bedrooms · 5 beds · 2 baths
Incredibly private historic mansion is perfect for a family getaway!
Ample yard for campfires or relaxing under the stars!
Vintage oven for those who love to cook!
Book your stay today!
★ 1.00 (1 review)
Steven
November 2020
House was dirty and cold, had clearly not been kept up. Strange smells in the basement and stains in the bathrooms. Would not recommend. Also, my husband went missing while we were staying here. Please let me know if you see him.

Anne Gare's Rare and Import Video Catalogue
October 2022

Jonathan Raab

<u>*Go to the Devil*</u> <u>– Dir. Terence Fisher, 1969</u>
<u>Starring Christopher Lee, Patrick Mower, Nike</u>
<u>Arrighi</u>

A middling Gothic horror film about cuckoldry paranoia and black magic. Features a laughable depiction of lower-demon summoning that is in fact a mishmash of lower-plane conjuration and various warding rituals against the interference of busy-body angels of the many-eyed and prophetic variety. The film's most notable characteristic is the presence of an authentic copy of the dreaded *Libellus Vox Larva* (as of this printing, a copy is available for sale in our book collection; inquire for current price and condition) and the improvisational and stilted reading thereof.

The film was never finished, of course, due to the subsequent destruction of London and the immolation and/or transmogrification of cast and crew wrought by the occult forces inadvertently conjured by the otherwise-admirable gesture toward authenticity via the inclusion of the *Libellus Vox Larva*. That you are not aware of this apocalyptic four-fold crossrip is a testament to both the degenerate wizard Einstein's perverse "theory" of relativity and the many-fold failures of the American educational system.

35mm incomplete work print on one-and-a-half two-reelers; includes case covered in a patina of human ash and dust from the tragic collapse of pre-war English masonry, very fine.

Thirteen thousand dollars.

HYMNS OF ABOMINATION

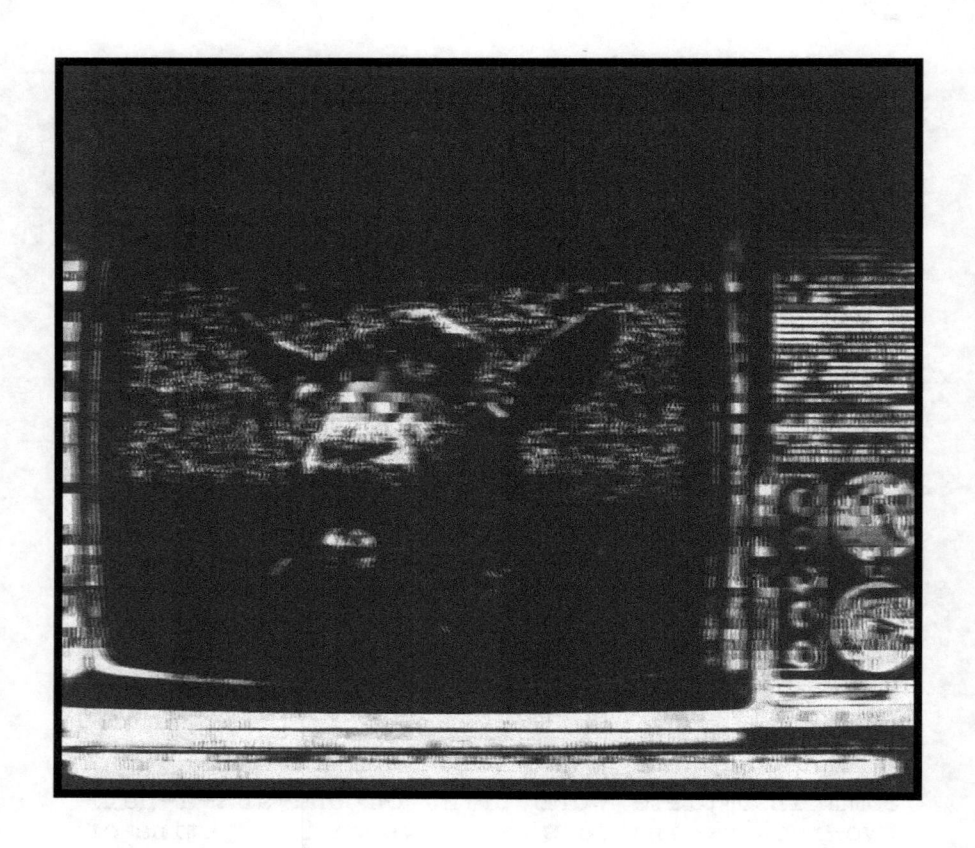

x158x

the house of lost sisters

That morning, after scraping her husband's cold eggs down the garbage disposal, Jillian Kettlewell ran away with the milkman.

Ah, the milkman! Trim, broad-shouldered, square-jawed, freshly shaven, with sinuous cheekbones and an Executive Contour beneath his eggshell-hued officer's cap. The milkman in his crisp uniform of black bowtie and pristine whites, where semen stains were indistinguishable from a slosh of curdled milk.

So unlike Vance Kettlewell. Vance with his ill-advised moustache, like pressing her lips to a hound's furry snout. A premature thickening at his stomach, its surface jiggling like an aspic at inopportune moments. His strange grunting orgasm, akin to his nasal laugh. The piebald patches of hair on his shoulders and upper back revealed on the moonlit wedding night, as though she'd married a roughly handled teddy bear. A mere five years had transformed that shy college boy presenting her with a lightly wilted bouquet from the corner drug to the ursine version of a werewolf bound up in a tweed suit.

The milkman came to extricate Jillian from the confines of the Kettlewells' raised ranch not in his familiar milk van, but a menstrual-red Cadillac convertible, procured from God knows where. Jillian's heart-shaped face was loosely anonymized in bug-eyed sunglasses and filmy chiffon headscarf to become someone glamorous: Liz Taylor, Audrey Hepburn, Jackie Kennedy. As he drove, her arm snaked around his, lifting the hem of her skirt just enough to reveal the snaps of her garters in his peripheral vision, inducing his sinister twitch of a smile.

Thus they cruised out of the suburbs and through the outskirts of Brookhaven, the milkman cheerfully recounting all the roadside spots where Doc Winterhalter vivisected those poor girls some 60 years ago. In fact, Jillian caught sight of a memorial plaque pounded into the bark of a thick old oak as she squatted to piss in the woods, its corroded metal surface bearing the lonely name of MRS. HEDDA VENABLE, drawing a line through time. A picture emerged in Jillian's mind: the doctor's horse's

l.c. von hessen

bored hooves kicking up dust, steaming equine bowel movements dropping from the horse's hindquarters as the sex maniac veterinarian did his bloody business under the trees, his carriage waiting on the dirt shoulder where the Cadillac was currently parked, where Jillian lowered herself onto the milkman's purple-tinged erection, her nipples pinched by his picket-fence teeth and buttocks clenched in his strong palms, all potentially visible to any strange automobile curving onto the highway.

I don't care, I don't care!! I want to go mad!!!

She had not asked him where they were going: it was simply Away. Away from Brookhaven. Away from Middle America. To the south was Mexico! On the West Coast was Hollywood! On the East Coast was—was her sister. And the old town. *Well.* Best not think about that.

"Oh, Johnny, can we have some music for the drive?" said Jillian as she nestled onto the milkman's shoulder.

And he switched on the radio.

The pair drove together past endless flatlands of hay bales and wheat fields and penned-up goats and cud-munching cattle and rotting barns with apotropaic symbols hammered out in metal above the door, rolling along to a soundtrack of buoyant, jangle-guitared rock'n'roll, mournful and vaguely necrophilic teenage girls' love songs about their dead greaser boyfriends, plaintive bewailing of what a Town Without Pity *caaan dooo*. Until, far enough from signals and civilization, the music was fully swallowed up in a static fog.

The milkman reached out and deftly switched the dial to the farthest left end. A pop song sprang out immediately, sharp and clear as a surgeon's scalpel.

"I saw your face on the *eee*vening news / they said that I should be a-*fra*-id of you, oh *nooo!*" sang a chipper young girl, backed by rhythmic handclaps. "Razorblade Johnny's got my heart in his hands / A trickle of blood at the tip of his glans / Razorblade Johnny, won't you *please* understand . . ."

As Jillian leaned on his arm, half-awake at best, the milkman smiled. And in that smile, it seemed, there were too many teeth in his mouth, three concentric rows of molars like malformed bathroom tiles. A mouth too large for its head, cracking apart in red ravines between cheekbones and earlobes. A head too large for its body, inflating like a tumor on a stiff-collared spindle neck. The crescent-shaped brim of the milkman's massive cap blotting out the sun surely as an eclipse.

And the DJ spat:

"This is Crackerjack Dan bringing you the hits, the grits, the banana splits, the peppermint clits, the maniac's fits, the crab-louse nits, the jackknife slits, the charnel-house pits, and if ya don't like it I'll *spit* where you *sit*, Mr. Splitfoot!"

—x x x—

That evening, Judy Cochrane sat before the vanity preparing for the House of Lost Sisters. She had selected a snug turtleneck sweater and cinched belt, settling on a pencil skirt over capri slacks since the latter might read as too masculine. A palette knife's thickness of makeup, applied under curled bangs.

Will I look like a beatnik? Oh, gosh.

Her destination was a certain apartment on the top floor of a certain building in a certain district of neighboring Leeds. The House—*that place*—was whispered about in the most discreet fashion by a select coterie of Judy's fellow secretaries, including some of the gals who were a little, well, long in the tooth not to have married out of the steno pool by now. The type who wore resolutely sensible haircuts and heels despite their employers' pinch-lipped "suggestions." The type who would not rat you out to the teenage boy manning the counter at the corner drug if they caught you slipping a paperback copy of *Odd Girl Out* or *The Sinful Sorority* into your purse. Go to the House of Lost Sisters, they said, and there you will find women brazen as the dawn, entwining their many young and shapely limbs and lips in every combination imaginable.

Take a taxi, they said, to Pleasant Street, where you can make a pretense of window-shopping for a time, then head down Tremens Terrace. (For this part of the pilgrimage, it is highly recommended that you carry a folding knife or somesuch other defensive apparatus concealed on your person.) You will come to the former shopping and warehouse district downtown, where all the buildings look much the same: the House in question will be distinguished by its topmost left window, which will glow a deep red. You are to knock on the front door, thrice and thrice again; and from the cracked gap of the doorway, if you have proceeded correctly, a voice will ask: *Are you looking for a good time?* And you must respond: *No, I'm a Sister of St. Anne's.*

In the back of the taxi, nestled in her car coat as the even beacon of streetlights swept over her face in the dark, Judy detached herself from grating memories of the workday, her boss, Mr. Hathorne, revising her shopping list for the latest company party.

"Vodka? That Russki swill? We drink *gin* in this office." He'd tapped the cocktail glass in his hand. "We vomit *gin* on our knees in the head just like our forefathers did, sssweety-cakes." Barely noon and he was already slurring. Judy smiled and nodded at Mr. Hathorne by rote, thankful her bottom was free of pats and pinches from his speckled hands as he already had a mistress in Reception.

The clack of her heels on concrete reverberated far too loudly as she walked past the shuttered crack-windowed factories and condemned storefronts with one hand tautly gripping the strap of her handbag. Truly, there was *nobody* else on these streets, not one living soul: no workers, no stragglers, no bums or—or loose women. Her eye was tricked time and again by warehouses with pallid mannequins arrayed on their upper floors, torpedo-breasted, hips cocked, elbows sharp, headless or blank-faced or coldly appraising: had they been manufactured in such places before the buildings, and this corner of town, were abandoned, or were they intentional decoys set up by the House to foil intruders?

A subtle motion in Judy's peripheral view: a live woman in lingerie, hands on hips, peering down at the timid steno girl on the street, backed in lush, pulsing red like an *anima sola*.

At her knocks, the door opened a cautious gap. And a raspy female voice queried:

"Are you looking for a good time?"

—x x x—

By late afternoon, Jillian was ensconced in a roadside motel while the milkman set out to collect dinner for them both. Dining out in a restaurant together would make them too conspicuous: he was still wearing his milkman's whites, and there were still not enough states in between themselves and Brookhaven. Vance Kettlewell was a salesman, and therefore dangerous.

Jillian sat alone on the bed with her biggest suitcase and her hat box full of prized jewelry and photographs: her sole souvenirs from the Kettlewell home. The bed's quilted spread was printed with impressionistic brown-and-yellow flowers distressingly reminiscent of the inside of a diaper. Mounted above the bed was a very bad painting, an amateurish attempt at a still life, which appeared to depict a plated brick of raw beef. On the nightstand, the tuning knob of the clock radio had been crudely yanked out, a couple of wires forlornly dangling from the hole like the frayed optic nerve of a skull socket. The clock itself was equally useless as its second hand was stuck, perpetually tock-ticking between 5:39 and 5:40. Opening the nightstand drawer revealed an obligatory Gideon Bible with pages crinkled and stuck together, bookmarked with a crumpled pamphlet that held several strips of pornographic Popeye cartoons. Jillian's bemused observation of Wimpy's improbable endowment was soon interrupted by a trio of sharp knocks on the door.

"Meat Man!" a muffled voice called.

She rose to open the door as far as the chain would allow.

"Meat Man here!" This gruff announcement was followed by a hard, phlegmy snort of heavy congestion.

"*Meat* Man?" she said, largely to herself, rolling the syllables around with distaste.

Unhooking the chain for further inspection revealed an emaciated figure with a neck and jawline encrusted in grey stubble and a squashed face like one of those dried shrunken apple heads Jillian's grandmother had taught her to make when she was young enough to fear the results. He was clad in a flat cap and long, ruddy peach-colored leather trenchcoat with a tattered hem.

The Meat Man patted his pocket. "Meat's here. Got your order, ma'am." He expectorated a purple clot onto the motel's unkempt lawn.

"I'm sorry, I didn't order any—"

"On the house, ma'am!" He grinned, revealing a gumline like a bombed-out city, and opened his trenchcoat flasher-style as she automatically flinched back. At least he was somewhat clothed under there, a pink-stained undershirt and boxers; the wet red lining of his coat actively dribbled into his sock garters. A hand squelched around in a hidden pocket of the inside lining and pulled out a fleshy cylinder recalling a bull's pizzle—but no, it was shorter and thicker, its outer casing disturbingly similar in tone and texture to the leather of the Meat Man's trenchcoat. She considered the mechanics of a kangaroo's pouch as he pressed it into her hand and immediately walked away.

The free meat was surprisingly hot. It squirmed sharply in her grip and she dropped it with a gasp and a splat on the pavement. One end of the meat retracted open, revealing a wet aperture baring multiple rings of round, yellowish nubs that looked uncomfortably close to human teeth. Jillian shrank back inside and secured every lock.

Shortly after dusk, the milkman returned with dinner in a pair of bagged containers, which he set out on the round table by the window. In Jillian's own container was a brick of rare beef that resembled the painting above the bed after a couple of minutes on a grill.

Before sitting down to eat, the milkman paused in the doorway, sniffing the air with a sour expression creasing his handsome features.

"Didn't let that Meat Man in, didja?"

—x x x—

With cautious steps, Judy ascended the groaning staircase, peering at tin ceilings and wainscoting draped in dust and cobwebs like a Hammer Horror manor. The building was clearly abandoned. She greatly hoped the House had working toilets and showers or else it could become quite unsanitary: after all, she had to return home to her furnished rooms at the Cowansville single ladies' boarding house afterwards, and just *imagine* running into the house mother while smelling of...

Judy was startled to find that the door to the top floor rooms, to the House proper, was guarded by an elderly woman in a houndstooth suit, with the mien of a decrepit librarian. Thin and petite, her frame compressed by a dowager's hump, she scowled at Judy through a round, pinched mouth and stringy strands of long, greasy hair fallen slack from an attempt at a beehive that was really more of a rat's nest. A pair of tiny watery eyes like those of a dead mouse appraised Judy.

"Now hold your horses, Goodwife!" The old lady blocked the door with the lacquered cane in her fist, its handle topped by a puckered asterisk, a tarnished metal effigy of a leech head or anus. She never rose from her rickety stool. "All in good time."

The old lady unfurled the drooping heap of fabric in her lap in a great whiff of must and mildew.

"What d'you think? Now give me your unvarnished opinion. Speak up, girl."

Hoisted in her speckled hands was a tattered quilt. Its materials and style fell somewhere between backwoods outsider art and the pearl-clutching content of modern-art museums, a crude patchwork of scorched, stained fabrics and used prophylactics, rubbery leather and reptile sheds, rank barnyard pelts, a chainmail square of rusty razorblades held together by twisted wire, even what appeared to be a tarantula molt. Judy's nose wrinkled involuntarily.

"Well…to be honest…it's a bit…garish?"

"*Garish!* Is that a *pun?*" She thumped her cane on the boards. "I don't like that. No puns." Judy was thoroughly confused about what the doorwoman meant. Even more confusing was the shift in Judy's peripheral vision whenever she flicked her pupils away from the old lady, whose outfit appeared to warp from staid tweeds to pinch-waisted Civil War widow to white-capped Puritaness to sequin-spangled cocaine-eyed flapper, but drained of all color in the crackling silver-grey of an ill-treated film reel.

Judy hoped she wouldn't be, well, a *participant*.

At last the door cracked open and Judy was invited in.

"Welcome to the House of Lost Sisters," said a girl in a pageboy and panty girdle, coughing into her fist. A girl in a short negligee arrived on her heels, brandishing a serving dish with a razor and a can of Barbasol "if you have a fear of the crab louse."

Inside were fewer women than Judy was expecting, or, more accurately, hoping. Nothing too naughty going on yet. A brunette splashing about in a shallow bathtub, dark mouth smiling through wet white panties. A woman with patchily-shaved hair—a remnant, perhaps, of electroconvulsive shock—sprawled out spider-legged in a green wing-backed chair. An imperious black-haired *maîtresse d'hôtel* with heavy winged eyeliner like actresses in Italian films watched over the proceedings with an elbow perched on the mantel of a bricked-up fireplace. Half the walls were stripped down to the insulation, the pronounced creak and clack of the well-trodden floorboards recalling a lowest-rent theatre, outfitted with tatty rugs and mismatched antique furniture with stuffing protruding from its seams like fungus.

In one corner, below the red light of the window, was an up-ended crate hosting a selection of gewgaws: a baby-sized goat skull, a compact mirror in the shape of an eye, a ribald novelty ashtray in which one deposited spent butts between the legs of a porcelain pin-up girl.

This, it was whispered, was a shrine to St. Anne, and beside it rested a transistor radio.

"You've been gritting your teeth to the dulcet tones of Benny Baxter's Broadway Orchestra," said the female DJ. "And now, an interlude of Sapphist sophistry with Fiona Foxcroft and her Phantasmagoric Fanny Finaglers. This one's dedicated to all you languorous lovers of Leedsbos." The ECT patient clapped her hands.

"'Holyoke to bed, Barnard to wed,'" said a honey-silk voice. "Or was it the reverse?" The speaker, an elegant redhead from the local women's college, tapped ash out the window, returning the cigarette to her crimson mouth and smiling at Judy with a conspicuous look up and down her body.

"H-hello, I'm—"

She pressed a pair of cold fingers to Judy's lips.

"No names, darling. We're all sisters here."

—x x x—

It occurred to Jillian that she had never seen the milkman fully divested of his uniform. Even now, with his jumpsuit dangling over the back of a chair like an old skin, he'd kept his milkman's cap on during this latest round of coitus. His black bowtie loosely knotted her wrists together above her head. His teeth glowed greenish-pale in the dark as he thrust.

From the silent dark emerged a squelching noise that didn't originate from the wet mashing of their genitals: and Jillian knew, she *knew*, that the meat leech full of molars had gotten inside, that it lurked under the bed, behind the beetle-gloss of the milkman's shoes, waiting. A sudden frisson of fear combined with the milkman's machinations to jolt her into orgasm. As he pulled out, the flood of his seed sprayed from her stomach to labia with the force of a punctured artery, growing cold and sticky on her skin like spilt blood. His sweat-moistened weight pressed her into the mattress and sleep.

The meat leech did not show itself until the morning, as she packed her suitcase on the sex-sullied coverlet in the milkman's absence. The air conditioner below the window emitted a gentle yet eerie ambiance, a faint ghostly chorus of the children she was too afraid to have. She glanced down at the carpet and gasped as the meat leech squirmed out from beneath the bed skirt, its misshapen, lipless orifice approximating a smile in Jillian's direction, visibly red and leaking inside as though it had been chewing at itself. By force of instinct, she punted it, hard, with the tip of one shoe.

As it sailed through the room, thwacking wetly against the wall to leave a pink-red stream of meat juice in its wake, the meat leech emitted a braying, squealing bleat of pain and protest, heavily distorted and unnaturally amplified, the dying screams of a slaughtered pig with a microphone caught in its throat L I V E ON THE AIR, a crushing wall of sound that pressed Jillian into a chair, fetally crumpled and covering her ears. The sound only stopped when the thing squirmed itself behind the dresser, as if ashamed.

Soon enough the milkman returned, bearing a grin and a crumpled flyer. On the front was a crude map depicting some obscure tourist trap nestled into a mountain valley; on the back, a faint mimeograph of a comically buxom Olive Oyl. The tourist trap had a name, handwritten in black, its letters alternately rickety and curled like bound sticks and scythe-hooks; yet somehow Jillian could not link them together into legible words to sound out by syllable in her mind, as if they were scrawled there in Cyrillic or Cantonese.

Here, the milkman informed her, was where they would travel next.

—x x x—

The redheaded college girl, kissing her neck in crimson trails, cochineal smears, with spit-moistened middle finger tracing an infinite spiral around her clitoris—the girl in the pageboy compressing her nipples between manicured nails with exquisite tactile timing—the girl from the bathtub massaging her feet, warm breath against her toes, hungry eyes gliding from her handiwork up to Judy's face and down again—the female DJ cheerily advertising a new-and-improved line of hemorrhoid cream—"And this one goes out to the beauteous Cochrane girls, by special request—"

"*What?*" Judy jolted up in shock, her interjection obscured by a deafening circus screamer march.

Sounds of a banging, thumping scuffle seeped through old wood and plaster. The hallway door timidly creaked open to reveal a moustachioed man in a fecal-hued suit, stout yet cringing, hat clutched in both hands. The other women disengaged themselves from Judy's supine body, ran and hid behind crumbling support pillars and old furniture. Judy herself jumped behind the couch, concealing her nudity with a sheet, heart pounding.

Judy allowed herself a cautious peek around the corner of the couch. The *maîtresse d'hôtel* stood before the intruder, arms crossed. Words were exchanged which Judy couldn't make out above the blare of the radio.

The man patted his suit pockets and held out a photograph as the music abruptly shut off.

"H-have you seen my wife?"

How, *how* had he gotten up here? He was sweating at the temples, a tremor in his hands. A pool of black blood nipped at his heels. His brown suit, dusted with dark spots. Judy knew, then, that he had beaten the doorwoman with her own cane.

The *maîtresse* leaned in and spoke, adopting a studied, soothing tone, dispatching the man in all his hesitance and threat with words Judy could not hear. She stared at the door and listened to his heavy footfall recede before storming behind the couch and hauling Judy up by the ear like a naughty schoolgirl.

"You're married? You've compromised us."

"No, I'm not married! I've never been married!" In desperation Judy held up a naked, untanned ring finger. "He must mean my sister, I have a twin—"

"Save it, toots." A cold sneer, the flash of a silver fang.

"No, please, listen. My sister went missing. She just disappeared from home one morning: nobody knows where she went. That must be her husband; I never met him. They moved to the Midwest after—"

Grim-lipped, the girl with the Barbasol can strode up behind the *maîtresse*; Judy's car coat and purse were thrust forward without a word. She swallowed a whimper and wanted to cry.

As Judy, sniffling and pushing back tears, hurried her clothes back on, the orgy continued without her in the adjoining room. Before her forced exit, she glanced inside at a sprawling jigsaw puzzle of women's flesh, its chorus of laughter and moans. No look back at Judy from any of the Sisters. Not even the pretty redhead.

Pressed to leave out the back way by the *maîtresse*, she was marched down a set of steep, narrow stairs without light or railing to guide her. A thick metal door creaked open before her with a rust-infused whinge and the *maîtresse* kicked her through.

Judy had expected an alleyway, but, taking in her surroundings on hands and thighs, she realized she was underground somewhere. A long, grey cinder-block tunnel with its opposite end swallowed in blackness like the distant drop of a well.

She had ripped one of her stockings on the cement floor in the fall, a clotted red mouth gaping open on her knee behind the laddered nylon. From some shadowed alcove a lithe tuxedo cat sauntered over to Judy on silent paws. After a perfunctory sniff of her fingertips, it crouched down and darted out a little pink tongue in order to lap at her wound.

"Oh, kitty. Kitty, no." She batted the cat away with chafed palms.

The cat cocked its head up at Judy with a quizzical stare, as if the strange disheveled human girl was the one behaving unreasonably.

Then its stance grew rigid, robotically retching until its small body hocked up a fleshy lump in a blotch of inky purple.

An oddly angular shape was concealed within. Carefully nudging the lump with a handkerchief from her purse revealed a car key.

The cat, with a rather smug smile, began trotting down the tunnel on brisk white paws.

Judy picked herself up and followed.

—x x x—

Through a cloud-curdled yellow-grey sky and featureless fields so barren and dusty they cracked apart like mummy skin, the flat horizon of a world without end, the milkman drove. Jillian had no idea where they were in the country and had given up hope of a real answer. The milkman's fixed grin did not meet his eyes.

As if on cue, the landscape erupted. An invisible Hand of God had turned the page of a pop-up book. The tents and banners and rickety rides of a traveling circus, a carnival, emerged fully formed from beneath the barren ground, flipping themselves over and onto the surface like the clockwork mechanism of a libertine's timepiece at midnight, a blank clock face abruptly beset by a reel of masqued revelers and dancing demons.

A clutch of panic in Jillian's innards as the milkman parked in the dry dirt.

"Oh, do we have to go? I don't want to go. *Please*, Johnny."

The milkman gripped her hand, striding through the entry gates past covertly rigged games of chance and pockmarked vendors of tooth-rotting refreshments. Around them, a stream of repetitive carnival music from an unseen fairground organ, at times so loud one couldn't think, at times drifting away to awkward near-silence, at seemingly random interludes. A crudely carved folk-art carousel cycled sluggishly with sneering red-eyed barnyard beasts in place of standard ponies. A wax-faced fortune teller in a glass cage tapped at a spread of cards with a stiff mannequin hand, eyes and lips stitched shut with black thread. A skeleton in a top hat and tailcoat swung its bony legs at the entrance of a ramshackle dark ride labeled C_ACKERL_ACK DAN'S L_VE _U_E. (*Love Tube?* thought Jillian. *Live Nude?*) A mechanical clown, his grin full of elongated yellow-green tiles, bowed stiffly in greeting to the couple and lifted his oversized bowler to reveal the quivering pink lobes of an uncomfortably realistic brain.

Jillian muttered into the milkman's ear: "My sister was deathly afraid of clowns. I pretended to be afraid too so we wouldn't have to go to the circus…"

"I didn't know you had a sister."

We haven't spoken about very much at all, have we?

"Yes, my twin sister. She's still in Massachusetts, or—or she *was*." A sudden Dread knotted into her skull, a sharp feeling as exposed as the clown's brain. "My sister went missing. She just disappeared one evening. She lived alone, and she wasn't going steady with anyone. I don't think she eloped or went away to have a baby: she was never all that interested in boys. Her boss, her company, nobody knows what happened to her." She paused. "One of the other secretaries said she was asking about a house—"

The milkman stopped short before a vendor's tent, its dubious wares protected from the elements by flapping canvas made of ruddy peach-pink leather. Strings of purple-grey sausages drifted in the breeze like the limbs of gibbeted criminals, their unsupervised links tracing spirals in the dust. Raw, bloodless chickens dangled above the counter, plucked skin lumpy and saggy as an old man's drooping scrotum. Jillian had no appetite.

Once again, the Meat Man appeared. He wore a nametag now, pinned to the increasingly ragged fabric of his trenchcoat:

I am an APPRENTICE
please be KIND

Seeing Jillian, he grinned in recognition, a post-nasal drip loudly snorted down the man's gullet.

"Didja like the meat?"

"I did not touch the meat."

"You're late for your act, y'know." From inside his awful trenchcoat, he retrieved a creased photograph, sticky with pink fluid. "Ah, yessss: the beauteous Cochrane girls!"

The photo held a pair of small girls, twins, perhaps five, dolled up in heavy theatrical greasepaint, in pinafores and Mary Janes, in forced grins and stovepipe curls. They wore identical crowns fashioned from twists of little plastic sausages. In Jillian's peripheral vision, the girls shifted into a chimera joined at the hip, now at the back, now plump cheeks melded together, skin stretched and distorted by the crude stitching. She turned it over to find writing in a spidery hand, which she deciphered as *J&J Cochrane, Little Leeds May Maids '41.*

As the sausage strings wafted in the dust, the radio on the counter burst forth a chirpy chorus of young girls: "Here's to milkshakes in the Ripper's hands / Here's to dear Judy and Jill / Sister, take me to the butcher's shop / I heard she was dwelling there still..."

She looked to the milkman for reassurance and found he had vanished from her side.

"Johnny? Where's Johnny?" No distinctive white uniform sauntered along the midway or bobbed around the Ferris wheel. "*Johnny?*" She realized then that the place wasn't just sparsely attended: there were no other spectators, no guests, at this carnival.

The Meat Man tossed her a patronizing smile. "Oh, I'll take you to *John-nyyy*." With a wave of his hand like a children's party magician and two hard stomps on the ground, a trapdoor opened into the earth.

At the bottom of the stairs was a dimly lit cinder block tunnel underground. As she advanced, lonely heels on concrete, Jillian noticed the walls to either side were broken up into several smaller rooms, old classrooms or simply made to look like them, with green chalkboards and rows of desks for small people, scattered pages of ruled paper and piles of plaster dust, a schoolhouse in the fallout of a Soviet bomb. Some rooms were completely bricked over with only a crude peephole bored through.

Where's Johnny?

A crisp *zzzing* rang out further down in the dark, followed shortly by a flat, flapping object that zipped along the length of the tunnel on a clothesline somewhere above Jillian's head. A man-sized, man-shaped sheet, like a target for shooting, but with the glossy, intricate detail of an anatomical cross-section. She was reminded, immediately, of her disgust as a child when a boy at school had told her that head cheese involved *brains*. And she realized the sound reminded her of a machine for slicing thin cuts of deli meat.

The man-shaped slice had dripped a trail of liquid onto the ground, atop an older trail in various stages of sticky coagulation. Jillian followed the trail into a cavernous room in which a line of factory girls in grey smocks and hairnets hunched over long tables laden with piles of clothes and rumpled leather sheets. The dart and flash of tiny silver tools.

A heavy stench of hot, wet copper, very faint at the bottom of the stairs, now clotted her nostrils.

"Where's Johnny?"

An imperiously pretty factory girl wearing decidedly non-uniform winged eyeliner, who had been taking a seamripper to the jacket of a brown tweed suit, stepped off the line. She brusquely took hold of Jillian's shoulder, marching her back into the tunnel and pushing her eye to a peephole emitting yellow light.

For Jillian, Mrs. Jillian Cochrane Kettlewell, little May Maid Jill, never did leave home: not her birthplace but that latter home, so far from Cowansville and her sister. Through the peephole she sat, an old woman in a rocking chair, silently perched in a locked room lit only by a sunbeam through which dust motes danced, there on that street in Brookhaven, that street in Middle America. Her wet lips parted slightly, shrunken eyes unfocused and magnified behind thick bifocals, as she brandished a box grater in one speckled hand. She lifted an arm, yellowing chicken-skin dangling from her bicep, and held it as steadily as possible with her antique joints as she pressed the large-holed side of the apparatus against her skin and mechanically began to grate. The old woman remained silent and expressionless as little balls of flesh dropped through the holes, curling up, rolling, and squirming across the bare floorboards at her feet, cannibalizing each other like animalcules under a microscope until there was only one left, a leechlike lump with an orifice full of molars, as bloody and screaming as a newborn.

—x x x—

Judy drove in her stolen murder-red Cadillac past mountains cloaked in robes of dried flesh, past forests unseasonably bare with trees burnt to black sticks, past parched, empty fields abandoned to desert under yellow-grey skies, leaving the entire Pioneer Valley, leaving Massachusetts, New England, the known world entirely. To stop and wonder if such things made sense was to surrender to madness.

The radio hissed, subtly narcotic, like a serpent in the garden. Someone, perhaps she herself, had torn out its knob.

She drove and drove in forgotten time until she reached that lone attraction on the roadside.

The ruin.

The last remnants of the great grey temple, clothed in dust, its foundations worn away by centuries of sand. Through a broken archway, only one full room remained.

The room stank with a perfume of must and musk from the decaying tapestries of barnyard pelts, rusty razors, reptile sheds, and spent prophylactics crudely adorning the walls. Dusty coils of sausages and unspooled intestines dangled alongside them, frail as communion wafers.

The discordant echo of laughter and moans brought Judy to a sheer, filmy curtain that clung to her fingers like the spiderwebs infusing its threads. She drew it back to see the girls, *all* of the girls, fused together in a single bulbous vessel of many-hued flesh, dotted with patches of hair and various apertures, endless limbs protruding like the bristles of a sea urchin.

Judy had never seen anything so beautiful.

For this, of course, was the *true* House of Lost Sisters.

She knelt down, arms forward, prostrating herself in prayer under a veil of cobwebs. Battered by the sand and wind, she waited, unmoving, for minutes and years.

She did not even rise upon hearing the rasping parchment shuffle, the steady tap of a cane pressing cautiously into the stone. A cool, dry hand reached down and rested on her head in benediction.

"Welcome, Sister Judy."

Anne Gare's Rare and Import Video Catalogue
October 2022

Jonathan Raab

<u>*Behold the Undead of Dracula* (The Moore Cut) — Dir. Macario Darcy, 1974</u>
<u>Starring Mara Pengrave, Timothy Gallagher, Daniel Daly</u>

Featuring a plethora of classic Gothic horror monsters and tropes, Camlough Studio's final film *Behold the Undead of Dracula* transcends its low-budget limitations through creative use of lighting, period sets and costumes rivaling Hammer's best, inspired camerawork, liberal use of fog, frequent nudity, sumptuous gore effects, and overwrought, scene-chewing acting and dialogue. Banned in Ireland, the United Kingdom, and most of the continent following the firebombing of an Ulster movie house where six teenagers lost their lives, few copies ever reached the New World, and fewer still remain. A well-preserved print exists within the Irish Film Institute's archives but is inaccessible due to political concerns over the period of violence, bigotry, popery, and rank occultism that the film represents. Fan edits and restorations such as the Moore Cut are most viewers' only option.

This cut is estimated to contain nine-tenths of the original film and some restored music, added sound effects, and judicious editing in the spirit of the original. The last known screening of the Moore Cut was at a private event at a historic and allegedly haunted ranch in remote Meeker, Colorado, hosted by an eccentric millionaire heiress who would prefer that her name not be mentioned

HYMNS OF ABOMINATION

in these pages, lest her ancient enemies catch her scent and pursue their vendetta with renewed fervor and ecstatic violence.

Letterboxed format on VHS, case vaguely smelling of smoke and the charred flesh of teenagers caught up in a conflict for which they bore no responsibility, fine+. Includes errant copy of the videogame adaptation by Lyceum Soft in CD-ROM format with jeweled case and insert, no manual or box, fine.

Eight hundred dollars.

crawl of the west

It was almost lunchtime for vultures. Lyle was climbing out of the arroyo where the camper with Oregon plates had crashed when Dot shouted at him that she'd won a prize off the radio.

"Ain't no radio out here," he said. "No cell signal, either." That was the whole point of being here, he didn't remind her. "Don't bother getting out to help, I got this."

"What happened down there." Dot always changed the subject when her logic jumped the track. "Are they okay."

He threw a couple shopping bags and an overnight case in the backseat and turned to look down the slope running alongside the curve of Sheephole Road, at the camper that had lost control and ended up on its side in the arroyo only minutes before. The flimsy shell cracked open and shockingly personal objects were strewn everywhere, like when a hawk dropped a turtle on a rock.

"Nope." He came around the Cadillac to lean in the open window. 110 degrees already and not even noon. Taking off his straw cowboy hat, he mopped sweat off his forehead and dripped it into her open mouth. "Three souls lost. Damn shame folks don't take more care on these old roads. Where's this damn station, anyway."

A voice out the radio like something cooking in its own fat squalled, "And congrats to our ninety-ninth caller, Dot out of Slab City, who just claimed that prize we discussed. But the offer expires at midnight, so Dot, you better dash…"

Dot always smiled patiently when she was about to eat his ass for lunch. Waiting for him to trip over it and dutifully take down his pants.

"I'll be damned," he said. "Where's the station."

A damp, crepuscular voice, like a nocturnal thing clinging to the underside of the Cadillac, rasped, "WXXT, the lifeblood of Death Valley…damn, did I do it again…?" The Emergency Alert tone screamed fit to liberate their fillings.

She turned it off. "Told ya. Been like that all day…"

"I'll be damned," he said.

He ambled around the Cadillac to slam the trunk when she leaned out her window and shouted, "You forgot something."

He muttered, "Did not," then slapped his forehead when she pointed.

"What would you do without me, hon." She batted her eyelashes and licked her lips.

"Drop dead, I guess." He shuffled back up the highway and grabbed the spike strip, came back and threw it in the trunk. Cheap city shits cost him the coolest part of the morning for thirty-eight dollars, some gas cards and a bunch of shit they'd be lucky to donate to Goodwill. This big prize better be worth it, he thought.

—x x x—

This was already turning out like the Cadillac all over again.

She won it at the Indian bingo and never let him forget it, though she forgot that she blew enough on bingo cards every year to buy the cumbersome, gas-guzzling lead-sled twice over.

He tried to beg or bribe, offered to buy her something nice with their fishing money, but she wasn't having it. We never win anything, she wheedled. He knew why it was so important to her. This land took everything from you, used you up and showed no mercy. The people, even worse. To win something, even if it was obviously a trap, was no small victory. In the end, Lyle could begrudge her nothing. He still got excited simply because she was excited, so the question was moot.

"Call that damn station back," Lyle said an hour later. They'd been from Cadiz to Ragtown and found no sign of any place called Leeds on the phone map, nobody who'd ever heard of it. She dug a mildewed Thomas Bros. guide out of the backseat junk and showed it to him, but the guide was from 1983, and it had to be a mistake. Said the town was inside Death Valley National Park. "If it ever was there, it ain't there now…"

She rubbed her thumb on the page and showed him the smudge of fresh ink. "Can't get any more up-to-date than that."

"Don't make a lick of sense," Lyle grumbled. Explaining the arcane niceties of FCC frequency and call-letter assignments did nothing to dissuade her. W stations are east of the Mississippi, he told her, but then he had to tell her what the Mississippi was (a big river), what a river was (like an ocean), and what an ocean was, (a desert made of water), and in the end, she just laughed at all the useless things he knew.

By noon, Lyle was desperate enough to get on the Needles Highway, expired tags and all, hungry enough to eat his own mouth, and they'd seen nothing open. He pulled into the first drive-thru they came across, in Ludlow. UNDER NEW OWNERSHIP was plastered over all the old signage. He was pretty sure it used to be an urgent care center.

The speaker crackled and spat like dry ice in boiling oil. The menu board was scorched, blackened and blank. Lyle ordered two lunches. The boy in the speaker, his acne sizzling, kept making Lyle repeat himself, then told him to take off his mask. Lyle worked himself into a fury. "This ain't no mask! *This my face!*"

The pickup truck in front of them in the drive-thru accepted a picnic basket that wailed like a spanked newborn. The truck rocked on its springs with its weight. It peeled out and Lyle advanced, hefting his tire iron in anticipation of an argument.

"Customer in front of you paid for your food." The boy pushed an open basket out the window and slammed it shut. The stink of it made Lyle's eyes water. He leaned halfway out of the Cadillac with the tire iron, but the glass was bullet-proof. The basket fell mewling on the pavement, but Dot kicked up such a fuss he had to scrape it off the ground and pass it to her without ever figuring out what it was.

—x x x—

HYMNS OF ABOMINATION

They drove on, but nothing looked right. The buckled lava fields of Lavic Lake were wreathed in mist and wildflowers. They had turned onto the 15 without seeing any sign of Barstow. Dot said he was lost but he knew perfectly well where he was, it was the road that was lost. His skin crawling at the sight of an armada of Highway Patrol cars speeding west, he ditched the interstate at Yermo and stuck to the old roads.

"How hard can it be?" Dot asked, half a hundred times. "Radio station's got a big old antenna, you can see it for miles."

The sun beat down like always, but the shadows were so cold you could see your breath. Lyle turned up the heater, stuck his hand out the window. Furnace wind scoured his melanoma'd skin. They passed through a cloud of locusts so dense they clogged the wipers and smeared yellow ichor on the windshield. He caught fistfuls of the swarming bugs and crammed them in his mouth. Dot laughed, so he did it again.

The bleached, rolling dunes he'd known all his life stuttered and flickered like frames of two films intercut. Staring and half-closing his eyes, he saw another landscape trying to overtake it, a cold forest of looming trees, driving snow.

Dot chased her station up and down the dial. The skittish signal would fade or squirt away just when you got a fix on it. Hiding behind the gospel stations as a sniggering jackass bray in the uplifting Jesus-freak choruses or lurking discordantly in the honky-tonk stomps of the country stations, always ducking out as soon as she found it. "Must be one of them pirate outfits," she muttered to herself, "but we're pirates too, ain't we..."

He pulled off the road and got out. A big, twisted tree, overladen with bloated crimson fruit, stood high over a ramshackle booth with an old woman sitting behind the counter. Wrapped in a coarse winter coat like a water heater blanket, she stashed a cashbox under her lawn chair as he approached.

The punishing sun was a fly's compound eye, its faceted light giving him a hundred jagged shadows like all the other Lyles creeping up behind him to steal his place in this world.

"How'd you get an apple tree to grow out here," Lyle asked.

"No trick to it," the old woman laughed. He blinked and she was naked and covered in blurry blue tattoos that bled and smeared under his bruising eyes. Her breasts swayed like gym socks filled with nickels as she stood up, and then the coat came back. A little transistor radio at her elbow squeaked like a lie detector as she chattered. "Used to be a town that was all whorehouses, and my grand the closest to a doctor in these parts. Buried all the aborted babies in this patch of ground. Reckon it's the most fertile soil in the region…" She leaned forward, squinting through the insect wreckage all over the Cadillac. "If she's got an unwanted visitor, one bite will evict it."

He knew she was lying about all of it. Only mercy of the desert was its lack of memory. When a place failed, the land ate it up and left no ruins, no history, to discourage you from starting over and making the same mistakes forever.

He tried to ask about Leeds, about the station, about the music, but found himself paying all the cash he had for an armload of the lopsided, overgrown fruit. He had to pick them himself, and when he blinked, the tree was not a tree but a sprawling prickly pear cactus, the hard, rosy hand grenades nestled among quills like knitting needles. His hand was swollen and furry with needles and he cursed them, but he couldn't stop picking them, couldn't resist biting into one with his pincushion hand to settle his upset stomach.

The radio cackled and a crippled marching band limped through a dirge for limbless wounded veterans. They couldn't hit a note to save their lives, but the music grew almost unbearably lovely as they were buried alive, the last stifled notes wringing tears from his eyes as the wet concrete closed over their heads and filled their instruments.

"That was the Damnation Army Marching Band with a medley of popular standards from undeclared wars. Before that, Tituba & The Old Familiars did a live set from the Chambre Argent Ballroom, and we started off with Raymond Scott's "Soothing Sounds for Babies" in its simultaneous entirety. Stay tuned for our special holiday season open-mic suicide program, where you can end it all on the airwaves. Don't be too shy to die. It's how I got my start..."

"It's louder," she said for maybe the hundredth time. "We must be getting warmer..."

Too loud. Lyle reached for the dial to turn it down and twisted it so hard, it came off in his hand. A squeal like a dental drill, so sharp and vivid, he smelled burning teeth. Behind it, a lost little boy repeatedly wailed, "I'm not listening…I'm not listening..."

"I've had enough," he said. "Let's go home."

"WHAT."

"FUCK THIS—" He pushed Seek but it scanned the empty airwaves in three seconds and came back to the dental drill. He pushed it again. Steel on naked nerves. Seek. Burning decay, gangrenous gums.

—x x x—

They rolled into town and the charnel stench made him roll up the windows. A bonfire in the town square, pyres on every corner. Folks rushing in and out of half the shops on Main Street, throwing merchandise into their trucks or onto the fires. Bodies danced on the desert wind under every traffic light and lamppost. The ones doing a ghastly can-can directly overhead included the Sheriff, a deputy, and something that might be the Mayor, only it had so little head left, Lyle couldn't figure how they got a noose to hold it up.

A ham-hock drummed on their hood at the crosswalk of Main and Pentecost Street. A man in a windbreaker with a big cross on the back circled round to the driver's side with a bloody hand splayed out. "Turn that damn radio down!"

Lyle choked a lump down in his throat. Stabbed buttons, cursing, until the radio fell mercifully mute. Rolled down his window. "Hey Early, how're you."

CRAWL OF THE WEST

"Golden calf days," his older brother said, hawking and spitting. "Half the town failed the test, so we mopping up. Used to be a righteous town. Can't figure what's gone rotten, but we cutting it away."

The wind blew and the dead men hanging from the traffic light did a soft-shoe on the roof of the Cadillac. "You sure this is all above board," Lyle said.

"Why wouldn't it be," Early's charbroiled fist-face broke out in what it thought was a grin. "We're licensed and bonded." Each of his teeth the size of a thumbnail. He held out his business card:

```
              Early Hopkins, Esq.
Skip trace, labor dispute resolution, limousine ser-
  vice, tree surgery, water-dowser, witchfinder.
```

"Got one, thanks," Lyle said.

"I'm powerful glad I still had it on the card. Never knew it'd come in useful." Shouting at the chain gang limping across the street, "Get along there, Greedyguts, Vinegar Tom, all you damned warlocks," then to their warder, "Won't you hang that batch out front the school. Fat boy there likes little kids." The fat one bleated that he was a teacher, pleaded to know what they did with his wife. Early pepper-sprayed them and turned back to wipe spittle off on his new uniform.

"How can you tell who's a witch," Lyle blurted. "You ain't never even been to church." He covered his mouth too late. A glut of locust carapaces lurched up the back of his throat.

Anyone else might've noticed. "Trade secret," Early said. "Most folks don't even know it yet. Lotta bounty in knowing where they suckle their familiars. Told you you should've come to work for me. Lot better outlook than roadkill detail." A slit opened in Early's face wide enough for a lazy eye to peek out. His mind cranked like a New Year's noisemaker. "What're you doing today, anyway."

"We off on some wild-goose chase for—"

"Looking for antimacassars for the family room," Dot cut him off. "Love to have you over, if nobody burns our trailer down today..."

x185x

"Wow," Early pinched Lyle's face. "You a fancy lad. Hope you get some out of it, little brother." Early waddled away spitting on his own boots.

Lyle floored it out of town, headed into Death Valley. "I thought we were going home," Dot murmured.

He held his breath until the last pyre fell behind the Cadillac before he cracked a window, another ten miles before he opened his mouth. "Fuck was that."

"You know how he gets..." She was in such a lather at Lyle's jealousy, she bounced in her seat. He needed to win a prize too, maybe more than she.

The desert continued to devolve as if the dying light was the only thing holding up the illusion. No vegetation, no rock formations, no terrain to speak of, no lights, no big shiny broadcasting tower. Only the blank white expanse of the alkali flat ahead of them.

The radio roared louder with every oncoming car. He noticed most of the westbound cars were encrusted with frost, their license plates wrong. He longed to lay out the spikes. Many had their heads stuck out the window in the ripping desert wind. Some looked lost, others despondent, as many more exultant, but none of them looked like they had any business operating an automobile.

The Cadillac almost lifted off the road as it crested the last hill. Lyle's scream was drowned out by the sound of the radio. He slammed on the brakes. They hit the road corkscrewing and nearly sideswiped the agricultural inspector standing in the road.

An improvised roadblock with government cars on the shoulders, a motor home and a few sawhorses with blinking lights. The inspector approached with his hand on his sidearm, shaking his head. "Did you not see the signs?"

"What signs," Lyle said. "Did you stop all those other folks coming in from out of state. Probably smuggling drugs."

"I only saw you, sir." The inspector bent and leaned into the car, mustache twitching. His uniform was forest green whipcord, glistening with spit. "Do you have any plants, animals, agricultural products or ritual paraphernalia? Don't lie to me. It's urgent."

"No," Lyle said.

"We're looking for this radio station out here," Dot leans across Lyle to touch the man's arm, smiling like she used to smile at Lyle, when he had a job.

The inspector said, "Cactus-apples."

"I don't know what you're talking about."

"Step out of the car."

Lyle opened the door. The inspector tugged him out and searched under the seat, coming up with four of the bitter fruits. "This is contraband," he said. Another uniformed inspector with a long beard came crashing out of the motor home, arms flailing like he was choking to death. The inspector ran to his friend, who staggered almost up to the Cadillac and fell to his knees.

"Well, I'll be," Dot said.

What he'd mistaken for a beard was a long, glossy hank of colorless hair protruding from the choking man's mouth. The more he convulsed and spat, the longer it grew, and something at least as big as his whole head seemed trapped in his throat. His partner tried in vain to feed him a cactus-apple, then dropped it and took hold of the hair. Planting a boot on the choking victim's shoulder, he shouted at Lyle, "Don't you move, I'm not done with you!"

"Drive," Dot said. He did.

Speeding away from the agricultural station felt pretty good, like they'd beat back every obstacle and earned whatever fool prize Dot was trying to win. Like Bonnie and Clyde, like—

"Honey," she says, "this just isn't working out."

He ripped something in his neck turning to look at her. "What d'you mean, we're almost there." He waved at the radio, the signal throbbing with unclean vitality, every uncanny sound throwing off sparks of static.

"I don't mean this, I mean us." Like a conjurer doing a magic trick backwards, her manicured hands negate herself and him, the Cadillac, the desert, the world. "All of this. I want a divorce."

Of all the—"What the fuck, Dot. Out in the middle of nowhere. In the middle of all this. Why now."

"That's exactly why. Look at us. We're powerless. We can't get ahead. Can't build a decent life. Can't even find a goddamn radio station in the middle of nowhere. We got no power. You, especially. No power over our enemies. No power over the weather. No power to...you know."

"Pretty sure I don't." The static roared up like it was laughing at him.

"Well, that's another problem. But I think it's for the best. We don't communicate effectively, we don't want the same things, and you're clearly happy with the way things are, or you would have fixed them."

He felt a foot in his chest. "I can't just wave a magic wand—"

"That's what I mean. That kind of thinking. Why should we stay together? Give me a reason."

He thought for a long time, looking out the window at nothing.

The flickering vision of the other place came back, the frames equally intercut, both places trying to be here now. Snow fell and rose as steam. The crowded trees wilted, softened, and sagged, writhing to the salted earth like gigantic slugs.

The radio chuckled like a gas leak. Catcalls from the studio audience. *TAKE YOUR MASK OFF...We're licensed and bonded...Ain't no trick to it...*

"I love you, honey. You're my whole world. If I lost you, I'd..."

"Die? Well, go on, then. I got insurance on you. Best for both of us if you were useful, just for once. Maybe Early's too much man for one wife..."

The foot in his chest became a spear about the diameter of a baseball bat that went clean through him. If he'd ever felt anything in his life and called it real, the foreign object transfixing his heart and pinning him to the sticky leather seat was the only real thing in this or any world.

He hadn't realized when they'd left the road, but they were flying across the alkali flat with no sign of the highway, or civilization, no vertical lines to speak of. The infinite blank plane of white and indigo spread out in all directions. There was only them and the radio.

"What's got into you. You're not my Dot. You're some kind of..."

"Witch? I wish, little man. What do real men do with witches, I wonder? I'd sure like to find out..."

He wanted to stop the car. He wanted to twist her head off and drop-kick it over the moon. He wanted to take her in his arms and love her forever and make all this go away. He couldn't do any of it with the goddamn radio blasting.

His fist smashed in the face of the stereo. The display cracked and buttons scattered like loose teeth, but the blood he dappled all over it seemed to have a more drastic effect. The shaggy static bearding every sound fell away, the raucous laughter, a firehose of scorn, directed at him. He punched again and again, until his knuckles were bloody shreds, until the sound went away.

"Well that's just fine, you ruined this too."

"What do you mean?"

"You imbecile, it's a contest. I had to make you try to kill me to win the prize...Now they can't hear it, you...you fucking idiot..."

He threw his hands around her neck and slammed her head into the window. She screamed, but not because he was killing her. She pointed out the windshield. He looked up and had only a moment to reflect on the unlikelihood, out in this emptiest of all places, of crashing into another car.

The Cadillac smashed into the little hatchback so hard it exploded in a cloud of rust, the chassis flipping end over end across the alkali flat. The airbags smashed them into their seats, then deflated amid a flurry of powder. He heaved into his lap, ears ringing, then reached for Dot, suddenly throttled with remorse.

Her neck was broken from the airbag impact. Incredible that a safety device achieved what he could not. He wept into the cooling hollow of her neck for a while before he noticed a noise.

From somewhere outside, he heard the radio.

He got out to find the abandoned hatchback all but disintegrated, its body so corroded that very little of it was not carried away by the wind. Not fifty feet away, a half-collapsed shed in the middle of the empty plain. Caked in savage impasto strokes across the wall above a half-open doorway in blood and shit spangled with buzzing flies: KXXT.

A low-wattage light, almost umber and flickering fitfully, leaked out the doorway and between the warped slats of the walls, but that was not what held his attention.

An antenna jutted out of a rude rip in the rusty tin roof to protrude maybe ten feet into the night sky. Even in the failing light, despite its sheer size and the blinking lights at its apex, he could tell it was not metal, but bone. The radio sounds were coming from the shack. The music reeled in pitch and clarity and the antenna itself bobbed and wobbled in the absence of any wind, jerking as if the strain of broadcasting had induced a seizure.

He opened the door and stepped back, wiping the sight from his eyes, covering his ears against the stabbing pipe organ chord that bellowed from inside.

The antenna grew out of the spine of a naked, emaciated human, starved past death and scabbed with glittering salt crystals. Their crotch was a blank slash of exposed bone and an apron of dried black blood spilling down their bowed thighs. Shriveled like a grape, the skull soft as cartilage, the head lolled against their collarbone between the stanchions of taut tendon anchoring the antenna tower to the shoulders, yet it jerked and twisted askew, trying to get a look at Lyle. The emaciated Atlas took a faltering step towards the door, but the antenna trapped them in the shed like a pin through a beetle.

The radio signal emanated from their slack mouth and the gaping wound in their groin. "And we have a big winner for the grand prize, which we're not allowed to mention on the air, and if you know us, you know what that means...But if you're still trying to win, we salute your efforts, and we'll never tell you to stop..."

His phone rang. Numbly, he held it to his ear. "Hi, is this Dot Hopkins?"

Lyle gasped for air and gathered the nerve to tell the oily radio voice what he'd done and what it cost him, but before the whickering breath could penetrate the dusty dam in his throat, he heard her voice.

"It sure is...did I win?" She sniffs, nearly hysterical. "I tried real hard but Lyle, he screws up everything..."

He almost threw the phone. He screamed her name into it, but the disk jockey's voice just got louder. "You sure did!" She screams like their wedding night. "That was an evergreen performance, Dot. We're gonna play that recording every Valentine's Day. So, when can you come collect your prize?"

He had forgotten what day it was. Maybe that's why all this got started.

"That's just it," Dot says, "we're way out in buttfuck Egypt, but we heard your show and I called in..."

"Tarnation...we got another repeater. Just between you and me, we had an intern run off with a carload of old studio equipment last month, said they were going to take us nationwide. Anyway, I guess it's your lucky day. But I'm afraid you still have to claim your prize in person...They'd never let us mail something like this." They share a knowing chuckle like guzzling formaldehyde.

Lyle punches himself in the face until his head clears. He turns to run for the Cadillac. He bounces off Dot and falls flat on his ass.

Dot gouges out her eyes and eats them. She begins to sing in a new voice more piercingly beautiful than any sound he's ever heard. It comes not from her bovinely chewing mouth, but from the new lips of her empty eye sockets.

The phone on the ground chirps, "How soon can you get to Leeds, Massachusetts, Dot?"

Dot pulls him upright by his hair and drags him to the Cadillac. Her voice comes out of the phone. "We'll be there before you know it, hon..."

Lyle mopped sweat and tears out of his eyes. His voice so low he barely heard it himself, he moaned, "Oh Dot...I thought I'd lost you..."

Anne Gare's Rare and Import Video Catalogue
October 2022

Jonathan Raab

Film Maudit — Dir. Anonymous, 1974

Known as a "snuff" film due to the producers' inspired employment of extras to "protest" its graphic violence and sexual content at the few theaters at which it played during its abortive single-weekend release in Germany and the United States. Critical reviews eschewed plot summaries in favor of accusations against theater managers and/or the filmmakers for dosing the audience with hallucinogenic drugs and playing sounds at vibrational frequencies that disturbed both mind and bowels. But when it comes to film critics, what's the difference between their heads and asses, really? Am I right? Am I **rite**?

No viewing of *Film Maudit* is complete without the accompaniment of the vibrational seductions of a RestoRed Oscillator. The Oscillator's custom-design magnetic tape must be fed through the device in sync with the film's projection to achieve maximum psycho-spiritual cascade resonance. Attempts to view *Film Maudit* without the Oscillator's accompaniment will inevitably result in missing time, head injuries, and only a partial dissociative break. The viewer would better spend their time bashing the frontispiece of their skull against a hard surface—preferably concrete, or the buttstock of a shotgun—over and over again.

Three 16mm cannisters (VG condition) with RestoRed Oscillator device (G) and oscillation pattern magnetic tape (VG+) in a plastic storage bin with blue cover (like new).

Seven thousand four hundred dollars.

HYMNS OF ABOMINATION

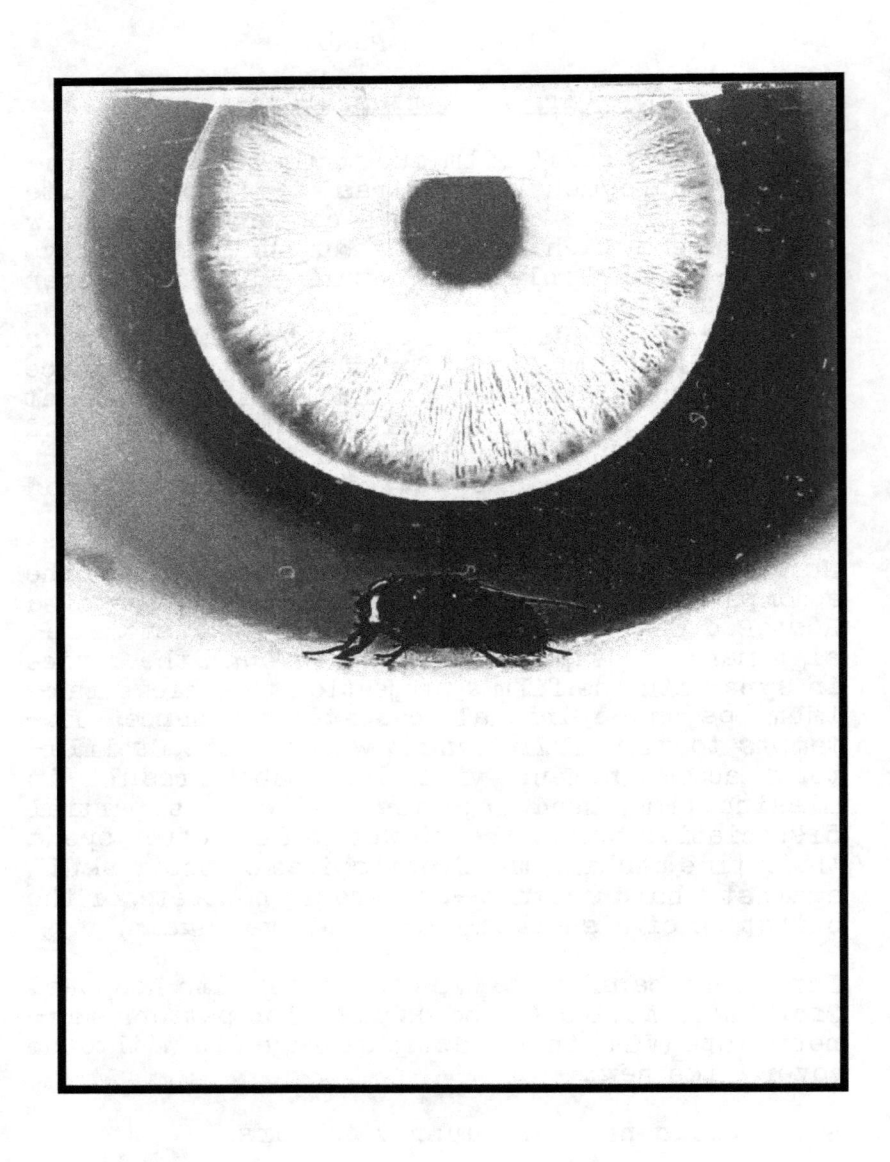

x194x

there will always be men like johnny

Johnny was halfway through murdering me when a serendipitous fist knocked on the hotel room door.

Always the same: a lady gets in the bathtub and someone shows up uninvited. Mine was no interrupted bubble bath, my flesh screaming through stab wound mouths and the porcelain slick with my shoulder's red slobber. Johnny had doubled me over the rim and meant to toss my stocking-clad legs in with the rest. Blood caked the nylon where he'd driven the knife toward my crotch, maybe trying to save me the surgeon's fee on my upcoming procedure, but he'd stabbed my inner thigh instead. He liked me the way I was and thought that made him special. Thought that meant I'd let him keep me. What a shock for him when I said we were through.

What a shock for me when he pulled the knife.

And one more shock for both of us when that fist hit the door. Over my bleeding shoulder, our eyes locked—what made for proper etiquette in a moment like this? Call a time-out, check the door, and then let the murder carry on?

No, proper etiquette said to elbow him with the unstabbed arm, scramble out the bathroom, and rush past the confused hotel maid in her pretty blue uniform, her arms loaded with fresh towels. Might have been smart to grab one and put pressure on my new slits, but I couldn't think straight until I hopped in the car and tore out of the hotel parking lot. Bloody handprints patterned my arms, neck, and chartreuse blouse.

If I was crying, it was for the pain. Not for him. That's what I told what remained of myself, losing blood pressure, darkness creeping into the edge of my vision, heart floundering. Halfway murdered, I'd left something behind with him thicker than blood. Only half of me drove out of there alive.

What became of the rest?

HYMNS OF ABOMINATION

—x x x—

Six months can change a lot. A tender, ladylike penis might shift into new shapes under skilled hands. A woman who used to sleep peacefully through the night wakes up, bladder screaming, heart pounding, terrified to cross her bedroom to the bathroom because he's there, she can't see him, but yes, he's blended with the darkness. Turn the light on and there's nothing, but couldn't you smell him? Couldn't you feel his unseen fingers prodding in the dark, slick with my blood?

I could. When I'd recovered from stab wounds and the surgery his stabbing had almost delayed, I gave him a call, told him he needed to make things up to me and break in the new organic hardware.

He hadn't changed. Any reprieve I'd found from his badgering in the past six months, chalk it up to his terror that I'd called the police. They had questioned me at the ER, but for once, I was grateful the cops around here don't care whether trans women live or die. None of their business what went on between us. Johnny wanted to call me his, and I would pretend to grant his wish.

He was the type to leave every task half-done. Only paid half of dinner, his half-focused kisses too focused on his downstairs, and even then he brought me only halfway to orgasm. A man of half measures can't see his double standards; he expected the whole of me in exchange for part of himself. He couldn't have gone any further than half-murdering me.

Knives don't cut minds, at least not directly, but they leave wounds. I didn't tell him that I no longer slept through the night. Let him believe what he liked when he strode out his townhouse door, dressed in button-down and jeans, a half-hearted try at cleaning up for our big reunion.

He hopped into my car, giddy as a Golden Retriever who's just heard *We're going for a ride* and hasn't figured out it's a vet visit.

THERE WILL ALWAYS BE MEN LIKE JOHNNY

In Johnny's case, the final kind. If I hadn't been ready to put him down the few months between hotel stabbing and steering away from his house, I certainly found the need on the long drive. He blathered about how he missed me and hadn't meant to hurt me. He filled the car with his musky scent that months back would drive a mild quake down my center. It still did as we crossed highways. Despite my pieces having rearranged, the nerves were the same. They remembered his touch and forgave him their disappointment, drawn deep into primal urges and a lip-biting desire.

My mind was less forgiving. There would always be a version of me bleeding out in that hotel bathtub. Old memories belonged to that dead half, who would never survive murder, undergo long-awaited surgery, recover, and plan how she'd never fear Johnny again. Those experiences and every new memory fell to alive me, the surviving half.

I had to do right by both selves.

—x x x—

Leeds made it simple.

A lumpy, wart-ridden toad of a region, its hills sagged heavy with thick woods and dissuaded prying eyes. There's a town, too, but online maps don't distinguish where civilization ends and wilderness begins. Main tourist attractions include nervous breakdowns, reports of strange phenomena, disappearances that leave no trace, and reappearances that carry too many traces of what caused the disappearances. New England knows graves, with Leeds its own forested Bermuda Triangle.

The car crept through the woods, over a slope, and around a sudden copse, until I felt safe that no one from town would hear.

Dusk settled while Johnny rambled. I stared, long and hard, driving an intense chill through my eyes, urging him to wonder why I didn't engage, desperate that he understand how I could never trust him. One wrong word might set him off again.

HYMNS OF ABOMINATION

I never believed in mixing signals, clear from the get-go that I had no need for long-term, short-term, just the right-now-or-never term when too much would change soon after our one-night stand. Past lovers of all genders had understood, but Johnny wanted me. He fancied himself a gentleman, called me goddess, but his worship felt less like man to woman and more like he pictured me his special, secret porno.

As if playing pretend could last longer than an evening. He wanted more, craving the lovely lady with the soft member between her legs, the kind of woman he'd never touched before and couldn't accept that he would never touch again.

If he couldn't touch with fingers, he'd touch with a knife.

Half-killing someone is easy. Anyone can go part of the way and then backtrack, the nerve hitching a ride on sweat drops as they dribble out your pores. Johnny couldn't commit. How did he think he'd handle a relationship with me if he couldn't see through murdering me to the end?

I reached over his lap, and maybe he thought we might be tender, that I'd grasp him and play with him and then pull him into the back. Thinking with the wrong head, as always. I popped open the glovebox and grabbed the kitchen knife I'd stowed there.

I wouldn't commit to a relationship, but I committed to murder. A shoulder wound sends a mixed signal, like you're already prepped to change your mind.

To go for the throat is to mean it.

He gurgled. Red muck poured down his buttons, onto the lap of his jeans, and through my mind, a mental porcelain tub turning white to crimson. I shoved him out the door where he wouldn't stain my passenger's seat, and his blood steamed in the autumn chill. He pawed at his neck. Knife. Earth. Pawed at nothing. Stopped.

I stared for another long while before I remembered there was digging to do.

—x x x—

THERE WILL ALWAYS BE MEN LIKE JOHNNY

I fell into ferocious shoveling, a physical desperation to get him out of my sight, but once I'd rolled him into his shallow, unmarked grave, I needed a breath before blanketing him in soil. Hormone treatment and recovery's lethargy had thinned my muscles.

Part of me wished I'd tricked him into digging his own grave, but that sounded complex, and complicated plans die in the cradle. Better to do the work. Bleed him in the Leeds earth, bury the body, and hope on every shooting star that I would eventually sleep through the night, knowing he wasn't coming back.

Static crackled through the car, injecting lightning down my nerves. I hadn't touched the radio in ages, but it reached for me, a warped, snowy hiss that whispered: *Sorry.*

"Johnny?" I called, white mist puffing through my lips in the chill.

I looked to his corpse. Had these woods brought him back, some apologetic ghost in the machine? I wouldn't have thought so; these were the kind of woods that swallowed souls along with corpses.

Sorry, the radio crackled again.

He could have been telling the truth. That door knock months back might have snapped him out of thoughtless rage. Maybe deep down, he never meant to hurt me.

But he had, and beyond that, he'd learned nothing. Thoughtless rage had subsided; thoughtless want was back, absolute and unquestionable. He might have been sorry for stabbing my shoulder and leg, but he couldn't be sorry for the sleepless nights since, how he'd haunted my bedroom while I lay terrified. He didn't even know.

This would be another haunted night if I didn't hurry. I finished burying him, and when I got in the car, I shut off the radio and left the woods.

Tried to leave, I mean. The trees had given each other wide berths when I drove Johnny between them, but they seemed to have grown curious and become good friends, clustering around the burial site, their trunks hugging too close for my car to slip through.

Outside, an owl cried to its fellow night birds, *Good job, woods of Leeds, we got her*. Insects cheered their approval, a grateful cacophony. Everyone seemed merry except me. They lived here, Johnny died here, but I was the one who had to traipse through dark woods with only my cellphone's flashlight mode to guide me.

Johnny was dead, and I still wouldn't sleep tonight. Some part of me, that dead half, said killing him wouldn't do any good, but how could I have heard her? It wasn't like my surgeon came trundling out of the dark with a skin of bleeding hotel me, *Oh Veronica, you forgot this, let's stitch her back in, dick and all*. I would have to get by being half alive for a while, maybe forever.

Half-souls don't grow on trees.

Their trunks moved whenever I turned the light. Every glance back shifted the path in the darkness, and I couldn't aim in every direction at once. I should've asked my surgeon to stitch eyes to the back of my head.

The insects cheered louder—no, not insects. I had misheard. The woods roared with radio static, an aural snow that threatened to bury me if I didn't find my way out. And above? No hooting owl, no answering crows. Birds don't have fingers. Long, crouching limbs clutched tree trunks or perched between branches. Angels came to mind, but I read once that true Biblical angels had lion heads and a hundred eyes, and besides, I didn't believe in angels. Nothing had come to the woods of Leeds to judge me for the blood on my hands or the dirt of the grave stuck beneath my fingernails.

Had something always been here? The woods seemed to like dead air, and maybe other dead things. Figures walked in the dark that, even when I shined my light toward their footsteps, I couldn't see, but they walked with me just the same. Or crawled. I couldn't ignore that rustling behind me, claws and feet and belly scrabbling over crushed leaves and pine needles.

THERE WILL ALWAYS BE MEN LIKE JOHNNY

My friend Charlie, who'd cared for me while I recovered from wound and miracle alike, used to tell me that some men never stop. They love the chase too much to quit. What a burden, to be so adored.

Or maybe it wasn't Johnny's fault that he came crawling out of that grave to follow me through the woods. There's the chance I'm only half a murderer myself.

I blamed Leeds instead. Dead air, dead earth. If I'd only murdered him halfway, then he'd been alive, and now the ground had spat him up as if it couldn't stand his taste. I knew the feeling. I didn't want Johnny; why should I expect these woods to be any different?

His voice rasped around the knife I'd left jutting from his neck.

I didn't answer, afraid the trees, angels, and static might think I wanted to chat, the way you might hear a strange man call, *Hey beautiful*, and hate that he's bothering you, but thrill you're passing so nicely that you get to feel a little misogyny, only to realize he's talking to some other lady. You watch; he's cool and casual, and if he gave you a minute, he'd rock your world and mercifully never call back, but you're stuck with a Johnny. There will always be men like Johnny.

He once told me that, when he was little, he couldn't quit touching the hot stove. The burns never dissuaded him. His mother thought he liked the pain, and he didn't have the words to explain that though metal conducts heat, it isn't instantaneous. There are seconds, a slim margin of error, where he could quickly touch a hot stovetop and not get burned. He craved that rare moment when he could get away with it.

Never said if he managed. Johnny and his half-stories, always with purpose, never with finality. Sometimes you don't outgrow those dangerous habits.

Hot stovetops take many shapes. Even mine.

Johnny rasped again, and I almost thought the static answered, warped by the trees. Another few steps, and the static spoke. Static meant a radio, and a radio meant people, and people meant a place I could escape from crawling Johnny.

HYMNS OF ABOMINATION

Clearer now, the dead air voice rocked the tree branches with a confident hiss. *You're listening to WXXT, voice of the radio land you can't understand. We come upon the witching hour, if that bears some meaning to you, and let me tell you a quick story before the hits resume. There once was a man who carried his broken heart on a long walk into traffic. Romantic, isn't it?*

There was a thought, Johnny's fate finished in a metal-on-meat instant. I liked that. Lucky, easy. Johnny was never so courteous.

You're listening to WXXT, the radio added, and then static swallowed the woods, a merciless, scrambling tinnitus that ran its nails down my chalkboard skull, *eeeeeee.*

I followed it just the same, misty breath streaming from my face. Something in the static wanted me as bad as the man who'd half-murdered me. Half this world, half someplace else, and that someplace else would swallow me whole. Johnny was the devil I knew, and maybe heading back to him would've made sense; not like a man of half measures could finish the job, right?

Unless this dead side of him was different. He could only half-murder me, but two halves made a whole.

Either way, I was never a fan of mixed signals, and I'd already made it clear that I didn't want him. I could not go back.

Instead, I dove for the static. For Leeds.

Dead air's pressure squeezed my body as if I descended the ocean's continental shelf to the abyss, the static so tight that my bones cried inside. If these woods killed me, at least I wouldn't have died by Johnny's hand. Disappointing him might have made dying worthwhile, but I wouldn't do anything for his sake. I wanted to live, and more than halfway. All the way.

Think this is bad? the static asked. *That's on account that you don't listen to the radio. We're nothing out of the ordinary. These days, everyone watches too much TV—*

The static broke for one split-second, silencing the woods. The voices of those who'd been swallowed up rumbled through some undercurrent and then came roaring back.

THERE WILL ALWAYS BE MEN LIKE JOHNNY

—kids on their phones all the time—
—those damn computer games—
—simple truth is, folks should listen to the radio daily and nightly. Folks must listen. We tell the real deal, the whole of it. You're listening to WXXT.

The roar rushed, my skin wishing it could fly with the wind and leave me. I hugged myself tight and promised my skin it would only get stuck in tree branches.

Twigs cracked beneath fingers. Closer now? Farther? I tried to remember any more of Charlie's wisdom, but I was starting to believe she didn't exist, my memories fragments of Johnny's half-stories. Charlie was a figment the radio made up to scare loners at night into thinking they had friends.

Or maybe this was just what listening to small-town radio does to people. The static might swallow them, digest them, and make them part of itself.

You're listening to WXXT, and we have a special message from one listener to another, the star-crossed lovers of Leeds woods. Veronica, you out there?

Voice and static boomed in every direction. I turned right without aiming the light, where the woods dripped pitch-black. The nearest tree trunks stood faint as a bathroom doorway across a bedroom, and sure as when I would lie in bed, needing to get up, too terrified to move, Johnny stood in the dark. Arms outstretched, he awaited me.

Johnny wants you to know he's sorry, Veronica.

Another twig snapped in the undergrowth. Behind me? To the left, right, ahead? Closer now, the static boomed, a sudden press of rushing footsteps.

Johnny wants you to know you're sexy, Veronica.

That familiar musk filled my nose. He was calling, a hundred yards away, or two feet, or six inches, reaching out with one once-bloody hand that had bent me over a bathtub. Not to hurt me, not to touch me wrong. He'd only screwed up killing me so that he could keep me, and if I'd died, I would have slipped through his blood-slickened fingers.

Johnny wants you to know he's forever.

A bathtub prison, a place for him to caretake my body and worship it. I would have been his altar for as long as he could keep me alive without being caught.

Johnny wants you forever.

Eventually, someone would have noticed. What would have been left of me, skin stuck to skeleton, grown into the porcelain? How much of me would he have taken?

Johnny wants you.

How much could he still take?

Johnny wants.

Fingertips brushed my ankle, and I dashed through the trees. Under low-hanging branches, over arched roots, the woods meant to knock me down to his level where he'd crawl atop, cling to me, cry half his heart out, the rest still dead in his shallow grave. Screaming and scrabbling past trunks, I dove deeper into the static.

—x x x—

I must have run for a lifetime before the house in the woods reared up beyond a tangled copse of black trees.

Its roof hid between clustered tree limbs, but the single floor's curtained windows flickered with pale blue and white light, giving definition to the outside. Rotted squirrels and sparrows, abuzz with flies, clustered to either side of the porch steps, their fur and feathers twitching in the unsteady luminance. The angels must have driven the animals from their natural habitats and taken their place. The house of static had called, but it wouldn't let them in. Dead air, dead creatures. Maybe here I'd find wholeness with my murdered half.

Better than letting Johnny's fingers stroke my skin.

The front door hung slightly ajar, a black line like a thin, sideways mouth. That static roar crept through, too sharp to ignore even before I swept the door open.

The living room was a mess of pizza boxes and Chinese food cartons. Across from the lumpy couch rested a sagging pyramid of bulky gray amplifiers, precious antiques amid the refuse. A boxy CRT television sat seemingly out of place, its snowy screen casting the only light in the house. Small portable radio sets dotted the windowsills, their speakers casting a shrill hiss. I thought my favorite song seeped from a corroded boombox in the corner, but the static was playing tricks instead of music. These woods didn't know songs outside their own.

Geological layers of trash led into a short hallway. The bathroom stank of cat litter, but there was no other sign of a cat. Across the hall, I found the bedroom, where a broad mattress hoarded candy wrappers.

This house might have been home to someone once, but it had become a transitory rest stop in these endless woods. No one broadcast from the radios here. Trying to find the voice behind the static was like questing for gold at the end of a rainbow. Sometimes, there is no ghost in the machine, no soul inside the chest cavity. Hollow soundscapes orbited this void, and not all travelers escaped its gravity. For some, the radios and amplifiers lashed their hushing white noise into a static spiderweb, dead air that might catch the dead inside.

Johnny would be lured here same as I'd been lured. The static had welcomed us to Leeds, my car radio perhaps playing just below hearing, a direct line to my brain. The house would become a new prison where Johnny kept me.

I had to kill the static. Without its call, Johnny would pass by this house, roam the woods of Leeds forever, and find someone else to drag his fingers over. Come morning, I would leave.

Back to the living room, with its altar of amplifiers and perimeter guarded by sentinel radios, I tried to unplug everything, but the cords tangled in a rat king's nest of tails. The radios outnumbered me. The boombox, then. Its speakers grew in swollen tumors to either side. I closed my hands over them.

The static went shrill, and then a new voice poured through. I recognized this one, its pitch and cadence and candy-coated sweetness the kind that hid hunger underneath. My own voice snowed through portable radios, amplifiers, and boombox, as if I'd been digested with everyone else who'd traveled down the static's throat to radio land.

> *Did you dream the ancient heavens where we used to dwell?*
> *Did you dream the holy She who crawled to Earth from hell?*
> *Where would one lonesome walk, this She of endless power?*
> *She'd stalk the sacred plains of time beyond the witching hour.*

Two hands closed around mine, around the boombox, and snatched it from me. I spun around expecting to find Johnny to have found his legs again, perhaps in some clearance bin at the Leeds trading post, right beside his will to finish what he'd started. A kiss, a partner's orgasm, a murder. Anything but that endless future in which he might keep me.

But this woman was no Johnny. She lowered the boombox past her stern face, eyes unblemished by gray bags from too many sleepless nights. I envied those eyes at first sight. A gaping mouth opened one shoulder, another slid sideways down her inner leg, beside her tender, ladylike penis. I recognized it.

Recognized her. Johnny had only murdered me halfway. Alive me had carried on to recover from stab wounds, have parts reshaped between the legs, and trespass into these woods.

But dead me had found her own way, caught in the static spiderweb. Had she been waiting the whole six months for her living half to show up, or just part of it? She stood naked, an effervescent, almost expectant ghost, knees still raw from striking the hotel room's bathroom tile. Stuck in time.

I didn't want to see this. I didn't mean to meet her—me. Anyone. I wanted to shout into the static for help, but it hissed through her mouths, the one on her face and the two cut into her body. Her hand climbed towards me. Were her fingers clean or slickened with blood like Johnny's? The television's flickering light made every surface murky, unclear whether covered in fluid or shadows.

"Sorry," I hissed out. "I'm—"

One fingertip slashed across my lips, its touch slipping a numb crackle through my nerves. She radiated springtime warmth, and I couldn't talk. Couldn't move.

Her lips touched mine next, and she tasted more alive than I felt. I kept staring into her eyes, looking for resentment, rage, even forgiveness, but she offered no feeling, the heightened awareness of a prey animal. In that way, she became a mirror. We were both prey, weren't we?

She drew a hand down my chest, reading my pounding heart through my breast. The dead craved that thunderous ache, and she was death's glorious goddess of pain like I'd never seen myself. Never appreciated. Sometimes indifferent, other times hateful, agonized, but seeing her from the outside, touching her? I loved her.

Was this the woman Johnny had seen when I first stepped into his life? I could almost forgive his obsession.

The static current swept us to the bedroom, my clothes falling faster than autumn leaves, where she took me, and I let her. Candy wrappers crinkled beneath my back as she mounted me. Her prick swelled soft, and I opened my lower lips and drew it inside. Touching myself. Inhabiting myself. Dead and alive, two halves made whole.

I was tired; she was tender. I wanted her, she wanted me, and we never believed in mixing signals.

She could keep me, if she wanted. Keep my beating heart.

Our sweet screams lured Johnny sure as the static. When we finished quaking against each other, I wanted nothing but to lie there holding her, listening to the radio land's snow, and feeling her tremble as if alive.

Instead, I heard the front door hinges cry. Johnny was letting the static out like furnace heat on a winter's day.

I grasped my dead half's arms, eyes urging her to run, but her lips closed on mine. She laid me back down, candy wrappers parting in a welcoming wave, and entered me again. Our shared heart thundered through two halves.

Johnny's severed throat rasped, and his footsteps padded the hallway, fingers dragging on the walls.

My dead half clutched tighter. She didn't understand. She thought he'd already done the worst thing he could to us, hadn't heard the radio signals warning that *Johnny wants you forever*. She wouldn't stop. We wouldn't stop.

I grasped her, sat up, rode her lap, and stared past her shoulder. Darkness filled the doorway, no different than on those sleepless nights when Johnny haunted my bedroom. He stood unseen in the blackness, a ghost who watched us fuck ourselves whole.

Beyond the bedroom walls, the amplifier altar, portable radio sentinels, and lonely boombox cranked their static through the roof.

You're listening to WXXT, one more love song sweetening the air waves, listener to listener. Do you hear his call, Veronica? Johnny wants you forever.

Blue light flickered at the doorway, the altar having followed through the house with its lone wayward television. I watched the blackness shift up and down in gentle waves and waited through each heartbeat, each tender shift in my dead half's embrace. He was here.

Johnny wants you, sweet heavens, does Johnny want.

Light cut his shape from the door. Soil, sap, and brown leaves plastered his shirt, its buttons sticky with blood. The television flicker slid shadows down his palms and fingers, and radio static sent rippling wind through his clothes.

Johnny wants.

Dead me turned her head over one shoulder so that we both looked at the doorway, a two-headed, dead-alive Veronica, a fresh new fetish for Johnny to chase.

"Which of us do you like more?" dead me asked, her tongue chucking a golden apple.

The static waned to catch and consider, a confused twinge in the spiderweb. *You're listening to WXXT, where Johnny's calling yet again to his favorite radio station. Johnny wants each Veronica to know she's uniquely beautiful.*

THERE WILL ALWAYS BE MEN LIKE JOHNNY

My fingernails clawed into dead me's back. I watched Johnny's silhouette, and for once in his half-assed life, he was right. We were beautiful. He would never realize that knowledge entitled him to nothing.

The dark doorway twitched. He was too used to haunting that space to unstitch himself right away, but after a moment he managed to wriggle loose and grow solid.

I started to rise from dead me's lap. If we dove out the window and ran, we might still make it.

Dead me wouldn't let go. She turned from over her shoulder and gazed an inch from my face. No bags hung under her sockets, but in the invasive blue flicker, I saw tired eyes, earnest and needing. She forced them shut, and her hand passed over mine. Warm fingertips drew my eyelids down. No more staring at the doorway, dreading Johnny in the night.

Darkness swallowed everything. My world became radio static.
Johnny wants each Veronica to know she deserves him.

He had craved our loveliness since that first and only night together. He thought we would want him back like he was someone special, the last of a dying breed of men, but there will always be men like Johnny aplenty.
Johnny wants each Veronica.

Dead me squeezed hard enough to bruise skin, and I echoed her. Bones popped under tensing muscle, and pain flared through my breasts, crushed against sternum.
Listeners, if there were ever a true thing in this world, it's that Johnny wants like nobody's business.

We kissed again, tongue in her mouth, her prick up between my legs, inside each other, inside me, a self-swallowing snake in that static crush. Almost whole again.
Johnny wants.
Almost one. Almost gone.
Johnny—

HYMNS OF ABOMINATION

His fingers stroked a cloud of misty breath-static that bloomed into an escaping flower. He pawed at the empty mattress, as desperate as he'd pawed at his neck when I first stabbed his throat, and then he clawed at the near-empty air. Radio airwaves slipped through his fingers. A dead thing for the dead air, caught in the spiderweb.

Better to become strands of that web, digested by static. Better to be free. Well, that's only half true. We're here. We're all here, one way or another.

Johnny still haunts that house in the woods of Leeds. He fiddles with the radio dials. If he tunes to the right signal, he might find an undercurrent of thought beneath the static, but more often he finds the roaring proper signal. Stories he's too dead to understand pour into his ears. They never tell him how to join along.

On some nights, he hears our voices, when it's our turn at radio land, and he lies on the mattress, hugs the boombox to his chest, and cries himself to some dead kind of sleep.

We don't believe in mixed signals. Only thoughtless, cruel obsession would make us keep him. Kinder to set the fly free from the spiderweb.

But you can't free a fly that clings to the web. Johnny wants to be stuck. Johnny wants. That he keeps finding our voices is no fault of ours. Hot stovetops take many shapes, even radio dials.

And I'm supposed to tell you not to touch yours, so don't. You're listening to WXXT.

Anne Gare's Rare and Import Video Catalogue
October 2022

Jonathan Raab

Rangel Bantam's Book Report on "A Skeleton Key to the Gemstone File" — Dir. Unknown, 198X

Purported to be the final known images of one Rangel Bantam, a young girl who went missing somewhere in the woods outside of Leeds, Massachusetts in the Year of Your Lord, Nineteen Eighty and Two. Unremarkable in every respect save for its suppression as evidence in the district attorney's grotesque and obscene gesture toward justice that was the investigation into her unsolved disappearance. This one minute and forty-five second short features the young girl in question—or a young girl who very much shares the appearance of Rangel Bantam—staring straight into a camera clumsily held by a person we never see nor hear. She recites, from rote memory, fragmented sentences about the machinations of one Aristotle Onassis, his connections to organized crime, the Bay of Pigs invasion, repeated references to synthetic gemstones, and the Kennedy assassinations. Her delivery is stilted and childlike, but the facts conveyed therein deserve the utmost scrutiny by any student of Serious History.

Super 8mm sound and film cartridge, acceptable.

One hundred and twenty dollars. (Available at a discount to substance abuse-prone private detectives and surviving Bantam family members suffering from various manias.)

HYMNS OF ABOMINATION

x212x

the wxxt podcast, episode 23: leeds regional high school

Archivist's note: As the popularity of terrestrial radio declined during the 2010s, the management of the Leeds-based broadcast station WXXT looked for new ways to reach audiences. This resulted in the creation of The WXXT Podcast, which ran for 28 episodes before the incidents that led to closed-door congressional hearings and the class-action lawsuit against Spotify, Apple Podcasts, and other podcast platforms, which is currently working its way through the US court system. Although the episodes have long been wiped from the major podcast platforms, and although playing those episodes—in public or private—has been prohibited under hastily passed federal legislation, samizdat copies and transcripts continue to exist in the shadowy corners of the Internet. This transcript, believed to be the only extant remnant of the podcast's 23rd episode, was found in the back seat of a car abandoned near the Calvin Coolidge Bridge in Northampton, Mass., its owner missing and a layer of black fungus covering the vehicle's interior.

tom breen

[Old-fashioned dance music faintly plays, accompanied by what sounds like lightbulbs being stomped beneath the boots of a heavy adult man]

VOICEOVER: From the heart of Leeds, Massachusetts, the number-one source of information, history, and fond recollections of this quintessential New England town: this is The WXXT Podcast.

[faint sound of an animal—possibly a fisher cat—or a human infant screaming]

BILLY BARLOW: Hello, listeners out there in podcast land, my name is Billy Barlow, and I am very pleased to be the host of The WXXT Podcast, the only podcast that covers the town of Leeds from every conceivable angle, and even from some inconceivable angles. Thank you for joining us this week, as we come to you every Wednesday absolutely free of charge, or even more frequently if you sign up for our Patreon, which I'll plug shortly. Joining me, as always, is more a legend than a man; the reigning and defending champion of the annual Leeds pie-eating contest; the guy who puts the "treat" in "Main Street"; the Christmas Cat himself: Big Daddy Jace. Hey, Jace.

JACE: Hey. Hey, everyone, thanks for lending us your earholes.

BARLOW: Jace, you sound a little hoarse, maybe, a little scratchy. Do my ears deceive me?

JACE: No, as usual, you're right on the money. We've been having such nice weather lately—

BARLOW: Beautiful.

JACE: Yep. So last night, like a genius, I decided I'd leave the bedroom windows open, forgetting that I do this every year, and every year I wake up with a nasty sore throat. I am, apparently, incapable of learning my lesson.

BARLOW: Speaking of being unable to learn lessons, that's a great segue for this week's show…

JACE: Hey-oh! I'm a pro at this.

BARLOW: You certainly are. But before we get to that, I want to introduce the third member of our triumvirate. He's well-known to Leeds residents and well-loved by Leeds ladies: Fly-From-Sin Rattlebones, who appears today in his most familiar form, that of an aged man dressed in filthy clothes of a bygone fashion, dripping clear pus from every orifice, and shaking horribly as if stirred by an inner fever-wind.

RATTLEBONES: I lay trembling, sweating, and smoking for the space of half an houre, afore I cryed out in a loude voice, Lord of eternal glory, what wouldst Thou do with me? And my bowels were shaken by a voice

THE WXXT PODCAST, EPISODE 23

amongst the trees, yea, and from the rocks, which spake unto me: thou shalt drink a bitter cup, a bitter cup, a bitter cup! Whereupon I was throwne—to my great and exceeding amazement—into the wriggling belly of hell (and take what thou will of it in this expression, which is beyond expression) and I was among all the devils in hell, even in their most hideous hew.

BARLOW: Today we're going to have, I guess, a little oral history of Leeds Regional High School, which I think a lot of our listeners will be interested to hear. Actually, this is something people have been asking for pretty much since we started this podcast, and so we're really happy to bring it to you.

But before we get to that, I want to take just a quick second to thank everyone who's signed up to support us on Patreon. You guys, we really are blown away by the incredible support you've shown us in these early weeks. It's enabling us to invest in better equipment, more episodes, and all kinds of goodies.

JACE: And it's something we can tell our moms when they say "Get a real job!"

BARLOW: Perhaps most important of all, yes! So if you are currently a patron—thank you, thank you, thank you. You are—and this is something that's been proven by the most rigorous science—physically attractive and incredibly smart.

RATTLEBONES: The devils hath their sport with me! All manner of torment and terrour my soul endured, in this very blacknesse of darknesse (you must take it in these tearmes, for it is infinitely beyond expression), until finally my soul was struck away, as if a man with a great brush dipped in whiting, should with one stroke wipe out, or sweep off a picture upon a wall.

HYMNS OF ABOMINATION

BARLOW: And if you'd like to become a patron, well, you're in luck, because this is the best deal in town right now.

JACE: Better than two-for-one hot dog day at Old Ep's Filling Station?

BARLOW: Even better! Somehow! For one dollar—one mere dollar! One li'l picture of George Washington!—you will get early access to each and every one of our weekly podcasts, plus access to exclusive content, like extended interviews, behind-the-scenes audio, and other goodies.

For five dollars, you'll get all that, plus an extra episode—an entire extra episode!—per week, plus the subscribers-only WXXT Podcast Email Newsletter, and—and!—a WXXT Podcast refrigerator magnet featuring our logo.

JACE: Boy, that is the best deal in town!

BARLOW: Hold on Jace, because there's more!

JACE: More? How is that even possible?

BARLOW: For ten dollars, you'll get all of the above, plus a WXXT coffee cup, a 20 percent discount on every item in the WXXT Podcast web store, including our popular "Don't Blame Me, I Voted For Ben Stockton" hoodies and t-shirts, and—and!—you'll get a drawer full of mismatched keys, one of which will open the safe in which your grandfather has been trapped for hours, his breath becoming heavy and labored as the air inside the vault grows thin.

JACE: Ten bucks to free grandpa from his subterranean prison! And discounted hoodies? Billy, how can we afford to give the patrons deals like this?

THE WXXT PODCAST, EPISODE 23

BARLOW: Jace, it's because we love our patrons more than we love our own lives! And for twenty dollars—the big two-oh—you will get: all of the above, plus your very own WXXT Podcast logo t-shirt, advance notice of our live Goat Night podcast tapings, three summer days taken from the life of a teenage runaway who made the mistake of loitering near the Inner Door at the train station downtown, and—and!—you can write a message that we will read on this very podcast! A birthday shoutout to your homie, words of encouragement for your classmates or your kids, hopeless curses directed at the unfathomable silence of God—whatever! You write it, and we will say it out loud! On a podcast! On this podcast!

JACE: We have to be crazy to be this generous!

BARLOW: Nothing's too good for our patrons! So just head over to patreon.com slash heaven is empty, and sign up for whatever tier you are able to. Guys, we know the economy is lousy, so in all honesty, any amount is a huge help, and we really appreciate it.

OK, enough plugging! Let's get to this week's feature. Do you remember your high school days, Jace?

JACE: I am trying to block them out, without much success.

BARLOW: Well, if you had gone to Leeds Regional High School, you probably *would* have some success! Lots of people have heard of this secondary school, few people can really remember attending, and for a select few, their high school days are a lingering terror from which they can't escape.

Our very own Emily Owens reported and narrated this piece, which we are very happy to bring you…right…about…now!

HYMNS OF ABOMINATION

[sounds that bring to mind a glacier receding quickly over rocky soil]

OWENS: For Leeds-area adolescents today, high school typically means attendance at Northampton High, the Northstar Arts Academy magnet school, or St. Julius Catholic High School. But intermittently, for several years in the 1980s, 1990s, and into the 2000s, there was another option: Leeds Regional High School.

Today there are websites and YouTube channels devoted to exploring the lore surrounding this institution of learning, but officially, it never existed. The Northampton Board of Education's files contain no mention of it; searches of the archives of the Daily Hampshire Gazette turn up no references to the school outside of vague allusions in the obituary pages; and state Department of Education officials say they have no record that a secondary school by that name has ever existed anywhere in the commonwealth.

That's small comfort to those who say they attended and even graduated from Leeds Regional High School. Absent from official accounts, their experiences have shaped them in ways both large and small. But the nature of those experiences is challenging for even the most diligent researcher to uncover. To begin with, there seems to be no agreement on just where the school was located.

[sounds of street traffic]

DON COLEMAN, FORMER STUDENT: I, uh, I was there in 1987, '88, and a little bit of '89. And it was located in the back of the old dye house down near the carpet mills. There wasn't a sign or anything, but you'd go up these rickety wooden steps. The school was in the second floor. The windows were painted white.

THE WXXT PODCAST, EPISODE 23

SUSAN LAMONT, FORMER STUDENT: Leeds Regional met in the house of my friend Tiffany. This was the early Nineties when I was there. School started really early—like, 5 a.m., 5:30, something like that—and you had to go in through the side door. The lights were off, and you had to go down into the basement. I remember every morning Tiffany's mom would be standing in the kitchen in her bathrobe, holding her finger to her lips, like "Shhhhh." She'd tell us "The babies are sleeping." In the living room, there were all these little kids on the floor.

KRISTA LOWE, FORMER STUDENT: The worst thing about it was that there was no building—they had what they called "a natural classroom." You had to walk through the woods on the edge of Leeds down where the ruins of the old ski tow were, and there was a little clearing with wooden benches in rows, and a wooden platform with a podium on it. That's where the teachers would stand. It was so cold in the winter.

NICK BELDEN, FORMER STUDENT: You could only get there by climbing into the back of a van. I think it was always parked in front of the charity store where they sell stuff to benefit the hospice. It was a white van, I remember, and it had the Northampton city logo on the doors. It didn't look like it would actually run, like it was rusted and covered in a layer of pollen. I never saw anyone at the wheel. We'd line up and climb in through the back doors, and this is weird, but it was so much larger inside than it should have been. They could easily fit 40 or 50 of us in there, with chairs and everything. The only light came from a couple of bare bulbs in the ceiling, and I remember falling asleep a lot.

OWENS: Regardless of where the school was located, what Leeds Regional alumni all agree on is that the curriculum was strikingly different from the lessons being offered at other secondary schools.

LISA RICKARD, FORMER STUDENT: On Tuesdays, we had to eat ghosts. I don't really know, now, you know, I don't really know what was happening. Looking back. The teacher would bring this cart into the classroom, and on top of it there was this old cardboard box painted white. We each had to go up and put our hand in the box, and everyone would get something different out of it. Some people got, like, kind of a porridge? Some people got these little pebbles. The teachers told us these were ghosts, and we had to eat them. Every time I put my hand in, I pulled out these little things that looked like white crickets. I hated eating them. They jumped around in my mouth.

SUSAN LAMONT, FORMER STUDENT: I think the idea was maybe an "alternative high school" type of thing? There wasn't a lot of structure. We would just be in the basement of my friend Tiffany's house, and you could kind of just talk to your friends, or read a book or whatever. There were record players set up along the walls, though, and you would go over and put on headphones and listen to records the teachers put out for us. Different records every day. I remember one was about how animals couldn't pray. Another one was called "Susan Had a Nightmare Last Night." I remember it very clearly, because it had my picture on the cover, and the record was my friends talking about something they thought I had done, something bad.

DON COLEMAN, FORMER STUDENT: It was basically a trade school. Every room was a different kind of machine shop. I wanted to learn to be an electrician, but these rooms had weird machines. I remember one class was all about teaching us how to connect these mannequin heads to things that were, like, mechanical spiders. They were called the Little Governors. People hated that class, but for whatever reason, I was just really good at it. They didn't give out grades; that was maybe a hangover from the hippie era? I don't know. But at the end of the semester, the teachers gave me this huge brass coin that I had to carry around. It was a big honor. They said I was the first student to earn it. It was the size of a dinner plate, though, and it was so heavy. Just touching it gave me this horrible rash, but nobody else in school had one like it. It was an honor.

THE WXXT PODCAST, EPISODE 23

AMY FLETCHER, FORMER STUDENT: Our classes met at night for some reason, and I remember one class was in this room with these long benches, with telephones on them. We'd sit at a phone and listen to conversations that people were having somewhere else in town. We'd have to take notes, and then write letters to the people whose conversations we listened to. I remember listening to one woman who was crying hysterically, I think she was on the phone with a doctor or 911 or something, because she kept talking about killing herself, and saying she was cutting into her arms, and the doctor or whoever just kept saying, "Don't you think you're overreacting?" I was kind of upset about that, but the teacher told me most of the calls were fake. "We don't have the budget for real suicides," or something.

BARLOW: We have lots more WXXT Podcast to cram into your head holes, but first, we need to pay the bills! Here are some quick words from our sponsors.

VOICEOVER: America runs on Dunkin'! Whether it's a handcrafted espresso drink, an all-day breakfast sandwich, or one of our signature classic doughnuts, we keep you refreshed and ready to take on the day! And now, you can help a hero run on Dunkin' as well. For every e-gift card purchased at DunkinCoffeeBreak dot com, we will donate one dollar to the Dunkin' Joy in Childhood Foundation's COVID-19 relief fund. So log on, and treat your hero to a coffee break!

VOICEOVER: Are you a guy between the ages of 14 and 45? Do you feel like your peers have all passed you by? Do you find yourself struggling with social protocols that other people navigate with ease? Does life increasingly seem like a maze with a map that you weren't given? If your answer is "yes," then you need the Bedlam Box. Shipped to your house once a month in discreet packaging, the Bedlam Box has everything you need to stop feeling left behind: audio recordings of war refugees describing their nightmares; drawings by children in special schools of the man who waits for them at the gates to the park; Etruscan curses expertly carved into wax tablets by artisans in Central Appalachia; a mask that looks like the place you go inside when your aunt hits you; and more. You don't need a doctor's prescription, and you don't need to tell your parole officer: the Bedlam Box has the ingredients for the new life you've been afraid to dream about. And now, for listeners of The WXXT Podcast, the Bedlam Box is more affordable than ever: just go to www dot bedlam box dot com slash WXXTPod and enter the code "Dad Doesn't Love Mom," and you'll get your first Bedlam Box absolutely free while saving an additional five percent every subsequent month. This offer is only available to listeners of The WXXT Podcast, and it will only be here for a limited time. So go to www dot bedlam box dot com slash WXXTPod and use code "Dad Doesn't Love Mom" to start saving—and start saving your life—today.

JACE: And now we're back with more WXXT Podcast!

[muffled sounds of a crowd]

OWENS: The students who attended Leeds Regional High School all describe an unconventional learning environment, but what was it like for their teachers?

MAY-ELLEN FITZER, FORMER TEACHER: I needed a job so badly. My husband got hurt—he was crushed under a tree, he was a lineman for the power company—and he couldn't work. I had been a homemaker, and I just thought, what do I qualify for? I thought I'd have to work in a shop, running a cash register, you know. Minimum wage. Then I saw an ad in the Red Circle, the little free newspaper that came out on Wednesdays, it said something like "Teachers Wanted: Preference Will Be Given to Those With No Experience."

THE WXXT PODCAST, EPISODE 23

IVAN GLANTSHOW, FORMER TEACHER: There was a phone call late at night. I looked over at my "mistress"—the bottle of bourbon I took to bed with me and clutched deep in my tangled bedclothes—and for some reason I thought it was God calling to tell me I was dead. Instead, it was the voice of my great-uncle Archibald, who had been lost at sea before the war, telling me to go into the woods behind my house. It was a night with no moon. I walked out in my robe and pajamas: I think it was maybe raining. Not far from my back door, I came upon an old television set, like one we had growing up in the 1950s. It was huge, a piece of furniture. On the screen, in black and white, I could see an old-fashioned classroom—a big Franklin stove in the middle of the room, students sitting at slanted wooden desks, using hornbooks. And I was standing at the front of the classroom, wearing an old-fashioned teacher's cape and wig. I was asking which student would become the spider's friend, whatever that meant. A little boy in the back shyly came forward, walking very slowly up the aisle to where I was standing. I recognized him right away: he was my brother, Reece, who had thrown himself out of a window while a student at Columbia in 1964. But here he was, alive and maybe 11 years old. I was holding a burlap sack out in front of me, and inside that sack was "the spider," but somehow I knew it wasn't any ordinary spider, and that it was going to do something horrible to Reece. I tried to turn the television off, but the knobs came right off in my hand. I started banging on top of it as Reece walked closer and closer to the bag I was holding. Finally, I picked up a jagged rock from the ground and used it to cut my throat. I fell to the muddy ground, dead. Or so I thought. The next instant, I was sitting at a desk in an unfamiliar building. Actually, in what looked like the lobby. There was a group of adolescent boys and girls sitting in front of me, waiting for me to say something. "Spiders have no friends among men," I said, and they began writing in their notebooks.

PAIGE ASTLEY, FORMER TEACHER: The hardest part of the job was that there was no school building. Every morning, I'd get in my car and drive to different spots around town, where little groups of students would be waiting. Usually this was outdoors: Look Park, Pulaski Park, the parking lot behind the ballet school, the bus shelter in front of the condos on Milk Street. I felt really bad for them when it was cold or rainy; these kids would be out there, shivering, waiting for "class" to start. I'd get the day's lesson plan by listening to the radio in the car; in between songs on the classic rock station, I'd hear someone I knew as the superintendent say, for example, "Today's lesson is that the Ice Age is not over," and I'd design the class around that. I liked it, the creativity of it. I liked that I didn't have some school board designing the curriculum for me.

MAY-ELLEN FITZER, FORMER TEACHER: The students were very bright, very creative. I remember one day they performed a song they had written for me, "The Wind Exposes the Many Lies of Mary-Ellen's Husband." Somehow they found out that he was being unfaithful to me, before I even knew it. Talk about smart! They were very sweet kids, in their way. One of them came to my house while I was teaching, and he brought a hammer and a tarp.

OWENS: After enduring a series of challenges, Leeds Regional High School finally closed its doors for good in the mid-2000s. Although many who apparently attended have almost no memory of the experience today, for others, it was a truly formative period in their lives, greatly influencing the adults they became.

DON COLEMAN, FORMER STUDENT: The dye house burned down one night, and that was the end of the school. Somebody said one of the teachers did it, and someone else said a student did it, but the cops arrested the guy who owned the old carpet mills. They said he did it for the insurance money. It's funny, people now don't even know where the dye house was, that whole area's changed so much. There's a fancy coffee shop there now. A couple of years ago, I went there to poke around and see if I could remember where the dye house had been, but for some reason I got sick, like throwing up sick, and sat in the coffee house bathroom for like half an hour, sweating and puking.

KRISTA LOWE, FORMER STUDENT: Everyone who went there, at least in my class, got a tattoo from one of the teachers. Mine is a little woodsman, on my ankle. He's holding an axe, and he's got a little word bubble where he's saying, "God is withholding his mercy, Marguerite!"

NICK BELDEN, FORMER STUDENT: Ever since I graduated, I've had insomnia. I can't sleep. I moved to Amherst to work in a restaurant, and my roommate and I lived in an apartment below the guy who was the president of the state Audubon Society. He had these bird feeders, seed bells, all kinds of things on his porch, and he attracted just huge numbers of birds. I would try to sleep, I had blackout curtains so I wouldn't see the sun, but every morning I'd know I had failed when I heard the birds. So many of them, showing up right at dawn. It drove me crazy. One day, when the guy was out, I climbed up there and left crushed-up Alka Seltzer in all the bird feeders. The next morning, when the birds ate it, it expanded inside their stomachs and they exploded. Just dozens and dozens of dead birds, guts and blood everywhere. The guy was screaming, full-on screaming. I learned that Alka Seltzer trick in high school, actually.

SUSAN LAMONT, FORMER STUDENT: I don't have many fond memories of high school. Every day at lunch they'd serve us doughnuts with big bunches of hair as the filling, instead of jelly or Boston crème or whatever. I remember going upstairs—this was senior year—into my friend Tiffany's kitchen, to throw out the hair doughnut, and Tiffany's mother was standing in the kitchen. She was still wearing her bathrobe, but I could see all these wires coming out from underneath. And in her hair, instead of hair curlers, her hair was wound around these thin mechanical arms, that were slowly moving, flexing like arms. "Susan, your mother raised you all wrong," she said. She didn't like to see anyone waste food.

JON PRICE, FORMER STUDENT: I don't know if we were the last graduating class, but if not, we were close to it. We had a graduation ceremony behind the old mansion on Thomas Street, the one where they found those kids. I remember running around that day to get my cap and gown, and by the time I was ready to go, it was already evening, and my mom and dad had left without me. I got on my bike and booked over to the ceremony, wearing the gown and keeping the cap under my shirt. I can't imagine what people must have thought. When I got there, no one was out front, so I went around the back. All the graduates were standing in this wading pool, about three feet deep. There were bleachers on either side, and they were mostly empty. I couldn't see my mom and dad, but I knew they had to be there somewhere. I got into the water and waded over to my friend, Justin. I asked him if I had missed anything, and he said, "The barbershop quartet drowned." I remember they got a pretty impressive graduation speaker, a guy who had been beheaded on a Greyhound bus, but who got his head sewed back on somehow. He gave a pretty good speech. I remember him saying we were the future.

OWENS: The school may be gone, but for some of the students of Leeds Regional High School, one thing is certain: the memories will never fade.

[sounds of muffled clapping, a suddenly alarmed voice in the distance is cut off]

BARLOW: Wow, really interesting stuff. That's Emily Owens, folks, doing a great job there.

THE WXXT PODCAST, EPISODE 23

JACE: If someone made an oral history of my high school experience, it would be a lot less exciting, and most of it would be devoted to the time I got an "F" in gym class.

BARLOW: Did you really get an "F" in gym? How is that even possible?

JACE: The gym teacher hated me!

BARLOW: Well. Folks, that's just about it for this week. Fly-From-Sin had to dip out; he's changed forms from a decrepit old man to tiny red flecks inside the apples of a tree on Henry Street. Anyone who eats those apples will experience the malady known locally as "the singing worms." But Jace and I are really glad that you joined—

JACE: Ahem. Forgetting something?

BARLOW: Oh! Yes! Wow, how embarrassing. We have some messages to read from twenty-dollar tier patrons! Again, thank you so much to all our patrons. OK. Jace, want to read the first one?

JACE: I'd be delighted. This one comes to us from, ah, from Grace Chantavong—Grace, please forgive me if I bungled the pronunciation there. I'm a basic white guy, you have to grade on a curve. Grace writes: "Dear WXXT Podcast, I would love, love, love it if you would give a shoutout to my roommates Sarah and Julia. We listen to every episode and have been to the last two Goat Night podcasts"—thanks, Grace!—"And we tell all our friends they need to start listening to the WXXT Podcast right now." And the words "right now" are underlined.

BARLOW: Grace, holy cow, you rule.

JACE: Grace, Sarah, and Julia: all three of you rule. Thank you for your support! You know what, we're going to put some swag in the mail for you. You already have the shirt, but there's a super limited edition WXXT Podcast beanie that not many people have.

BARLOW: If anyone deserves the beanie, it's Grace. OK, I've got one here from Breckin, who writes: "Please give my sister back to us. I know you have her. She started listening to your show and after a while that was all she could talk about. She started spending all day in her room, listening through headphones. Things started happening around the house. I woke up one morning and there were 30 or 40 black rabbits sitting in the back yard, looking up at her window. All the kitchen drawers would fly open on their own, and everything would spill out on the floor. We started getting letters from someone named Wendell Holcomb who kept inviting us to visit him 'on the site of the bombing.' He knew things about us, about my mom and dad, about me, about my sister. She was on the dance team, she was popular, she had friends, until she heard your podcast. Then, it was like all the happiness had gone out of her life. One night I had a dream that she was being pulled into the Bluetooth speaker in her room; I grabbed onto her hand and tried to pull her back, but all the skin came off in my hand, like when a piece of fish comes apart if it's been cooked too much. When I woke up, I had a nosebleed, and someone had written on the ceiling of my bedroom, 'A sharp sickle, thrust in, to gather the vines of the earth, for her grapes are now ripe.' That was the day she disappeared. My mom and dad have completely broken down. They hired a private detective, they hired a psychic, they spend all night on the Internet, in these Facebook groups for parents of missing kids. But I know the truth. I know where my sister went, and I know who took her. I gave you twenty bucks so you'd read this on your podcast, and so people would know what kind of show this really is. What kind of people you really are. I'm asking once, because after this, I won't be polite. I won't ask. I'll demand. I'm not afraid of you. The people of this town might be, but I'm not. This is your last warning: give my sister back, or I'm coming after you."

THE WXXT PODCAST, EPISODE 23

JACE: Huh.

BARLOW: Yeah.

JACE: Breckin, man, how do I say this…

BARLOW: I don't know what you've heard or read online, Breckin, but…

JACE: Your sister's not coming back.

BARLOW: Not ever.

JACE: Doesn't work that way.

BARLOW: We do appreciate the support, though. Our patrons mean everything to us.

JACE: Until next time…

BARLOW: I'm Billy Barlow, he's Big Daddy Jace, and you're listening to The WXXT Podcast. Keep one ear on the ground and the other in your pocket, because you never know when you might need it.

[sounds of breaking glass, as of many windows in succession]

VOICEOVER: The WXXT Podcast is a Rexroth Slaughton Studios production. Our theme song was written and performed by Curtis Bachelor, and our closing song was written and performed by The Night Glumps. This episode was written and produced by Billy Barlow and Emily Owens, and performed by Billy Barlow, Emily Owens, Big Daddy Jace, and Fly-From-Sin Rattlebones. Technical assistance was provided by Paul Flynn. Special thanks to Norm Dimble, Dunkin' Donuts, and Bedlam

HYMNS OF ABOMINATION

Boxes LLC. Follow us on Facebook, Twitter, and Instagram at WXXTPodcast.

Thank you for listening, Leeds.

Anne Gare's Rare and Import Video Catalogue
October 2022

Jonathan Raab

Star Trek: The Next Generation unaired Halloween episodes — Dir. Various, 1987–1994

These holiday-themed episodes were disavowed by cast and crew, and immediately consigned to the studio archives after production, never to be seen publicly. And yet, each season, a new Halloween episode was produced, each more nauseating than the last.

In the first season, Data, the star vessel's resident soulless mandroid—a character generated solely as a personal insult to the Living God—discovers the history of "Hallow'd Eve," a pagan-Christian mishmash of assorted superstitions. He convinces the crew to participate in ever-more spastic recreations of the misinterpreted rituals of this ancient human tradition until the body count is high enough for him to "obtain one human soul, patched together from the charnel house runoff of your suffering," as he tells it to Geordi La Forge, shortly before slitting the chief engineer's throat with a straight razor.

The episodes that follow are increasingly upsetting, spawned as they are from the subconscious minds of series creators and renowned sex perverts George W. Lucas and Lafayette R. Hubbard. Notable examples include: "Trickers' Treating," in which the crew wears racist Ferengi costumery and makeup as they demand candy and "gold-pressed latinum" from passing ships they hold hostage with their advanced space weaponry; in "The Beast of the Void," Lieutenant Commander Worf becomes a

HYMNS OF ABOMINATION

blood-crazed vessel for Q'a'glah—the demon of Klingon legend destined to consume time itself—when a spirit board session goes awry; Counselor Troi and Doctor Crusher develop a fixation with black gloves, trench coats, and razorblades as they experiment with vivisection on the enlisted crew in "Calliope of Madness;" Captain Picard's thinly veiled sexual obsession with a totemic archaeological find results in the microwaving of Vulcan scientists at a remote star base in the sickening "Called Beneath the Earth;" in "The Mind is Plastic," Commander La Forge presents a paper on advanced warp theory at the Daystrom Institute, resulting in the spread of a higher-dimensional mimetic virus that heralds the return of elder gods; Lieutenant Barclay discovers a digital copy of the *Necronomicon* in the ship's archives in "Lessons of the Ancient World" and proceeds to conduct a series of murderous, grisly rituals before being strangled to death by Wesley Crusher in the episode's final moments.

Low-resolution MP4 files on a DVD-R marked "Halloween" in black magic marker scrawl, very fine.

Thirty-five dollars.

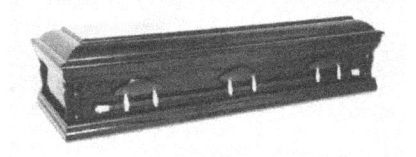

on hunger hills

They meet by stone and stagnant water; they meet by stands of alders, root and rot.

Moll of Ledston with her rope-broke neck; Mary Bateman, with cake which no one cares to eat, and Old Wife Green, crabbed and bent, dragging her skin behind her. Blind Demdyke and Sly Ursula are here, and others walk the half-world in their wake, even the Simmerdale Hag—alone, apart, always, dancing to drowned tunes as the alders tremble.

The sky is small and does not want to see them.

But Alizon Crosse has called, and this must be. She twists in the thin Yorkshire daylight, feeding on shadows between the trees. Her face—her terrible face—is hidden by a torn felt hat with a price tag hanging from the brim.

"This morn I pissed both sulphur and blood," she says, and somewhere a church bell cracks, a new-born rat goes blind. "Childers are swole and dark with petty flux; the hooded crows are silent. Something comes."

Moll's head lolls, her cheek upon one shoulder.

"What is the work, that you do need us?"

"Naught as yet. No spite or purpose lies on Elmet but that it is ours; no harm but that we will it." Alizon wraps herself in thought. "We mun watch, and be ready for the kisses of strangers."

"What if they do spurn our will?" A whisper from deeper in the woods, a shade of doubt.

"Then fuck 'em," says Old Wife Green.

There is laughter, and it is not kind.

—x x x—

LUMBRICORP. FASTER, SMARTER, BETTER.
WHAT YOU NEED, WHEN YOU NEED IT.
LUMBRICORP. WE CARE ABOUT YOU!

No one at work seemed to like Chad, however good an earthworm he tried to be.

And he really did try. He squirmed on the touchline at every company game; he bumped the thick foam rings of his costume against indifferent fans, and made those noises that an excited earthworm might make, if it were an overweight twenty-seven-year-old with no other job in sight.

john linwood grant

"Go, Annelids!"

A muffled shriek, a twitch of his pink-brown tail through the discarded plastic cups and half-eaten hot-dogs. No waving of his arms, unless he really had to—it spoiled the "magic," they said.

His supervisor called it an internship. Exhibitions and conventions, trade-meets and local fairs. And at those times when there was no call for an eight-foot-long earthworm, Chad, suitably de-foamed, wheeled mail from one cubicle to another, or watered the plastic plants, gleaming and gaudy under flickering strip-lights, along the corridors.

"The clients don't realise," said his supervisor, a man called Mr Slaughton who insisted on being addressed simply as Gerald, "but it *looks* like caring, nurturing. That's what we're about."

Chad nodded eagerly. "Absolutely, sir. But if there were other opportunities, something I could do which helped more…"

"You're doing fine, Chad. Doing fine. Hey, great job at Saturday's game."

Which was always the end of their "little talks." Back to the mail trolley and the suspicious glances of his co-workers. Back to being the mascot that no one cared about.

At first, he had thought it was because he was Black, but weeks of trundling in and out of offices gave the lie to that one. Marvin in Accounts, who had skin the colour of tyre burns on tarmac, stared at him as if daring him to come closer; Marjeane, working security by the front desk, fingered her taser whenever he hung around in the atrium too long.

If he'd known what the company did, what it serviced or produced, he might have tried to insinuate himself into the mechanism—*earthworm* his way into their confidence. But he didn't. People typed incessantly and whispered into headsets, hour after hour. Chad was never too near their cubicle-encampments. Never offered anything which might inform or challenge him…

Until one March morning, three months after he joined the company.

ON HUNGER HILLS

"Chad, my boy." The supervisor, mostly pockmarks and hair-oil, called Chad from his mail route, ushered him into an office half the size of a football pitch. There didn't seem to be room for it in the building.

"This is the future," said Gerald.

Chad shuffled his feet. "It's empty, sir."

No furniture, no computers, not even the usual junction boxes, wires and lighting tracks, waiting to be hooked up.

"Exactly." The supervisor seemed pleased. "And we're going to fill it. The Board at A.I.I. Corporate have signed off on it. We're setting up a new branch of Lumbricorp in Britain."

"Oh. In London?"

Less pleased. "Of course not. A.I.I. itself is already active in London, but they want us to test the water for them, to go back to our roots. Here we are, in Leeds, Massachusetts, ripe with history, ripe with the future. Where better to go next than the original Leeds?"

Chad had never heard of the place, had no idea there was somewhere else with the same name. "That's in...?"

"The North of England. Some weird little county called Yorkshire. And guess what, Chad? We're sending you with the team. Eddie the Earthworm will be just what we need to put a smile on the faces of those stiff-lipped, gap-toothed Brits. The common touch, the friendly face of Lumbricorp."

The earthworm outfit didn't have a face. It had two eye-slits, barely enough to see through, and that was it. Chad decided not to mention this fact.

"Yes, sir."

A conspiratorial lean forward with a blast of acrid halitosis. "Chad, you'll be the most important person there. We'll be relying on you—we expect you to report back every day on how it goes. That part is vital, remember. Vital."

"But—"

"That's the spirit. Go pack your bags, my boy, and don't forget your costume. Your flight leaves Sunday morning."

—x x x—

Britain, England, or Yorkshire—Chad wasn't entirely sure where he was. As soon as they landed and had been through passport control, he was bundled—along with three other company employees—into a large airport taxi. More people were on a following flight, apparently. The driver was a young, heavily bearded Asian man who kept his foot on the accelerator and his eyes on his mobile phone.

The Lumbricorp staff stared out at fields stiff with gorse and thistle; fields which seemed nothing but furrowed mud, and fields which sprouted low, malevolent-looking sheep. Leafless trees hung over the road as if ready to pounce.

"Is Leeds far?" The smoker's rasp of Mary-Beth Selowski.

"This is Leeds, lass," said the driver. "There's just less of it round here."

And soon there was more of it, though the houses clustered by the roadside were strange as well. They came in clumps, some large and imposing like sets from a historical film, others modern structures, all red brick and satellite dishes. Every so often a grey stone cottage sat sullen amidst these interlopers.

"So these are your suburbs, yeah?"

The driver looked round at Mary-Beth, ignoring the growing traffic.

"Towns. Villages. Leeds is a greedy bugger—she eats 'em up, year on year." He laughed, and accelerated between two buses to the sound of angry horns.

Their destination was on the edge of the modern city, a former market town which huddled around a heavily wooded hilltop. Just off the main road, set in its own grounds, stood a pale, two—storey rectangular building which bore the sign "Lumbricorp" in gaudy plastic lettering.

"Is that it?" Jay Pringle sounded less than enthusiastic.

Chad felt oddly pleased as the taxi pulled onto a long driveway. None of them had talked to him during the flight, but now…they were unsettled, maybe disappointed.

"It's so cool, guys," he said, grinning. "We're here, in Leeds, England!"

The original Leeds.

He felt the words in his belly, in his big chest, in his bull-neck, coming up like something that had been waiting, a belch that had to come out…

The driver hauled out the case which held the Eddie the Earthworm costume, and Chad's moment passed, because there it was—the sweat, cloth and polystyrene reminder of his role.

Tom Wolton clapped his hands.

"Get your gear over there, guys."

He pointed to a large Victorian house behind the offices and explained that the building had been divided into tiny apartments through the wizardry of plywood and plasterboard. Each apartment, said Tom, held a toilet and shower, as well as a bed, table, and chair.

The others moaned, but Chad was excited. His grandmother read the B of Baptist as meaning Brutal, swishing her cane and muttering for the Lord to preserve her good-for-nothing grandson. If she loved him, she didn't let that stop her poking her nose into his garage-room at all hours. Here, he would have his own little space.

Inside, Tom stood on the narrow stairs with his arms out as if to deliver a blessing. "OK, guys, working dinner tonight in a restaurant up the road."

A mix of groans and curiosity.

Tom took Chad aside.

"No need for you to come, Chad. Corporate talk—not your sort of thing, huh?"

A clear dismissal. He'd expected it.

"Uh, what do I do about food, then?"

The other man slipped a company charge card out of his jacket, pressed it into Chad's palm.

"Plenty of food joints around here. Eat out, relax. Busy day tomorrow."

Four more employees, none of whom Chad recognised, turned up before the end of the day. Tom pumped hands and assigned work details. Unable to face the world outside head on, Chad unpacked, and when the others had gone, he checked the address and rang for a takeaway pizza, which tasted awful when it arrived.

He slept fitfully, his belly gurgling its objections well into the night.

—x x x—

Chad was surprised to find that he had his own desk, his own computer. Not in the main open-plan office where the other would work, but in an alcove off the corridor to the washroom.

"What am I supposed to do here?" he asked Jay, the other member of his immediate team. Jay was five foot six of pettiness and resentment, his moustache in a sneer most of each day.

"You can use a computer, yeah? You type up what you've done each day and send it to head office. It's all on-line, under your user ID. 1700 hours, every day. Simple as that. If they want to know more, there's a videolink they use."

When Jay bristled off, Chad logged on and looked at the report form he was supposed to use. How many sites he'd visited, how many leaflets he'd given out—much as he'd done in the States.

The screen flickered, and a second form came up.

TO BE SHARED WITH SUPERVISOR ONLY

- *Estimated height and weight of co-worker (0900hrs daily)*
- *Number/length of comfort breaks observed*
- *Skin tone (see schedule D1)*
- *Facial tics/hour when observed*
- *Ambient temperature of office (0900 &1630hrs daily)*

The list went on. Most of the items were very personal observations, things which made Chad feel uncomfortable. And yet…it wasn't like anyone on the "team" paid him any attention or showed any camaraderie. He might as well do it.

The route for his first week was laid out for him on a laminated sheet. He read the flyers before setting out, and didn't see the point. All they said was:

LUMBRICORP IS COMING!
FASTER, SMARTER, BETTER.
WHAT YOU NEED, WHEN YOU NEED IT.
LUMBRICORP. WE CARE ABOUT YOU!

No product or services mentioned; no address, website or phone number.

Little wiser, he trod the streets. Through narrow alleys, down broad avenues where the windows stared in suspicion. Along meandering lanes that intertwined and turned him round at every corner.

Old women stopped him and asked if he knew where their parcel was; children circled him and threw crude insults, cheerful on their discount roller skates. Some people took flyers; others discovered sudden reasons to cross the road, and one flustered woman thrust loose change into his hand.

He'd had worse jobs.

It rained a lot in Yorkshire, a cold, heavy rain that cut through anything. At those times he sorted the mail and photocopied the incomprehensible charts that others passed to him. Or he played solitaire with the computer. The computer won every game.

"Keep up the good work, Chad," Tom would say, walking straight past him without looking.

One afternoon, finishing early, he found the door to his apartment open. Thinking automatically of a break-in, he picked up the fire extinguisher from the corridor and edged around the door, fairly confident he could out-bulk most intruders.

The woman crouched by his bed was thin, about his age, her skin so white that he felt oddly self-conscious about his own colour. She was surrounded by packs of wipes, dusters, and a partly-dismantled vacuum cleaner.

"Nearly done, mate," she said, without looking up. "Fucking machine's playing up." She shook the vacuum in frustration. "Bollocks!"

Chad went over and took the tube and hose from her.

"We had one like this." He slammed the flat of his hand over one open end, and a shower of dirt came out the other, along with some sort of British coin. "They jam easy."

"Oh. Ta." She fitted the vacuum back together again. "You're a big bugger, aren't you?"

It was said with a crooked grin, and Chad was taken by how pretty she was—dirty blonde hair scrunched up away from her face, and large hazel-green eyes.

"Afraid so."

"I do for all these flats. Five times a week."

"Do? Oh, clean, you mean?"

"Yeah."

They stared at each other, and her grin widened. He ought to say something.

"I'm Chad. With Lumbricorp, you know, the American company that's taken the offices."

"Well, obviously, duh."

His cheeks were warm. "I guess...I guess you don't see many Black folk here."

"You kidding? Three quarters of a million people here, Chad. Not that many Yanks, mind you."

"Oh. I didn't—"

"No reason you should. Right, I'll get my crap out of here."

As she left, she waved a duster at him.

"The name's Isobel. Catch you later, big feller."

―x x x―

Trying to get a handle on this other Leeds, Chad began to read the local news on his phone. And to notice things. This city was a thousand small communities, sharing some loyalty to the soil beneath them but not necessarily to each other. It thrummed with localised events—what they called car-boot sales, and flower shows; church coffee mornings, evening classes, drop-in centres, and jumble sales (?). They seemed proud of being part of it all, though, of being Yorkshire.

Chad couldn't remember being proud of anything.

The team had been there two weeks, and Tom looked...bigger. His skin was stretching to accommodate the pounds, taut over full cheeks, forming a pink expanse from which Tom's pale eyes stared. Chad was no lightweight, but he didn't think this was healthy. And when he glanced at the others, he realised that it was true of everyone else. They were...fuller, bulkier. He, on the other hand, had dropped a few pounds after spending so many days on the streets in that hot, sweaty costume.

He noted all this in his reports.

It didn't bother him much, until one overcast morning.

Mary-Beth was at her desk, humming and painting her nails, whilst Jay argued loudly on the phone, his moustache bristling. Tom walked into the room, and both of them fell silent. No one noticed Chad as he crouched behind the mail trolley, trying to free a manilla envelope which had jammed itself in the wire surround. He looked up, wondering why the room had suddenly gone quiet, and…

Tom's mouth was open, and a purplish protuberance quivered between the man's teeth, a second tongue. Confused, Chad waited, maybe for his vision to clear, or for this hallucination to pass.

Neither happened. Instead, Tom closed with Jay—the other man opened his own mouth wide, and the two of them pressed their lips together. It wasn't a kiss—more a docking of flesh. The skin of Jay's neck rippled, bulged, and then it was over. The two men wandered away.

Mary-Beth had obviously seen what happened, yet showed no alarm.

Chad crept away, feeling nauseous.

—x x x—

Blind Demdyke lifts her head and her nostrils flare, her butter-milk eyes turned to a disinterested sun.

"What dost tha smell?" asks Peg, but her choking speech is lost on the others. Her throat has a pewter spoon jammed halfway down it, her plan to save herself from choking on the gallows. It worked, so they skewered her on swords instead.

"She has found the taint we seek," says Alizon Crosse, pleased. "Beldame, you bring spoiled milk to my cup, a rotting bowel to my platter, at last."

For this is the first sure touch they have had, and once on a scent, the women of Elmet do not falter…

—x x x—

He hadn't seen what he'd seen in the office, because he couldn't have. So, he buried it as best he could. Instead, he began to calculate when Isobel, the cleaner, would be on duty at the apartments. It made him feel like a stalker, but all he wanted was someone—anyone—to whom he could talk. About anything. His closest friend so far was the bad-tempered Polish delivery boy who brought pizzas.

When he knew she would be there, he slipped over from the office and took an extended break. She didn't seem to mind.

"So where you from?" she asked, sipping the Coke he'd brought her from the office vending machine. "I mean, America? Is that like New York, or California, or..."

"We're from Leeds."

She frowned. "This is Leeds."

"Yeah, but there's another Leeds, over there. Named after this one, I guess. It's on the East Coast. Massachusetts."

"What's it like?"

What was it like, back there? It was just...just what it was. He tried to describe the place he'd grown up in—the dark, heavy woods and the white frame houses, interspersed with the lichen-spotted roofs of buildings which had once been mills and finer homes of an earlier town. Gleaming new offices growing from New England soil; WXXT and bad country music on the airwaves, and sodas at polished counters. He tried to give her the feel of his home, and failed, because he didn't know what that feel was.

"Sounds like the usual shit," she said.

Frustrated, he spoke of the death of his parents in an auto accident, years ago, and his life under a resentful grandmother as he wandered from one low-paid job to another.

"But then I got this call from the company, Lumbricorp. They were looking for paid interns, said I fitted perfectly. Not even an interview."

"Like them apprenticeships we have over here. Slave labour."

"It's work."

"Yeah." She kicked off one trainer and flexed her toes inside the lime-green sock. "What do they do?"

Chad shrugged. "They're part of something bigger, some sort of international set-up. We're a service industry, I guess. Offices, computers, and headsets. I don't think they—we—make anything."

"No one does, these days."

—x x x—

He did his job, but noticed changes. Visitors were coming to the office now—locals, by their accents. He recognised a few of them as people who had taken his leaflets.

A small Chinese or Korean looking woman with a shawl wrapped around her head and shoulders, and two thick-necked blond men (brothers?) with Leeds rugby shirts and cans of strong lager; a lame old man with mud-spattered workman's overalls. None of them made eye contact. They looked distracted—or ill.

As far as he could tell, Mary-Beth greeted each arrival in the lobby and showed them into one of the small side-offices where Tom or Jay would see them.

"Are they going to work for us?" Chad asked.

Mary-Beth formed a cold smile with fat, lipstick-greased lips.

"Isn't everyone—in time?"

He counted perhaps a dozen visitors some days, and there must have been more when he was out on his leaflet rounds. How did they even know where to come—and why were they there?

During the third week, one of the Lumbricorp people died. Bo Svensson, a tall, slightly hunched man who did something in Finance. Two of the other staff took the body away on the mail trolley, presumably to an ambulance or a coroner. No one made any time to explain it to Chad.

"Heart attack," Tom announced in the general office. "Not entirely unexpected."

There were a few more words, but he might have been talking about the demise of a faulty microwave. No one seemed alarmed.

Chad held up one arm, as if he were at school. "Will there be a funeral?"

"Oh, it'll all be dealt with."

Tom placed a large, damp hand on Chad's shoulder.

"Don't worry yourself—Svensson was weak. Not everyone adjusts."

That evening, when the others had left, Chad dared to call his supervisor on the video-link. He couldn't shake what he'd seen between Tom and Jay, and now...

Gerald's pockmarked face appeared in moments, close enough to the screen to show whiteheads in the craters like tiny moon landings.

"Getting some great figures at this end, Chad. Strong conversions, all very organic."

"Thank you, sir." Chad was fairly sure that the supervisor was referring to the new Yorkshire-based website. Fairly sure, because when he himself clicked on it, all he could see was "Lumbricorp is coming," and a background image which reminded him of over-boiled spaghetti.

"I'm a bit worried, sir."

"Worried? What about, Chad?"

"I, uh…well, with what happened to Mr. Svensson—"

"You know what they say, Chad—always boil the water when you go abroad."

"I thought it was a heart attack."

"Well, we're not doctors, are we, you and I?"

How was Chad going to build up to what he wanted to say? That he thought there were worms inside his colleagues, that something was horribly wrong here?

As he tried to form the words, he saw it—a purple-grey moistness in the supervisor's left eye-socket, caressing the edge of the eyeball as it slid into view.

"Anything else?"

"No, sir." His lips spoke the words whilst his mind made small, mewling noises.

"Keep those reports coming. That's why you're there, remember. You carry on like this, Chad, and you'll be ready to join the big boys." Gerald chuckled. "Maybe, if you're lucky, you'll end up like Tom…"

And the eye winked at him.

Chad cut the feed.

A day later, he noticed that the corner desk by the lobby was empty. Chad had vague recollections of a small, quiet woman. Wells, Wills?

He asked Tom about her.

"Oh, she's probably around. We're all busy people, you know?"

Chad took a handful of vitamins that night and vowed to eat more salads, drink less beer. He wondered about other jobs over here, and then remembered that he was a low-grade American intern on a company visa, far from home.

This was it, for him.

Not everyone adjusts...

—x x x—

"What's that hill in the middle of the town? The one that stands out?"

"Bit of old woodlands. They call the area Hunger Hills. Want to go up there?"

"Sure."

They tramped up past a church, past a school, and onto a narrow, sunken track between hedges, a track which rose higher all the time.

"This is an old pack-horse road," she said, kicking back a patch of nettles. They kept climbing until they reached a ridge thrusting out from the woods.

"There you go. That's Leeds."

The view was impressive. North and west lay fields and scattered farmhouses; south and east was the enormous sprawl of the true city. Swathes of tight-packed housing and complex suburbs, nothing like the suburbs in the States; church spires and massive Victorian buildings, interspersed in the city centre with blindingly bright office blocks and telecommunications masts. None of the roads were straight—there was no obvious way to get anywhere.

He remembered what he'd said to her about his own Leeds.

"It's…big. Different."

She grinned. "Way old, as well. They called this whole area Elmet, once, you know? The Kingdom of Elmet. Like, over a thousand years ago, and more."

"That's pretty cool."

He dropped to his knees and slid his fingers into the bare soil. It was warm, and slightly sticky with clay.

"Once it has you," she said, "it keeps you. Unless you turn on it, of course."

Unless you turn on it.

Here, under stark lime trees, his hands filthy with Leeds, he felt somehow free of Lumbricorp for a moment.

"Look, the company—there's something wrong. Or weird. And I can't get my head around it."

And he told her everything.

She listened until he ran out of anything he could put into words. He knew it wasn't enough, and that it sounded insane.

Magpies clattered in the branches above. A lean cat wandered past, ignoring them.

"Let's go back down," was all she said.

Back in his apartment, she cupped a mug of coffee in her hands, without drinking.

"Show me this stuff they make you hand out."

He opened his shoulder bag and passed her one. She read it, turned it over…

"That's…sick." Isobel pushed the flyer away from her. Her clear distaste made no sense.

He picked the flyer up and read it out loud.

"'Faster, smarter, better. What you need, when you need it.' What's wrong with that? I don't get it."

She stared at him. "That's what you see?"

"Of course." Sweat trickled down the small of his back. "What do you see?"

She told him.

Chad was stunned. What he'd been handing out, what was printed there…

"No one ever complained. No one said anything!"

She thought about that.

"Maybe most of them don't see it," she said eventually. "You didn't. And the ones who do, maybe it's their thing." She paused. "Maybe it speaks to them, specifically, and that's the point."

He thought of the visitors to the office, the slightly fevered look to their eyes.

"But you—"

"I'm different." She didn't sound thrilled about it. "On Sunday, I broke an egg for breakfast. It had two yolks—one was just yellow, like normal; the other was sort of grey, like, you know, spunk." She pulled a face. "That afternoon, my mum sat up in bed and sang 'Death a-Wandering.' She hasn't done that for twenty years. Can hardly speak after the stroke. I knew trouble was coming."

"Lumbricorp?"

"How the bloody hell would I know? Now, though—yeah, seems it's your lot."

"Not me!"

"Nah, not you. I get that."

"God, my head hurts. What am I supposed to do?"

Isobel stood, up paced.

"Hang in there. 'It'll be reet', as we say here." She tipped her cold coffee into the small sink. "You're in Leeds, with me—and that wouldn't have happened if it wasn't meant to. Trust me."

"I don't think I trust anyone."

She grinned. "Yes, you do."

He let her out, and collapsed onto his bed.

ON HUNGER HILLS

With Svensson and that other woman gone, he was stuck in the office with five people who might or might not have segmented monstrosities crawling around them inside them, for a purpose which completely escaped him.

Chad was not a happy earthworm.

—x x x—

Isobel's trainers are soaked, and her head is low, but she is a dutiful daughter, sent by her mother's stroke-slurred demands.

There will be women, in the copses by Breary Marsh, and they will listen to you...

More rain is coming, and the woods smell of decay. Alders bow and whisper in the chill North wind; crows pick entrails from a frog which rots in the stream.

The six or seven figures between the trees might be women; they might be anything. Isobel finds it hard to focus on them, but she has seen these faces before, loomed and clustered around her mother's bed—the same sharp, spiteful faces from when Isobel was a kid.

She clears her throat.

"I'm supposed to tell you—"

The bent figures grimace and titter.

"Spawn of a spoiled crotch."

"The carline's soft, unwanted get—"

"Enough!"

Alizon Crosse's voice is a whip from under the lowered brim of her hat.

"Speak up, child of Jennet Payne."

And Isobel tells them, spills out all she has heard from Chad. Fragments and fancies, small truths and greater fears. They are not good listeners—they stalk around her at a distance, muttering—but she manages to finish.

"Mum said you needed to know."

Peg Fyfe makes a sound which not even Alizon can understand. Old Wife Green crouches and urinates into the stream. She is singing to herself—"Death a-Wandering," and "The Worthy Butchers."

The words crawl on the air, sliding between each gathered figure; mouths gape and swallow them, and Alizon Crosse smiles, which is Death-in-Spring, and fearful, and an abomination. Sheep give voice on the hillsides, a deep lament; magpies rise raucous and bloody-hearted.

"This ay night, and the morn, then. It must be done." she says. *"Pretty Moll, you shall make merry with those who bring this taint."*

Isobel, ignored, has had enough. Turning, she heads back to the bus stop on the main road. She wonders if she will be late for her shift at the supermarket. If her shoes will ever dry out—and if she will end up like her mother.

Mad.

There is something she needs to say to someone, but the icy wind stabs at her ears, and it is hard to concentrate.

—x x x—

Sirens haunted the early morning. Chad woke with a headache and the realisation that the cries of police cars and ambulances had not been part of his dreams. The Doppler wails of speeding responders, the repeated heavy whoop of fire engines. They were still sounding.

He looked at his phone. There were news alerts, bands of white text on crimson across the bottom of the screen.

A twenty-three-year-old walked into the Leeds-Liverpool canal yesterday evening. Witnesses said they saw black oil running from the corners of his mouth. It took three men to drag the body out, at which point they found his abdomen crammed with parts from a vintage BSA Fury motorcycle.

Two brothers in nearby Bramley, popular rugby players, emasculated each other with bread-knives around the same time. They managed to bleed all the way from their kitchen to the local store, where—before collapsing—they told shop owner Faizal Aziz (57) that a crow suggested they do it.

Chad scrolled down, appalled. A family had immolated itself in a third floor flat; an elderly man, Solomon Gertz, shaved himself with an open razor until the bone of his jaw gleamed pale and clean.

The reports were oddly matter-of-fact, interspersed with a weather update—cloudy, but little chance of rain—and a request for volunteers at the Headingley vegan fair on Saturday.

And he had to go to work, regardless.

ON HUNGER HILLS

The atmosphere at the office was feverish. Tom, Jay, and Mary-Beth kept going into huddles, unpleasantly close ones, whilst Rav, their IT guy, stared at endless screens of code, complaining about "the site" being down. The other team member, Beverley, was cloistered upstairs in what Tom called "the hub." Chad didn't have the passcode to that part of the building.

Unable to think clearly, he followed routine, and tinkered with the copier. The earthworm costume was slumped in the corner; he had seventy-five English pounds in his wallet, and five changes of underwear in his room.

If he ran, where would he go?

Tom's grumble rose from the adjoining lobby as a slim figure pushed past him. Chad's eyes widened.

"Isobel?"

She took hold of his arm, dragging at him.

"Listen, Chad, you really don't want to be here. Not today."

He looked around, feeling helpless. "I can't just leave."

"No indeed, young lady," said Tom. His face creased with irritation. "This is a busy—"

It happened then.

The whine of the automatic doors; the sharp, involuntary jerk of heads.

What entered was the odour of cinnamon and carcasses, brought by a gaunt figure in a tattered dress of plain black cloth. One filthy foot was bare, the other thrust into a dirt-encrusted pink ballet pump. She had dried blood around her eyes, half-hidden by a mat of hair, and her head was bent to one side as if she couldn't raise it.

She sniffed the air.

"Pretty Moll remembers. Once-brothers, who left to pomp and pule across the seas. Buckle-hats and bluster. Be thou their spawn, come back to play?"

Tom stepped forward.

"I don't know who you women are, but this is a private—"

A broken-fingered hand shot out and clutched his throat, lifting him from the floor. As he gasped, open-mouthed, for breath, Chad could see a wet mass slithering upon his tongue, a blind worm-head protruding under his upper teeth.

It hissed; the woman hissed back and tightened her grip. The worm retreated, writhing under Tom's skin, but her other hand drove into the man's belly, blunt surgery which parted muscle and membrane. She hauled out a glistening tangle of intestines, and more—swollen things which squirmed for a moment only, and died.

Tom slumped to the floor, more blood now than business suit; the woman turned on scabrous feet and eyed the rest of them.

Isobel thrust herself in front of Chad.

"Not this one! He's with me."

The woman snorted and turned to other prey.

Pressing themselves by the lobby vending machine, Chad and Isobel held each other tight, watching—and not watching.

Jay ran forward, the flesh of his neck swollen and pulsing; Pretty Moll dragged him down and spread him out carelessly as she worked, ignoring the moans and whimpers. His moustache kept moving after the rest of him was still.

"The 'hot chocolate' isn't hot chocolate," said Chad, close to losing it. "You just get some kind of watery beef soup."

"I don't like soup."

"Unless it's Chinese. That stuff with egg in it."

The computer guy had passed out; Mary-Beth waddled for the emergency entrance at the back, but the woman was faster. The American shrieked, exposing nicotine-stained teeth, and then an arm was reaching down her throat, down into bloody, worm-ridden vaults…

"I want to leave here." Chad was clenching every sphincter. "I really, really want to leave."

The intruder swivelled.

"Tha mun burn this place," she said. The bulging, blood-shot eyes were unfocussed, but she seemed to be talking to Isobel. "Burnt it round Moll, and go. Let her do as she is bid."

She placed one twisted foot on a bloated, segmented thing which lay on the floor—Chad had seen it come out of Mary-Beth moments before. The worm burst, a torn bladder whose juices soaked into the beige carpet tiles.

"Tha hears me?" Moll glared at them.

Chad nodded, and watched her go to the door which led upstairs. The security lock opened at her touch.

Isobel took a cigarette lighter from her jeans and raised her eyebrows.

"Hell, yes," said Chad. "Whatever she says."

There was a lot of paper in the offices of Lumbricorp (Yorkshire), and some surprisingly flammable plastics, designer wooden window blinds, and in the storeroom, bottles of cleaning fluids marked "Fire hazard." Chad and Isobel used them all, trying not to look at the bodies.

"What...who was that?" he asked, shoving an improvised torch of copier paper into a heap of his flyers.

Isobel lit some shredder waste.

"You don't want to know. I think...I think she's a friend of my mum's."

—x x x—

Pretty Moll does not walk often, or well.

Once, long ago, they had shattered her feet with stones and snapped her neck. The first part had not been quick, and somewhere during the process, her temper took a turn for the worse.

Today she moves through the flames; between them. She forces a man's limp form into a long, lumpy tube, some sort of costume. She moves the body as if it were no more than air and foam itself. The latex is starting to smoke and darken in patches.

As she drags her burden out of the building, she kicks away a last few jerking, twitching things. Someone screams inside, but then is silent.

Jennet Payne's daughter is there on the grass outside, with the man black as a Barbary Moor.
Moll looks to Hunger Hills and remembers what she was told.
"Let there be witnesses, and those a-plenty," she mutters.
Crooking a finger at the two, she starts up the rise, hauling the smouldering mass behind her.
Doors open; net curtains are tugged aside. People struggle out from the crown of houses below the rise. The slick mud and broken stones of the paths slow them down, but they come, in carpet slippers and cheap stilettos; in trainers, hobnailed boots and blue suede shoes.
Brickies lay down their trowels; a postwoman leaves her cart. A taxi-driver, sired in Kashmir but born on this soil and of it, steps out of his cab—his grandmother taught him to listen to the land before all else.
The witch-wise call to them, an ancient call.
Oak and elm, sycamore and briar—they part for Moll of Ledston, and for those who are following her. Whatever these people are at other times, in this moment they are Leeds, and the North, and the dank, boar-haunted woods of Elmet; they are the heavy clay on which the hopes of outsiders smoulder and die...

—x x x—

Chad and Isobel stood on Hunger Hills, watching Eddie the Earthworm burn. Latex smoked and bubbled; cloth flared. He didn't know who was inside the costume. Didn't care.

The woman called Moll was drifting awkwardly away; dark figures danced on the edge of sight, and songs wafted through the smoke, tunes he'd never heard.

"'Grismond's Fall,' and 'The Bloody, Black Bull,'" said Isobel. "They like their traditions round here, you know?"

The locals were also leaving, wondering why they had left their soap operas and X-boxes and shrieking, snot-nosed children. Wondering what they had seen, but somehow satisfied.

Far down the slope, the Lumbricorp building was collapsing, consuming itself. The roof had fallen now. Photocopiers hissed and sighed as they melted; a single telephone cried out in the ruins, desperate for attention.

"I was a good earthworm," he said, as his past was consumed by the flames. "Better than they deserved. But what do I do now?"

"Fuck knows. I'm supposed to be stacking shelves in half an hour."

"I could manage that."

"Doubt you'll get a reference, though."

He managed a strained laugh.

"I don't suppose you have a spare room, do you? Just for a couple of days..."

"Yeah, I reckon I do." Isobel linked her arm in his. "And hey, Chad..."

"What?"

"Welcome to the real Leeds, mate. I have such sights to show you."

He recognised the quote—and, quite reasonably, was not amused.

—x x x—

In a place across the ocean, radios crackle with venom, with resentment, calling out through the dark woods of Massachusetts. Emails and voice-mails fly, a thick chatter that sours the streams and wakes the near-dead...

It makes no difference, for Old Wife Green is deaf to threats or entreaties; deaf to the lures of their constructed world.

She crabs and scuttles along corridors lined with dying plastic plants. Hounds—or creatures that might be hounds—slink at her heels. If they were meant to guard this place, they were swift in their betrayal, licking her flayed thighs with the eagerness of pups. They have seen their masters fail, and seem to be reconsidering their employment options.

With one hand she drags her blackened skin; the other holds a gift acquired here, this very morning. She believes in shopping locally.

In her wake, the surviving office workers crouch and whimper, their eyes as tight shut, as blind, as they can manage. Alizon Crosse wanted the work to be known, and—with some reluctance—Old Wife Green has left many alive. They are maggot-breed, anyway, not of the elders.

The room she wants, huge and empty, is easily found. And in the centre of this thwarted space, she leaves a reminder for New England.

HYMNS OF ABOMINATION

She puts it down carefully, so as not to spoil it...
The lapel badge says Gerald Slaughton, Senior Supervisor.
Gerald himself says very little.

He does not whimper, not with his lungs splayed outside his shirt, not with the fat, segmented mass that is dying in the ruin of his throat. Nor does he move, because she left his limbs elsewhere along the way, finding that they vexed her.

There are others coming—more important, darker others, perhaps. She can hear the clatter of goat-hooves and heavy boots on tarmac, and many voices outside, but she does not care. Her task here is done, the point made.

"Fuck 'em," says Old Wife Green, and the hounds growl with pleasure.

Soon the alderwoods will be in leaf.
Soon she will be back in Elmet, singing.

Anne Gare's Rare and Import Video Catalogue
October 2022

Jonathan Raab

Super Dogs II: Super Puppers incomplete assembly cut — Dir. Monty Blackwood, 1991

The unfinished feature film of an amateur apothecarist and UFO crank, *Super Dogs II: Super Puppers* is Blackwood's last major Hollywood project before his death at the hands of sexually frustrated government agents some years later. Nominally a family friendly movie sequel about talking dogs with super powers and their illiterate moppet companions, the film was sabotaged from the start by its own cannabis-addled director, who insisted on on-the-fly reshoots of scenes with recontextualized dialogue and setups. The producers cited a number of these stilted, odd additions to the script in their eventual dismissal of Blackwood, claiming that the lines were inappropriate and possibly seditious, considering they were to be delivered by the canine stars and their children sidekicks for a general audience. Such phrases as "New World Order syndicate," "unlocking your third eye through chemical experimentation," "the satanic alliance between President Eisenhower and the Greys," and "this country produces children for the killing fields of war and a bloodthirsty judicial system," drew special attention.

Three 35mm reels with case, very fine.

Five thousand dollars.

HYMNS OF ABOMINATION

x258x

station maintenance

Abe took the last step and then walked over to the railing. From five stories up he could see for miles in every direction. There was a slight sway there at the top of the steel tower but he didn't mind. He had been working for the District for almost thirty years and had an abundance of faith in the engineers who maintained the structure, just as they had faith that he and his partners would keep the transmitters operable. It was a mutual trust that bordered on symbiosis, two systems that were entirely dependent; neither could operate without the other. In staff meetings, the two engineering groups were adamant concerning the way things were done. Everything, every station, every process, every part, was documented in large, red, three-ring binders that were treated like holy texts. There was even a zealously maintained index to the binders, and cross-references too. The managers were like religious fundamentalists who had not only drunk the kool aid, but were actively mixing up a batch for the next generation.

Zac followed him up on to the platform. Zac was in his early twenties, and fresh out of trade school. He still had that lean and hungry look that young men have when their whole lives are ahead of them. He had only been with the District for a few weeks, and Abe had only worked with him once before. Abe thought that he seemed nice enough, a little slow on the uptake, but a decent electrician. If only he could just learn to follow the damned SOP.

Abe handed him the clipboard. The Standard Operating Procedure checklist was there, laminated right onto the tablet. "You've seen me do this twice, your turn at bat. Follow the checklist and it shouldn't take more than thirty minutes."

Zac chuckled, took the clipboard, and sat it down on top of the open mesh grating that surrounded the control panel. He fumbled through the key ring at his belt and unlocked the panel.

Abe sighed. "Gloves," he growled. "You have to follow the SOP, its not just there to make sure you do your job, but to keep you safe."

"Right, right." He put on his thick gloves with the rubberized palms and opened the four-foot panel door. Something angry buzzed past his head and he jerked back in surprise. "Looks like some wasps have made a nest in one of the junctions."

Abe nodded his head. "This is why we wear gloves. Wasp, bee, and fire ant colonies are all pretty common. Rats, mice, and snakes can also be a problem. When we're up this high, you might see some bird nests too, owls, ospreys, and eagles."

Zac took a brush and a can of pressurized air from the kit and went to work on the wasp nest. "What about vultures and bats?"

Abe nodded reluctantly. "They love it up here, but the bats only hang out if the tower has some sort of non-metallic roof. If the whole structure is metal, it gets too hot. Vultures sometimes roost overnight though." Abe looked east at the sea of green sugarcane that filled the landscape. Something glinted on the horizon, beyond the high voltage lines, and then was gone, a truck out on US 27, maybe. "The thing is, with bats and vultures, you'll smell them before you even get close to climbing the tower. Bats smell like piss, an ammonia smell that'll burn your eyes. Vultures," he paused for a second, "well vultures smell like death."

"You have a way with words Abe." Zac chuckled again. "You kind of remind me of my father."

"Was your father a badass too?"

"Ha," the younger man blurted out, but immediately regretted it. "Sorry, no, my dad was a washing machine repair man. He worked Monday through Thursday, eight to eight."

"What did he do when he wasn't working?"

"Rye," Zac said reluctantly. "He drank from Friday night to Sunday night, put himself in the grave at fifty-two."

"I'm sorry." Abe watched a pair of spoonbills glide silently across the sky.

STATION MAINTENANCE

"Don't be." Zac finished cleaning out the nest and picked up a screwdriver. Then he glanced at the checklist and quickly traded the screwdriver for a small electrical meter. "My father wasn't an easy man to live with, let alone like. I don't think he even liked himself that much."

"And I remind you of him?"

The young electrician shrugged. "You talk like him, always about work, never anything personal, careful with what you say. My father was rather economical with words, as if language was a limited resource, something precious that had to be paid for and horded and only released when absolutely necessary." He checked a connection and then another. "A kind word now and then would have gone a long way." He glanced up at Abe. "Still would."

The older man frowned and looked west. There were clouds forming out there, hinting at a storm. It wouldn't be long until they became something more than a rumor. It would be best to be out of here by then; off the tower, off the levee, out of the marsh, and back to something that looked a little more like a road.

Forty-five minutes later and they were back down on the ground. Zac had done well; he had gone through the checklist and only run over by five or six minutes. Abe double-checked everything, found the work to be satisfactory, and they both signed and dated the checklist at the bottom.

They secured the tool kit in the back of the truck. It was a beat up 4x4, with off-road tires and a large antenna stabbing into the sky. On the front, a winch had been attached to the bumper. The whole thing was painted a sandy tan, but around the edges another shade was still visible, and under that a third peeked out as well. Clumps of sand were imbedded in the tires, and a crust had built up on the mud flaps and the wheel wells.

They tumbled into the front bench seat and Abe turned the engine over. After a few moments, Zac leaned back, letting the AC wash over him. Without opening his eyes, he reached out with his left hand

and turned the radio on. It popped to life, and the speakers emitted a soft crackle.

Abe shook his head. "High tension lines interfere with the reception."

"This wouldn't happen if you had FM radios in the trucks."

"AM is standard. Management sees no reason to upgrade."

Zac turned the dial, scrolling slowly through the static until a thin voice peeked through the white noise. He fussed with the tuner until the transmission resolved into something intelligible:

That was du Hond's Third Symphony performed by the Borderland Orchestra. I'm William Hope and this is WHHX. We're in the middle of our pledge drive. The operations and programming at WHHX don't come cheap. We're asking you to donate today, to make a contribution, a sacrifice if you will, and keep the voice of God on the radio in Moriah County...

Abe snapped the radio off. "I would rather not listen to that, and you shouldn't either. Always begging for a donation of one sort or another."

Zac laughed but then jumped when the other radio crackled to life. "West Palm to Unit Six, Unit Six respond."

Abe wrenched the microphone from its cradle. It didn't want to come free, but with a judicious application of force, it finally released. "Unit Six responding, go ahead West Palm."

"We've had Tower Thirteen go silent. You're the closest team. We need you to go and do emergency maintenance."

Abe frowned and looked over at his young partner then he spoke into the mike again. "The kid and I just finished our fourth tower, I'll run into overtime. Can I do this tomorrow with a contractor?"

"Don't you be giving away my overtime Abe," whispered Zac.

Abe scowled at the young man.

"Negative, it has to be done today. All expenses are authorized."

Abe nodded to no one in particular. "Understood. I'll contact you once everything is resolved. Unit Six out."

STATION MAINTENANCE

"West Palm out."

While Abe put the truck in gear and began to rattle down the levee road, Zac pulled a map out of the door compartment and unfolded and refolded it while scanning the grids. "Where the hell is Tower Thirteen?"

"Grid D-18, there's a town called Tophet at the junction of county road 832 and 833. A couple miles south and west there's the Golgotha, a kind of wasteland. Thirteen is in there."

Zac flipped through the map and scanned it with his finger. "I still don't see it."

"Look at the 't' in Golgotha."

"I see it," the kid exclaimed. "Hidden in the 'o' and the 't'. Seems odd, to make a map and then hide what it's suppose to show you."

"It happens. Sometimes things just get lost, even on maps." He reached down to his waist and unclipped his keychain from the loop of his pants. He let the keys jingle in his hand until the one he wanted fell free. It was a fat thing, old and rusted. Abe handed it to Zac and brought the truck to a slow halt. "Gate."

Zac took it and turned it over in his hand, it was heavier than he thought, and worn from use. The head was an oval decorated with stylized leaves of some sort—a fruit, maybe. Zac looked up and out the windshield. There was a gate; he hadn't even noticed it before. "Where are we?"

"A private road through a farm."

"What farm?"

"Gethsemane."

Zac opened his door and stepped out, keys rattling in his hand. "Never heard of it."

Abe watched as Zac slammed the door behind him. It took a moment for the kid to free the lock and swing the gate wide. Abe took his foot off the brake and let the truck creep through. He watched in the rearview as Zac closed the gate and fumbled with the lock until it snapped closed.

With a swagger in his step, Zac made his way back to his seat and the comfort of the meager air conditioning. "So what do they grow here?"

Abe waited for the kid to fasten his seat belt and then gently moved the vehicle forward. "Gethsemane is an orchard." Then he reached out and flipped the radio back on, still tuned to the last station with that thin voice.

We must all make sacrifices when called to for the things we love. Recall that God called on Abraham. He said to him, "Abraham!" And Abraham said, "I am here Lord." The Lord said, "Take your son, your only son Isaac, whom you love, and go to the land of Moriah, and offer him there as a burnt offering on one of the mountains that I shall show you."

As they drove up the bank of one levee, the radio crackled and the voice was suddenly replaced by static. From the top of the bank, rows upon rows of trees were laid out in a grid for as far as the eye could see. The trees were short with thick branches reaching out so far they needed poles for additional support. The leaves were thick and dark green and tinged with small dots of gold.

"Oranges," exclaimed Zac.

Abe nudged the car down the levee and made his way into the trees. He moved slowly, cautiously. Fallen branches and leaves crunched under the tires. Lizards and squirrels scurried away from the trail. Off to one side a large shape weaved through the trees like a fish—a rafter of turkeys heading into the deep gloom of the woodland.

"Keep your eyes open for deer, hogs, maybe even an ewe," Abe suggested.

Zac's eyes were wide and full of wonder. His neck whipped to one side as a pair of zebra butterflies danced over the hood of the truck and past his window. He opened his mouth to speak, but then thought better of it. Finally, his curiosity overwhelmed his sense of caution. "Abe have you ever…you know?" He had this sheepish look about him as the radio crackled back for a second.

STATION MAINTENANCE

So Abraham called that place "The Lord will provide;" as it is said to this day, "On the mount of the Lord it shall be provided."

"It's best to stay in the truck. We're only meant to be passing through. You stop and get out, you draw attention to yourself." The light in Zac's face dimmed a little. Abe took pity on him. He eased the truck towards the right and with his left hand hit the little button that rolled down the front passenger side window. "Just one."

Zac reached out his hand and let it crash through the passing foliage, his eyes evaluating the various options presenting themselves. His hand closed around a particularly golden piece of fruit and yanked it into the cabin. The stem held fast at first, and a cluster of leaves followed it into the truck, but it finally gave way and the branch flexed back and out, thumping against the window frame and scraping the side of the cab.

In his hand, Zac cradled an oversized citrus fruit, but it wasn't an orange. It was oblong and curved and comprised of multiple segmented sections that were anchored at one bulbous end and opened up at the other. Except for the color, it bore a striking resemblance to a human hand with a dozen slender fingers.

"What the fuck is this?" Zac was so repulsed he almost dropped it.

Abe laughed. "It has a bunch of names. In Latin markets, it's the fingered citron, but in Asian shops it'll be the Buddha's hand."

"People eat this?"

Abe bobbed his head. "It's considered a delicacy. The flesh can be candied, the skin used as zest or in traditional medicines. There are religious uses as well."

"You mean it's sacred?"

"Buddhists consider it a symbol of good fortune." Abe paused, mulling his words around in his head. "Some obscure Christian sects think that what you're holding in your hands was the forbidden fruit in the Garden of Eden."

Zac grimaced in disbelief. "Obscure Christian sects?"

"The Ophites, from the first century. They believed that mankind was created by a lesser god and held in Paradise as prisoners. The snake was the true God and entered into Paradise not to tempt Eve, but to set her free with the truth." He paused as the radio cut him off.

Like living stones, let yourselves be built into a home for the Lord, and offer up to Him a home acceptable to Him through His Sons.

"Well, aren't you just a bucket of crazy facts." Zac flexed his eyebrows in jest. "You should join a trivia team."

Abe looked over and gave Zac a stern look before turning back to watch the trail. "I play at the Brew Garden on Wednesday nights, if you want to join. What do you know about sports?"

Zac waved a hand and went to throw the fruit in the back seat, but Abe stopped him.

"You stole that, now you've got to eat it. Can't just waste it. Who knows, it might be the best thing you ever tasted."

Zac stared at it for a moment and then reached into his pocket and pulled out a penknife. Clear juice leaked out as he cut into it. The skin was thick and flakey, the flesh a pale white. He popped a small fragment into his mouth and crushed it between two molars. Suddenly his eyes lit up.

"Delicious, right?"

Zac didn't even bother to respond, he just cut into the fruit and ate another bite and listened to the radio as it spouted scripture.

And the serpent said to the man and the woman, you may eat of all the fruit of all the trees of the whole of the garden.

It was twenty minutes before they came to a paved road. The gate was open, so they drove through. Zac thought they should stop and close it but Abe just kept driving. "There are rules about gates on a farm that isn't yours. Leave everything as you find it. If you find a gate closed, leave it closed. If you find a gate open, leave it open. You have no business interfering."

The road was barely that, with no swale between it and the canals of still, black water on either side. Along the edges the asphalt was cracked, crumbling into chunks that were slowly working their way toward the edge of the bank. Alligators and turtles hurried out of the way as the truck barreled down the oily strip. A caracara swooped down and snatched something from a low hanging branch. Zac whipped his head to see what it was but only caught a blur of something small and brown. As he watched the landscape fly past, he saw something large, furry, and black move through the reeds on the far side of the canal. He tried to track it but it was gone.

Why then have you broken down the walls, so that all who pass may pluck at its fruit? The boar of the forest ravages it, and all the beasts of the field partake of it, even the proffered goat. Turn again, Lord of thy flock, look down from heaven, and see; have regard for this vine, the stock that your right hand planted. They have burned it with fire, they have cut it down; may they perish at thy image. Let your hand be upon he who serves you, the one whom you made strong for yourself. Then we will never turn back from you; give us life, and we will call on your name.

Abe slowed the car and let it drift to the left. There was a building there, not much more than a concrete box with a barred window and an aged ice machine on one side. There was a faded bear in a sweater painted on the wall above the ice machine. The bear had been white once, but the paint had long since flaked away and revealed the ash grey brick beneath.

Abe pulled into what passed for a parking spot. He left the engine and the air conditioning running. "Cold drinks for the both of us," the older man announced as he got out. "You stay here, they don't take kindly to your kind in these parts."

As he slammed the door, his partner answered in puzzlement: "These parts? Where exactly are we?"

Abe waved a hand at the store where red letters said WELCOME TO TOPHET.

And they went to build the high place, which is in the valley of Gehenna, to burn their sons and daughters in the fire, which I did command in my name, the name of Moloch. This is WHHX and I'm William Hope, asking you all to sacrifice and keep the voice of God on the radio in Moriah County. And now, a little something special from master composer Bernard Herrmann, I hope you enjoy it.

A choir of strings broke across the radio, something raucous and terrifying that Zac felt in his bones. He had thought a musical selection would have been a welcome relief from the incessant preaching, but this wasn't comforting at all. If anything, it seemed to make things worse. He felt uneasy, almost anxious. He stared out the window at the cattails swaying in the wind. They were tall, taller than they had a right to be, or at least so Zac thought, with long, brown spikes as thick as his arm. The growth was so thick that they didn't move in the wind. His eyes went to the sky; the clouds were building in the distance, but that was summer in Florida for you. Storms were always building in the distance.

Abe swung the door open, sweat glistening on his black skin. He had two bottles with him, green glass bottles. Both of them were marked "Bartlett's Carbonated Water," but one was clear while the other was dark. "Your choice Zac, cola or lemon-lime flavored?"

He took the cola. "What the hell is Bartlett's Carbonated Water?" He took a swig. "Not bad, kind of like Doctor Pepper with a cherry kick." He squinted to read the label's claim that the soda had been manufactured in Leeds, Massachusetts since 1863. That was in the middle of the Civil War. "Who decides to invent a soda in the middle of a war?"

"People do all kinds of things when the need strikes them," said Abe as he backed out of the dusty parking lot and back onto the crumbling road. "They find a way. It might not make any sense to you or me now, but back then they figured something out, something that worked for them, and they just accepted it." He put the truck into drive and put his foot on the accelerator. "They made it work, and stuck with it. As long as it works, why make a change?"

Zac shrugged and then took another swig from his soda bottle. "That really is tasty."

On the radio the musical piece ended and the announcer returned.

A magnificent piece, if I do say so myself. Stirs the soul. Invokes something of the Old Testament. They come for violence, their faces pressing forward, gathering their prisoners like sand in the wind. WHHX continues its pledge drive. The voice of the Lord must not waver. We must all make sacrifices.

"This guy is all about the sacrifice. I wonder if he has ever had to give anything up?" pondered Zac.

"I'm sure he gives, in his own way." The radio echoed Abe.

We all must make sacrifices And Abel, for his part, brought forth the firstlings of his flock, and the Lord of Shepherds had regard for Abel and his offering.

They drove down the road. One would think out there in the middle of nowhere, no other cars to get in the way, that Abe would drive at breakneck speed. But he didn't. The road didn't allow for it. The outer edge of the lane was too damaged, too warped and rippled, like waves in a stream, to allow for speed. The only smooth portion of the road was in the center, but Abe refused to straddle the centerline, just in case there was another vehicle. They just drove, slowly, listening to the radio as it implored its listeners to donate.

We're so close ladies and gentlemen, so close. I'm William Hope and here at WHHX, I'm proud to tell you that we can see our goal. All the donations, all your efforts and sacrifices...we're almost there now. So close. You will be enriched in every way for your great generosity, which will produce thanksgiving to the Lord from all of us.

Abe turned off the road and onto a sandy trail overgrown with weeds and shadowed on both sides by stands of massive cattails that seemed too thick. Beneath them, Zac could see nothing. The canopy swallowed up the light and left only gloom.

They crossed a metal culvert and then pulled through an open gate. The tower loomed in front of them. It was old, steel painted black that twisted into the sky. At the top there was a wood and shingle roof. At the base there was debris scattered about, the remnants of logs burnt down to brittle cinders and ash piled about in what had once been bonfires. There were four or five piles of ash, and some seemed more weathered than the others. Off to the side there was a stack of fresh timber waiting for the fire.

"Popular place with the locals," muttered Zac.

The radio crackled and then began to hiss. Abe stopped the truck, put it in park, but left it running. Then both men opened their doors.

The stench made Zac gag. "What is that stink?" His eyes were watering as he walked toward the back of the truck and popped the topper open.

"That is the smell of vulture. They like the roof."

Zac scanned the sky, but there wasn't a bird in sight. He also didn't like the look of the platform beneath the roof. "Are you sure this thing is stable?" He made his way to the ladder that ran up the center.

Abe walked over to one of the guy-wires on which metal tags had been clipped. He inspected one, and then another. "Passed inspection last week." He looked up and down the tower. "Think you can handle this one without me? I'm about ready to sign off on your certification."

"You drive back?"

STATION MAINTENANCE

Abe nodded, and while Zac climbed the tower ladder, he climbed back into the cab and rolled down the window so he could watch his young apprentice. From the dashboard, the speakers crackled to life.

And the Lord said, "What have you done? The ground has opened its mouth to receive the blood that you have spilt with your own hand. It cries out to me and begs for consummation."

"You know," called out Zac. "He really does have a flair for the dramatic. And he certainly does know his Scripture. I don't know half these verses." He climbed up those metal rungs, his boots clanging as he hauled himself and his toolkit up, one step at a time.

Whoever flees at the sound of the terror shall fall into the pit; and whoever climbs out of the pit shall be caught in the snare. For the windows of heaven are opened, and the foundations of the earth tremble.

In the distance, a peal of thunder rolled. A cold wind blew across the surrounding swamp. Abe took a deep breath and sighed. Above, Zac reached the top and set his kit down.

Though they dig into Sheol, from there shall my hand take them; though they climb up to heaven, from there I will bring them down.

"It really is beautiful up here, a true wonder of the Lord," shouted Zac.

Abe turned the radio up.

Blood shall drip from wood, and the stone shall utter its voice; the people shall be troubled, and the stars shall fall.

"He was right about sacrifice. At least I think he was. We must all give of ourselves, you know, but of what use to an idol is a sacrifice? For it can neither eat nor drink."

Abe tried to close his eyes but couldn't. He couldn't help but watch. He had to.

Zac had taken off his shirt and removed the safety chain that stretched beneath the winch where the guardrail was missing. "It all has to be done in order. It's important to follow procedure. All by the book. Otherwise, the ritual isn't a sacrament. It's an affront, and he who affronts the Lord shall be punished. But he who pleases the Lord will be forever loved by the Lord of Shepherds."

And the houses of Tophet shall be defiled like all the houses upon whose roofs offerings have been made to the whole host of heaven, and libations have been poured out to the other gods.

"Praise be to God." The wind made Zac's words barely audible, but Abe had heard them, and then he watched as Zac fell. He fell, he fell and hit the tower, smashing in part of his skull. He bounced away from the main structure and then wrapped around a guy-wire. He hit at speed, and the body suffered for it, splitting in two. The two pieces hit the ground. Blood and gore spattered across the sand, some of it hit the truck.

He is your praise; he is your God, who has done for you these great and awesome things that your own eyes have seen.

Abe wheeled the microphone out of its base. "Unit Six to West Palm. West Palm, please respond."
There was a pause before a thin voice crackled into being. "Go ahead Unit Six."
"I'm at Tower Thirteen. Isaac has fallen, he's dead."
"Stand by."
Abe crossed the sand and began stacking the wood. Even now there were still things to be done. The wood had to be stacked in the right way, the fire brought to the right temperature. There were rules. Beyond the gate, the others had gathered as Abraham prepared the sacrament the proper way, as he had been taught. One radio sparked and then spoke:

STATION MAINTENANCE

You shall present your burnt offerings, both the meat and the blood, on the altar of the Lord of Shepherds; the blood of your other sacrifices shall be poured out beside the altar of the Lord of Shepherds, but the meat, that which is the Lord's portion, that you may eat.

When the announcer finished, the other radio crackled to life, but it was the same voice that came out:

Confirmed Unit Six, Golgotha is fully operational

HYMNS OF ABOMINATION

x274x

seven-second delay: in which terrible things happen to tender young girls

Lauren Anne Michaud, age seventeen and a virgin more or less, was driving home from play rehearsal at the high school when the car radio came on by itself. The play was that dusty old wheezer, "Our Town." Lauren had been chosen for the role of Emily Webb. She had big plans to parlay her performance as the doomed Emily into acclaim on the Broadway stage and eventually, into starring film roles.

    She thought it wasn't impossible that a Broadway producer would be in the audience when the play opened and would be instantly mesmerized by her talent. Anyone with half a brain would realize how unlikely such a break would be, but Lauren was young and naïve, having been brought up on animated Disney films in which plucky young women achieved seemingly impossible goals.

    She was jolted from her reverie by a chipper, friendly voice booming from the speakers in the dashboard of her mother's Toyota Camry. The voice was that of Lauren's father, dead for two years from pancreatic cancer. It was indisputably him. Lauren would know that voice anywhere. Her mouth fell open in shock as it said:

    "…so come on down to Paint 'N Sip and guzzle wine while you create beautiful works of art you'll be proud to display in your home. You'll get absolutely shit-faced on the selection of cheap wines that Gary, the filthy Nazi degenerate who owns Paint 'N Sip, provides for the imbeciles who patronize his establishment. Mention that you heard it on WXXT and Gary will give you a ten-percent discount, as well as a complimentary hand job."

    Lauren was flabbergasted. Was this a joke? Surely, she hadn't heard correctly, had she?

    Her father's voice went on. "This is Lauren's dead daddy, that old Yankee trader, that old masturbator, coming to you hot and heavy from WXXT, the poison dart in the heart of the Pioneer Valley, hitting your brain like an aneurysm full of jizzm."

The jovial voice became confidential. "Now, folks, make sure and mark your calendars, because next Friday is going to be a big night at Unity Grange Hall, located at the intersection of Route 43 and Whippoorwill Road. It's the annual bean-hole supper! This year's guest of honor will be County Road Commissioner Mitch Ginter. Come on out and say hi to Mitch and thank him for his many years of service. Doors open at six-thirty, sharp. Veterans and children four and under eat for free. Five dollars for the rest of you dipshits. Get there early and heap your plates with baked beans and cornbread like the disgusting gluttons you are. After you've chowed down, join the grange members for some excitement as they chase Mitch into the woods and dismember him in a good, old-fashioned ritual sacrifice."

There was the sound of high-pitched shrieks, as if a litter of kittens were being pureed in an industrial blender, followed by raucous male voices eagerly chanting, "Go! Go! Go!"

Lauren clutched the steering wheel, breathing hard. She tried to push the button to turn the hellish broadcast off, but nothing happened. She couldn't change the station, either. It was stuck on WXXT.

There was a rustling as of papers being shuffled. The voice coming from the speakers cleared its throat. "We have a very special announcement. It's a promposal from Kyle Engelman, the starting quarterback for Pioneer Valley Regional High School's fighting Mohawks. As you may know, the Mohawks have been undefeated this season, having kicked ass like the fucking beasts that they are. Kyle has taken tremendous amounts of steroids and smoked enough meth to kill a platoon of Marines, all for the love of football, can you dig it?"

The voice was getting choked up. There were sobs and the sound of a nose being noisily blown. "Gosh, sorry folks," it apologized. "I got kinda teary thinking how wonderful it is that there are fine young men like Kyle Engelman in today's rotten world. I'm even prouder that

Kyle, that over-medicated slab of beef who's hung like a goddamn elephant, wants to invite my daughter, my little girl, my baby..."

More sobs, more nose-blowing. "He wants to ask her if she'll go to the senior prom with him. He'll pick her up in a stretch limo and dance with her all night, holding her tenderly in his arms and making her the envy of every girl at Pioneer Valley Regional High School. At the conclusion of the evening he'll take her to where the dumpsters are behind Dewey's Auto Body and strangle her and rape her with a broken bottle. Lauren, honey? What do you say? You down with that?"

In a blind panic, Lauren clawed at the radio. Her fingernails tore off as she fought to make her dead father's voice stop talking. Tires screaming, the Camry swerved into the opposite lane, hurtling into oncoming traffic. It ran head-on into a tractor-trailer and burst into flames.

Lauren lived for a week on life support. Another girl replaced her in the role of Emily in "Our Town," and life went on as usual in Leeds, Massachusetts.

—x x x—

In the control room at WXXT sat broadcast engineer Marlee Greenglass, age nineteen. Although it was June, she wore a crown made of shiny, silver-colored cardboard with HAPPY NEW YEAR on it, outlined in sparkly silver sequins. Draped around her shoulders was a moth-eaten fox fur. Other than that, she was naked. At her feet knelt a misshapen old man. He was exfoliating her legs with a loofah while absent-mindedly playing with himself. Marlee didn't notice. She was beyond noticing much of anything.

Marlee had been hired four months previously, after graduating from Windham County Community College in Putney, Vermont. At that time, although she didn't know it, she was a dead ringer for Lizzie Siddall, the pretty redhead who was the favorite model of pre-Raphaelite painter Dante Rossetti. Marlee was into technology rather than the visual arts.

Like a lot of artists, Rossetti was a handful, and Lizzie ended up severely depressed and sickly, addicted to laudanum. She died after giving birth to a stillborn baby. Rossetti, a drama queen if ever there ever was one, carried on like a lunatic, berating himself for having failed to take better care of her. In a typically flamboyant gesture, he buried her with a manuscript of some of his poems tucked into her long, red hair. Six years later, thinking better of it, he had her coffin dug up in order to take the manuscript back. The book of poems was in rotten shape, stinking to high heaven of decomposition and full of worm holes. Lizzie herself was a wreck, her once-pretty features clotted and scabbed.

Marlee, while technically still alive, had deteriorated to the point that she wasn't looking much better than poor dead Lizzie. Tragic as Lizzie Siddall's fate had been, it was a day at the beach compared to Marlee's. Running the control room at WXXT had a deeply unfortunate effect. None of the previous engineers had lasted long.

Marlee was young and might last another eighteen months. When she arrived at WXXT for her first day of work, the station manager showed her into the control room. He was a stocky, potato-faced man who had with the glazed-over, bored expression of someone waiting in an airport terminal for a flight that has been delayed for hours.

"Left or right-handed?" he asked.

"Excuse me?"

"Are you left or right-handed? Which is your dominant hand?"

"I'm right-handed," Marlee said, embarrassed that she hadn't understood the question.

He opened a drawer and took out a pair of shiny steel handcuffs. Without further ado, he snapped one cuff around her left wrist. The other he attached to a wide leather belt, which he buckled around her waist. The belt had a heavy chain about eight feet long attached to it. The other end of the chain was attached to a ringbolt cemented into the floor.

He stepped back, surveyed his handiwork and nodded. "You're all set," he said.

"What's going on?" Marlee asked.

"FCC regulations," the station manager said.

"Are you sure? I never heard of it," Marlee said, nervously eyeing the handcuff on her wrist. It had to be a joke, she thought, a prank they played on all the engineers on their first day of work.

"There are lots of things you never heard of," the station manager replied and left the room.

Marlee was soon to learn that she was a permanent fixture at WXXT, on a continuous 24-hour shift. She was supplied with food—venison steaks from deer that had been slaughtered and inexpertly butchered in the woods, Ritz crackers, and chocolate-covered peppermint candies from the vending machine in the lobby, which was sponsored by the Benevolent Order of Odd-Toed Ungulates. She obediently opened her mouth and ate when she was commanded to. If she failed to eat, she was punished.

While her hands moved efficiently, continuing to operate the mixer deck with machinelike precision, Marlee had gone blind. After she had ceased to blink, her eyes became as dried-out as the exoskeletons of the cicadas that littered the ground outside. In a way, it was a blessing. While her eyes were fixed in the direction of the window between the control room and the on-air studio, she couldn't see what howled and ranted into a microphone on the other side.

No one could remain sane after taking a good look at what was in the on-air studio. It was currently in there, screeching, "Go on down to Dinettes Plus today and get yourself a new dinette. There are deep discounts at Dinettes Plus, you stinking sacks of lard, you fatty bombatties! I never lie and I never tell the truth. I vote Republican. I fuck your mama. You can trust me. Get your asses over to Dinettes Plus or I'll come looking for you. And now let's hear Charmaine Gilbert sing 'I Got a Gun and I'm Gonna Blow All Y'all's Brains Out.'"

Lively music began with the strains of a twangy Country Western guitar. Marlee moaned. It was the plaintive, despairing wail of an animal caught in a trap.

"Please kill me," she whispered.

The thing in the on-air studio shook a finger capped with a long, black fingernail at her. It spoke through the talkback system. "Not gonna happen, sugar buns. You're in it 'til you win it. Set up the cart for the next commercial. We got broadcasting to do."

—x x x—

The baby was crying. Brandi Drucker wearily got up out of bed and went to tend to it. The baby had been a surprise. Brandi never had a baby before, which wasn't all that unusual, considering she was only twelve. The baby hadn't become Brandi's in the usual way; her parents had brought it home from bingo night at St. Scrofula's Church.

"Looky here! We won you a baby. Ain't that great?" her mother slurred as she threw open the door to the trailer and stumbled inside. She shoved something wrapped in a stained yellow flannel blanket with smiley faces on it at Brandi.

No longer encumbered by the blanket-wrapped bundle, Brandi's mother lit a Marlboro Red from the pack on the kitchen counter. Her breath stank of the wine they served at bingo nights at St. Scrofula's. They kept it in the baptismal font and it tasted horrible, like old puke and cherry cola mixed with motor oil, but it was free and the bingo enthusiasts eagerly swilled down plastic cup after plastic cup of it.

The people of Leeds, Massachusetts held the adamant opinion that free stuff was not to be turned down. Not ever. No matter how bad it was. If the hospital had offered free castrations the men of Leeds would have lined up to get one. Fortunately (or perhaps unfortunately), it did not.

Brandi cautiously peeled back the folds of blanket and peeked at the small pink creature. Its eyes were shut. She thought it looked more like a newborn rat than a human baby. "Is it alive?" she asked.

"Course it's alive," her father said indignantly. "You think we'd give you a dead baby? Show your mother and me some respect, fer

Crissakes. You said you wanted a pet. Some fucked-up flying squirrel thing called a sugar glider. Now you got a baby. It's a boy. We checked. A boy baby's better than a sugar glider."

He went to the refrigerator and yanked open the door. The light from inside threw him into pitiless, glaring relief: a big man in a grimy red-and-black Buffalo plaid jacket, his face lined and surly from a lifetime of disappointment. He rooted around on the bottom shelf and got himself a beer. Popping the top he took a long pull and belched loudly. Then he sat down at the dinette in the kitchen and glared at Brandi.

"No respect. No appreciation," he muttered. "After all your mother and me do for you, feeding you, giving you a roof over your head, putting clothes on your back, you got no appreciation."

"Lots of girls your age would love to have a baby," her mother said.

"I guess," Brandi said dubiously, staring at the baby. Its chest rose and fell. Its eyes were clenched shut and it made a rattling sound in its throat. Already Brandi knew she wasn't going to like this baby. As if in response it farted noisily. A terrible stench filled the cramped kitchen.

"Phew!" said Brandi's father fanning the air with his hand.

"Is it on loan? I mean, isn't somebody going to come and get it?" Brandi asked hopefully.

Her father finished his beer and tossed the empty can in the direction of the overflowing kitchen garbage. It missed, and rolled clattering across the scuffed linoleum floor, coming to rest at Brandi's feet.

"Pick that up, willya? And get me another," her father said.

Brandi complied. "So, is somebody coming to get it?"

"Nope. It's yours. We won it and now it's yours," her mother said. She rose and crushed out her cigarette in a turquoise-colored ceramic ashtray shaped like a smirking whale, a souvenir from Mystic Seaport Museum. Going to her purse, she opened her wallet and took out a wrinkled twenty-dollar bill. "It's gonna need diapers. Walk down to Bub's and get some. Be sure and bring back the change."

Yawning, her mother shuffled down the trailer's narrow hallway, toward what she grandly called the master bedroom. Her father followed, carrying his beer. He spoke over his shoulder to Brandi. "Take the baby with you. The night air will do it good. Blow the stink off it," he said before disappearing into the bedroom and shutting the door with a firm click.

Brandi was on her own. Sighing, she put on her hoodie, stuck the twenty-dollar bill in the pocket of her jeans, and hoisted the baby to her shoulder. "Come on, Giles," she said

She had decided to name the baby Giles after the lead singer in a band she liked called Seven Layers of Ants. She'd always imagined she'd have a baby boy someday and would name it Giles as a tribute to the handsome, pouty-lipped rocker. She just hadn't anticipated it happening so soon.

The trailer park where Brandi and her parents resided was about a mile from Bub's Day 'N Nite Grocery. At that hour of the night the road was deserted. Brandi trudged along the shoulder, carrying the baby. It was the first of many trips she was to make to the wretched little convenience store over the next months.

Giles grew rapidly. At first, he devoured jars of baby food filled with pureed vegetables. Then he moved on to bits of smushed-up hamburger. Then he moved on to actual hamburgers, four or five at a clip. He had a formidable set of teeth by then and a thick head of brown hair and, rather alarmingly, a clump of thick pubic hair. His eyes were a muddy brown, like those of a chimp's. They betrayed a sly intelligence, beyond that of a beast, below that of a human.

Brandi dressed Giles in toddler clothes she bought at yard sales, t-shirts with cartoon characters on the front and little blue jeans. He was never toilet trained. No matter how hard Brandi tried Giles either failed to understand what he was supposed to do or he simply didn't want to.

He was walking by then, stomping around on a pair of sturdy legs, getting into everything, pawing through dresser drawers and kitchen cabinets and leaving the inside of the trailer in a tremendous mess, as if a burglary had taken place.

Brandi's mother's orange cat, Gingersnap, disappeared. She thought it ran away. Brandi suspected that Giles ate it.

Giles knew two words: "mama" and "hungry." He'd stomp over to where Brandi sat watching TV and shake her arm. "Hungry! Hungry! Mama! Hungry!" he'd say, showing her his teeth in a ferocious grin.

When Brandi was in school she kept him locked in a cage in the shed behind the trailer. One day, she came home to find the cage door unlocked and the door of the shed wide open. There was no sign of Giles. Brandi must have forgotten to lock the cage.

In a panic, she ran into the woods behind the trailer park, calling for him.

"Giles! Giles! Come here! Want steak? I've got steak. Yummy steak," she shouted.

Giles loved steak. If anything could lure him, it would be steak.

There was a sound of crashing in the underbrush. Then Giles appeared. "Mama! Hungry!" he shouted happily.

And then he was upon her.

—x x x—

From a broadcast on WXXT:

"Continuing with our look at life in the Pioneer Valley during Colonial times, Grace Bingham of the Leeds Historical Society was kind enough to share with our listeners a diary written by Reverend Ezra Harpwell between 1690 and 1698. Here's Reverend Harpwell's entry for June 15, 1692:

"A female infant was taken from its cradle in ye dooryard of Goodman John Spaulding's cottage while ye childe's mother, Goodwife Anne Spaulding, was hanging washing. Goodman Spaulding believed a wilde beast had taken it and was much aggrieved. However, upon hearing of ye occurrence, an Indian woman who had embraced Christianity and was of a gentle and kindly nature, not at all savage as is ye wont of most of her kind, did go to Goodwife Spaulding and with much sorrow told her of creatures called Mogupopowat in her native tongue, which meanith Men 'O Ye Woodes.

These creatures, said she, resemble men and inhabit ye forest in this vicinity. They are bold and ferocious and greedy for meat and will abduct and eat infants and any persons who are too feeble to fight them off. They have always lived in these parts and always shall, or so she averred.

If she spoke true or if she was repeating a foolish tale handed down by ye ignorant people of her tribe who know no better than to believe in monsters and ghouls, I know not. I only relate what was repeated to me."

Anne Gare's Rare and Import Video Catalogue
October 2022

Jonathan Raab

<u>Assorted horrors previously screened at the Red Hand Movie Palace — Dir. Various, 19XX-2001</u>

To the undiscerning eye, the various shorts assembled together on this unique collection of strange and eldritch reels may first appear to be run-of-the-mill snuff films, what with their depictions of wanton bloodletting, cruelty towards the youthful victims on-screen, and the animalistic fervor in which the proceedings devolve into a colonization of violence against patches of unblemished and innocent flesh. But you would be mistaken, dear patron, in assuming these sights were something so simple, or that they were for *you*, one of the lesser entities that pass through the periphery of awareness of these films' intended audiences. That you are acknowledged at all is a wonder; that you may have caught a glimpse of the religious rapture preserved on these shreds of celluloid-skin is an affront to me, to *us*, personally.

These are the most prized former possessions of the sorcerer-bastard Ramsey Crowley—an enemy of certain Parties here in beautiful Leeds, Massachusetts—whom we believe and prayerfully hope to be dead and buried, rotting in a cemetery in blasted and haunted Black Knot, Oklahoma, itself a preserve of the perverse and paranormal, a province of decay and dismemberment, a Southern-Fried funhouse mirror reflecting Leeds in all the Worst Ways Imaginable. Crowley was a bastard and a charlatan, a fecund failure and a hoplite of harlotry. He was a menace and a foil, in opposition to

HYMNS OF ABOMINATION

and concert with the dread energies we sought and seek and will find for our own ends. May the bastard *rot*, may he rest in *pieces*, may his works come to naught and his soul toil slavishly as an attendant to some lesser god that we will soon conquer and subsume!

We shall miss him.

Pitch-black, heavy, leather-like stock on 35mm reels... but this can't possibly be 35mm. It can't possibly. It can't possibly be—

One thousand seven hundred dollars.

all your fathers here and gone

k. h. vaughan

You are at the diner in a booth with them because it is a Monday and you always eat at the Bluebonnet Diner on Monday unless there is a funeral. Tuesday is mac and cheese, Wednesday is spaghetti with meat sauce, Thursday is Elio's frozen pizza. The other days are your fathers' choices, Ant on Friday, Lute on Saturday, and Odd on Sunday. You have to eat what they pick. There will be nothing else, and it would be impolite to decline.

You prefer the diner. The diner is scratched chrome and red vinyl patched with black electrical tape, every surface a palimpsest of burnished and forgotten memories. The menus are in plastic sleeves and have not changed in decades. There are tiny jukeboxes on the tables in the booths, except for the one you always sit in. Only the metal stand it was secured to remains, and you have scraped your elbow on it and added blood and skin to the brown gunk in the crevices on more than one occasion.

The special today is Salisbury steak and creamed corn. Yesterday—Sunday—was half sheep's head. "You have to eat the eye first while it is still hot. No one wants to eat the eye when it is cold," Odd says cheerily and laughs. The man in the next booth mutters to himself over his third coffee refill and complains about the radio. His face is scarred like the surface of the moon. He asks the waitress to turn it down again and again she tells him the radio isn't on, the mole on her lip wobbling as she does.

"He was filled with leeches," Lute says, continuing his story from before the waitress left your food. Lute works as an undertaker at Morentz and Teale.

"Of course, he was filled with leeches, he was in the water," Ant says. "You should expect a body in the water to be filled with leeches."

"He was walking around after that," Odd says. "That is what they say. That is the interesting part of the story."

"But it does not explain the leeches," Lute says. "One is not the other thing. They are separate things."

The man in the next booth slams his hands on the table. The waitress, who has returned to your booth with the coffee carafe, startles but does not respond.

"Refresh you cups, Hun?" she says.

"Turn the radio down, I can't take it anymore," he yells and jams his hand deep into his mouth, pulls out a tooth and flings it at the waitress. The tooth bounces off her bosom right where you imagine her right nipple to be and falls into your creamed corn. It sits there, brown and yellow enamel with black spots surrounding the filling that stares at you like a dull silver eye, and, reversing your attention, the silver filling sits surrounded by yellow-brown, surrounded by the paler yellow-brown of the creamed corn, surrounded by the dark brown gravy from your Salisbury steak, and little threads of blood spread from the tooth along the soft topography of the niblets and looks like an aerial view of the town. And for a moment you hear unsettling words vibrating from the filling until one of your fathers reaches out with his spoon to pull the tooth from your plate and tucks it in his pocket as if nothing unusual has happened. And, in reality, nothing unusual has. This is a normal day in Leeds.

—x x x—

The parlor on the second floor of Morentz and Teale is an odd shape, more of a wide hallway that leads from the main hallway straight to the outside wall. Ancient, baroquely textured wallpaper, a French provincial couch, and a black and white television. Wacky Racers is your favorite when you can find it. Sometimes, the television tunes in a station that is just audio, patterns of repeating tones or numbers that have no identifiable meaning. Sometimes radio. A man preaching an unknown and unknowable gospel of obscenity into the airwaves.

ALL YOUR FATHERS HERE AND GONE

On some days, your fathers let you ride your bike home from school, and on other days, you are to go to the funeral home until dinner. Why is a mystery. This is where you do your homework while Lute works downstairs in the embalming room, lying on your stomach on the faded carpet with your sneakers flapping in the air while the voice on the television drones on: "And I will give you twelve names. And I will give you twelve names, sirrah! Twelve...names, Amen!"

Homework has become strange, as your eighth-grade teacher, Miss Lobenstein, believes that President Reagan will start a nuclear war with the Soviet Union and is distracted. Some days there is none, others, too much. Often, it has nothing to do with the material in your classes. It does not appear that any of it is ever graded. The biology homework is difficult because the frog diagrams in the worksheet do not look like the specimens you are dissecting, with their tiny human hands and aberrant internal architecture.

This is where you wait to go home after school. The second floor of the funeral home is covered in dust like the silt of an ancient and immobile lake, as still as death itself. No one comes here. The preparation space and the casket showcase are in the basement. The public rooms and parlors are on the first floor. These rooms are abandoned, except for you. No one disturbs the dust and desiccated dead flies except for you. If you were to trace a line along the top of a library table in the hallway, that disturbance in the silt would remain, to be covered over in time by layer after layer of accreted dust until the outline of your presence had been completely obscured.

"The day is the time and the time is the place and it is the number too. I tell you this brother. This I tell you," the voice on the radio says. "All things will rupture like a putrefactive pustule and be revealed. Break yourself upon the wheel in righteous slavering! Break yourself! This is your only salvation. You're listening to the Soul of the Pioneer Valley, your bleeding third eye-hole, the lotion in your motion, the pain in your vein..."

You do this and, in the basement, Lute attempts to reconstruct the face of a man with a shotgun injury. He works in putty and makeup. It will look like the doll in your closet—*Hugo, Man of a Thousand Faces*—when he is finished. The family will say he looks so lifelike, despite the plastic features and nylon wig. *Hugo—create thousands of pretend friends!* You do. They are so lifelike.

—x x x—

Your bedroom looks out over the town, a dense warren of old houses and small commercial buildings with apartments on the second and third floors. Some nights you look out the window and watch the residents. There is a secret behind every door and the drawn shades always have shadows and silhouettes in varying acts of life, mundane, sexual, and violent. Once, a man hanged himself and his shadow-puppet image dangled for two weeks, slowly deforming, growing bloated, collapsing, then hanging limply until the neck gave.

At night, men in tall hats scurry from building to building. There are others in robes, some with horns of stags and others of goats. Sometimes, they collide in the streets and tumble helter-skelter in desultory fisticuffs that lead nowhere, each group running away in a panic, often with someone from another faction mixed among them until they discover the accidental infiltrator and beat him until he escapes to find his own.

When it is very late and you cannot sleep, you listen to the radio or, when that fails, a tape recording of your favorite television program. It is *Victory at Sea*, taped from the television broadcast on a dictation microcassette you found in the secretary desk in the front hall. You listen over and over again to the sounds of merchant sailors floating in the vast dark sea, ships sunk beneath them, nothing left but the dark cold ocean for a thousand miles in every direction as the light of oil fires on the surface gutters and dies. The narrator talks of rescue, but this is propaganda. They drift, forsaken and alone, until they sink themselves. No one will find their remains deep in the cold and dark. No one will even look. All security vanishes beneath you in fire and thunder and you drown.

Your fathers each have a bedroom on the second floor of the house, with its tall ceilings and windows that rattle with the wind. The walls are filled with knob and tube wiring and newspaper, among other things. There is another bedroom on the second floor that still smells of decay, the mattress stained black with rank decomposition fluids, long since dried out. No one speaks of her.

She never existed.

—x x x—

Satyros House of Pizza II has an Asteroids Game, and you play there after school when you can. Mr. Vardopoulo will let you play all afternoon as long as you buy a slice and a Coke and don't fight over the machine. Mr. Kittieb, a paunchy insurance man with a mild face and a graying beard, sits with that professor from the college who affects a fez and who no one likes at one of the small Formica tables. They share a pie and a pitcher of thin domestic beer. The light of exploding asteroids flashes across Mr. Kittieb's glasses and swept back receding hair. They talk quietly, their words covered by the clatter from behind the counter as Mr. Vardopoulo and his wife yell back and forth about orders, the slamming of the steel oven door, and the crunch of the big curved pizza knife dissecting pies. The oven is hot and the heat from it when it opens washes over you with the smell of grease and pepperoni.

"Sometimes I wonder if it would be better to leave," Mr. Kittieb says. "I don't know. I think that sometimes. But then I don't." Sweat runs into your eyes. You slam the fire button on the console as fast as you can, dodging bits of electronic wire-frame rock and flying saucers.

"That's the thing," the Professor says, scratching his beard—he always does—and bits of dandruff and beard hair accumulate on his gut. "When you've lived in a place, grown up there, no matter what it is, nothing else looks quite right, does it? The soil, the trees, the houses. Everything else is just a bit off."

"Even if it was bad."

"Even if it was bad."

The high siren-like trill of the small UFO runs over the rapid heartbeat of the game as you are cornered by fast-moving debris from strange angles. You slap the hyperspace button to escape and the white triangle of the spaceship vanishes and reappears in a worse spot to be immediately smashed. You are out of lives.

You place 10th, beneath two scores by GAB, bumping the lone RGB from the bottom of the screen. Someone has taken all the higher scores on the machine—they are so far out of your league you will never get in the top six until the machine is reset—and they have entered XXT for their initials.

—x x x—

The Sisters of Perpetual Misery at the Lying In Hospital are in a panic, screaming that the building is on fire. You don't see any smoke as you sit on your bike with a Dr. Pepper, waiting for the fire trucks. They run to and fro frenetically, feverishly. The sirens wail like something sad and desolate you cannot identify. The nuns shriek for help and throw swaddled infants from the third-floor windows to save them from the flames. The firemen find no fire, not even a candle, but the melon-splat corpses on the pavement are all blackened and charred.

—x x x—

"I was bitten by a goat."

Odd has come into the kitchen from the backyard, where the house sits against a moist stone slab from an incomplete blasting project left abandoned after the Civil War for unknown reasons. It is always in shade, and anything left there mildews and rots. The weeping shingles are covered in mushrooms and slugs, except in the deepest winter when an impenetrable sheen of ice takes hold.

"Well, you should expect to be bitten if you approach a strange goat," Ant says.

"How do you know it was a goat?" Lute says.

"Look!" Odd says. "Look at my leg!" His left pant leg is torn and soaked in blood below the knee. Lute stoops to inspect it.

"Oh, you are a hysteric," Lute says. "Going to pieces over a mosquito bite. Bitten by a goat! Ridiculous."

"If you bother a goat and it bites you, you deserved it," Ant says. "You should leave strange goats alone."

"It is my backyard! I will not be held hostage in my own house by strange goats!"

"Well, this is what happens."

You go to the bathroom closet and find the small glass bottle of Mercurochrome and the tin of Band-Aids. The rubber bottle stopper has become dry and stiff with age. The hinges on the Band-Aid tin are stained with rust. When you return, they have removed Odd's pants and moved him to the couch, placed a newspaper under the leg to catch the blood. His legs are thin and hairless, mapped with varicose veins and bound with sock garters. Odd teaches Mathematics at the Unified District High School. It will embarrass you to have one of your fathers in the same school, but that is later. There is always chalk on his hands and coat. He has a glass eye, and cocks his head to the side so that he can see you with the real one.

The wound is a garish slash across the shinbone beneath the knee. Crimson oozes from the jagged edges. The band aid tin reads "A speed bandage for minor injuries" and contains exactly four small band aids suitable for wrapping a pinkie finger and the backing strips for several larger ones that have been used. You return to the closet and find gauze and electrical tape. You go back to the living room and Ant is painting Odd's leg with the Mercurochrome, staining the skin, the newspaper, and the couch orange.

"Hold still," Lute says. "You don't want Orf."

"Orf?" Odd moans.

"Pustular dermatitis," Lute says. "Common in sheep and goats. If a goat has indeed bitten you, that's what I would worry about. Perhaps we should use Iodine tincture instead?"

Ant grunts and waves his hand dismissively. "Rabies, if anything," he says. When the wound is dressed they make Odd a whiskey toddy and shoo him off to bed. You clean up, throw away the sodden newspaper and wipe the blood from the kitchen floor with paper towels. You can hear Ant and Lute continue on in the living room down the hall.

"It would be just like him to get rabies on us," Ant says.

"But why would a goat want to eat Odd?" Lute says. "That's the strange part. It's very curious."

"Why would anyone?" Ant says.

—x x x—

You are thirteen. Rumors have spread around school about something called "HBO" that brings R-rated movies into your living room, complete with full-frontal nudity, but it will be a long time before cable television reaches you here. Mrs. Belanger runs the video rental store and won't let you take out anything with a girl in a bikini on the cover—never mind even peek behind the bead curtain into the adult-only room in the back corner—but she doesn't care at all if you bring R-rated horror films to the counter. "You boys and your scary movies," she says. She has a white streak in her black hair and a slight mustache, and she watches soap operas all afternoon on a small television on her counter. She is rotund, goitered, and smells of feet. Even though you find her repellent, you peek at her deep veiny cleavage when she isn't looking.

Your bedroom is by the back stairs, so you can sneak down to the living room after your fathers have gone to sleep. You don't find any of these films frightening. At most, a jump cut will startle you, but they are mostly comical and inept. The blood is fake. The plots, ridiculous. You will watch a ninety-minute feature in the hopes of catching a minute or two of a shower scene somewhere in the middle. Sometimes there is nothing. Rarely, a brief glimpse of pubic hair. The women are live and moving, and it is better than the Penthouse magazines that Mr. Saccone causally leaves strewn about the waiting room of his barber shop. One night you watch Cannibal Holocaust, and the actors murder and eat a turtle for no reason other than that they are there to make a horror film and it fills you with indescribable grief and guilt. You can't masturbate for weeks afterwards.

—x x x—

Of your fathers, Lute is the one you spend the most time with. Tall and bulky with a bald head fringed with stringy gray hair. A cigarette hangs from his mouth at all times. He smokes when working. He smokes when cooking dinner. He smokes in the bathroom, which makes the bath towels reek. "I smoke too much?" he says. "Harry Walsh over at Oulette and Charbonnier smokes four packs a day. I only smoke two. How can anyone say I smoke too much?"

You participate in embalmings, listen to stories of exploding caskets from anaerobic activity. "Oh, that's a mess," he says. "Never let them seal you in. It's worse that way. Bacteria release gas and the pressure builds and builds and builds. Brown slurry explodes like a pressure cooker all over everything. Once, this happened during a murder investigation at the Memorial Park Mausoleum. They said she poisoned him because he was fucking her little sister. Well, they barely had the casket out of the crypt when baboom! A big wet ka-thump, all over the police detective and the grieving widow in her prim black dress." You imagine them. Putrescent goo drips from their faces and bones poke up from the sludge around their feet. You watch as he inserts the long steel trocar into the abdomen. The distended purple-green balloon of the gut gurgles and deflates. The ancient transistor radio on the stainless-steel counter plays tinny music while the announcer tells deeply personal tales of humiliation and weeps between songs.

—x x x—

A girl in your class—Martha—lives a street or two over. On some afternoons, after school she invites you and some other neighborhood kids over to watch television on their color set. No one is allowed in the house until her mother comes home at four, so you all watch from the screen porch through the living room window. Match Game, Emergency, Batman. One afternoon it is just the two of you and she invites you into the house and upstairs to her room. You kiss and take off your shirts. You tremble as you touch her tiny pointed breasts. Neither of you have done this before and it is exciting and embarrassing and you are about to explode in your pants. Excitement turns to terror at the sound of a car door outside, and you scramble to dress and compose yourself. Martha tells you to pretend to use the first-floor bathroom. You had to go badly so she let you in so you wouldn't have to run all the way home. But it wasn't her mother. Just a car across the street. You do this several times, exploring further, becoming more daring, more insistent. You return home one day, the smell of her on your finger, and spend the entire night sniffing it compulsively as if hypnotized by a secret that you have known all along. The first time you pull down your jeans, you whimper. She slides your underwear down, and you are as engorged and distended as a leech. Rigid and purple with anticipation. You gasp as she touches you, awkward and uncertain. There has been nothing like this before. She strokes you once. Twice, and you explode, howling, cum in her hair and face and all over her hand. It is overwhelming, your knees buckle and you could pass out from the intensity of it. It takes a moment, a thousand moments, before you realize that she is distressed by your semen on her face, eye twitching and grimacing. Her bangs are sticky and it drips in pearlescent globs onto her breasts. You realize with horror that you have killed her with AIDS, as the Health teacher has warned you. Your head spins with terror and tainted ecstasy. Uncertainly, you help her clean up, and clean yourself, and go home.

The next day at school you see her talking with her friends. They whisper amongst themselves, look at you and giggle while you try to hide your hard-on with your notebook, face red as a carbon monoxide victim. It is hard to talk with Martha afterwards and eventually you don't speak anymore.

—x x x—

You gather in Odd's room, where he lies in bed smelling like rot and urine. The leg has gone putrescent with putrid yellow pustules, and he has been sent home from work following numerous complaints. Ant frowns. "Well, there's only one thing to do," he says. Lute presses a rolled towel into his mouth and holds his head down against the pillow. Ant gestures for you to hold the good leg. You grab his ankle with both hands but he kicks when Ant starts sawing, kicks you in the chin so hard that you see everything through a narrow tunnel of red and you bear down on his leg with all your weight with your split lip bleeding on the mattress while Ant saws with big jagged strokes. He works as some sort of machinist at Annelide, so does all the chores involving tools and repairs around the house. The leg comes free with a gout of dark septic blood that smells of corruption and bile. Odd moans. Lute inspects the cut and nods approvingly. You consider bandages, as no one thought to prepare any in advance. The blood is sluggish, oozing tepidly from the stump. Ant paces about the room in a state of increasing agitation. He drops the dripping saw with a clatter on the hardwood floor.

"Perhaps we should have got a tourniquet," Lute muses.

Abruptly, from the far side of the room, Ant takes a running start and dives right into the stump of Odd's leg with a meaty smack. He is frenzied, clawing his way inside, forcing himself up into the meat, slowly working his way into the resisting tissue until you see his hand press against Odd's stomach from the inside like an enormous, hideously past-due baby and his feet finally vanish and you see him peer out through Odd's one good eye.

That night, you listen to the radio as you watch from your window: "I could tell you five things, but only believe two of them, my friend. Things are happening. That much you can count on. Wheels within fucking wheels, brother, and they'll never find those bodies the way I hid them. Next up we have The Roy Smeck Trio covering *Closer* by Nine Inch Nails."

A man in a long dark coat and slouch hat shambles drunkenly down the street. He must be eight feet tall, and there is something deeply wrong with his anatomy, as if a tall man were riding on the shoulders of a dwarf beneath the coat. He bends in unusual places. The gait is strange. He turns down a dark, wet alley and you are relieved that he has passed out of sight.

—x x x—

Bobby Marderosian got braces over the summer and said he could hear the radio through them. He looked worse and worse each day, grayer and grayer, unable to sleep. He took to wandering the streets at night while his mother worked as the night clerk at the Motel Divine Chateauguay near the highway. He tried to cut out the wires and was found with blood pouring down his chest from the tattered flaps of his lips. They sent him to a special hospital in Worcester after that. He came back to school in October when the leaves are mostly gone from the trees that twist and bend like the bones of arthritic hands against the slate grey sky. They took the braces off, and he grew a wispy metal-head mustache, but you can still see the scars from where they stitched the dangling strips of his lips back together. He still mumbles "WXXT" under his breath like he is saying "Our Fathers" but has no idea he is doing it. You don't want to hear the radio in your head like the man in the diner or Bobby Marderosian. You brush each tooth thirty-two times every night. It is better to be able to turn it off.

ALL YOUR FATHERS HERE AND GONE

—x x x—

No one thought about Halloween costumes, so they throw together some rags and tell you you will be a hobo. They use makeup from an embalming kit to give you a red nose, but it stings like murder and you have to wash it off. You are out with a few kids from school. Not that you like them that much, but there are only so many of you who like horror movies and comic books. Cast offs and NPCs, all of you. You and Terri, Phin, and Davey. You are careful to evade the houses whose pasts are hushed by adults but talked openly about by children. Likewise, you skip the houses where they give out religious tracts or raisins, and the one on King Street where the soil pipe for the upper floors drains directly into the basement. The smell of sewerage permeates the property and the fourth-grader who lives there. At some point after eleven when all the porch lights are off, you realize there are five of you. You accept this. A straggler among the losers. You know what that's like. He wears a bag on his head, with button eyes and a coat that must belong to his father. He smells of mothballs and doesn't speak and worms fall from his pants legs. You decide that perhaps this is unusual. You are all thinking it and suddenly you decide to ditch him. He runs awkwardly after you, until he trips with a wet splat and the maggots and leeches explode from the coat in every direction, then crawl away leaving trails of putrescent slime that smells of bile and corpse wax. You go back the next day and the coat is gone, but the burlap sack remains, slimy and reeking. A man walking his dog struggles to control it as it whines and pulls away, finally biting him until he lets go of the leash and it runs down the street, to the sound of horns and screeching breaks at the intersection. Phin picks it up with a stick and you carry it to the woods, dump lighter fluid on it and burn it. You watch the maggots squirm as they brown and pop.

—x x x—

HYMNS OF ABOMINATION

Saturday dinner is stewed chicken hearts and gizzards. It was liver the day before, although there is some contention in the household as to whether Ant and Odd get to pick two days a week or one. Ant-Odd. Odd-Ant. You are confused by it. "I wish we could cut him out of there," you tell Lute after he (they?) have stepped away from the table.

"You can't," Lute says. "It's all one thing. Impossible to separate. How would you tell them apart?"

"There has to be a way."

Lute shrugs, pops a gizzard in his mouth and settles his bulk back in his armchair and takes a drag from his cigarette. Crosses his arms across his gut and tells you a story about picking body parts from train tracks and the technical challenge of assembling the puzzle. "Even if you have all the pieces, they're not in any condition to put together cleanly. But, when people refuse advice and insist on an open casket, you do what you can. It's the kindness of the job, you see." Once, you watched him wire a head to a mannequin in order to fill out the casket. Another time, a volleyball for a head, a face drawn on with a magic marker. If the family noticed, no one said anything. You push your organ meats around the plate in the thin grey gravy and consider, but Lute is obviously unwilling to discuss the situation with your other two fathers (or one father) any more.

—x x x—

"You just keep telling yourself that's a fisher cat crying in the woods! It's safer if you can talk yourself into it, but we all know better, you heartless sack of shit! You're listening to WXXT, the voice of the Pioneer Valley. The sheen on your bean, the burnin' in your urine, the psychosis by osmosis, the clots in your cot, the abortion in your portion, the abomination in your vacation, the…what's that Lou? No, I don't smell sulfur. Oh, wait. I'm supposed to do a public safety announcement from the Leeds PD, but what's the point of that? So, we'll be back after these messages from Morentz and Teale Funeral Home, The Ancient and Honorable

ALL YOUR FATHERS HERE AND GONE

Order of Dead Birds Lodge 398, and the Community Meat Marionette Theater, always looking for new participants."

—x x x—

Another Saturday evening. You watched wrestling in the morning and *Creature Double Feature* on WLVI Channel 56 in the afternoon. *Attack of the Mushroom People* and *War of the Gargantuas*. Dinner was some sort of sausage that you could not identify, and you were prepared to not ask questions about them. In the evening, you and Lute watch the Bruins on channel 38. The signal is snowy and you adjust the electric roof antenna with the control dial by the television until he is satisfied. You don't really care about hockey. Sometimes there are fights. Mostly, you plan a Dungeons and Dragons campaign that you would play if you could find people to play with. After the second period, Lute frowns and looks at his watch. Snorts.

"Odd is at The Antler," Lute says. "It's late to be out. Go and tell him it is time to come home."

The sign for the Velvet Antler Bar and Restaurant features a graphic image of a bull moose shedding its velvet in bloody shreds. Dripping, clotting tangles hang from its massive rack like the remnants of a sublime and grotesque crucifixion. The exterior doors are tall slabs of wood with ironwork hinges. Heavy. They yield only with effort, into a dim vestibule and second set of doors. You hear polka music and voices. The smell of cooked meat. The door handle is sticky with an unknown fluid.

You pull open the doors and are confronted by a dizzying scene. The tin ceiling is low and spattered with stains and rust. Candles provide most of the light. Indistinct forms crowd a long bar and carving station. There are booths around the perimeter, but the chairs and tables are piled haphazardly against the back wall and the occupants wander through piled filth on the floor between fires set in oil drums. Slavering, they strip greasy meat from bones with their hands and teeth, dance strange, drunken reels to the sounds of accordion and screaming. Old men with skeletal faces howl and pull their hair in abject agony. These things are not the worst abominations on display, not by any measure. Odd sits stiffly at the bar, a nearly full Manhattan in front of him, hair askew. He is composed and appears oblivious to the chaos and noise around him. His casual sport coat with the patches is dated (you will not think of the leisure suit experiment from the previous decade) but not nearly so much as the old-fashioned long jacket and waistcoat of the man to his left—the side with his good eye. They are having some sort of conversation. It is not tense, but not casual either. There is a certain formality that you can apprehend in it. The man on his right's jaw hangs to his breastbone. He sits unmoving except for the worms pouring from his mouth. Flat, wriggling things, ten to twelve inches long with jaws and spike-like parapodium that pool in his lap and on the floor around the feet of his stool in a growing pile. But this is not the worst.

The music changes without transition or warning and suddenly the Sisters of Perpetual Misery have their leather habits hiked up to their waists and are grinding ecstatically to Frankie Goes to Hollywood. They gyrate and thrust violently on impossible stilettos except for the one on hooves with cigarette burns all over her inner thighs. The one with the hook hand drops a pigeon with broken wings from her cooch and it is immediately swept up and taken to the kitchen. You are transfixed. The nun with raven hair pulls her black leather skirting higher to reveal a scabrous Cesarean scar across her midriff, makes eye contact with you and touches herself and you nearly cream your pants. You can barely see the horrors that surround you. You can barely see anything except the tangled black forest of her sex. Glimpses infiltrate in the periphery of your vision. A man in a business suit lies tied bent over a table with his pants around his ankles and a hood over his head. His buttocks are raw and bleeding. She undulates, strokes the dark tangled thatch of her vulva and eyes you with unspoken and forbidden promises. Young children sit packed in booths, heads lolling on broken necks, eyes stabbed out. She parts the dense thicket, inserts two fingers and beckons. Her overwhelming, unimaginable display, raw and horrifying, fills you with revulsion and desire.

But even this is not enough. The server at the carving station scrapes his rusty jagged knives together over his dubious and familiar cuts of meat and stares at you. He has the eyes and horns of a goat, and a mask-like face. Other things invade your senses. Small rent bodies. Sexual perversities. As the obscenities surrounding you force their way into your perceptions—these and ones infinitely worse—you tear yourself away from the nuns and their terrifying promise of corporeal salvation. You run until your side stitches and you stagger to vomit in the gutter. As you puke, a thing with a massive head like an overripe wheel of cheese emerges from the alley, regards you with its three baleful eyes, and crosses the street whistling an off-key song that sounds like despair.

You return home and tell Lute you could not find Odd.

—x x x—

Mr. Grindley, the math teacher, sets up a media cart with a television and VCR, as he does most days. Today it is about the construction of the Great Pyramids, which is arguably related to geometry. He sits in the back, splayed, shirt untucked, and covered in yellow stains and cigarette ash. A string of bloody mucus hangs from his nose as he snores. No one pays attention to the video and you draw while other kids play "Break Your Finger" or "Hide the Bruise" and make fun of Sarah Gates for her manifold physical deformities or Jared Cleaves who wets himself because of the things his family lets the neighbors do to him at night. The fluorescent lights hum and flicker and are so full of dead flies that they are almost opaque. Occasionally the intercom sputters to life, mostly static, with occasional mumbled curses or orgasmic moaning involving people in various configurations. The Class Treasurer comes through and announces that she is collecting donations. They have found a high school football player who will tackle Mr. Stork, the sadistic gym teacher, right in his colostomy bag at the next track and field meet for a hundred dollars. You have forty cents for lunch, but it seems like a worthwhile investment. Lisa Hirtmann sits passively in the corner while Travis Fell strips off her shirt and gropes her. She began fourth grade with a sudden D cup, and you still remember the way she hunched over her desk with her arms crossed over her breasts while boys tried to worm their fingers in for a feel and the teachers just ignored it all. It took three years for them to break her in, and she'll go to the janitor's closet with anyone now. She says she doesn't care and just goes somewhere else in her head until they finish, but you think she minds.

—x x x—

You and Odd sit at the dining room table. Lute has promised something special for dinner, but the kitchen has been quiet. Odd browses the Weekly and asks indifferent questions about the school day and homework without listening to the answers. The table is a long, dark oak slab, with room for twelve. Your remaining fathers sit at either end, and you along the side, equidistant between them. Ancient china lies in the cabinet opposite your seat, along with an assortment of dusty knickknacks of uncertain provenance. You have never seen the cabinet opened. Dust also lays thick on the chandelier over the table, with threads of cobweb between the dangling crystals. It is late for dinner, and the cold November wind shakes the drafty window panes. The cobwebs drift like seaweed.

Lute lumbers heavily from the kitchen behind Odd and stands beside Odd's chair. You watch as he opens his mouth, jaw unhinging like a snake over Odd's head. Blood runs from the corners of his mouth as his round face distorts and splits to fit and stains Odd's coat. Odd struggles and howls muffled obscenities from inside, but Lute's bulk holds him firm and he forces his mouth wider to envelop Odd's shoulders. His eyes roll back in his head, his gut expanding like a constrictor eating an animal far too large for it. The buttons on his shirt pop off. One hits you in the chest, rattles on your empty dinner plate. He is down to Odd's paunchy belly. The point of his brown paisley tie peeks out. Odd shudders and spasms.

You run.

Up the wide-open front stairs and down the hall to your room. Look around in panic. Smash your piggy bank and grab up the loose bills. Your denim jacket. Backpack. Throw aside Star Wars figures and the Six Million Dollar Man trying to find the notebook with your game and comic book ideas. Down the back stairs.

Lute is in the hallway. His pallid, veiny nakedness touches the walls.

"Where are you going son?"

He expands as he shambles, oozes, toward you, knocking picture frames from their hooks and now dragging along the ceiling as well. A wall of flesh. There is no way past. No escape except to go back up. No. Forward.

You push against his vast pallid gut, slick with perspiration and covered in stretch marks, umbilical herniated and purple. The overwhelming smell of cigarettes and body odor. His mass is suffocating and you can hear Odd and Ant muttering within. He embraces you and you fight and punch with wet slapping noises. And then you push through into a warm, thick, curdled mayonnaise of adipose fat, choking you. Drowning you in smothering thickness. The tangle of intestines, the sound of Odd mumbling geometric proofs and warning you about the perils of more worldly Sophomore girls. His glass eye drifts past you, empty of sentience. You struggle, running out of air. The pounding of Lute's heartbeat like an enormous drum and his cancerous lungs wheezing like a rasp along electric violin strings. Ant advises that this, too, is all your fault. You should give up. The thick resistance of liver, kidneys, spleen, and then a final desperate push that leaves you soaked and gasping behind him as you break free on the other side.

You turn and watch his face slide around from his front to the middle of the vast, spotty bulk of his back, now filling the hallway and spilling into the side rooms. He continues to expand. His bones splinter like wet saplings as he pours into the vents and spaces between the walls and floors, infiltrating the radiator pipes and sewerage lines. You hear the sickening sound of bone fragments grinding together as the horsehair plaster bulges beneath the heavy wallpaper. You run outside, and the entire face of the house appears to be his face until it is only the house again. For a moment you think that you could burn it down. But you know that one day you will want to return.

—x x x—

You run through the park where feral children throw bottles as you pass. They are naked and barefoot, their skin raw and inflamed from bites and flagellation with briars. They scourge the skin from each other in bloody strips and rub nettles and poison ivy in each other's wounds, and eyes, and orifices.

You steal the bicycle that someone got for his birthday last year. Ride as fast as you can through the streets, past the drawn shades with monstrous shadows, the houses with trees pushing through their rooftops, the thousand abominations and crimes of all size and severity that layer every structure in this place. You brave the terrible woods and bare grasping trees, make for the lights of the truck stop on the highway. Ditch the bike when you hit the gravel moat that lines the edge.

Ahead, a massive slab of eighteen-wheelers under lights.

The 24-hour service station.

The smell of carrion from a ditch.

Women and teen boys wander the periphery of the lot, smoking cigarettes, eyeing you over. Their postures change once they get a good look at you and they ignore you. Others walk between the lines of trucks.

Broken glass crunches beneath your feet and the pavement is littered with crushed cigarette packets and used condoms. A trucker cleans the remains of some animal from the spattered grill of his cab. Blood and hide, scraps of black wing.

ALL YOUR FATHERS HERE AND GONE

    The passenger side door of a cab opens and someone spits thickly. A long lanky boy in cowboy boots and jeans emerges and climbs down without speaking or looking back. He's a few years older than you, pale with sunken eyes. You make eye contact briefly and he pushes past you, hitting you roughly with his shoulder.

    There are trucks heading all across the country, or at least to the bus station. You hope that, starting now, everything will be better.

    But you know it won't be.

    Leeds extends a thousand miles in every direction.

    And you will carry it with you no matter what.

HYMNS OF ABOMINATION

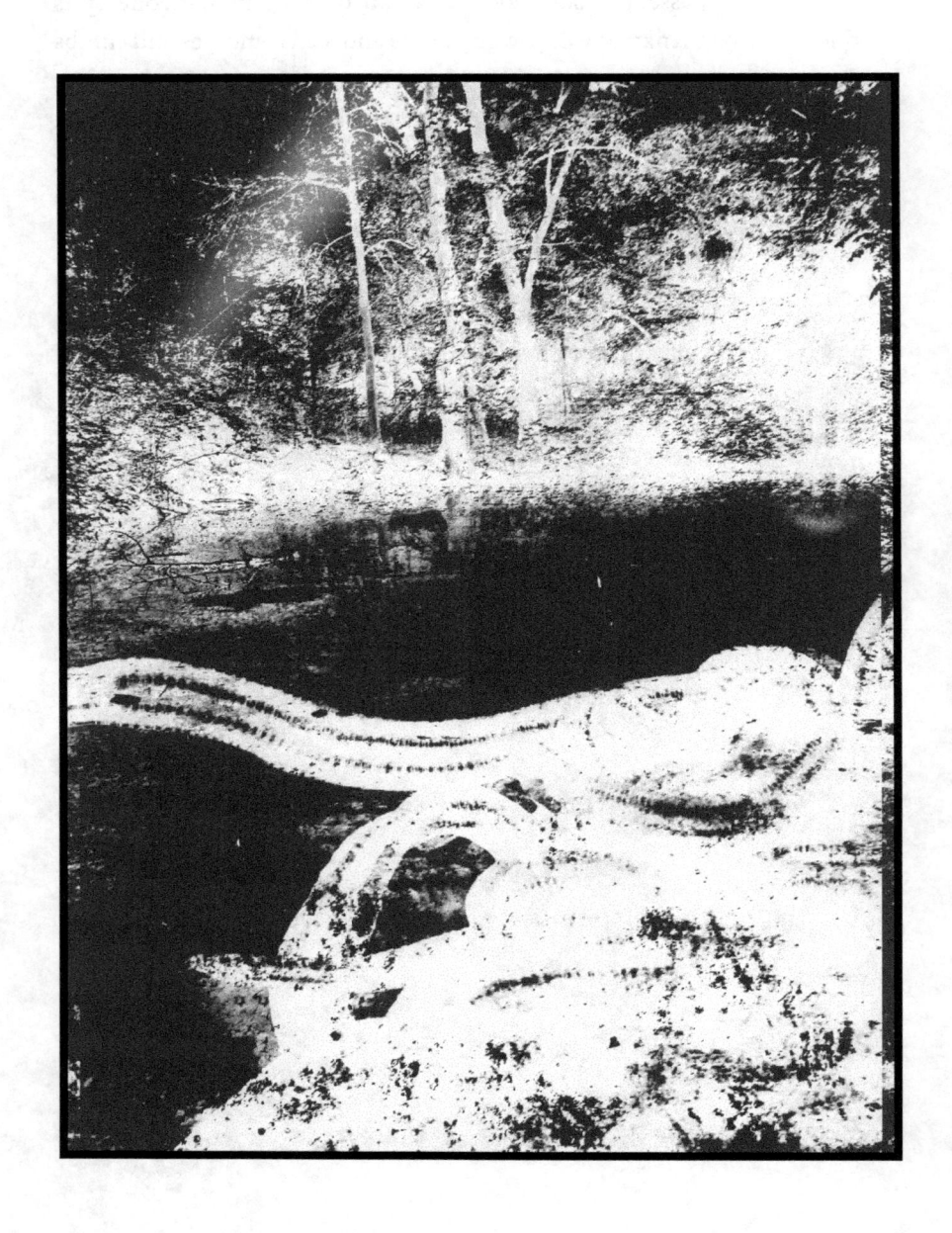

x308x

itemized human sacrifices, q4

Skeletal pines lean in to hear the men speak as they prowl over the dead leaves and worm-riddled dirt of Leeds. The sun is blotted from the sky by encroaching rain clouds, darkness enveloping the businessmen like a living thing, an entity longing to embrace these decrepit specimens as its own. Leopold is panting and heaving his enormous bulk along, wheezing like an asthmatic, sweat and blood alike pouring down his face in a prodigious waterfall of pungent fluids. Ignacious staggers along resolutely with his cane, while Invictus adjusts himself most crudely, grunting with a lascivious mirth as he stares at their captive. Chatham Choronzon, by contrast, practically gambols ahead; his steps are delicate, even dainty, as he traverses the rough terrain with the grace of a dancer.

After half an hour of walking they break for a late lunch. Bartholomew has four packets of baby jerky hidden in the numerous interior pockets of his lined uniform; he distributes them amongst the cohort. Invictus rips into his portion with particular relish. "Ah, this invigorates me anew," he smiles, tearing the meat between his teeth. The wet mastication of gristle slurs his speech. "Nothing like infant flesh to get the blood pumping."

At this point, the boy cradled in Bartholomew's arms utters a single, stifled moan through his duct-tape gag. He stirs, convulsively, in the tall man's arms, then slumps back again. Ignacious watches with interest.

"Sounds like baby blue is starting to wake up." Ignacious turns to Leopold, face still smeared with blood, gnashing the jerky between his teeth. "Say, Frunksplatter, where on earth did you find such a charming specimen?"

"At the country club," mutters Leopold, pink saliva dribbling down his lips. "He served me and Marnie drinks one night. The opportunity of mutilating his pretty little face was too tantalizing to pass up."

"Yes, he'll be a more than suitable offering for our benefactor," Invictus agrees. "And he won't be missed?"

"Missed? Ha! I *paid* his father for him," chortles Leopold. "What's a son compared with a check for seven hundred thousand dollars, a new Bentley, and a Cape house? He practically shoved the wretch into my hands."

"Just like little Annette's mother," smiles Ignacious, lost in the throes of sweet memory. "Do you remember her, fourteen years ago? Our darling Annette? All of twenty, and what a sacrifice to see..."

"My favorite shall always be our first," says Invictus, firmly. "Curtis Gagnon. The night we offered up his towheaded carcass, those thirty five years ago, to our terrible dark deity Cläwneck, I felt for the first time what true power tasted like. The power to beat a secretary to death in front of a full staff without a single soul uttering one word. The influence to bring politicians begging for our favor on their hands and knees, naked, trembling. The wondrous wicked freedom to burn to the ground the houses of anyone who dares to oppose us, to snatch babes from their cribs and stomp them to sanguinary extinction in broad daylight upon the main street, and not see one iota of consequence. And all this for the miniscule price of a single human life every seven years! Yes, my friends," he declares, "upon my honor as a businessman, that is a most judicious bargain indeed."

"Truly, the Cläw is the law," Ignacious affirms, staring wistfully into the trees.

And the other two gentlemen sagely nod in agreement, each reliving their own memory of that fateful day. But before they fall too deep into their nostalgic reveries, Chatham sharply stomps his foot and gestures at the darkened sky: the sun has almost set. The quartet rise and plough forward, their strength renewed, and as they grow nearer to the scene of their celebration, they become almost giddy with excitement. Even Bartholomew has a greater spring in his scraggly step. Only the boy remains unmoved. From time to time his eyelids and fingers twitch, and from his nostrils short bursts of breath cloud the cold evening air.

—x x x—

ITEMIZED HUMAN SACRIFICES, Q4

The clearing is situated at a depression in the land, so that the hills seem to crowd and smother the barren area. About thirty feet wide and fifty feet long, shadowed by a thick canopy of branches, it's situated far enough from any roads or hiking paths to be completely and absolutely secluded. Not a sound could escape that lonely spot; the roads are too far, the woods too thick.

As the six step through the gloom into the clearing, they are met by the orange glow of a bonfire and the panther-like whirring of industrial lights. At the far end a black passenger van is parked, with a ridiculous, cartoonishly airbrushed woman possessing a pair of prodigious breasts on the side of the vehicle. The logo printed above her reads "Shimmyin' Shirley's" in pink script. At the right end, beneath a black banner which reads in red letters "35th Anniversary!," there is a plastic folding table offering muffins, a box of powdered doughnuts, three coffee machines, cocktail shrimp, and bottles of Mad Dog 20/20 in garish pinks and blues.

The left end is altogether different. There lies another table with neatly arranged implements and devices of unclear purpose. A melon baller, a cheese grater, two fondue forks, a car battery with cables, and a meat tenderizer. Upon this table an auburn-haired woman of middle age, dressed in a black robe with red trim revealing an ample amount of cleavage, taps her bright red stiletto press-on nails with an air of disdainful impatience.

"Well, look who finally decided to show up!" she yells, spotting the businessmen, her lips parting to reveal a front tooth made of tarnished gold. Two other women sit in plastic folding chairs by the fire, vaping, in matching pink combat boots, black booty shorts with "Cläw" printed on the ass, and overlarge black t-shirts featuring the very logo airbrushed on the van looming close by.

"There better be a fourth girl, Mildred," spits Leopold. "We're paying you for four."

"Tut, Leopold," says Mildred, sauntering over to him, running a finger down his expansive midsection. "Patience. Of course there's a fourth girl. She's resting in the van. We'll bring her out once we get things started." She smiles lewdly, a fat pink tongue peeking out beneath that golden tooth. "She's one of your favorites, you know."

"Where's the damn podium?" Ignacious demands. One of the seated girls gives him the finger. She exits the light of the fire into the darkness between the trees, and upon her return she slowly pulls a crude wooden podium on wheels and positions it before the blazing bonfire.

"Satan be praised!" cries Ignacious. "We've only done this ceremony for fucking ever, you'd think we could start on time for once!"

"Hey, we ain't the ones who showed up forty-five minutes late!" the other half of the pink combat boot ensemble yells at the wrinkled, black-besuited man.

"Ladies, gentlemen, please!" Mildred says, "That's enough! Let's get this infernal show on the road, shall we?"

"By all means," Leopold says, through a mouthful of donut, crumbs tumbling from his chin in tiny avalanches.

Bartholomew, who has been lurking on the outskirts of the clearing, hands the hogtied boy to the two girls, then scampers back into the woods, taking his leave. The pair of booty-shorted hoofers drag the dazed young man, his head lolling on his chest, up to the altar before the fire. They grab him by his shoulders and feet respectively, count to three, and hoist him onto the platform.

With all the rapidity of a memorized speech, Ignacious begins: "Cläwneck the mighty! Beloved of Lucifer! Servant of Syrach! Idol of all the financiers of the world! We call upon ye, this Tuesday, the twenty-fourth of September, to accept this offering in your infernal name!"

"Evaluate the asset!" incants Leopold. And Ignacious adds in chorus: "Let us know if the exchange rate is sufficient for your infernal acquisitiveness!"

The young women lift the duct-taped young man to a standing position. His knobby knees sway before the heat of the flames. For a moment, the great bonfire flickers purple, then settles back to orange. The girls drop the duct-taped boy from the podium to the ground, and high-five. The boy lies flat on the grass, his polo shirt besmirched by dirt. Suddenly, he emits a brief groan. The assembled participants turn to look at him.

"Took him long enough," Leopold observes. He dabs the still-dribbling blood on his forehead curiously. "I always forget how delicate mortal flesh can be."

"Shall we remove the duct tape?" suggests Ignacious. "We'd be able to understand him."

"And what purpose would that serve?" Invictus shrugs, his eyes coolly regarding the soon-to-be victim. "It's not like he has any voice in the matter."

"But," protests Leopold, wiping his sweaty palms on his belly, "but I should dearly like to hear him scream."

"Au contraire, my dear Leopold," rejoins Invictus, "there is a pleasure in the thought of the scream being stifled, of the asset lacking even a vocal respite from its suffering; that, to my mind, is significantly finer and vastly superior to the vulgar thrill of cheap theatrics. But, Chatham shall have the final say," he concludes, turning to their veiled companion, "it is only right; he *is* C.O.O."

Chatham, his deep-set green eyes glinting, steps over to Invictus and places his gloved hand on his partner's crotch, clearly indicating his preference. Leopold does not dispute the ruling, but, frustrated, whirls around and faces the three women. "Some preliminaries, ladies!" he roars, and stumbles toward Mildred, who receives him in a rough embrace. He starts sloppily sucking at her face, the blood from his head wound spurting into her hair. She cackles, throatily, and starts to undo the buckle of his bulging belt. "Girls!" she calls to the combat boot duo. "Show our other clients a good time, ay?"

Cordially, Invictus and Ignacious turn to the lovely seductresses, politely undoing their belts for them. To return the favor, the girls lift up their baggy black t-shirts, revealing not breasts but the snapping black beaks of octopi. Invictus traces the pink fleshy rim of his girl's beaks, tickling them gently before leaning in for a taste of their pale white tongues, while Ignacious' strumpet lowers her booty shorts to reveal an enormous white mass of pubic hair poofing out from a nearly engulfed g-string. The huge mass of alabaster pubic hair ruffles against Ignacious' face and awaiting open mouth, long strings of the curling tendrils catching in the old man's elongated, jaundiced teeth.

After a few minutes of similarly charming pastimes—punctuated by the nasal moans of Leopold and the hoarse roars of Invictus—Chatham, cock stiff against his black dress pants, claps his hands, indicating the beginning of the ceremony. The girls depart from their lovers, much to Ignacious' despair; as his inamorata exits his embrace he extends one feeble, bereaved hand after her, mewling despondently through a mouthful of pubic hair.

The dames strut over to the boy, who has heretofore been a mute observer of the festivities. They undress him, tugging off his pants, his t-shirt, his underwear, leaving only plain white athletic socks. They haul him to a lone red chair set before the fire and redo his bonds so he is firmly secured. The harlots then make their way to the van, swinging open the back doors. A shape accordions out, all purple-grey flesh, segmented joints and snakelike movement, unfolding like a slinky from its narrow confine.

A disembodied DJ's voice, low and distorted, rumbles above the clearing.

"Ladies and gentlemen, now entering the sacrificial field we have the one, the only: *Haaaagaaaathaaaaa*!"

"I will never understand how he does that," Leoplod says, looking around, baffled.

The shape snaps to full height, ten feet tall at least—bloodstained teeth as long and keen as butcher knives. Her countenance bears the frozen rictus of a cadaver dolled up by the needle and makeup of the mortician. Her blonde hair is peculiarly full, and upon closer inspection one can see there is a wig stitched onto her scalp. The hair falls along her slender grey neck as she tilts her head back toward the sky, emitting a croaky, guttural wail.

At this sight the boy begins thrashing violently against his restraints, showing true fear for the first time.

"Look who's finally decided to join the party!" cackles Invictus, mid-coitus with Mildred against the poorly constructed wooden altar, slapping meat sounds like rotting pork tenderloin swung against an old dead branch. "Don't be afraid, now; you're in a position of privilege. Not many young men can claim to have received a lapdance from the mighty Hagatha!"

A tuneless, feverish jazz score begins its unearthly whine as Hagatha stalks over to the boy's chair. Slowly, sensually, she begins to sway and gyrate in rhythm to the discordant notes. Her buttocks are oddly plump, her immense breasts strangely full; even the young naïf cannot resist the hypnotic spell of this voluptuous physique. His eyes, evincing both revulsion and fascination, follow his monstrous courtesan's massive anatomy along its sickeningly sultry curves and rotations. As Hagatha bends low to gyrate against his crotch, the innocent youth shudders and twitches, and Hagatha giggles in a bizarrely high-pitched tone.

"There you are, boy!" Ignacious cries, pausing from his slobbery tonguing of Mildred's mouth. "Spurt away! Spurt for Cläwneck!"

The sweet youth's eyes roll back in his head and a gentle sigh pushes through the gag. Hagatha withdraws from her boyish patron, looming above the fire, all tensed muscles, teeth, and pale grey skin. Chatham struts over and inspects the young guest's crotch. After a moment, he rises again and signals a firm thumbs-up to his fellows.

Ignacious smiles, rising up from coupling with Mildred. "Darling," he says to his paramour, straightening her clothes out by the altar, "please bring out the sacred gown."

From the van the venerable madam retrieves another oversized t-shirt emblazoned with a *Shimmyin' Shirley's* design, only this one is as white as snow. She drapes it over the boy's head, hanging it on him like a dress, and indeed for all his fairness he could be a comely maiden in her evening shift, save for the pale, wrinkled testicles protruding from the bottom of the garment.

Leopold, ever hasty, emits a grunt. "Enough of this gentleness, now," he states crisply, "it's time we were onto more piquant pleasures," and, gesturing to his co-workers to follow, he walks toward the table laid with curious instruments. As they arrive, each in turn salivates over the neat arrangement of devices, a lecherous glisten in their aged eyes.

Invictus leans over to one of the fondue forks and turns it in his coarse hands. "For starters, I think this will do nicely for me," he announces. "Its lightness, its delicacy, contrasts so neatly with the keen pain it can inspire."

"To hell with your contrast and delicacy," sneers Leopold, "bluntness is what's needed," and he grasps the meat tenderizer with his stubby fingers, weighing it in his sweaty palms as he grins in dissolute contemplation of its possibilities.

The boy, still secured to the red chair, remains very still as Leopold and Invictus advance with their instruments. He inhales deeply through his nostrils, brow furrowed, a look of mortal terror in his wet blue eyes. Next to him, the pink combat-booted girls with the snapping beak breasts stand symmetrically, ready to further subdue him if necessary.

"Now, to work," Leopold says.

Invictus contemplates the boy's scrunched, anxious face for a few silent moments. Then he rams the fondue fork, hard, directly into his ribcage. The boy convulses and emits a muffled, wretched yell. He manages to stand up, wobbling, but unfortunately, Leopold is waiting at his side. In one rapid motion, Leopold whacks the meat tenderizer into the youth's right kneecap. A sound like celery snapped in half, and the boy drops to the ground in agony, wailing through the tape.

"My turn," Ignacious says, carrying the cheese grater as he slowly approaches. Leopold and Invictus hoist the boy back onto the chair, Leopold holding his right shoulder, Invictus securing the left. With terrible purpose, Ignacious pushes back the boy's bangs, grasps the young man's head hard with his wiry fingers, and proceeds to violently rub the cheese grater across the young man's forehead. Bits of pinkish red flesh flake away in tiny strips while the boy bucks and flails. The pieces that plop to the ground squirm, turning into bloody red worms that wriggle toward the fire.

"Well," Ignacious says, "I'm having fun, but this is going a little fast, don't you think? Cläwneck prefers a deliberate pace."

"Yes, and a trifle more ceremony," admits Invictus. "We've been a bit too eager to get to the bodily emissions, I fear."

"'Pace,' 'ceremony,' get over yourselves," snarls Leopold. "This is transactional. We're delivering payment in exchange for goods. No need to be fancy about it. Now," Leopold says, having picked up the melon baller, "what on Earth am I even going to do with this?"

"If you put enough force…oh, let me just show you," Ignacious says, snatching the instrument from the fat man.

Ignacious drives the melon baller into the flesh of the boy's left thigh, leans with all his weight until the spoon breaks the skin, and proceeds to dig out a perfectly shaped crimson ball of bloody flesh, dusted with light brown hairs. The boy howls. Ignacious throws the chunk of bloody meat into the air, and catches the flesh ball in his open mouth, chewing hungrily.

By the time Leopold is done, the youth is missing tiny circular hunks of his flesh from his other thigh, his right buttock, his left bicep, and the shin of his left leg. The boy appears woozy, eyes fluttering, head dipping low as if he's about to pass out. Ignacious slaps his forehead, tiny bits of his own putrid flesh sticking to the boy's wounds.

"Time to start wrapping this up," Ignacious yells. "Everybody strip!"

In a flurry of discarded vestments—suits, dresses, robes and booty shorts all—the participants disrobe. A mass of wrinkled and sagging flesh is shortly exposed to the horrified gaze of the young man. Even Chatham begins to peel off his clothes, although his face remains ever-concealed behind his black scarf and hat. But oh! What a frightful body lies beneath those executive garments! Dry and desiccated as a mummy, covered in the wounds and scars of a burn victim, his arms are as thin and brittle as a skeleton's, his rib cage visibly taut beneath charred, brown skin. Only his leathery ass has substance and shape; the rest is so scorched and worn away it might as well belong to a corpse. Beneath his grotesquely protuberant pelvis, swinging idly between his legs, hangs a worm-like cock of narrow girth but monstrous length, still dripping from its earlier onanistic indulgences. From behind the scarf, his green eyes flicker with the perverse glee of an exhibitionist.

"Come now, mesdames," Invictus says, whispering to the two young ladies, "fetch your beau." In perfect unison, they grab the young man by the shoulders, dragging him up to the podium. As his shattered knee makes contact with the hard surface of the wood, he emits an anguished, gurgling wail. One of the girls holds his arms down. He begins to resist, so Leopold walks over to duct tape his arms together.

Invictus approaches with an iron hatchet. "Here goes," he murmurs drolly to himself, raising the heavy leaden instrument directly above his head. In a single motion, he brings it smashing down onto the young man's right wrist. The blow severs muscle from bone. Squirting blood, the boy faints again from the pain. Invictus continues to clumsily hack until the hand is set free. Then, he moves onto the left wrist. Several more gory swings and the other hand is cut clean. Mildred collects the hands from the grass where they have fallen and tosses them into the flames, screaming "FOR CLÄWNECK!" with her distinctly theatrical flair.

Ignacious, rather bored with these childish frivolities, regards the boy with an air of bemused curiosity. "Look," he calls to Invictus, who begrudgingly stops sucking Mildred's nipples.

The boy is stirring in his place on the podium. His eyes don't seem to see at all; they roll about, aimlessly, without focus. His face is alarmingly pale.

ITEMIZED HUMAN SACRIFICES, Q4

"Boy!" calls Ignacious, and the youth's head lazily swivels in his direction. Ignacious smiles warmly. "You're free to go now, if you'd like." A pause, and then: "We won't stop you."

The boy stares dumbly at the pair of them, seemingly uncomprehending. Then, miraculously, with an enormous effort, the young man manages to hop down from the pulpit and land on one of his still working legs. He slowly gets to his feet, hobbles a few paces, then pauses, swaying as if drunk.

"He's making a good go of it," remarks Invictus.

The young man takes a few more steps, stumbling almost to the edge of the clearing. Then he collapses into the dirt.

"Why what's wrong, son? I thought you would want to leave?" Ignacious calls.

The young man struggles and strains, inching through the dirt like a worm. Invictus stands before him when the boy stops moving just before the tree line.

"I guess he wants to stay," shrugs Ignacious.

"A valiant effort. The big one please," Invictus says, motioning to Leopold, who walks over with a cartoonishly oversized ax.

The boy looks up silently; he doesn't even move. Invictus swings the huge ax down and swiftly severs the boy's feet from his legs. He convulses once but doesn't scream. Chatham grabs the severed feet and carries them to the fire.

"We beseech thee, Cläwneck!" Ignacious bellows, "accept these, in your name!"

The severed feet are thrown into the flames. A moment's pause, and the fire turns black. Everyone applauds

"Alright, main event," sighs Ignacious, who at this point is rather tired. "Ladies, grab the Unspooler."

Mildred and the girls head to the back of the van and begin unloading a strange, wooden contraption; it's enormous, situated on large truck wheels, with a huge wooden stake as thick as a telephone pole protruding from the center. Chatham grabs a line of rope, which he feeds into a metal rod hammered into a sturdy oak tree. There is a mechanical contraption attached to the tree and rod resembling an enormous fishing reel.

    Chatham hoists the young man from the ground, still bleeding profusely, and places him beneath the wooden pole. The pink-booted strippers use strong leather clasps to secure his arms and torso to the wooden stake. Chatham claps his hands twice, signaling everyone to take their place. Once all is ready, the offering begins.

    "Chatham, slice open his belly," Invictus says, with a flourish.

    Chatham takes a bowie knife and slices open the boy's abdomen. Guts spill from the wound's pink lips.

    "Attach the other end of the Unspooler to this fellow's intestines, Invictus," Ignacious says.

    Invictus does just this. He fetches the fishing reel-like hook and unceremoniously swings it into the dying boy's bowels.

    "Let the Unspooling commence!" intones Invictus, his manner a little forced. Then, with more vigor: "For Cläwneck!"

    "For Cläwneck!" the rest yell in unison.

    Mildred flips the switch on the machine attached to the tree, and the rope begins to pull, the young man's guts unspooling, foot by foot, over the fire. There the taut intestines singe and scorch like cooking sausage. The celebrants observe it rather impassively; the best parts are over, and they've seen this all before. At this stage, all the disemboweled boy can do is tremble. Blood spurts from his nostrils and drips from the edges of the tape covering his mouth. With a final paroxysm, his eyes roll back into his head, and he is gone. Strapped to the pole, he looks like a broken doll.

    There's a lull as Chatham makes sure the intestines are fully stretched. Then: "Is this to your liking, Cläwneck?"

    "Cläwneck says this is totally wicked!" the disembodied strip club DJ voice says from nowhere.

    There is polite applause. The guts char and catch fire over the black flame, falling to the ground in clumps. Soon, the viscera begins to coil in the heat, transforming into crude, fleshy dolls. Still alight with obsidian tongues of flame, the humanoid creatures begin to dance around the fire. After some time, the tiny dolls break from the circle of flame and dance off into the forest.

As soon as the last doll vanishes in the tree line, the dead boy begins to buck against the restraints. Chatham unties him, and the corpse floats into the dark sky above, eventually disappearing into a mass of shadowy clouds.

Mildred and the girls turn to the old men.

"The money, gentlemen," Mildred says coldly, suddenly all business.

"Yes, yes," Invictus sneers, grabbing a large wad of sealed hundred dollar bills from his pocket. The rest of the men stack their money in Mildred's awaiting hand.

"Thanks for your patronage, as always," Mildred says bluntly. Then she and the girls quickly pack themselves into the van and drive back into the unknowing strangeness of the woods of Leeds.

"Well, my fellows," remarks Invictus, "here's to another successful year." And they shake hands, smile, and affectionately rub each others' cocks. But they are all tired, and they sigh once the niceties are done. They have been doing this for so long, and they are so very old.

The board of Leeds grabs coffee and donuts from one of the tables. The caffeine livens them, the sugar invigorates them. Chatham, as is his habit, paces over to the fire, still carrying his donut and coffee in each hand. He regards it brightly, almost tenderly, and then squats beside it and quivers out a rotting pile of feces. White maggots worm their way out of it and disappear into the grass. The pile of shit grows a host of tiny insectile legs and begins rooting through the leaves in search of food.

"Okay, gentlemen," Invictus announces. "Which one of us shall fill out the paperwork?"

HYMNS OF ABOMINATION

what am i?

This is a place where the dead should be still. It's a place where things last far too long, climbing up from charnel graves and into the blistering howls of long winter nights.

I turn myself into the maelstrom and slow beneath flickering yellow street lamps. The village is unnerving in its stillness. Bone-colored trees break and snap in its ice and wind.

I have been here before, when every home was made of wood and orange-red leaves fell upon the dirt. I was here in the winter of 1654, when this ground was first bloodied with a ritual made in the honor of a colder, darker place. Before the people were wise enough, before they had learned to lock their doors and shutter their windows in fear of the rot they had drawn from the dirt, I was here. When the town was a tempest, a place of swirling fire and constant dying, I was here.

Now the town is dark, quiet, silenced by the storm I ride.

I walk the streets alone, surveying the new buildings and sidewalks that have cropped up since my last secret visit. I expect to find no one, this weather too hostile even for the bravest New Englander.

But, to my delight, I find one man. One man, walking along with some greasy brown bag in his hands. One man, gaunt and shaking with cold and age alike. He turns to me, eyes milky-white green even in the night.

He should have expected what happens next. After all, what fool goes out into the middle of a snowstorm for *burgers*?

I dig my fingers into him, ride his veins and blacken his blood. I look into his eyes and he knows me. Through choking coughs and pink spittle, he *knows me*. Because he is *one of them*, the initiated hundreds who guard the deeper Leeds.

Not a *fool* at all, but a *watchman*.

The burger bag falls to the ice as my fingers work their way through his mouth. I wiggle them inches away from my face, marveling and giggling at the webbed liquid between them.

HYMNS OF ABOMINATION

And I smile.

I leave the felled sorcerer a mass, a pile of spent bones and steaming innards.

I walk a little farther into town, into the biting frost of this blasphemed place.

The dirt beneath the snow is diseased and desecrated. I scoop my hands into it and the maggots are fat, wriggling like so many profane fruits. I bring one to my mouth and bite, letting the juice split across my teeth and tongues.

Awful. Acrid. Birthed from spoilt dirt entirely beyond redemption.

They brought their grudges to this country, those thieves and murderers, those simple things who found holiness in blasphemy. Oh sure, there are "innocent" people here, but most of them pretend not to notice. Just as *you* may walk past a fight between children, just as *you* hear a scream and only wonder *for a moment* if you should call the police before nervously resuming your reading.

But then, the fact that these "innocents" are here, harboring their grudges and celebrating their rot, means so very little to me.

Behind closed doors, one of those "innocents" lies sleeping.

I will do to him what his fathers have done to this world.

My long legs rise to the ice-sleeted roofs as so many shadowy, spidery tendrils. I crane my face upward, into the shuttered window of some coughing child's room. I slip through the seal and listen for his dreams.

His room is dark and messy, strewn with stuffed bears and plastic soldiers. He is soft-faced, an angel sleeping through the roaring storm outside. But there is a monster across his bed, a curled dragon breathing fire at some gallant knight.

The child is even *dreaming* of *dragons*.

And so I sing a song of *dragons*.

In the morning, the child will grow scales. He will sprout little bloody wings, spastic flapping things that will stain his room with red

WHAT AM I?

spatter as he weeps like a bleating chicken. His teeth will sharpen in his mouth, tearing his gums and ripping his tongue. Its mind will narrow and drown in its own screams. The parents will attempt to take it to the hospital. But what doctor would know what to do?

I picture the bleeding thing, pale and shimmering scales beneath pink-red blood, and I know it will be *hilarious*.

I leave the child to his nightmares, to the flames already singing and blistering the top of his mouth. From the top of the house I can see the forest, the sacred seat of this place's unholy power. I lift myself into the air, letting the ice tear across my faces. I rise higher, delighting in the whimpers of the child growing louder and more panicked below.

The city is pock-marked with dying lights, jaundice-yellow lightbulbs peeking out from houses where men and women strip themselves of their flesh and play with the pulsing truth beneath. I rise higher, sickened and intrigued by the fetid odors wafting so high above the winter wind.

I lift my feet from the snow and ride the wind, soaring over the corpse-finger branches of the trees. For an innumerable eternity, it is peaceful. Calm. Exactly what any town should be.

And then I see the Little Ones.

Their settlement deep in the woods, a sprawling camp of tents orbiting around an infernal fire. I see them dancing, stained and red with raw, unidentifiable meat at their lips. Impure, wicked things that they are. Perhaps they, more than anything else, represent the inescapable permanence of what has been done here.

I free-fall and sprout black wings wider than the night sky. I drum them against the wind, inspiring fear in the hearts of Little Leeds, a fear these awful children have never known before.

They see me and cry out in fury.

In horror.

I make sure they see my grins.

My thousand rows of teeth. My burning, swirling eyes.

Their black-and-red tents crumble as my talons dig deep into the bonfire at the center of their camp. The savory smell of my own flesh curls up as my shadow-arms shoot out, ripping their little homes like so many stained sheets of paper.

A man (god?) emerges from the woods. He invokes a terror in me, and in that terror I snap his body between one of my many jaws. His gore tastes of copper wires, sparking along my tongue in electric hums. Languidly, he casts his eyes to a few of mine, and I know that even dying disinterests him.

My jaws meet in his middle and I split him in two, hot and sparking gore pouring out between my fangs.

Around me, the horrors of Little Leeds scream, the corrupted fruit of their great-great-great grandfather's consequences. They're quicker work than the man from the forest, who's spent torso is already worming itself back together.

When the ground beneath them is as red as their canvas homes, I rise once again into the air.

And there they are.

The leeches have grown wings like my own, batting against the snow and crying out in the voices of sobbing priests and terrified nuns. Throbbing, purple things as wide and long as a man's arm dig their teeth into me. They wrap around my arms, my wings. They bind and bite me, forcing me to the earth. I crash against the trees. The trunks break off, stabbing and ripping me to shreds.

The leeches burrow into me, bringing a cold that pulses from my own heart.

I will not survive this.

But, I was never meant to.

They're finally before me.

They emerge from between the trees. Some are tall, gaunt things reaching the top of the forest ceiling. They wear flowing black robes that beat against the storm, white faces stretched tight by the bovine skulls beneath their pale skin. Others are hulking men and women,

WHAT AM I?

wide shoulders and stained thrift-clothes hanging tight to their tumorous, acne-scarred forms.

But above all of them is Stockton.

Stockton, whose smile will crack the world open.

He reaches for one of my faces. His touch is crawling, one million writhing movements at once. His voice is soothing, the sweetest song I've ever heard.

But in his eyes, in those brown-yellow eyes I see his concern. His fear.

"What are you?"

"What am I?"

I tell Stockton.

I tell him that he was wrong to imagine that he would go unnoticed. That the *only rule* for his kind was that they *must stay dead once dead.* He could have been an emperor in hell, a greater daemon in the fire than he could ever be on Earth. The ritual had only furthered this perverse carnival, only made its lights and sounds brighter.

I warn Stockton that he has *not* gone unnoticed. The wheezing warlocks of Dunnstown, witches along the other, far coast of this massive nation. The Stone Mother, moving through her dark web-catacombs beneath the earth. The antlered men. The White Woman who walks the water. The Winged Queen of the mountains. The bellowing gods of the salt marshes.

They've all *seen you*, Stockton.

They've seen you and *they know what you are.*

"What am I?"

I am warning shot. I am an emissary and an omen.

I am *laughing.*

HYMNS OF ABOMINATION

x328x

Anne Gare's Rare and Import Video Catalogue
October 2022

Jonathan Raab

"A Black Triangle Appears in the Sky Over Whispering Pines, MA" — Dir. Unknown Private Aerospace Security Contractor, 2015

An all-too-brief digital recording, captured on a DSLR held in shaking hands by a man whose breathing and vulgarities of shock and surprise are the only accompanying soundtrack to the sound of the wind moving through the trees. As soon as we get a sense of the scene—a dark, ominous sky with distant, grey stars peeking through the forest canopy—an object arrives at the edges of the break of the lush pine branches: black and purple and terrible, seeming to glow darkly in some impossible, inverse, negative-film way. It is sleek and angular and decidedly synthetic, and to any viewer with a modicum of self-preservation instinct, it will not inspire wonder, but *fear*. It is the triangular, dread disc-obelisk of the truly unknown. It is a passing wraith of extradimensional menace that perhaps you have seen before, that recalls suppressed childhood memories of being drawn to stand under the gaze of the wide and terrible night sky, that enveloped you in a beam of anti-light and drew you into its waiting portal, a maw that consumed you and returned you an hour later, with no memories or explanation, but a change in your flesh, a new marking on your arm or leg or neck or behind your ear, and unseen changes to your physiology, to your mind, *to your very essence*, held within.

MP4 video file on USB flash drive, excellent.

Twenty-two dollars.

HYMNS OF ABOMINATION

x330x

leaving leeds

On the way out of Leeds you travel south perhaps a dozen miles until a stray comment that you think you catch on WXXT as the signal fades in and out makes you aware that your stove might be on, that you might have *left* your stove on, that your house might, right at this very moment, be filling with billowing smoke, the windows shattering from heat, the flames creeping up cedar-shake walls. This is no common house. This is the house that used to belong to your mother before you killed her with an axe and buried her in the four corners of the basement earlier this summer. And so you turn around and head back.

      You almost got out that time, you really almost did. As you drive back, you wonder why the radio keeps turning itself on, even when you have very deliberately turned it off. Why do you keep hearing it, even after you tore the speakers out from where they were lodged in the side panels and buried them down in the basement alongside your mother? And why does it seem like the voices from WXXT are louder when your mouth is open as opposed to when it is closed and why does your mouth keep dropping open no matter how hard you try to keep it closed? There are, no doubt, more questions, but as you drive and the signal grows stronger, your mind goes hazy and you find yourself forgetting them. Soon, all you can hear is the secret voice of Leeds whispering sweet nothings in your ear, with the emphasis all on the nothing.

      And then, abruptly, without quite knowing how it happens, you are back at your house—or rather at your mother's house, because once again her hands have dug themselves out of the cellar floor, gathered the rest of her, and laboriously sewn herself back together. She is in charge again. You make a mental note to sever and burn her fingers next time so you can have some peace. She is sitting at the kitchen table, leaning at an odd angle in her chair, and you know she would probably fall over if she wasn't so stiff and if the slick, single-eyed worms that have taken up residence within her weren't so muscular and sinuous. Probably it would do no good to sever her fingers. Probably the worms would figure out a way to squirm her out of the ground anyway. Probably better to just let her wander the house dead: if you keep on cutting up her body, eventually the worms are going to get tired of living in what's left of your mother and decide it's time to come live in you.

Of course the stove isn't on. Of course the house isn't on fire. And now that the radio is no longer playing, you realize. *What would it matter if it was?* You were leaving. You were never going to come back: why not let it all burn? Once again, WXXT has tricked you into coming back.

You stand there, looking at your mother, warily. "Hello, mother," you finally say.

Her empty face creaks toward the sound. Her sockets are eyeless, her face still encrusted with dirt. She doesn't say anything. She just smiles. You think it's a smile, anyway. What else would it be? Her tongue that is not a tongue moves in a slow rhythmic pattern as if tasting her lips, leaving a viscous mucosal coating behind. You catch glimpses of other tongues behind it in the darkness of her mouth. Her hand suddenly jerks out and you see it has been attached wrong side up. It heavily thumps the splat of the chair beside her, inviting you to sit down.

You do not sit. Instead you go to the kitchen to fetch a knife.

As you reenter the room the radio turns on suddenly, the volume blaring. *This is WXXT coming at you from the nadir of the dial*, you hear, but after that it's hard to make out what is said: it is felt more than heard, the sound coming in bursts, pummeling you like surf. You can see your father now—the man your mother claimed was your father—standing near the old lacquered Fonovox Kobold radio set. The front plate of the radio glows, its light pulsing brighter and darker, which is strange because you know it isn't made to glow, but it is glowing all the same.

Your father, truth be told, is both there and not there. His outline becomes firm and sharp, then the sound recedes and he becomes blurred again until can see through him and he almost isn't there. But here he comes again, roaring back. You can smell the cordite in the air, even though you fired that gun days ago. The hole, just left of center in his forehead, slowly trickles a line of blood so dark it's almost black and you suspect if you could get him to turn around you'd find the back portion of his skull to be gone, a slurry of blood and brain dripping onto the back of his collar. You also suspect that if you were to tear yourself away and climb the stairs, your father would be up there as well, lying on the floor in the room where you shot him, his corpse beginning to liquefy and become part of the carpet.

The jangling of the radio dips briefly and your father turns transparent. You can see through every part of him except for the fillings of his teeth which stud the air like nailheads. You shake your head to clear it and try to shake your leg out of the grip of your mother who, without you realizing it, has left her chair and crawled across the floor to take hold of you. To get free, you have to hack her hand off, and even then the hand still clings to your pantleg, a black ichor oozing from both it and the stump of her arm. She just smiles. You can see the worms again, blunt heads flicking in and out of the surface of her stump. For a moment you work to pry the fingers of the severed hand free but then, instead, hack off the cuff of your pants and rush for the door before the music can get loud again.

It is only once you're out, off the porch and scurrying down the driveway toward your car that you realize you've left your keys behind. In your head you can picture them lying on the kitchen counter where you must have dropped them when you chose your knife. You turn and start back toward the house, but you can hear the sound of the radio so loud through the door that the door itself is vibrating. If you go back in, you know, you probably won't be coming out again.

You'll have to walk your way free of Leeds.

Better that way, you think. *No radio.* You set off down the street, hands deep in your pockets, knife slid into your belt, keeping your head down, trying your best not to be noticed. In your head you picture the map: a mile or so to the courthouse, then a mile and a half through to the other side, to where the road takes a long curve skirting the county border. Then you can take a shortcut through the woods and that'll speed things up a little, let you get outside of town limits before dark, or pretty close anyway.

But by the time you get to the edge of the woods, you think *What sort of fool am I?* And the answer, you know, is the sort of fool who knows better than to take a shortcut through the woods. That's where the broadcast comes from, somewhere in there—you're not sure where exactly, but you know it's in there. Even here, on the shoulder, you can sense it, almost hear it. If you hear it, you'll be sunk. Standing there staring at how the darkness gathers just a few feet in among the branches, and then gets darker, and darker still, you realize you cannot bring yourself to go through the woods.

And so, you continue down the road, following its gentle curve out of town. Cars pass you, some slowing before roaring away. A truck comes close enough to clip your hand, making it sting even though the truck's not going all that fast, making you stumble into the gravel.

A sheriff's car pulls up and shadows you for half a minute. You tell yourself no, you're not going to look over, you'll just keep walking. But, in the end, the act of not looking and imagining what's in the car feels worse than seeing what's actually there. When you do look, it proves to be two officers who at first glance seem ordinary, and then you see that their staring eyes are all whites, no pupil, with a glaucous sheen. You look quickly away, heart pounding. A moment later they speed off and you're left wondering why they're letting you go. *Because*, the cynical part of you tells the rest of you, *they know you can never really get away*.

And yet, by the time darkness falls, by the time the red moon starts to slice its bloody path across the sky, you've made it. You've successfully passed the signs warning that you're exiting Leeds, have hopped over the small fence made of the polished thighbones of children. You've even passed the dead and chained old man with the paralyzed face who incessantly waves the stump of his arm, some teenage vandals having no doubt cut off the hand itself. He makes a gurgling noise as you sidle past, trying not to get too close to him but trying also not to get too close to the road and, above all, not too close to the edge of the forest. And then you are free.

Your feet are blistered, your legs aching, but you're jubilant. You're free! You're also hungry, starving even. You haven't, you realized, had anything to eat today, maybe nothing for a few days.

You keep walking.

There are no cars on the road, maybe because so few people ever leave Leeds and even fewer ever visit. After a while, you realize that every other streetlight is either turned off or burnt out. And then, perhaps a quarter mile farther along, the light poles vanish entirely and it's just you tramping along in the darkness, shivering a little as it grows colder, just you and the sound of your soles against the gravel.

You walk for perhaps an hour, perhaps two: who can say? You took your watch off when you first chopped up your mother so you wouldn't get blood on it or break it and you forgot to put it back on. How many days ago was that? Why did it seem so important at the time not only to kill her but to cut her body up and bury it in the four corners of the cellar? Now, alone in the darkness and the silence, miles from Leeds, you have a hard time remembering, but you know it felt right at the time.

And then, far ahead, you see a glimmer of light. At first you think it might be a solitary car, making its way toward you, but it doesn't get bigger fast enough to be that. And, after a while, as you keep walking, you realize the light's the wrong shape for a car, and the wrong color too. You squint and keep walking and soon the road curves a little and you see where the light is coming from: a glowing sign over a building just off the side of the road.

Wu's Noodles and Blues, the sign says. It's a place you've never seen before, despite having driven down this road earlier today. Maybe you didn't notice it because you were in a hurry to get out of town. Maybe you were hunched over trying to turn off your already disconnected but somehow still broadcasting radio as you passed. Or maybe, somehow, you're on a different road than you thought you were. Or maybe, just simply, in daylight there wasn't anything to notice: without the glow of the sign the place might be mistaken for a deserted building. But it's clear it's not deserted now: several dozen cars are in the gravel lot. You're hungry, you're tired: you want a bite to eat, maybe a drink, a little rest, before you continue on. You're out of Leeds, you tell yourself, you're over the border: you should be safe. So, you push open the brushed metal door and make your way in.

It's warm inside, and moist, like walking into a room that holds an indoor pool. Just inside the door is a black velvet curtain, thick and plush. A man in a tuxedo stands before it, behind a podium, and when you enter he raises his finger to his lips. You come in and close the door behind you and then look for a way through. But when you try to sidle around him and pass through the curtain, he straight-arms you.

ID, he whispers, but you can't see his lips move. You're well past the age when anyone should be asking you for ID, but you fumble your driver's license out anyway and give it to him.

He stares at it for a long time, frowning. You lift out your hand for him to return the card but he doesn't seem to notice, just keeps staring, and finally you let your hand drop.

You from Leeds? he whispers at last.

You hesitate, then nod—you are from Leeds, even if you're never going back.

As soon as you nod, he returns the card to you and parts the curtain. With a little shove, he sends you stumbling through.

It's dark on the other side. You stop, waiting for your eyes to adjust. When they do, you realize you're at the back of a large room, soaked in darkness except for, at some distance away, a stage. The stage is dark too, only not quite as dark as the rest of the room, and you can see the vague hint of figures standing on it, motionless, as if ready to perform.

You look for a place to sit, making your way between the round tables, but they all seem full. In the darkness, you can see the forms of bodies in the chairs but you can't see heads turning toward you, eyes looking at you. The only noise is the noise your feet make swishing across the concrete floor.

At last you spot a table right near the front, just inches from the stage. Not empty, no, but with one seat not taken. It may be the last seat in the house.

Half-crouched, worried that the show will start at any moment—are they waiting on you? they can't be waiting on you, can they?—you make your way there. You clear your throat but the woman doesn't look away from the stage. It's like she's frozen. You bend down, just behind her, and whisper in her ear: "Is this seat taken, Miss?"

She still doesn't speak, but her hand jerks out and awkwardly pats the back of the other chair at the table, inviting you to sit. And so, a moment after she withdraws her hand, you do.

You sit and wait for a waiter to arrive to take your order, for the music to begin. You've always liked the blues. The dim glow from the stage grows slightly stronger, but still the figures don't move. None, you suddenly realize, are holding musical instruments. They are not, in fact, holding anything at all.

A moment later the lights blaze fully up and you wonder how you ever could have mistaken the figures for human in the first place. There's the fur, for one thing, and the fact that the appendages are neither the right number nor bend in the usual way. Some of them have more than one head and others have no heads at all. You can't stop yourself from counting, to see if the total number of heads add up to the total number of bodies, but every time you reach the end of the count, it seems as though one more figure has appeared on the stage.

Then the ones that have heads open their mouths wide enough to split the flesh of what can loosely be called their faces and the broadcast begins.

You tear your gaze away from the stage and stand, knocking your chair over. The lights in the house are rising too, and everybody seems to be looking at you. You recognize neighbors and friends and relatives, people you've seen on the street, the two officers you saw earlier, the ice cream man, the used bookstore owner, the butcher. It's as if all Leeds is here tonight, here for the show. The woman at your table looks unsettlingly like your mother, you realize—at least during those brief moments when she looks like anyone at all. You wonder if you were to make the mistake of looking again at the stage would you see someone up there who is a dead ringer for your father?

You try to cover your ears with your hands, but it's too late. The broadcast is already too far along, has wormed its way too deeply into your skull and is busily jimmying door after door of your soul.

The broadcast extrudes itself from the mouths on the stage, each a little out of sync with the others. And then it is coming out of your own mouth as well, and your head is turning of its own accord and you are staring at the stage and there, in the middle of the stage, warbling into a 1940's Unidyne microphone, is Ben Stockton of WXXT, broadcasting live.

You listen, because you can do nothing else. Already you can hear the words squirming within you, hollowing you out, making room for them to breed. Eventually, you know, the show will come to an end. Eventually, the night will come to an end as well, and you'll have to go home to Leeds.

But then the transmission sharpens and you realize that, no, you're already home. In a very real way you never even left.

father ezekiel shineface sermon hour (after david wilkerson's hell, what is it like?)

I tell you, it's something isn't it? Brothers and sisters, I'm going to talk about the thing gospel preachers hate to talk about more than anything else. I'm going to talk about hell this evening. Gospel preachers hate to talk about it; gospel preachers, a lot of them, don't even believe in hell anymore. They say how can a God of mercy and love send anyone into an eternal fire?

Let me explain to you good people what hell is going to be like.

There was a little boy who lived in Leeds, where I grew up. His name was Amos. Little Amos was in our church congregation, and he was mocked for his beliefs by a bunch of tough kids, you know the type. Well, one day he was out in the barn behind his house praying, and those tough kids came in there and started taunting and mocking him, and soon they were grabbing and beating him. A lamp got knocked over, and the barn caught fire.

Little Amos ended up with burns over ninety percent of his entire body, just in pain like you wouldn't believe, unending pain. But that's nothing compared to what happened to those other kids. Almost all of them died horribly in that fire, eventually, and little Amos, he told me that once he escaped, badly burned but not dead, he saw one of those bully boys running out of the barn, literally on fire, and that boy ran right up to Amos. This boy, his ears were burned off, his nose was gone. Everything. His head was nothing but charcoal. And what do you think that burnt shell of a boy said to Little Amos? Did he cry out, "Jesus, save me?" Or, "I beg forgiveness for mocking your belief, little Amos?" No, not at all. Little Amos, he said that the boy, still smoking and burnt coal black, asked, "Is my nose okay?" Then that boy fell down in a heap, dead, his spirit bound to hell.

Little Amos himself spent the whole rest of his life in the greatest physical pain, but he never lost his faith till the day he died, many years later. I remember on his death bed, on his way to Glory, little Amos

jon padgett

said to me, "Father, they gave me morphine and laudanum and alcohol, everything, to deal with the pain of my burns, but none of it ever worked. I felt it all, every second of it, for decades, and, Father, I know better than I ever did before that there's a hell. Hell is real."

Hell is real.

Hell is a kingdom of total darkness. Endless night. No sun. That's hell, brothers and sisters. Eternal darkness. A darkness created by God. Forever. Brothers and sisters, it's beyond all human reasoning. We can't imagine it. Thick darkness like they experienced in Moses' day in Egypt. But an eternity of it. A literal darkness.

But you say to me, Father Shineface, what about all the hellfire? There's hellfire, and that casts light, right?

No, brothers and sisters. Hellfire casts no light. It is what God calls outer darkness. There is a fire without light. Imagine a lake of fire casting darkness, not light. That's what it is.

Sinners like those bully boys in that barn will be cast into outer darkness. Burning in blackness.

Some people say hell will be in the heart of this earth, but it won't. It's a different planet entirely—a hell planet cast into an outer cosmos. Away from all light, into outer darkness. Drifting further and further away from God.

And I'll tell you something else you don't know about hell. Those in hell have a kind of eternal knowledge that everything that once gave them cheer is gone forever. You may think that this hell planet is a world filled with the worst of the worst: child molesters and dictators and the worst transgressors. Nothing and nobody but the ungodly, but you're wrong.

It is true, though, that men and women prefer darkness. God knows this, and can you imagine His wrath at this knowledge? Men and women prefer darkness, and it is the Devil—not God—who they most believe in. And I'm here to tell you that hell is worse than being *abandoned* by God. It isn't the Devil who rules there. God Himself will punish the damned. The vengeance of God, the flaming black fire, everlasting

FATHER EZEKIEL SHINEFACE SERMON HOUR

destruction at the hands of the Lord. *Vengeance is mine*, sayeth the Lord. *He* will repay sin. That task is not in the hands of Lucifer, oh no. Lucifer is going to be occupied with his own torment, day and night. The Devil is the punished—not the punisher. God will be hell's jailor.

Can you imagine it? No, I'm here to tell you, you can't.

People mock the idea of hell. Mockers and scoffers, just like those boys who got burnt up and hurt poor little Amos so bad all those years ago.

You can't conceive of the vengeance of God. Sodom? Serpents? Egyptians covered in boils? Noah's flood? That was just the slightest touch of God's vengeance.

I'll tell you how bad it's going to be. Everyone in hell will receive an eternal, new body. Inviolate. Unbreakable. The perfect vessels for God's instruments of torment. A body that can never be consumed, can you imagine? No, you cannot, brothers and sisters.

There are those listening to my words right now who feel rage towards God. Right now. Blasphemers, and they have repented not.

I've seen and heard them talking right here in Leeds. Men and women who have been cursed, who have been plagued. You'll never hear worse blasphemy and rage towards God than from these damned Leedsians. Banging their heads with stones, drunk on whiskey or worse, and just cursing the Lord. No repentance in them. None. I know them, and I've heard them.

Rage and hatred towards God, brothers and sisters. And you know why hell will be filled with the gnashing of teeth? Why the terrible weeping and rage towards God? Because they are going to realize how simple it would've been to be saved. All that time they were alive. Even people who have done good deeds, studied all the six hundred and thirteen commandments, felt like they listened to and followed God's revelation throughout their whole lives. But because they didn't simply believe in Jesus Christ on a cross, didn't quite believe in their heart of hearts that something so simple could be true, brothers and sisters, those people will wake up in hell. And they will curse God because he made it too easy.

"It was too simple! I was fooled by God! That one thing was all I needed to do!"

And I'll tell you another thing: In hell, men and women's lust will burn forever and never be satisfied. These new bodies will be burning to the unbreakable bones with the desire to do the worst things to other bodies in hell, let me tell you. They'll be like walking skeletons, still trying to work a trick.

And lust will take many forms, brothers and sisters, like an old woman dying of lung cancer, sucking smoke through the hole in her neck, this lust will rage and will never be satisfied.

There are five times the Bible calls hell a lake of fire. A place where men and women will seek death and will be unable to find it. Everlasting. Don't try to think about the beginning of God, brothers and sisters. Don't do that. You'll go crazy.

A teacher of mine once in a Sunday School class told us to imagine a whole earth that was nothing but a ball of sand, and that once every twenty five million years, a little bird would fly in and take a grain of sand. Then my teacher, he said it would take billions of years for that bird just to fill a cup of sand. That's a tiny sample of what eternity is. And eternity is how long the damned will burn.

And The Bible said the majority of humans will go to hell. Straight is the gate, narrow is the way.

Athens went to hell. Rome, Sodom, New York City are going to hell. Leeds is going to hell.

Can you imagine God sticking out his hands, trying to stop all the hordes rushing into hell? Stop! Stop!

In Noah's day, during the Flood, how many were saved? Eight human souls.

In fact, the majority of churchgoers today are going to hell. That's right, even most of you listening to me or maybe reading a transcript right now. Some of you who were saved way back, joined a

FATHER EZEKIEL SHINEFACE SERMON HOUR

church, maybe shook a few hands around you. Some of you are not living for God.

We think about hell as a place filled with the most abominable: sorcerers, whoremongers, and liars.

But there is a book in God's keeping: The Book of Life. And your name is either in there or it's not. God knows. Do *you* know if your name is written in the Book of Life?

In heaven, the Holy Spirit once revealed it to me, nothing is static. It's ever-increasing glory. You get there and it becomes brighter and brighter and richer and richer, and the ecstasy grows more and more powerful. Your memory of your life on earth will be erased so you don't feel bad for your loved ones bound for hell, but you have an ever-increasing knowledge of joy. It never ends.

In hell, there's an ever-increasing knowledge too. Ever increasing torment, an ever-increasing sense of being cast away.

But I'll tell you, the largest multitude in hell will be the neglecters who never took the time. Who lived carelessly. I tell you, brothers and sisters, your own desolation will come suddenly. You will hear the word and miss it. You're going to forget. You'll even forget the words I'm speaking to you over the radio today. Except for this last part I'm about to tell you. I'm going to burn this part into your brains so that you'll never be able to forget it. Because God loves you, he's going to allow me to do this.

I am calmly telling you right now that there is a living, everlasting hell. You've heard this elsewhere, but let me tell you, God told me first. I've heard it in churches and on the radio. They don't tell you where they got it. They got it from me. I saw it.

There is a worm that never dies. Your conscience.

Can you imagine waking up in hell? The touch of eternal death on your shoulder? The stench, the darkness? You hear the roar of your adversary in your mind; ever more cast away from the presence of God.

I can't describe to you what it's like to be in hell.

You are in hell. You are lost, brothers and sisters.

HYMNS OF ABOMINATION

If you knew you'd get a week's break in ten million years, it might be bearable. But there's no hope, no chance. You are in hell. Forever.

And then suddenly, the worm turns. Your conscience. You remember every word of this sermon. You hear me preach it through eternity. Every word of it. You will replay it. Your conscience will transmit it back to you. Conscience is memory. It drifts back and forth between time and eternity.

The worm turns. I'm suddenly back in my house as a child, in my bedroom. I pinch myself. My mother is bringing me a cup of warm milk, and I say to myself, I can't be in hell. I tell her to put the cup down. I had a dream I was in hell. She says, don't worry. I feel the warm milk; taste it. I get down on my knees, and just about the time I'm about to feel the warmth and grace of God, it all goes dark.

I lost. I'm in hell.

Then the light goes on again. The worm has turned.

I'm in front of the microphone relaying my gospel message, sitting alone in the radio booth stunned, and if this is a nightmare, God please let me wake up. Drugs in my drink? I scream God, save me, looking at the hanging lightbulb, pulling my ears and hair, and I feel pain, and how can I be in hell? I can't take it anymore. I want to pray for mercy for forgiveness and just before I do it all goes black.

I say oh God I'm in hell. I sit through it all—my whole life, again and again, and wake up in hell in a moment.

Let me tell you something, brothers and sisters: I walked out on God a billion years ago when I mocked little Amos and set that fire in the barn as a kid and slipped out back, while Amos and my friends burned, and I've been back in this seat a billion times talking to you, never able to repent, never able to even feel the mercy of Jesus because this worm in me never dies.

What really saddens me, brothers and sisters, the worst torment of all is the opportunities lost and missed tonight. Because the love of Jesus, the forgiveness of Jesus, even the cross of Jesus, is not enough.

FATHER EZEKIEL SHINEFACE SERMON HOUR

God has sent me for you to hear this message even while I burn in the darkness of living and everlasting hellfire. God knew you'd be there, where you are. You may think this message is God's embrace or maybe even his warning, but I'm telling you it's His thunder and a piercing sword. Because in spite of Jesus and the Holy Ghost, in spite of the Word of God speaking through me, through these speakers and on this page, I know this sermon has settled over you tonight, moving you, waking an invisible, invincible worm within your heart. Maybe you can't imagine that now. But, oh my brothers and sisters, one day…I know you will.

Hallelujah and Hallelujah and Amen.

You're listening to WXXT. The gristle in your gravy. The rancid fart in the broken elevator of your life.

HYMNS OF ABOMINATION

x346x

Anne Gare's Rare and Import Video Catalogue
October 2022

Jonathan Raab

"An Unpatriotic Dissident Takes Their Medicine" – Dir. YouTube User Benbackstheblue, 2020

Forty-five seconds of a single shot set in a wide, dimly lit room with a stage in the background—perhaps a local high school gymnasium or theater, repurposed for some more clandestine use. Black iron candelabras hold long-stemmed white candles, their wicks sputtering with white-hot flame, set at the right and left edges of the shot.

Four figures appear at the five-second mark, their faces covered by ill-fitting, insectile gas masks. Their bulging, distended bodies are wrapped in jet black robes, the fine cloth smeared with dirt and streaks of wet. They drag a person from stage left to the center of the frame. We cannot see a face, as it is covered with a black hood, and their voice is indistinct and mewling in its pleas for mercy, cries of defiance, or its hopeless appeals to a God that is indifferent in practice—if not in propaganda—to the evil of men.

The beating is mercifully brief, but the victimizers take turns growling threats and slurs while they place their hands on the victim's throat, denying them breath for short, interminable spans of time. This is an act of good old-fashioned *terror*, and its violence is merely one tool of many carried out to a greater end: the vast and terrible American Project.

Text flashes across the screen during the course of these outrages, and appears again as a final

HYMNS OF ABOMINATION

card over the darkness that precedes the end of the video, underpinned by the laughter of men and women who, through training, personal trauma, cultural conditioning, and professional experience, understand only obtuse, ever-present cruelty:

COMMUNITY ENGAGEMENT
FROM LEEDS
TO YOUR CORNER OF AMERICA

Online video, available on a social media feed of your choice.

Free.

With thanks to Tom Breen, Gemma Files, Logan Noble, Christopher Slatsky, Sean M. Thompson, and Mer Whinery.

uncle bart's map

I
The Perils of Alleyways

Uncle Bart lived over in Leeds, Massachusetts, a three-and-a-half-hour drive at the speed my father insisted on (a minimum of five miles an hour beneath the speed limit, the consequence of an expensive speeding ticket and a run in with an aggressive state trooper a few years prior). Once a year, on a Saturday in reasonable proximity to Christmas, my brother, sisters, and I would sacrifice the day to join our parents in a holiday visit to Uncle Bart's apartment on the top floor of a modest building on Broadway, within the couple of square blocks of what you could call downtown Leeds, if you enjoyed your humor dry. The apartments had at their base a discount store of the kind ever more popular these last years, as the economy has struggled to recover from the Great Recession and its lingering aftermath. At the time, the store was something of a novelty to my siblings and me, and we would spend the first part of each visit to Uncle Bart's wandering its aisles, armed with the three dollars Father had distributed to each of us before he and Mother began their climb to the fifth floor. (There was an elevator, but it was perpetually out of order, so we didn't bother trying it anymore.) We would linger in the toy aisle, deliberating over cheap, knock-off versions of the toys we had written on our Christmas lists, the names on their boxes and backing strange, Excellent Cowboy and Beautiful Princess Girl and Angry Monster, their color schemes off, probably to avoid legal action from the companies whose originals they were copying. When we opened our selections in Uncle Bart's, we found the action figures and dolls were made of brittle, acrid-smelling plastic liable to snap at the slightest provocation. The first time this happened, to a figure I purchased named Mean Space Knight, Father sent me back down the wide

john langan

stairs from Uncle Bart's apartment, armed with my receipt, to demand an exchange from the impassive teenage girl stationed at the register. At Father's direction, my younger brother accompanied me. The girl behind the register took the receipt and the broken Space Knight and told me to find a replacement. I did, the girl scrawled something on the receipt in black ballpoint pen, and my brother and I made the climb to Uncle Bart's on the stairs, which reeked of lemon and ammonia cleaner. A short time later, this toy broke, too, but I opted not to share this information with my parents, thus saving myself the exertion and stress of another round trip to show the girl at the register my latest poor choice.

If the weather was mild, or at least, if it wasn't Arctically frigid, my brother and sisters and I would be sent out later, after our early afternoon holiday dinner in Uncle Bart's living room, to venture the two blocks along Broadway to the municipal playground, where a scattering of local kids in threadbare jackets and knit caps stood along the chain link fence enclosing the area, watching us suspiciously as we sat on the swings whose seats were molded plastic, cold through our chinos and skirts, attached to chains threaded with long strands of hair snagged in them. It was difficult to maintain your seating on the swings, and before long, we would be scaling the ladder of the slide, which rose unnervingly high, the entire structure swaying as we reached the top. Possibly due to the cold, the slide's metal was not especially slippery, and we had to push ourselves most of the way down. After a couple of tries, we moved to the next entertainment, a merry-go-round suspended about two feet above the ground that one of us spun faster and faster while the rest lay flat on it, watching the sky twirl overhead like a poor man's kaleidoscope. Because I was the biggest, I was in charge of accelerating the platform, which was plated with stippled metal whose purpose, I believe, was to keep any child on it from sliding off. I would push the platform until it had achieved sufficient velocity, then run alongside and attempt to leap onto it. The ride shrieked metallically as it turned, the sound growing louder as it picked up speed, drawing stares and snickers from the local kids in their clusters next to the fence, which made me self-

UNCLE BART'S MAP

conscious, embarrassed, and although my brother and sisters wanted to go a second time, I refused, insisting we had to return to Uncle Bart's. My siblings grumbled in protest, but I browbeat them until we were walking through the opening in the chain link fence.

On the way back to the apartment building, we passed a pawn shop, a record store, a storefront church, a 7-11, and a Chinese takeout, each of them surmounted by one or two stories of apartments. Interspersed among the businesses were large, run-down houses whose front porches abutted the sidewalk. I set a brisk pace for my siblings, who had practically to run to keep up with my long legs. From a variety of sources—conversations between my parents overheard when the family went food shopping, mostly, but also bits of the nightly news on channel seven (also overheard, as Father and Mother forbade our viewing it, declaring it unfit for children), conversations with my peers at school, and the comic books which constituted my principal reading—I had internalized the view of cities as sinister, dangerous places, urban jungles whose brick and concrete flora concealed fauna lying in wait for an awkward kid from the country. Granted, Leeds was nothing like New York City, the typical setting for these narratives real and invented, but to my anxious imagination, it was near enough.

Although I did my best not to turn my head as we hurried by them, I was particularly nervous about the alleyways separating the various buildings. Strange as it sounds, I didn't really understand what alleys were for. They played an outsized role in the comics I read, as both the place a hero like Spider-Man could run to change into his costume, and the place criminals lurked, ready to grab you by the arm as you passed and haul you in to mug you. Alleys were full of trash cans clustered together, and larger dumpsters, and assorted other junk, old mattresses, wooden boxes, and piles of clothing. Fire escapes lowered their final extensions into alleys. Featureless doors marked their walls. They might connect to other alleys, or open to courtyards, just as dingy and dirty as the alley(s) leading to them. I couldn't understand why whoever had designed even so small a place as Leeds had incorporated alleys into it. The house in which I lived was separated from our neighbors on one side by a half-acre of land on which grew corn whose stalks my brother and sisters and I were not supposed to play among; a high, wooden fence lined the boundary between us and our neighbors on the other side. Those borders made more sense to me. The alleys whose mouths my siblings and I passed compressed the space I was used to into a narrow strip between buildings whose height rendered it perpetually dim. From my reading, I knew that people sometimes used alleys as shortcuts between the street they were on and another they wanted to reach, and in bigger cities such as New York, these shortcuts formed almost a secondary system of streets, but the risks hazarded in employing such a network seemed to me to far outweigh the benefits.

UNCLE BART'S MAP

II
Christmas Tree in the Corner

Uncle Bart's apartment was a strange place, crammed with sufficient contents for a house considerably larger than the modest one my siblings and I shared with our parents. A significant portion of its five rooms (living room, kitchen, bedroom, bathroom, office) was given over to books, which filled the bookcases stationed along the walls to overflowing, spilling off the shelves into teetering piles on the floor. They gave the apartment an underlying odor something like dry wood, a library smell I always appreciated. For our annual visit, Uncle Bart would make a cursory effort to shift enough of his books out of the way to allow some freedom of movement around the living room and to the bathroom, which mostly consisted of pushing the stacks against the bookcases. I never made an exact count, but it appeared to me slightly less than half the books were science fiction and fantasy paperbacks, their covers a brightly colored range of exotic scenes involving aliens, dragons, castles, spaceships, forests, and starscapes. The titles were as suggestive as the images they adorned: *The Three Stigmata of Palmer Eldritch*, *Dhalgren*, *There Are Doors*. The other half of the books were a mix of regular and oversized hardcovers, most without their dust jackets, the titles printed along their spines of less interest to me than those of their gaudier fellows: *Economic Theory: An Introduction*, *Special Equations*, *Tropical Diseases: A History and a Guide*. Paperbacks and hardcovers had been stacked on the floor or grouped on the shelves according to a principle of organization known solely to Uncle Bart, or which had been known to him at some point in the past. In response to a remark uttered over the dinner of the small turkey and fixings he served, he would push back his chair and set off on a journey through the apartment in search of the book he insisted Father, or Mother, one of my siblings, or myself read. He would begin with certainty, heading directly to a particular spot on the shelves or floor, his certitude becoming confusion as he did not find the volume where he had expected it. In the process, he would shift parts of one stack on top of another, move books from shelf to shelf or shelf to floor or floor to shelf, all (apparently) without noticing the changes he was making, thus explaining his current difficulties and setting up future ones. Complicating his searches further, he had strung Christmas lights around the apartment, anchoring them to the taller bookcases, using one or two heavy volumes to hold them in place. Inevitably, he would have to shift these books, allowing a line of colored lights to slip loose, swinging across the table and knocking over someone's glass of soda, or the gravy jug, unleashing a wave of fluid which had to be sopped up with our napkins right away, before it rained from the table and threatened the books. To his credit, Uncle Bart always found the title he was looking for, and it was through his intercession that I first read many of the novels I would go on to study in graduate school years later, *Kim*, *Nostromo*, *Mr. Fortune's Maggot*.

There was, it will come as no surprise, not enough room available for a Christmas tree, live or artificial. Uncle Bart's solution to this drawback was unique. He shifted enough of his books to allow him access to one of the corners of the living room, where a window set in either wall had prevented him from placing a bookcase, and on the narrow juncture of drywall there, he painted a seven-foot-tall Christmas tree, using thick oil paint whose petroleum odor lingered in the room, competing with the dusty scent of the books and the heady smell of the turkey. Some peculiarity of Uncle Bart's technique lent the tree the illusion of looming from the corner instead of receding into it, an impression strengthened if you saw the painting from the corner of your eye. At the foot of the painted tree, he arranged our presents. These were not books, but an assortment of gifts from countries near and far. I remember one year, he presented Father a portable chess set whose figures were hand carved into characters of a medieval French court. Mother received a silk dressing gown from Japan. I unwrapped a compact German camera Uncle Bart had loaded with film, while my brother lingered over a pair of binoculars ("Military grade," according to our uncle), and my

UNCLE BART'S MAP

sisters removed the paper from dolls dressed in the traditional garb of Georgia (the then-Soviet republic) and Kenya. The first several pictures in my camera were devoted to documenting my family's gifts from and to Uncle Bart (we gave him a pair of flannel pajamas, a new comforter for his bed, and a Yankees cap at which he grunted with all the outrage of a diehard Red Sox fan). I snapped a few more photos of us around the dinner table, then of the Christmas tree, a bookcase draped with colored lights, and a couple of Uncle Bart's maps.

These last hung framed in whatever wall space was available, which is to say, mainly above the bookcases, though a few found their way into spaces between the bookcases, and some hung from the sides of the bookcases. They were hand-drawn by Uncle Bart on thick white paper, using black ink and watercolor, as he sat at the same table around which we ate our holiday meal. About a foot square, they were closeups of places in countries I could identify only by the names he had lettered on the base of the frames: Guatemala, the Dominican Republic, Vietnam, Chile, the Philippines, Indonesia, Iran. The level of detail was incredible: buildings rendered in three dimensions with such vividness they seemed to rise from the paper; rivers and lakes whose surfaces sparkled with sunlight, which must have dazzled the eyes of whoever was at the helm of the tiny boats traversing them; forests whose leaves you would swear you heard the wind moving through, stirring unfamiliar birds to song. Uncle Bart's careful handwriting identified streets, monuments, public parks. At random spots on each map, he drew small, fanciful creatures, blends of the human and animal, or of different animals, which resembled the inhabitants of a Bosch painting (I had not seen any of Bosch's work at this point, and thought they looked like something from my comics, the kind of gamma-radiation-mutated foes the Incredible Hulk faced on a regular basis). I asked Uncle Bart what they were, but he evaded the question, describing them as "mere adornment" with an awkwardness that revealed they were nothing of the kind. Nor was he willing to explain his maps' other peculiarity, a fold running across each of them in different places. As far as I could tell, this crease did not affect the map's design, but it drew the eye, disrupting the map's aesthetic harmony. This bothered me in ways I couldn't quite articulate.

UNCLE BART'S MAP

III
Meat Pies

Uncle Bart was Mother's second cousin. His mother and her mother had been cousins in the old world, Ireland, Dublin. As a young woman, Uncle Bart's mother had immigrated to the US, Boston, where she had met, married, and raised six children with his father, a city of Boston policeman. Her letters home played a not-insignificant part in my parents' decision to repeat her journey a generation later; in fact, for the first six months after they arrived, they stayed with her, until a chance conversation on the T led to Father taking a job with Central Hudson, which relocated him and Mother to New York, outside Poughkeepsie. His family's eldest son, Uncle Bart had become an Army chaplain (I was unclear whether he had entered the seminary or basic training first), a position responsible for sending him around the world, to locations he would talk about at our holiday meal. He had been stationed in Okinawa for a short time, and I, who was fascinated by such ambassadors of Japanese culture as Godzilla and the *Battle of the Planets* cartoon, thrilled to hear him drop tidbits of information about his travels off base around the Japanese islands. Because his mother had been something like a decade and a half older than my grandmother, whose youngest child Mother was, Uncle Bart had been ordained and in the service while Mother was still a girl. By the time we were visiting him, he was living in semi-retirement, on call for both his religious duties (at St. Sebastian's, the nearest Catholic church) and his military ones (at the air base over in Westfield—or maybe I should say, *via* the base, because from what I could tell from his conversations with my parents, every so often, Uncle Bart would be picked up by a driver who took him west to the air base, where he would board a plane to a destination far removed from Massachusetts. Exactly what he did upon his arrival at these places was discussed in only the vaguest terms; certainly, neither of my parents pressed him for details.

Instead, they were content to listen to him describe the peculiarities of wherever he'd been).

(Even at this young age, I was aware Uncle Bart living on his own was unusual. He should have had a bedroom in a rectory, probably St. Sebastian's. One drive home, I asked my parents about this. Father answered that, since Uncle Bart was not of the same religious order as the parish priests, he was not required to live with them. I'm sure Father told me the name of the order, as I am equally sure it was the Fraternity of St. Martin de Porres, an order I have tried and failed to find much evidence of. At the time, I accepted Father's answer, the same way he accepted it from Uncle Bart. Both my parents were devout Catholics, but there was a certain ferocity to Father's faith, which combined with his intense loathing for all things English, and which manifested in a vigorous admiration for all manner of Catholic clergy, especially the priesthood. While I imagine Uncle Bart's order would have been unfamiliar to him, and had he attempted to find information about it in the twelve volume *Encyclopedia of the Catholic Faith* in the bookcase in the living room, his efforts would have been frustrated, still he would have accepted the existence of the Fraternity of St. Martin de Porres and Uncle Bart's place in it without question.)

He was a handsome man, our uncle, tall, broad-shouldered, with a head of thick black hair maintaining itself against the silver intruders seeking to undermine it. I thought he looked like Gregory Peck, who had enjoyed a late career resurgence for his roles in *The Omen* and *The Boys from Brazil*, if the actor's eyes had been a little bigger and less squinty and his nose more generously proportioned. Though he dressed in his priestly blacks, he also wore cardigans whose worn surfaces were as comfortable to hug as his low, calm voice was to listen to. When he wasn't talking to my parents, or telling us details of his trips abroad, he would attempt to entertain my siblings and me with stories whose promise was always greater than their fulfillment. I recall one year—I was maybe nine—he told us about a woman he had heard of who baked the most delicious meat pies anyone had ever tasted. He pronounced

UNCLE BART'S MAP

"meat pies" with lip-smacking relish. People came from blocks—from miles and miles for them. What none of them knew about was this woman's secret ingredient, the source of their distinctive flavor: the people she ground up to fill them with! He delivered this plot twist with great verve, clearly expecting myself, my brother, and my sisters to be aghast, which we were not. Much of my brother's and my reading material, which we discussed in front of our sisters, featured details, if not quite as lurid as this, within the general vicinity. I remember the glances my brother and I exchanged with one another, with our sisters, the feeling I had of, *Is that it?* Finally, we smiled and offered mild expressions of disgust, which seemed to please Uncle Bart.

IV
The Stockade Wall

Our final visit to Uncle Bart's took place when I was twelve. The following year, we would have to cancel our trip due to my brother's emergency surgery to remove his appendix. The year after, my younger sister requiring the exact same operation would keep us home again. Throughout this time, my parents said we would see Uncle Bart on another occasion, maybe he would come to us, but neither of these things happened. About six months after my sister's dangerously swollen appendix was excised, we received news that Uncle Bart was moving, all the way to Alaska, Juneau. There was no time for even a quick jaunt to say goodbye to him before his departure: the night he called with the news, his books and other belongings had already been boxed and taken by the movers, and he himself was scheduled to board a commercial flight out of Logan airport early the following morning. We had to exchange goodbyes over the phone, an arrangement which, if I'm being honest, suited me just fine. By this point, I had no desire to return to Leeds, ever, even to hear Uncle Bart describe his tour of a Japanese castle. Mention of the city's name filled me with a terrifying lightness, as if myself and everything around me were ready to fall *up*, into the sky. I hadn't told my parents, though I started to on several occasions but lost my nerve, what I'd seen during our last visit, after I lost my way in an alley chasing my brother and sisters. Aside from the general unbelievability of the event, I was also perplexed by Uncle Bart's apparent connection to it, which I couldn't work out how to articulate. In Father's case, this was because I heard the note of suspicion enter his voice whenever any of us said anything related to the Church, as if he was readying himself to defend it. In Mother's case, my reticence was because I suddenly couldn't bear to expose her to what I had experienced; I was overcome by the need to protect her from it.

UNCLE BART'S MAP

What happened began with a trip to the playground. For the only time I can recall, Uncle Bart was not well for our visit, regularly wracked with coughs which lingered at the tail end of the flu he had struggled with over the weeks leading up to our visit. He assured us he was feeling better, proving this by the table set in the living room and the food cooking in the kitchen, but his skin was pale, his hair unwashed and uncombed. He hadn't shaved in a couple of days, and the white stubble on his cheeks and chin aged him, made him an old man and not the vigorous contemporary of my parents I typically saw him as. Twice, his coughing interrupted the grace he offered when we sat down to our turkey, and after the second round, which lasted a long, painful minute, he was dazed, momentarily unable to recall where in his prayer he had been. A similar fit gripped him during dessert, prompting Mother to insist he relocate to the couch while we cleared the table and did the dishes. Once the last bowl was dried and put away, the tablecloth removed and placed in the laundry hamper, my siblings and I were sent on our yearly excursion to the playground.

I had the impression my parents wanted us to stay out for longer than usual, to give Uncle Bart a reprieve from his hosting duties. Unfortunately, the day was astonishingly cold. Over the previous month, a series of strong winter storms had roared up the eastern seaboard, leaving feet of snow in their wake and sinking the mercury in the thermometer to a depth it had yet to climb out of. From the look of things, Leeds had received even more snow than we had, and the municipal authorities had done little to clear it. Great, dirty piles of the stuff covered the city, transforming it into a polar outpost of a particularly run-down stripe. A steady wind whistled across the Siberian landscape, snatching the breath from you when it rushed against your face, flooding your eyes with tears already half-frozen. As we were pulling on our boots, wrapping our scarves around our necks, and zipping our coats, I tried to explain to my parents that conditions outside were not ideal for extended play. They downplayed my concerns, insisting our heavy coats and lined gloves would keep us warm. Mother and especially Father were possessed of an almost mystical belief in the benefits of playing in what they called the fresh air, which was rooted in childhoods spent (they claimed) roaming the streets of Dublin in hand-me-down coats and mittens full of holes. Accompanied by one of Father's frowns, which seemed to punctuate most of our exchanges these days, I led my siblings down the apartment building's stairs and out the front door.

The sidewalk we struggled along was a channel in the snow, its walls varying shades of yellow from the dogs that had decorated it. Maintaining our footing was a challenge, and several times on the way, each of us almost tumbled into the tainted snow. My calves burned with the effort, and I was relieved to reach the playground. My relief curdled as I saw our destination had received less attention than the sidewalk, its entertainments mired in snow that drifted halfway up the slide's ladder. Someone had begun digging a slender path into the space, but had abandoned their efforts almost immediately; nonetheless, I marched along the abbreviated trail to the end, so I would be able to tell my parents we had gone as far as we could into the playground and found it unusable. Mother and Father would probably greet this news with skepticism, but if my brother and sisters backed me up, there was a chance I'd walk away with minimal reproach. At least the snow and cold had kept the local kids and their mocking looks away (though I could imagine them lurking behind the snowy mounds, snickering).

Our reconnaissance complete, I was ready to return to Uncle Bart's and take my chances with my parents' displeasure. My siblings were in agreement, but in spite of the cold, they were in no hurry to trudge back to the apartment building. Instead, my brother proposed venturing along the street to see where it went. He was pretty sure, he said, there was a park a couple of blocks on. I had no recollection of any such park, but my sisters immediately agreed to this plan and so, outvoted, I consented to proceeding further into Leeds.

We did not find a park. After four blocks of struggling past low brick buildings and shops, including a fishmonger's, an electrical supply store, and a used bookstore whose window display I lingered on until

UNCLE BART'S MAP

my younger sister called for me to catch up, our exploration halted in a parking lot. Bordered on the near side by a locksmith, and at the back and far side by two-family houses, its portion of snow had been plowed all the way to the far side and heaped into a ridge several feet taller than I was, a miniature mountain range. Instantly, I pictured my brother and I playing with our G.I. Joe figures and vehicles on what presented itself to my imagination as a gigantic playset. (This was the time when the G.I. Joe toys were reconceived as a line of three-and-a-half-inch action figures, each with a different military specialty and individual backstory; the same was done for their principal adversaries, the terrorist organization known as Cobra.) I tried to express my vision to my brother, but both he and my sisters had been distracted by the cat who appeared at the far end of the snow mountains.

He (I couldn't determine the cat's sex with any certainty; I simply observed the prejudice of a twelve-year-old boy who takes his gender as the default) was as big a cat as I had seen, his size emphasized by his gray fur, which, though matted and filthy, gathered around him in flaps reminiscent of a samurai's armor. He walked along the foot of the ridge, picking his way among chunks of snow, for all the world as if coming to meet us. Not many sights could have drawn us from the sidewalk into the parking lot. Even the snow mountain was something to be admired, not actually climbed, but presented with an apparently friendly cat, all our hesitation crumbled. In the perennial divide between cat families and dog families, mine stood firmly on the feline side. Our most recent cat, Andromeda, had been an All Saints' Day casualty of the fast road on which we lived, and this may help explain the eagerness with which the four of us rushed from the sidewalk. Nor did the cat flee from us; instead, he stayed where he was as we advanced in a group, each of us uttering some form of half-nonsensical greeting. When we were within ten feet of him, we halted, so as not to spook him, and stood in admiration. This close, he was larger, more massive than he had seemed from across the parking lot. Tufts of hair stood up from his ears and between his toes. Tail swishing, he considered us from eyes green as sea ice as we babbled away. Then, to our mutual delight, he resumed his approach until he was winding his way among us, rubbing his head against our coats, his eyes squinted, his purr like the engine of a small car. An odor of vegetation, like freshly cut grass, only more pungent, clung to him, strong enough to register even with our frozen noses. This did not discourage us from reaching tentative hands to pet his head and back, which he met with chirruping approval. For a moment, we basked in the pleasure of the cat's presence. The cold, if not forgotten, was then of less concern, and our shared enjoyment, explains why, when he began to draw away and back toward the other end of the snow ridge, we followed. On the way, he paused a couple of times to allow us to shower more attention on him. We went all the way to the back of the parking lot, where the snow ridge terminated, leaving ten feet of open space into the alleyway between the houses there. With a burst of speed, the cat sprinted across the tarmac to the alley's mouth, slowing there to glance over his shoulder at us, as if inviting us to catch up. Snow boots slapping the parking lot, my brother and sisters raced after him. He turned and ran down the alley, and without breaking their stride, my siblings did, too.

 I did not. It was as if my feet were caught in concrete, held fast by a combination of fear of the narrow corridor between the houses and concern at my parents' displeasure. Had either Father or Mother been present, none of us would have dared enter the parking lot in the first place. A single warning would have arrested my brother and sisters in their tracks. As far as authority figures went, I was less successful at keeping my siblings in line, which would not prevent Mother and Father from reprimanding my failure. I could have run back to Uncle Bart's and summoned my parents to my aid, if doing so would not have left my brother and sisters alone in a strange place. Nor was waiting for them to reappear a better option. There was no other choice: I would have to venture after my siblings and hope they had not traveled too far down the alley.

UNCLE BART'S MAP

No more than a minute or two had passed, and yet I could neither see nor hear them. The only indication they had gone this way was the imprint of their boots in the snow. I did my best to hurry between the gray siding to my right and the wide porch to my left, but the snow here had not been shoveled at all, the residents relying on their own boots to clear a rough path through it, and my feet kept slipping, threatening to dump me on my face. I had the uneasy impression I was being watched by someone on my left, not on the wide porch crammed with junk (an old TV, stacks of wooden crates, an easy chair turned on its side), but from one of the windows behind it. Attempting to mask a glance as a consequence of my latest slip, I searched for a face at the glass but saw only a reflection of the alley. Overhead, I heard wings flapping. I looked up and saw only a strip of blue sky framed by the blank gray wall on the right and the peaked black roof opposite.

The alley t-junctioned another, this one running along the back of a single story building whose bricks were a faded yellow blackened with age and grime. I checked both ways and saw no sign of my siblings. The panic I was fighting to control sped my heart. To the right, I heard a shout the wrong note for either my brother or my sisters. It might be someone shouting at them, though, so I headed in that direction, passing on my right the back stairs of a house crowded by tall plastic garbage cans, and on my left a black door with a black-tinted window in the dirty yellow building. This alley was shorter, emptying into a small courtyard. Its margins were defined by the dirty yellow building and another brick structure across from it, this one brownish red, its three stories scaled by a fire escape clinging to it like a giant metal insect. To my right was the back of another gray-sided house, its stairs surrounded by a deployment of plastic trash cans, and on the other side of the courtyard from it on what I judged the street side of the courtyard, was a wall.

Maybe ten feet tall, it consisted of a row of logs, each roughly cleaned of its bark and hacked into a crude point. Mud caulked the seams. The structure was curiously free of snow, which should have drifted against it instead of stopping a yard or so from its base. Unlike every other thing I encountered in Leeds, which possessed a palpable sense of age and exhaustion, the wall looked brutally new, its raw wood bright, yellowish white. In the approximate center, a doorway had been cut through three of the logs, a sheet of dull metal hung in the opening. The door stood ajar and there, rubbing his back against its edge, was the gray cat.

Relief flooded me. I ran across the snow, once again almost losing my footing. By the time I reached the doorway, the cat had slipped through it. The door was heavy, but I was able to pull it open wide enough to follow him.

To find myself on a street that would not have been out of place illustrating the reports of the fighting in Lebanon my parents didn't know I overheard on the nightly news. The majority of the buildings had been reduced to heaps of brick and wood and metal from which single walls rose, their window frames empty of glass. Beyond them stretched muddy fields whose trees had been snapped and splintered, whose soil was a muddy mess. In the distance, I saw the rounded tops of hills. The street itself had been churned into broken chunks. There was no snow anywhere, and while the air was by no means warm, neither was it as cold as it had been on just the other side of the wall. There was no trace of the cat, or my siblings, or anyone.

From those same comics and TV shows which had made me leery of alleyways, I knew every city had what Father and especially Mother called its bad part. Clearly, I had found it, though it was far worse than any of my reading or watching had prepared me for. The mingled smell of smoldering wood, plastic, and trash fouled the air. Quiet, utter and profound, hung over the place. I could not hear the rumble of cars and trucks, the squeal of brakes and the echoes of horns; given the condition of the street, not exactly a surprise, but they should have been audible from over the wall at my back. I could not hear the shouts of kids playing, and no matter how much their parents might have forbidden it, most of the kids I knew would have been helpless to resist the allure of a landscape such as this, of its opportunities for exploration and mischief. I could not hear any of the noises constituting the aural backdrop of a small city: the barking of dogs, someone playing the radio so loud you could hear it despite their closed windows, the unexpected grace note of a bird warbling its song. I could not hear my brother or my sisters.

Possibly, they had not come this way. The cat might have lost them, as it had lost me. They might have made their way back to Broadway and be waiting at the mouth of the alley, wondering where I was. Or worse, they might have assumed I had left in a snit and decided to return to Uncle Bart's, which meant my parents would know I had let them separate from me, which would make the long car ride home longer still. At the same time, they *could* have crossed the threshold of the metal door into this strange, silent neighborhood. If this were the case, I wasn't sure why I couldn't hear them—unless something had happened, some kind of accident I should have been there to prevent. Within my gloves, my palms were sweaty. My face was heating the way it did when I had to present Mother and Father with a report card on which there was anything less than a 90. I decided to walk along the street a couple of blocks in either direction, in hopes I would come across my siblings. Maybe they were playing a joke on me; maybe they were about to leap out and shout, "Boo!" (The prospect filled me with relief and fury). Already, I was whispering a prayer to St. Anthony of Padua, patron saint of lost things. "Dear St. Anthony," I murmured, "please come around, my brother and sisters are lost and they need to be found." On my left, the front of the dirty yellow building stretched undamaged, the sole structure intact. Boots clomping on the sidewalk, I headed that way.

As with its rear, this side of the yellow structure ran undisturbed except for a black door with a black-tinted window. I reached the end of the building and saw that the rest of the block was devastated, leveled, the sole exception the shell of an apartment building across the street from me. Its face was missing, its interior gutted, its four stories brimming with shadows. There didn't appear to be any way my siblings could be hiding in it; the place was all but unreachable over the enormous gouges in the tarmac. I couldn't see anywhere the three of them could remain concealed among the devastation, whose end was not visible, reaching farther than seemed possible, but duty (and anxiety) prodded me forward, even as the darkness opposite seemed to thicken.

Before the end of the block, the street and the wreckage lining it sloped down to a tremendous crater. The size of the soccer field I played on in the fall, it was filled with the shattered remnants of wood and brick structures from which the ends of cars and a single delivery truck protruded like huge metal fish caught mid-dive. About two-thirds of the way to the bottom, water bubbled up from amongst the wreckage in a weak fountain.

Obviously, there had been a disaster here—some kind of explosion, perhaps. But why hadn't I heard anything about it, not only from my parents or Uncle Bart, but from the wider world? This degree of devastation in a state adjacent to the one in which I lived should have been all over the news I wasn't supposed to watch; my friends at school should have been speculating about it while my teachers reassured us. Why was there no indication of the catastrophe anywhere else in Leeds? Once we turned off the Mass Turnpike, I put down whatever book I had been passing the ride with and stared out the window in order to avoid the car sickness brought on by the winding local roads. I didn't pay attention to street names, preferring to focus on familiar landmarks, distinctive buildings, weird confluences of streets, and the occasional weathered statue. Shouldn't I have seen sawhorses and barrels blocking certain side streets, signs routing traffic around the stricken area? From what I could remember, the city itself made no acknowledgment of this place.

When I was directly opposite the remains of the apartment building, the sidewalk began to tremble under my boots. So strange was the sensation, so disorienting, it stopped me where I was. Around me, broken bricks clicked and clattered, while a low rumble filled the air. Dust and dirt trickled from outstretched lengths of wood and metal and

UNCLE BART'S MAP

fell hissing onto the ground. I had seen movies in which earthquakes occurred (*Godzilla vs. Megalon*) but never experienced one directly; as far as I knew, the phenomenon in the United States was confined to California, which was destined to drop into the ocean (I hadn't paid much attention in Earth Science). What was happening now, the intensifying trembling, the sidewalk shifting like a funhouse floor, was not possible.

As was what was happening within the confines of the apartment building's walls. The mass of shadow contained there was moving, writhing, rising up and up and up, growing as it did, expanding until it had risen above the brick walls, an enormous, squirming mass held aloft on stilt legs impossibly long, an ebony cloud against the blue sky. The quaking of the ground tumbled me to my butt and I scuttled back in the direction of the stockade wall, whose function now seemed incredibly obvious, if its dimensions woefully inadequate. All the time, my eyes were on the thing whose surface appeared at one moment to be a coat of shaggy hair rippling over enormous muscles, the next a forest of rubbery feelers, and the moment after that something like ink spreading across a glass plate. The sidewalk bounced under me. I spilled onto my left side, came up in a half-crawl, and scampered toward the barrier I had not realized was so far away. A moan like the hollow groan of metal parting from itself mixed with the rattling and crashing of bricks. I glanced over my shoulder and saw the great mass turning, its long legs shuffling as a new side rotated into view. There was something on this part of its black coat, a long white adhesion whose contours I couldn't make sense of. I was beyond afraid; I had vaulted past fear and into a stunned blankness. A heavy green odor, full of the smells of freshly cut grass and boiling Brussels sprouts, rolled over me. The ground almost pitched me from my hands and feet, but I kept my balance through a combination of speed and willpower. I had scrambled all the way to the dirty yellow building, which, incredibly, had not collapsed with the earthquake (if that was what this was). The wall lay not much farther, which may explain why I chanced another look at the monster behind me.

The attachment on its side had swung fully into view. A slender oval at least the length of a city bus hung vertically amidst the writhing black hair. It was flanked by a pair of enormous, bone-colored growths which appeared to be horns, until they liquefied, unrolling into arms that swatted the air. Between them, what looked like a huge piece of fabric had been stretched across the oval, leaving only the bottom third of it exposed. *Like a mask*, I thought. The lower section of the oval swung open, revealing huge, blocky teeth, and I saw I was right: the expanse of material covering the oval was a mask, pulled tight against the contours of a long face like that of a goat. From its open mouth, the metal groan sounded, vibrating my skull. One of its legs was lifting, raising a splayed hoof the size of my family's car and swinging it toward the street. How many strides would the thing need to reach me? Two? Three?

I had slowed almost to a stop in front of the dirty yellow building, all my attention focused on the monster whose enormous hoof had come crashing down on the rubble outside its shelter. Between the ongoing noise and the motion of the sidewalk, I wasn't aware of the black door behind me opening, nor did I witness the short, stout man in the pea-green army greatcoat tottering out of it. The first indication that anyone human was with me was a gloved hand which grabbed the back of my jacket and hauled me toward the doorway. At first, I thought I had lost my balance yet again, and only when I did not strike the pavement did my situation dawn on me. Instead, I moved away from its second hoof, which smashed into the street next to the first, leaving the monster half-submerged in the building's shell. Struggling against my abductor, I tried to wriggle out of my winter coat, but it was securely fastened, and I couldn't reach to free myself. The man dragged me across the threshold and into the dirty yellow building before dropping me onto its wooden planks. He hurried to push the metal door closed, locking it by sliding a trio of heavy bolts I did not believe for a second would keep the monster from shoving its vast head into the room. From beside the door, the man hefted a heavy rifle (an elephant gun, I thought); retreating a couple of paces, he settled the stock against his shoulder and aimed the barrel at the door. The gesture was entirely serious, but I had no more faith in the gun's ability to halt the thing than I did the door's to keep it out. The shaking was enough to prevent me from taking in any more of the room than the walls and ceiling, both constructed from the same broad planks as the floor. A pair of lanterns swung side to side from the ceiling, their yellow beams racing around the space, illuminating the streaks and swirls of dark mud on the walls. Another door was set in the back wall. It hung open, clapping against its frame with the shaking. I assumed it was an escape route, one the floor was moving too much for me to reach before the squat man in the long coat caught me.

Now, the front door's tinted window filled with the face of the monster. This close, it was too big for me to see in its entirety, but I could glimpse the ragged edge of its mask. The covering was stitched together from dozens—hundreds of what I took at first for small pieces of leather, each more or less square and pierced by a series of holes elongated by tension. I fancied they resembled human faces and at almost the same instant saw this was exactly what they were: faces of men, women, and children, old and young, all colors, skinned from their skulls in one piece and joined into a mask for this thing, whose gray flesh I could see through the empty eyes and mouths adorning it.

Until that moment, I had been overwhelmed by the immensity of the monster; now, a piercing scream burst from my throat. Seemingly in response, the creature's great mouth opened, revealing its blocky teeth, each large as a trash can (all manner of debris caught between them, including the remains of a human leg, half-crushed), and unleashed another metallic groan. This close, the moan drowned my tiny shriek, shuddering the room and everything in it. Sure the monster would crash into this wooden room imminently, either to catch me in its mouth or to crush me under one of its enormous hooves, I squeezed my eyes shut, the scream still pouring from me. My ears were ringing, blasted by the thing's groan. Deep in the recesses of my brain, a small voice counseled me to pray. If I was going to die, I should at least say a final Act of Contrition, but the words were pieces of a puzzle my quivering psyche could not fit together, and the best I could manage was, *Forgive me forgive me forgive me.*

I hung in that screaming darkness for what seemed an eternity, my hearing a dull circle whose circumference was a steady ringing, until I realized the wood planks on which I was lying were moving less, their shaking subsiding. Before I could think better of it, I opened my eyes and saw the man in the greatcoat standing with his rifle aimed at the window, whose tinted pane was empty. Suddenly, I was sobbing, a flood of tears fracturing the scene in front of me, my chest hitching as my screaming crumbled to a hoarse keening. My nose ran, my face burned, and misery overwhelmed me. Through watery eyes, I watched the stout man lower his rifle and, keeping hold of it, turn in my direction. He crossed the space between us and knelt beside me. Once I had wiped my tears he hooked a powerful arm under mine and helped me to my feet. I saw that he was older than I thought. His uncovered head was bald, and the walrus-like mustache drooping over the lower portion of his face snow-white, as were the heavy eyebrows over his bright, wary eyes. Gesturing with his rifle to the door in the back wall, he propelled me forward. I went, mostly because there was nowhere else for me to go. Already, the lanterns had slowed their wild swinging; though their motion had not ceased entirely, the two lights giving the impression I was crossing two rooms slightly out-of-sync with one another. My throat was raw; my eyes kept filling with tears. Nonetheless, I managed to exit the wooden room with the old man.

We stepped into a corridor with walls and ceilings composed of rough red bricks thickly mortared into place. Its floor was of packed dirt, and all of it was illuminated by lanterns hung every ten or fifteen feet. The air smelled of mildew and dirt.

My guide steered us left. He still had his arm hooked through mine, but the looks I stole of his face revealed an expression more of duty mixed with concern than of malice. Those same glances showed me his dense mustache rustling, and I realized he was speaking. I considered explaining that my hearing hadn't recovered from the monster's groan, but decided against it. For one thing, my throat felt full of broken glass; for another, I was afraid he might halt our journey until I was able to listen to whatever he had to say.

He released my arm and I continued beside him. Gradually, as we trudged along the brick corridor for what seemed like far longer than it had taken me to reach the stockade wall,

(my thoughts already turning to my parents, whom I was certain my siblings would have summoned and who, when they found me, would be furious at me for abandoning my responsibilities and for lying to them, because there was no way they would believe what had happened to me, for which I couldn't really blame them, because I was having trouble with it myself, the memory too much for my brain)

(and a secondary thought: if this man was a soldier stationed behind the black metal door, was it safe for him to be away from his post?)

the ringing space surrounding me contracted, bringing the man's speech nearer. In a voice that swam around inside his mouth, he reassured me, telling me not to worry, I'd seen old Matthias's script, hadn't I? As long as that mess was on the walls, the Goat could threaten all she wanted, but there wasn't anything she could do. I repeated, "the Goat," understanding as I did he was naming the monster in whose teeth I had seen a human limb. It was what he called her, the man said apologetically, since her actual name was too much of a mouthful—not to mention, he didn't want to risk uttering it, in case doing so contravened the script's potency. None of which made sense to me; nor did what followed, a rambling discourse on Leeds which kept circling back to what he referred to as the "porousness" of the place. This area was a block of limestone; it was a hunk of Swiss cheese. He was talking about the holes, which he also called pockets and, once, bubbles. They were what allowed so much more to fit into the area than what the eye saw. You could have the Market Procession, and Katrina's Hearse, and the Goat, whose acquaintance I had almost had the pleasure of making more directly. Why, there was a whole *other* Leeds...Here his monologue subsided, as if the mention of the other city had summoned it to his mind's eye and the vision had quieted him.

Then his voice returned from whatever vista had swallowed it. "But what good are all these holes and their residents if you can't do something with 'em? All they'd do is torment locals who stumble across their thresholds. This is where your mapmakers come in, your followers of Sainted Martin. One of the fraternity draws a map in his special ink, with all its *flourishes*, and you can send one of the holes' inhabitants somewhere else for a little while, let 'em indulge their appetites far from the good citizens of Leeds."

I didn't follow, and although saying so hurt my throat, I did.

The man started to answer, but we had come to a black telephone set in the brick wall on the right. The cord joining the receiver to its base was short and straight, and there was no dial. I was aware of no ringing (and this looked to be the kind of phone equipped with a trilling bell), but the man picked up the receiver and held it to his ear. "Yep," he said. Whoever was on the other end spoke for a little while. "She'll settle down," the man said. "Might want to let her have a walk, just to be on the safe side. Ortega's due for a visit, isn't he?" More talking from the person on the other end. "It's fine," the man said, "I'll take care of him. You let Martin's friend know." He paused. "Right," he said and hung up the phone. "Come on," he said to me, "we're almost there," and continued in our original direction.

For a moment, I remained where I was, held in place by the sudden, terrifying certainty that our destination was not, as I had assumed, the alley leading to the log wall. I had witnessed something incredible, something I wasn't supposed to see, and the penance for my trespass was to be a mortal one. Only three children would return to Uncle Bart's apartment and, search however they might, my parents would be unable to locate the fourth. From farther along the corridor, the man in the greatcoat glanced over his shoulder, saw me standing there, and waved for me to catch up. "Move it along," he called, "you don't want to be here on your own." The warning in his words was sufficient to break my hesitation and send me running after him.

After I'd rejoined him, the man resumed his monologue. "You see," he said, "there are people—most of 'em in other countries—who don't have what you could describe as the best intentions towards the good U.S. of A. Some of 'em have different views from us on important matters; others are outright belligerent. Now, great as our military is, they can't fight everyone at once, can they? I mean, they would if we told 'em to, but it would be too much. We have a secret weapon, though. We have a city full of monsters and we have one of Martin's fraternity at our disposal. The good cartographer composes one of his special maps, which allows a sort of a bridge to open, and then, well, you wouldn't want to be living in that part of Iran, or El Salvador, or North Korea, or--you get the point."

I did not, but chose to keep quiet.

"Afterwards, when we bring back whichever one of 'em we let out, chances are they'll be quiet for a little while. Or, at least, not as restless."

We passed the remainder of our journey in silence, until we arrived at another black metal door, this one set in the wall to our left. Instead of a tinted window, it had a single slot set head-high and covered by a metal strip. The man slid the cover aside and peered through the aperture. He grunted, pushed the metal strip back into place, and turned the lock set over the doorknob. "I don't have to tell you," the man said, "mum's the word about all of this. You look like a smart guy. I'm sure you're thinking, 'What's this old fellow talking about? Who's gonna believe me if I tell 'em I saw a monster big as a building, in Leeds of all places?' Well, maybe your folks wouldn't, but they might tell their friends: 'Can you believe this crazy thing my kid said?' And those friends might pass it along to their friends and so on, until it reaches the ears of someone it ain't supposed to, and then…" His expression indicated consequences whose exact parameters I couldn't discern but whose general nature was clear. I nodded. "Good," the man said. He turned the doorknob, revealing a flight of concrete steps ascending to an alleyway. "Go right at the top of the stairs," the man said. "When you reach the street, you'll meet your brother and sisters. Remember," he added as I started past him, "not a word."

"Not a word," I mumbled, nodding, then hurried up the steps, which, I saw with relief, were covered with a scrim of snow and ice. Behind me, the metal door thunked shut; I did not risk looking over my shoulder at it. To the right, the alley I crawled into was crowded with garbage cans on one side and stacks of wooden pallets on the other, drifted snow high between them. Beyond, I could hear the honk of a passing car's horn, see the tops of buildings across the street. I rushed into the dirty white barrier, frantically pushing it aside with my boots and legs, sweeping it away with my gloves. The cold, which had abated while I was on the other side of the wooden wall, grabbed me, numbing my face. With a final effort, I staggered out the other side of the drift and stumbled the remaining distance to the alley's mouth, where I almost ran right into my brother and sisters.

UNCLE BART'S MAP

V
Present

They were on their way back to Uncle Bart's apartment. Having been evaded by the gray cat, they quickly realized I was not with them. Retracing their steps, they had found no traces of me. They climbed the massive heap of snow at the end of the parking lot to see if they could spot me, but to no avail. They called my name, and I did not answer. Descending from the miniature mountains, they returned to the alley in case they had missed me wandering through. I was not there. Finally, they decided I must have abandoned them and started for Uncle Bart's on my own, although it made no sense, since I would be walking into all sorts of trouble if I entered the apartment without them. I did have a temper, which their pursuit of the cat could have ignited, sending me raging on my way. My brother was concerned at my behavior; my sisters were looking forward to the trouble I was going to be in. None of them expected me to stumble out of an alleyway in front of them a block from Uncle Bart's.

Whatever conversation they had been in the midst of died, replaced by a flurry of questions: What happened to me? Where did I go? Didn't I hear them shouting my name? How did I get here? Why did I leave them alone?

Despite the sensation of thumbtacks coating my throat, I retorted right away: They were the ones who had run away from me, I said, to chase that cat. *I* had been trying to find *them*.

My defense was ignored in favor of another question from my brother: What had happened to my voice? My younger sister asked if I was sick, while my middle sister suggested I had caught whatever Uncle Bart had. In an instant, my sister had handed me the explanation that would account for the hoarseness of my voice and allow me to gain the upper hand in our unfolding argument. I was *feeling* pretty sick, I confirmed, and they ran away and *left* me. "To chase a *cat*!" I added with some feeling. Regardless of the obvious holes in my lie, my siblings accepted my story, afraid of the same parental anger they had imagined descending on me. Together, we agreed on a simple narrative keeping within sight of what actually had occurred: finding our usual playground inaccessible, we had proceeded a couple of blocks farther, until we had reached a parking lot where we had played for a short time with a cat. When I had complained of not feeling well, we had departed. A surge of love for my brother and sisters moistened my eyes, which I wiped with my glove before any of them noticed.

My parents weren't thrilled with our admission of having left our usual play spot in favor of a parking lot, and our mention of the cat caused Mother to wrinkle her nose and admonish us for touching a strange animal, but my (apparent) sickness overshadowed their concern at these trespasses. Both Mother and Father pressed the backs of their right hands to my forehead and declared it hot, and the state of my voice seemed a clear indication I was coming down with something. The decision was made to leave for home early, which Uncle Bart, who had watched me closely since my return to his apartment, acknowledged was probably for the best.

This was, as I've noted, our last visit to Leeds. The removal of first my brother and then my younger sister's appendixes kept us home for the next two years, after which Uncle Bart was transferred to Juneau. I remember wondering how he had managed to pack all of his books; Father told me the Army would have provided movers to take care of that. Mother exchanged letters with him every month and sometimes she read us his descriptions of Juneau, of the Alaskan landscape, which made my brother and sisters ask if we could visit him in his new home. I don't think my parents ever seriously considered such a trip, but I recall one night, after the dinner dishes had been cleared from the table, Father brought out his Rand McNally road atlas and my siblings clustered around him as he plotted a course from our house to Juneau on the oversized pages, using a pencil to mark stops on the way. I stood behind them with Mother, drying and putting away the dishes she passed to me.

UNCLE BART'S MAP

Every so often, I expressed enthusiasm for their hypothetical odyssey, and although my interest was entirely feigned, I was convincing enough for no one to question me—or, more likely, they were too engrossed in their project to notice the false notes in my voice.

I was thinking about the package the mailman had delivered a couple of weeks after that last visit to Leeds. The note Uncle Bart included within the cardboard box explained that he felt bad for having been sick at our annual get-together and wanted to send us a little something to make up for it. He concluded with the hope I had made a full recovery; he had offered special prayers to St. Martin for me. (After a couple of days in bed with an actual low-grade fever, I had improved; though my throat took longer to heal.) The box's contents were surrounded by layers of crumpled newspaper pages, many of them from foreign countries. Father was as interested in these as he was in the contents of the heavily wrapped bundle they protected; he smoothed them out on the kitchen table, marveling at their locations: Istanbul, Karachi, Tokyo. Mother, in the meantime, had removed the bundle from the box and instructed my brother to bring her the sharp scissors, the ones she kept in her sewing basket. This he did, and like a surgeon slicing her way into a patient's abdomen, she cut slowly and carefully through the layers of brown wrapping paper and packing tape protecting the gift. Mother's exertions revealed the edge of a smallish picture frame, then the edge of the sheet of paper it contained, then the map Uncle Bart had sent us, the map of our house and yard, executed in black ink and watercolor with all his usual attention to detail. Here was the silver birch outside the kitchen window, and the two crabapple trees behind it, and the row of peonies to their right. Here was the line of apple and pear trees whose tiny fruit my parents would not let us eat because they hadn't sprayed them for pests, and which demarcated the back end of our third of an acre. In front of the house, he had placed the six of us, standing to either side of the fold in the paper running at a slight angle from the bottom of the page to the top, bisecting our house on the way. Where the fold terminated among the fruit trees, there was a blob of black ink which might have been intended to indicate the shadow of the trees on our neighbor's fence to the left, but from whose spiky outline I heard a metallic groan reverberate in the folds of my brain. The other fanciful figures Uncle Bart had drawn on the map clustered most densely around this spot.

Although they expressed surprise and delight, I heard notes of disappointment in my siblings' words. Mother and Father seemed confused by the gift. In the midst of my family's disappointment and confusion, I stood shocked, my face so pale Mother asked if I was feeling all right, following her question with a hand to my forehead. I was fine, I said, a response her hand confirmed. Of course I wasn't. The arrival of Uncle Bart's present confirmed everything I had suspected but resisted acknowledging about the connection between him in his apartment, his maps, his travels, and what I had discovered beyond the stockade wall, one of the pockets or bubbles the old soldier had said Leeds was rife with, a link too fantastical to believe, even for a boy who had been raised a devout believer in the Church and all its mysteries. I stared at the fold in the map slicing through our house, understanding the mingled warning and threat in it, the most shocking thing of all. It was as if Uncle Bart had pulled off the mask he had been wearing all the years I had known him, revealing a face whose eyes had the rectangular pupils, whose mouth had the blocky teeth of a goat, whose voice was the squeal of tearing tin. Mother decided to hang the map in the living room, on the wall across from the couch, where I had spent every possible minute of the years since seated, supposedly doing my homework or reading, but always keeping one eye on Uncle Bart's gift. Would he have to come here to activate the map? I wasn't certain. Leeds wasn't too far, though, especially compared to some of the places he'd visited. I imagined the fold in the paper shining with a crimson light, a hellish light, the map unfolding, bursting the frame as it expanded into a vast, infernal opening, an aperture to the hidden street in Leeds where the monster the old soldier had called the Goat was ready to push its enormous bulk into our little house. Would I run, I wondered, try to rouse my family to empty into the yard, or would I sit where I was, transfixed by the emerging horror? If we did succeed in escaping the house, would it do any good, or would the Goat eventually scoop us into its mouth and crush us between its teeth? These questions and others like them plagued my waking hours, haunted my dreams.

The map served its purpose: I did not breathe a word of what I had witnessed while lost in Leeds. On the whole, I was relieved when my brother's appendix kept us home the following Christmas, and when my sister's organ fulfilled the same function the year after. Uncle Bart's relocation to Juneau and the added distance it put between us eased my anxiety somewhat, but it was not until Uncle Bart's death a full decade later (from a heart attack precipitated by a severe bout of pneumonia—the official cause, at least) that I felt myself finally able to release the breath I had been holding for half my life. All the same, during my visits home from college, then grad school, then from the position I took in Pittsburgh, I spent at least part of one night seated in the living room, after my parents had retired to bed, contemplating Uncle Bart's map. Could its occult agency be accessed by someone else, another member of his unique fraternity? I couldn't say. The research I had done into the Friars of St. Martin de Porres had yielded almost no usable information. Once my parents decided it was time for them to downsize and move into senior housing, the map came into my possession, a responsibility I did not feel I could relinquish. I hung it in my office at home, where I continued to study it.

All those years of contemplation have led me, at length, to a new question, one I don't think I will ever be able to answer, but which haunts me nonetheless: What if Uncle Bart's map was not a threat, but an invitation?

For Fiona

HYMNS OF ABOMINATION

About the Authors

s.j. bagley is a multidisciplinary artist, philosopher, and critic what lives at the bottom of New England and produces the nonfiction journal THINKING HORROR; A JOURNAL OF A HORROR PHILOSOPHY and the zine/journal/thing SOFT TEETH. they enjoy spending time in the tops of trees and they are not available for parties.

Aksel Dadswell is an Australian writer of horror and weird fiction. He has a PhD in creative writing and cosmic horror, and he is a sessional lecturer at Edith Cowan University. You can find him on Instagram, Facebook, and standing right behind you.

Yves Tourigny is a greying biped living a quiet life in Ottawa. He has two sons, a dog, a wonderful partner, and too many interests.

Jonathan Raab is the author of *The Secret Goatman Spookshow and Other Psychological Warfare Operations*, *The Crypt of Blood: A Halloween TV Special*, *Camp Ghoul Mountain Part VI: The Official Novelization*, and more. He is also the editor of several anthologies from Muzzleland Press including *Behold the Undead of Dracula: Lurid Tales of Cinematic Gothic Horror* and *Terror in 16-bits*. You can find him on Twitter at @jonathanraabl.

Farah Rose Smith is a writer, academic, fusion dancer, and the author of the novellas *ANONYMA*, *The Almanac of Dust*, and *Eviscerator*. Her writing has appeared in Lackington's Magazine, Vastarien Literary Journal, Nightscript, Dead Reckonings, and more. She is a book reviewer for Publisher's Weekly and BlueInk Reviews, a writing tutor, and works as a literary agent. Smith is an affiliate member of the Horror Writers Association and a member of the International Gothic Association, North American Society for the Study of Romanticism, and the Science Fiction and Fantasy Poetry Association. A native of Rhode Island, she is currently a graduate student at CUNY Hunter College in the English program. She lives in New York City with her husband, author Michael Cisco, and their three cats.

Gemma Files was born in England and raised in Toronto, Canada, and has been a journalist, teacher, film critic and an award-winning horror author for almost thirty years. She has published four novels, a story-cycle, three collections of short fiction, and three collections of speculative poetry; her most recent novel, *Experimental Film*, won both the 2015 Shirley Jackson Award for Best Novel and the 2016 Sunburst Award for Best Novel (Adult Category). She is currently working on her next book.

B.R. Yeager reps Western Massachusetts. He is the author of *Negative Space* (Apoclypse Party), *Pearl Death* (Inside the Castle) and *Amygdalatropolis* (Schism(2)).

Scott R. Jones grew up in a weird cult. Now he writes weird fiction, such as his 2019 collection *Shout Kill Revel Repeat* or his LOCUS nominated debut novel *STONEFISH*. Is there a connection? Only his far-future biographer (an infradimensional hominid cryptid) will know for sure, so we all have to wait until *their* new book comes out, probably in some format that's difficult for humans to read, like a void-crystal or an aerosolized meta-narrative you inhale. Yeesh. Publishing.

Christine Morgan's works span the horror gamut from historical to cosmic to extreme, including the Splatterpunk Award winning *Lakehouse Infernal*. She was a longtime contributor to The Horror Fiction Review and occasionally dabbles in freelance editing. Her other hobbies include weird crafts and baking, when she's not being bossed around by her cats.

S. P. Miskowski has received two National Endowment for the Arts Fellowships. Her second novel, *I Wish I Was Like You*, was named This Is Horror Novel of the Year, received a Charles Dexter Award from *Strange Aeons*, and was a finalist for a Bram Stoker Award. Four of her books have been nominated for a Shirley Jackson Award. Her stories have been published in *Supernatural Tales*, *Black Static*, *Identity Theory*, and *Eyedolon*, and in numerous anthologies including *The Best Horror of the Year Volume Ten*, *There Is No Death There Are No Dead*, and *Darker Companions: Celebrating 50 Years of Ramsey Campbell*.

Betty Rocksteady's cosmic sex horror novella *The Writhing Skies* is the winner of the 2018 This Is Horror Novella of the Year award, as well as being nominated for the Splatterpunk Award. Her latest work is surrealist extreme horror collection *In Dreams We Rot*. She also draws spooky cartoon illustrations and talks to crows. Visit www.BettyRocksteady.com for more.

Joanna Parypinski is a Los Angeles based writer and professor. She is the author of *It Will Just Be Us* (as Jo Kaplan) and short stories appearing in *Fireside Quarterly*, *Black Static*, *Nightmare Magazine*, *Vastarien*, *Haunted Nights* edited by Ellen Datlow and Lisa Morton, and the Bram Stoker Award nominated anthology *Miscreations*.

LC von Hessen is a writer of horror, weird fiction, and general unpleasantness, as well as a noise musician, occasional actor, and former Morbid Anatomy Museum docent. They have recently appeared in *Vastarien*, *Nightscript 6*, *Planet Scumm*, *Oculus Sinister*, and *Beyond the Book of Eibon*, with previous works collected in the ebook *Spiritus Ex Machina*. An ex-Midwesterner, von Hessen lives in Brooklyn with a talkative orange cat and has loose ancestral ties to WXXT country through their mother, who attended Mount Holyoke College.

Cody Goodfellow has written eight novels and five collections of short stories, and edits the hyperpulp zine Forbidden Futures. His work has been favored with three Wonderland Book Awards for excellence in Bizarro fiction. He also wrote, co-produced and scored the Lovecraftian hygiene films Baby Got Bass and Stay At Home Dad, which can be viewed on YouTube. He "lives" in San Diego, California.

Hailey Piper is the author of *The Worm and His Kings*, *Queen of Teeth*, *Unfortunate Elements of My Anatomy*, and other horror fiction. She is an active member of the Horror Writers Association, and her short stories appear in *Year's Best Hardcore Horror*, *Dark Matter Magazine*, *The Arcanist*, and elsewhere. A trans woman from the haunted woods of New York, she now lives with her wife in Maryland, where their paranormal research is classified. Find Hailey at www.haileypiper.com or on Twitter via @HaileyPiperSays.

ABOUT THE AUTHORS

Tom Breen is a writer, freelance journalist, and podcaster whose fiction has appeared in numerous anthologies and periodicals. He is the author of the 2016 novella "Orford Parish Murder Houses." His introduction to the writing of Matthew M. Bartlett came via a local punk band in the 1990s, who had a song penned by the author, which concluded with the line "Your dream is a broken payphone that spits back your last quarter with a clink like laughter." Breen lives in eastern Connecticut, where he works for a large public university. You can find him on Twitter @TJBreen.

John Linwood Grant is a professional writer/editor from Yorkshire, UK, with some seventy short stories and novelettes published during the last five years in venues such as Lackington's Magazine, Vastarien, and Weirdbook, and in several award-winning anthologies. He writes dark contemporary fiction and period supernatural tales. His novel *The Assassin's Coin* (IFD), features the feared Edwardian assassin Mr Dry, from the collection *A Persistence of Geraniums*, and the related novel *13 Miller's Court* (with Alan M Clark) won the 2019 Ripperology Books award. He is also the editor of Occult Detective Magazine and various anthologies. His second collection of weird fiction, *Where All is Night, and Starless*, is out now from Trepidatio. He is ageing, sarcastic, and has his own beard. He can be found regularly on Facebook, and at his eclectic website greydogtales.com.

Pete Rawlik is the author of more than fifty short stories, the novels *Reanimators, The Weird Company*, and *Reanimatrix*, as well as *The Peaslee Papers*, a chronicle of the distant past, the present, and the far future, and the short-story collection *Strange Company and Others*. As editor he has produced *The Legacy of the Reanimator* and *The Chromatic Court*. His short story "Revenge of the Reanimator" was nominated for a New Pulp Award. He is a regular member of the Lovecraft Ezine Podcast and a frequent contributor to the New York Review of Science Fiction.

Jill Hand is the author of the Southern Gothic novels *White Oaks* and *Black Willows*.

K. H. Vaughan is a refugee from academia with a Ph.D. in clinical psychology. In his other life he taught, published, and practiced in various settings, with particular interest in decision theory, forensic psychology, psychopathology, and methodology and philosophy of science. He writes and edits dark speculative fiction including horror, science fiction, and fantasy.

Cheshire Trask was born in Hartford, Connecticut in 1969. He was raised in a strict Mennonite household till the age of twenty four, a period of life he would later immortalize in his memoir *Tears in a Salty Well*. He served as Executive Compliance Director at JP Morgan Chase for twenty years, eventually retiring following the untimely death of his wife Martha Ann, and returned alone to Hartford. Since then he has taught French literature and theology at the University of Hartford, writing memoirs and short stories in his spare time. Two months before the publication of this book, he embarked on an expedition to the Appalachians and has not been seen or heard from since. Anyone with knowledge as to his whereabouts are urged to contact the Hartford police department immediately.

Sean M. Thompson grew up in New England, and currently lives in the high desert of New Mexico with his partner. He is the author of the collection *Screaming Creatures*, the novel *TH3 D3MON*, and the novella and novelettes *Farmington Correctional*, and *Astrum*. He's had work featured in Vastarien, *Nox Pareidolia*, Unnerving magazine and many other publications. He is owner, and editor of Nictitating Books. You can find him on Twitter @SpookySeanT.

S. L. Edwards is a Texan traveling this wide, wide world. He enjoys dark fiction, dark poetry, and darker beer. His short story collection *The Death of An Author* is available from Journalstone and his debut novel *In the Devil's Cradle* is forthcoming from Word Horde in 2022.

Brian Evenson is the author of a dozen books of fiction, most recently the story collection *The Glassy Burning Floor of Hell* (2021). His previous collection, *Song for the Unraveling of the World* (2019) won a Shirley Jackson Award and World Fantasy Award, and was a finalist for the Los Angeles Times Book Awards Ray Bradbury Prize. He is the recipient of three O. Henry Prizes as well as an NEA fellowship. His work has been translated into a dozen languages. He lives in Los Angeles and teaches in the Critical Studies Program at CalArts.

Jon Padgett is a professional—though lapsed—ventriloquist who lives in New Orleans. His debut collection, *The Secret of Ventriloquism*, was named The Best Fiction Book of the Year by *Rue Morgue Magazine*. His work has appeared or is forthcoming in *Nightmare Magazine* and *PseudoPod*, among others, and his collaborative box set project with Matthew M. Bartlett, *Secret Gateways*, should be published by Nightscape Press in the coming months.

John Langan is the author of two novels and four collections of stories. For his fiction, he has received the Bram Stoker and This Is Horror awards. He lives in New York's Mid-Hudson Valley with his wife and younger son, and swears he doesn't hear anything strange coming from the radio. Do you?

Justin A. Burnett is the author of *The Puppet King and Other Atonements*, to be published by Trepidatio Publishing in 2022. He's also the Executive Editor of Silent Motorist Media, a weird fiction publisher responsible for the creation of the anthologies *Mannequin: Tales of Wood Made Flesh*, which was named best multi-author anthology of 2019 by Rue Morgue magazine, *The Nightside Codex*, and *Hymns of Abomination*, a tribute to the work of Matthew M. Bartlett. His quarterly chapbook, Mysterium Tremendum, explores the intersection between horror and the holy. He currently lives in Austin, Texas, with his partner and children.

Thank You

I owe thanks to a lot of people for this one, not in the least the man himself, Matthew M. Bartlett, for his support and enthusiasm. Discussions with my fellow Texan, S.L. Edwards, were invaluable to the development of this project. Also, the constant and unwavering support of Matthew Henshaw contributed more than I can say to my ability to keep moving forward, even when things were a bit overwhelming. Thank you for that.

This book would've <u>never</u> happened without Robert S. Wilson, who helped me figure out how to set up a Kickstarter. Equally important are those who backed the project. You are the true heroes of this beast. That also goes to the dedicated supporters of Silent Motorist Media on Patreon. Y'all make this whole thing worth it. I can't even begin to express how much I appreciate you being there.

I'm deeply indebted to s.j. bagley for the lovely introduction. Also, thank you Rohit Sawant, Scott J. Couturier, and Philip Fracassi for your patience while I stumbled through this production. Vincenzo Bilof—you're more help than you can possibly know. Same goes to you, Erik Mann.

I'm most certainly forgetting people, and I'm going to feel like shit for it later, but I'll try and make up for it by reaching out to them in person as I remember them. Most of all, thank *you,* reader, for being here. A special, special, *special* thank you to Chelsea, Chris, and the kiddoes for forgiving the long hours I've spent in front of the computer.

—Justin A. Burnett